Always Another Dawn

By

Torena O'Rorke

Pittsburgh, PA

ISBN 1-56315-262-2

Paperback Fiction
© Copyright 2000 Torena O'Rorke
All rights reserved
First Printing—2000
Library of Congress #99-65312

Request for information should be addressed to:

SterlingHouse Publisher Inc.
The Sterling Building
440 Friday Road
Pittsburgh, PA 15209
www.sterlinghousepublisher.com

Cover design: Michelle S. Vennare—SterlingHouse Publisher
Typesetting: Kathleen M. Gall

This publication includes images from Corel Draw 8 which are protected
by the copyright laws of the U.S., Canada, and elsewhere.

All rights reserved. No part of this publication may be reproduced,
stored in a retrieval system, or transmitted
in any form or by any means—electronic, mechanical, photocopy,
recording or any other, except for brief quotations in printed reviews
—without prior permission of the publisher.

This is a work of fiction. Names, characters, incidents, and places, are the
product of the author's imagination or are used fictitiously.
Any resemblance to actual events or persons, living or dead,
is entirely coincidental.

Printed in Canada

Dedication

To Angela, my friend,
and to Joe Moe, my grandfather,
who taught me how to fly.

I

As a girl, I remember Lizzie's life was ensconced in secrecy. The grisly scar on her right hand, her relentless penchant for danger, even the whereabouts of her mysterious father tickled my darkest curiosities, yet she skirted discussion of her brief, but seedy past. Her opaque eyes set in a narrow, elfish face, refused to reveal the slightest suffering, but Lizzie's eyes also had an ancient look, one that indicated wisdom beyond her years and a wistful yearning for something lost. The day I met Lizzie, I was thirteen and she was nearly so. Despite her youth, she'd already learned the meaning of the word survival. She was a spitfire and a champion of the weak and outcast. I soon learned that Lizzie often accompanied her mother into the treacherous hovels of Seattle's Skid Row to distribute handouts from the Unemployed Citizen's League. When I first saw her near the old stone church she was draped, like a limp flag on a windless day, near the wrought-iron gates, squinting with annoyance as though the sun was too bright. Yet the gray Seattle sky gave no indication of the celestial's glow. In fact, the third Sunday in May of 1933 was possibly the dreariest day of my childhood. That is, until I met Lizzie.

Although Black Tuesday had occurred over three years ago, my family had been fairly undisturbed by America's economic upheavals. My maternal grandfather, Joseph Danfrauer, had acquired his fortune during the Alaskan Gold Rush and had subsequently developed one of the largest shipbuilding firms in Washington. My father, George Strong, was a decorated war hero and highly successful attorney. Yet despite my family's social persuasion, on that joyless day in May, the Great Depression invaded our home like boll weevils in a cotton field.

I knew something was up months before when Papa Joseph sold his vintage cars. Angry conversations seeped into my bedroom in the middle of the night, but I'd ignored the heightening tension. After all, I'd lived with their turbulent waves all of my life. Yet that awful morning when I awoke to the clanging of an echoing bell at the first light, a deep chill settled in my bones. Trudging sleepily down the stairs, I joined my family in the parlor. The radiators hissed in a gallant effort to warm the enormous house as we stared into the hard face of my grandmother. The cavernous room was wrapped in shadow, though the large picture windows invited in the pale hint of day. While I perched on the settee, my brothers clung together on the chaise lounge. My pretty mother sat on the leather ottoman while my sleepy father reclined nearby. My grandfather was nowhere to be seen, but that wasn't unusual at our house. Papa was nearly always at the office.

I glanced over at my brother, Ernest. He'd turned 11 the day before and was still wearing his birthday hat. My parents had named him after the capricious literary genius, Hemingway, though the only talent our carrot-topped Ernest possessed was an incorrigible knack for trouble. Seven-year-old Jack, named after the canine lover, London, was the youngest of three. He was the apple of my parent's eye and not only because he was the baby. His hair was blonde and his eyes beamed sky-blue above his high cheekbones and adorable dimples. According to Papa Joseph, Jack was a perfect Aryan child. Though the boy had the face of an angel, I couldn't help but feel nauseated as he thrust his finger up his nose. Meanwhile, my grandmother's foot tapped in time to the Grandfather clock as she surveyed her clan impatiently.

"Children, I have bad news," Grandmother Ginny stated sternly. "Papa's firm hasn't received an order for 13 months now. As a result, we've had to release Robert, Charlie and Eloise. Most families no longer keep butlers or chauffeurs for that matter. Now that you children are all in school, we won't be needing Eloise. Your mother will have to cut down on her social activities to be available to you."

Ginny shot my mother a withering look, causing her to subdue any protest, but tears ran down her beautiful alabaster cheeks and her green eyes were clouded with sorrow. I knew my mother was less sad for herself than for those we were losing. Eloise had been our nanny since my birth. She was a funny old bird, but I loved her like no other. In the nurturing arms of Eloise, fairy tales became real events. She hunted for caterpillars for us to raise, caught baby crabs for my sand castle moats and fashioned tea parties from paper doilies, saltwater taffy and honey water. From the underpinnings of familial conflict, she had created a world of make-believe that melted despair like butter in the sun. Whether it was the cold slap of my grandmother's hand or a night without supper, Eloise had always soothed my indignant pain. Now Eloise, my savior and ally, was gone! I couldn't grasp the reality of it. Where would she go? Whose children would she now love? My wicked grandmother! Of course she would keep our cook, Josephine, to ease her burdens. Stunned, I stumbled from the parlor, unwilling to meet my parent's doleful gaze.

I rushed to my room where I collapsed into sobs on my lace canopy bed, cursing my grandmother without restraint. "Stupid, mean, old witch," I mumbled into the pillows while my Golden Retriever, Chippy, comforted me with scratchy licks on my leg. A few minutes later I felt a little better. Wiping my tears with the back of my arm, I stood up and went to the wardrobe. Pulling out my red taffeta dress and Mary Janes, I hurriedly dressed for church. By the time my mother knocked on my door, my tears were dry.

Mother was lovely as always—dressed in a paisley skirt and lace blouse, her auburn hair piled into a soft chignon. She smelled of almonds as she bent closer to me. Her eyes were shadowed by sadness, but she attempted a smile as she offered to fix my hair.

"I know Eloise always did this for you, but now I'll have to learn."

"Why does Grandmother always decide things without telling us? Doesn't she care about our feelings? I could have given up my allowance!" I groaned, surprised by the rancor in my voice. My grandmother and I were often at odds, though I kept my mouth shut most of the time.

"Your grandmother doesn't know any better. Her upbringing causes her to act this way. You know she was orphaned at two. She knows nothing about her parents. Then those cruel nuns raised her. She's just not able to show much compassion. Please don't worry. I'll find Eloise other employment, I promise," Mother insisted woefully.

As she tugged on my rag rolls, I struggled not to scream. Screaming wasn't allowed in our house, only angry whispers and chilling glares. Mother brushed my ringlets into a mass of amber fluff and placed a straw hat on my head. After she left to help the boys, I ripped the flimsy parcel from my head, throwing it to the floor in exasperation. Stealthily I crept out of my room and down the stairway toward the front door while avoiding my grandmother's study. I could see her sitting at her writing desk from the hallway.

"I'm going to Sunday school. See you at the service," I shouted, running as fast as my skinny legs would go.

The street was empty as I crossed it, though the churchyard was filling with a mixed assortment of jalopies and bicycles. I scanned the parking lot, looking for friends. About that time I caught sight of a strange girl leaning against the gate.

Her black hair hung in two long plaits and her arms were folded loosely at her waist. Her dress was entirely black and looked to be at least two sizes too large. The sleeves drooped well past her hands and the skirt dragged on the pavement. Her face had a scrunched-up appearance of someone with very bad gas. I hastened toward her, my curiosity stirred.

"Hello," I murmured as I drew closer to her. She continued to lean against the gate, eyeing me suspiciously.

"A little dressed-up, ain't ya?" she asked in a soft purr. I felt my face turn red as I summoned courage.

"My mother makes me wear this stuff, " I replied casually while silently congratulating myself for pulling off that ridiculous hat.

"Yeah? My mama don't make me wear anything I don't want to."

"What's your name?" I asked.

"Elizabeth Coomes, but you can call me Lizzie. How abouts you?"

"Emily Strong. Are you going to Sunday school here?"

"Guess so. Mama come here to find her friend, Melanie Strong. Ya know her?"

I gasped. Why would this filthy-looking waif and her kin be looking for my mother?

"She's my mother," I replied cautiously.

"Ain't that a coincidence? Our mamas was friends in school. I hope you can help me and my mama. We need a place to live. She was hoping your mama could ... well, shit," Lizzie clapped her hand to her mouth as she spoke. Tears sprang up in her eyes. She struggled to gather up her skirt and before I could stop her, she'd run across the street in the direction of the shops.

"Wait!" I called, racing down the road in pursuit. By the time I'd caught up with her, we'd reached Gerstein's Five and Dime, a favorite haunt of mine. Mr. Gerstein was just opening up the shop, as he did every Sunday morning as he was a Jew and didn't have to go to church like the rest of us. He was the best maltmaker in the city and I knew if I got within 10 feet of his store, I'd stop for one. Lizzie was breathless by the time I reached her. Her face was as white as an eggshell and she looked as though she might faint. I wondered how long it had been since she had eaten.

Mr. Gerstein peered out from the door and smiled. "You ladies like a little *chocolatta milch*? Come in Emily and I'll fix your favorite."

Temptation had called my name. I grabbed Lizzie's arm and led

4

her into the cool shop smelling of Pine Sol and licorice. We sat down on the red leather stools at the chrome-topped counter, watching as the friendly shopkeeper dropped mounds of creamy ice cream into the metal cup. With a yank on her braids, Lizzie drew a breath and mumbled, "I ain't got no money."

"That's okay," I whispered. "My grandfather has an account here."

"Ain't ya going to get into trouble, coming here instead of Sunday school?" Lizzie asked as an earnest look of concern crossed her pixie features.

"To tell you the truth, I don't give a damn," I pronounced in a burst of anger. Encouraged by my daring expression of opinion, Lizzie began to laugh. Rich and deep, her laughter boasted of freedom as it filled my head with its happy roar. Looking over at Lizzie, I grinned and nudged her with my elbow. Instantly I knew everything was going to be okay.

Lizzie slurped the malt, occasionally wiping her lips with the sleeve of her dress. As she drank, I observed her from the corner of my eye. Her skin was beige and as smooth as a kid glove. As hard as I tried, I couldn't find a freckle on her anywhere, unlike me who attracted freckles in the summer sun like flies to a picnic. Lizzie's almond-shaped eyes were as black as a coal and her small nose was turned up at the tip. Her wide grin revealed a set of bright white teeth that were perfect, except for a small space between the front two. She licked her spoon and the inside of her glass with her pink flower petal tongue. Then with slick precision, she slid her finger around the sides until the glass looked like new.

She glanced over at me and smiled. "That's how I keep my dishes clean when Mama ain't around."

"Where did you live?" I asked as curiosity got the better of me.

"In the basement of the Olympic Hotel, near the laundry. Our little room was just big enough for us two. We had a big old mattress on the floor and a picture of Mary Pickford on the wall. Mama got that from a garbage can. I got my own little crate where I kept my clothes and mama had two. Once I found a can of paint in the janitor's cupboard. Now don't you tell, okay?" Her voice dropped to a conspiratorial whisper. I'm sure my eyes were as big as saucers as I nodded slowly.

"I stole it and painted them crates a beautiful soft pink. I know that you might think that was bad, but there was about three zillion cans of paint in there. I don't think that one would go noticed, do you?" She looked shameless.

"Well ..." I stuttered. "God says it's a sin to steal."

"Of course, it ain't nothin' to you rich folks. You can think what ya want about me, *Miss* Emily, but I don't feel a bit guilty. After all, God don't really exist anyway, so what do I care."

I was aghast. Not believe in God? I'd never met anyone who didn't believe in God. The very idea of going through life without God was a fearsome prospect to me. Why even Jews believed in a God!

When I spoke, my voice was a hoarse whisper. "I've never met anyone who didn't believe in God before. What do you believe in if you don't believe in God?"

She gave me a rueful smile. "Oh, girlie, don't look so terrible sad. I believe in me, that's what. My mama and me's what ya call atheists. Don't believe in anything invisible, ya see. We just believes in ourselves. Maybe someday you'll understand." Her voice had a caressing quality to it. "Now, let's get going before my mama starts to worry. She'll be lookin' for me now that church is over. Geez, I'm gonna to feel like a big dope goin' in there. I don't know the first thing about church stuff."

I stifled a giggle. Lizzie was so matter-a-fact. She was the type of person my mother would say 'doesn't mince her words' and my grandmother would call a 'hooligan'. I called her grand!

"I have an idea. Why don't we go to my house? You can see my room and I'll take you through the secret passage to the east tower. Nobody lives there now, not since Eloise left." I hung my head and sniffed.

Lizzie reached over and tousled my hair. "Why so sad?" she asked.

"Oh, it's nothing."

"Come on, now. Nothin's that bad. Tell me or I ain't comin'."

That was all it took—someone who wanted to listen. I gritted my teeth and spun around on my chair. "Okay," I hissed. "But let's get out of here first."

I smiled politely at Mr. Gerstein as he looked over in our direction. "You young ladies, you like my *chocolatta milch*? Come again for the Mrs. Gerstein's cherry strudel."

"Thank you, Mr. Gerstein. Say hello to the Mrs. for me." I gave him a smile and grabbed Lizzie's hand, pulling her out the door passed the shelves of romance novels, kitchen items and fancy glass knickknacks.

As we strode up the sidewalk toward my house, light raindrops began to fall. I glanced over at Lizzie. She was frowning at me.

"What?"

"Now you tells me how that wasn't stealing, the way you walked out of there with no money on the table."

"I told you. My grandfather has an account."

"What's that?"

I rolled my eyes up. This girl was going to take some work. "Mr. Gerstein sends my Papa Joseph a bill once a month for whatever our family buys. I don't have to have money that way, see?"

Lizzie's eyes became pools of wonder. "I never heard a such a thing. How does a person get one of them?"

"I don't know. I guess it's because Papa is rich, but not that rich anymore."

Again she must have detected the sorrow in my voice, because she prodded me with her sharp little finger. "Okay, I's a dang good muckracker, so dump it on me. What's the scoop?"

I laughed again. "Lizzie, you speak another language, do you know that? Scoop. Isn't that what journalists say?"

"Yeah, my mama knows lots of 'em. She's a lefty, ya see. A socialist. There's lots of lefty journalists in her crowd."

"You mean she's a Bolshevik?" The faintest of shivers ran down my spine.

"I dunno. You ask her. She'll tell ya. My mama ain't afraid of nobody. Now, what's the scoop?"

"My not-so-rich-grandparents fired my nanny yesterday. I'm so mad I could boil my grandmother in a pot of stew. She didn't even tell us; ran out my wonderful Eloise without even letting us say good-bye." I stopped and turned to Lizzie. "Eloise was my best friend, Lizzie. She loves me more than anyone. She laughs at my jokes and played with me. Now that she's gone, I don't know what I'm going to do!" My tears sprouted like grass between pavement stones.

Though she was a good five inches shorter than me, Lizzie placed one grubby hand on my shoulder, lifted my chin with the other and said solemnly, "I'll be your friend."

Minutes later we passed the church, creeping along my neighbor's hedge like two secret agents on a hot trail. From the street we could hear the booming tirades of Reverend Norpucker, whose fleshy jowls wobbled to the rhythm of his tiresome speeches. I was glad to miss one of the Reverend's lectures on the evils of the world. Sin and damnation weren't my favorite topics, particularly now when the worst sinner in

7

my opinion happened to be my grandmother. Lizzie grew quiet as we reached my house. Her mouth dropped open in surprise as we came closer.

"You live here?" she marveled while staring at my grandparents' home. Smack-dab atop Capital Hill, our ivy-wrapped gothic mansion loomed like a haunting vision from a Jane Eyre novel. Two medieval-like towers banked the enormous structure. Dense Fir trees hugged the property's border while azaleas bloomed a brilliant crimson along the brick walkway.

"Yes, now come on," I urged as we scurried around to the servant's door leading into the kitchen. There were no signs of danger, but the house was silent. I ran to the icebox and pulled out a bottle of milk. Next I yanked the pineapple-upside-down cake from the top of the icebox. Lizzie's eyes lit on whatever form of sustenance they could find.

"Here, eat," I instructed, handing her a plate. Lizzie quickly wolfed down two pieces of cake.

"This is so dang good. Thanks ... ."Her voice stopped as her eyes traveled to the door behind me. An odd mixture of fearless surprise and mild chagrin crossed her face. I turned to see my grandmother standing in the kitchen doorway, her face a mask of controlled fury.

"Emily Strong, what are you doing home so soon?" she demanded.

As I began to reply, I caught Lizzie's eye and to my astonishment, my fear dissipated.

"I was on my way to church and I met Lizzie. She and I were so hungry, we couldn't imagine sitting through the Sunday school with our tummies rattling like old freight trains, so here we are." At that moment I was saved. Lizzie stood up in her wrinkled dress and with a voice right out of a British radio show, said,

"How do you do, Mrs. Danfrauer. It's such a pleasure to meet you. I thank you for your most gracious hospitality." Then Lizzie did something I wouldn't think of doing in a million years. She stepped toward my grandmother, daintily took her hand and kissed it. To my delight and relief, a faint smile crept over my grandmother's gaunt features.

"It's a pleasure to meet you as well," she replied, completely charmed.

Moments later, the front door burst open and the sound of rapid footsteps echoed into the room. My brothers careened into the kitchen, jostling one another and arguing over who would get the last piece of chocolate cream pie. As my brothers squabbled over the pie, my grandmother hastily left the room, unwittingly letting me off the hook.

Soon I heard my mother's voice and then another, softer voice. I turned to Lizzie, but she had disappeared like smoke on a fan. In the foyer I found her again, standing next to a petite, rosy-faced woman dressed in a navy wool dress and torn plaid cape. The woman's hair was as dark as a raven's wing and her pale blue eyes twinkled merrily. Instantly, I knew she must be Lizzie's mother. My own mother was giggling at something that the woman had just said. As I came closer, I caught the words that made my heart sing.

"Now that the servants are gone, we have extra room, Claudia. We couldn't pay you, of course, but if you would help Josephine with the cooking and cleaning, you two would at least have a roof over your heads." At my mother's suggestion, Claudia's face was touched by raw emotion. Then my sweet mother bent down to Lizzie, and added, "My daughter has always wanted a little sister, Lizzie. It looks like God has answered her prayers." Lizzie beamed.

Once the introductions were made, I grabbed Lizzie's hand and we raced up to my room. Compassion rose in my throat as she gazed in wonder around at the glowing pink space. With careful steps, Lizzie walked to my doll cabinet and gaped through the glass.

"You can open it if you want. My grandfather bought them for me," I announced with unbridled pride. I loved my dolls. There were over 100 in the gleaming cabinet. Madame Alexander dolls adorned in rows of lace and ribbon, storybook dolls from England, porcelain dolls from Germany with faces the color of fresh cream, funny Russian stacking dolls made of wood and painted in bright colors and kimono-clad *geishas* from the Orient. Lizzie reached out and touched the Indian doll, which was six inches long, dressed in buckskin and carrying a peace pipe. His ornate headdress was made of miniature feathers and beads.

"That's an old one from the Lummi tribe," I said. Entranced, Lizzie became as stiff as a statue. Watching her, I thought of the Indian women I had seen on Lopez Island. "Why do you like that one?" I asked. When Lizzie met my gaze, I saw the oldest eyes I'd ever seen in a human being. I stared back at her, trying to understand her expression, but Lizzie broke the spell with the flip of her wrist.

9

"Knew an Indian once." With that, she closed the cabinet door. She took a leap at my bed, her braids flying as she howled with glee. "Oh, Emily, you are so lucky. I love your room!" She clapped her hands and squealed, "Show me the secret passage now."

I obliged wholeheartedly; happy to have a new friend who would enjoy the house as much as I did. Lizzie followed me down the hallway past my parent's room, stopping every so often to gaze upon the paintings on the wall. Eventually we made our way to a narrow door, which led to the attic. I opened it. The space was pitch black. Lizzie's hand grasped mine tightly, but she didn't utter a sound.

"Here," I whispered. "Duck down and follow me." We climbed into the compact opening. The tunnel ran along the east wing of the house between the second floor and the attic. It measured 2 feet in height, extended 14 feet and exited by way of a trapdoor on the east tower staircase platform. Once inside, small cubed windows offered some light in the tunnel while electric bulbs lit the tower staircase.

Eloise had lived in the room at the top of this tower. Grandfather's study was in the west tower. Though I had found the tunnel that led there, I'd never dared to sneak through it. Papa's eyes grew sinister at the mention of possible intrusion and I'd once heard he'd forced my mother to sleep in the basement after finding her in his sacred domain.

Dust bunnies clung to our hands and knees as we climbed through the tunnel and out of another trapdoor onto a landing. I heard a deep moan and realized with a start it had come from Lizzie.

"What's the matter?" I asked. She shook her head and gestured for me to keep climbing up the stairs. When I turned back to her, I saw she was trembling.

"Are you okay?" I asked.

Lizzie nodded. "Just hate bein' up real high like this, but I guess I gotta get used to it, huh? I mean, if my room is up here and all."

"You can sleep with me if you want," I replied, hoping to calm her fear. "I'm lucky I guess. I've never been afraid of heights. My father's a pilot. He often takes me flying with him. It's great fun."

Lizzie clenched her fists, her eyes frantically darting around the confined space until we entered Eloise's room. There was little trace of my beloved nanny's prior existence, though a porcelain doll sat on the bare dresser. I rushed up to it; it had been my favorite of Eloise's collection. Under the delicate toy was a note with my name on it. Tears filled my eyes as I read my nanny's farewell letter to me. Lizzie stood by, silent and respectful of my moment. I shuddered and whispered, "She really loved me." Lizzie smiled agreeably and gave my hand a reassuring squeeze.

By the time we'd returned to my room, Josephine had clanged the dinner bell, announcing Sunday dinner. As we washed our hands, Lizzie exclaimed, "I hate this old dress. I hope Mama brings my other one today."

I gulped. She only had two dresses? I thought quickly. Mother had saved a bag of my outgrown clothes, with plans to take them to the orphanage. Lizzie would probably fit into them just fine. Would I offend her? I didn't give myself time to consider it, but instead blurted out, "Hey, I've got some clothes you could have. I grew out of them and I doubt my brothers will wear them." I gestured at my taffeta and waited with baited breath as Lizzie's face changed from a defensive pout to genuine humor.

She shrugged her shoulders and grinned. "Okay," she replied. By the time we left my room, she was dressed in my old plaid jumper and a white cotton blouse. The difference was astonishing. She looked like a little girl instead of a Halloween gremlin. I could tell she was pleased. Though her gratitude was whispered with downcast eyes, she grabbed my hand and squeezed it again as we hurried to our midday meal.

The dining room sparkled with twinkling light as we entered. Sitting down, Lizzie's face glowed with delight. A mental picture of her pitiful life at the Olympic Hotel's basement had formed in my mind. The thought of it made me want to cry. Poor girl!

As Josephine served the meal, I worried that my new friend's terrible table manners and horrible slang might cause another world war. To my relief, the little elf kept a sly eye on my choice of silverware and followed suite. Though my brothers and I were accustomed to our prim Sunday suppers, I wondered how long Lizzie could hold out. During most meals, Grandmother Ginny spent the entire time correcting our table manners while Mother and Father discussed current affairs. When Papa Joseph did eat with us, a rarity these days, he was moody and unpredictable. Reverend Norpucker's presence only added to our family's rather peculiar mealtime banter.

Still as nervous as a fox, I watched Lizzie as George Bernard Shaw's *Pygmalion* surfaced in my brain.

"Mrs. Danfrauer, this meal is most delectable," Lizzie commented as Ernest snickered at the far end of the table.

"Thank you, Elizabeth. We are very fortunate to have Josephine. She comes from a long line of cooks, dating back to President Lincoln." I almost burst into giggles. Grandmother Ginny was absolutely beside herself with pompous self-satisfaction.

"How interesting!" Lizzie continued, delicately dabbing her mouth with the starched napkin. I thought my brothers would explode with uproarious delight when Lizzie winked at them right under Ginny's nose. Jack began to laugh so I gave him a swift kick under the table, but I missed, instead kicking the Reverend who, in order to remain the epitome of composure, simply grunted, though his florid face turned as red as the soup. Recovering with a cough, he engaged Ginny in conversation by commenting on her recent gesture of goodwill, namely the taking in of Claudia and Lizzie.

"She is a great servant of God who will embrace the homeless, Mrs. Danfrauer," he said in his annoying whine. The Reverend loved to hear his own voice. With his current commentary came a rolling of the tongue as well as a rolling of his beady eyes. "I can't tell you how much you have pleased our Father with your gesture of concern for little Elizabeth and Claudia. You are a saint, my dear." He leaned across the table and patted my grandmother's hand as her lined face twitched with pride.

Meanwhile Lizzie leaned over, whispering in my ear, "I bet he'd like to get his hands on her pocketbook as well." She shot me a wicked grin and batted her lashes at Ernest who responded with a typical schoolboy's snort of embarrassment.

Soon the conversation moved to the state of the economy. Bored with the adults, I listened as the boys challenged Lizzie for rights to their territory. They began showing off for her, entirely enjoying her teasing, playful responses. Obviously there was no disagreement among my family members regarding this unexpected turn of events. Already Jack seemed to take a liking to Lizzie, though he was watchful of his big brother's reaction. When Ernest grumbled about having another girl in the house, Lizzie quickly put him in his place by mentioning that she was an excellent marble marksman, willing to provide instruction. All and all, the entire family seemed quite pleased by our new visitors. Of course, Lizzie and her mother would never take the place of our glorious nanny, but I was promised that Eloise would visit soon, and was therefore satisfied for the time being.

That night when I tiptoed into my mother's room to say

goodnight, I learned more about Lizzie. As my mother brushed and rolled my tangled mane, she told me about her close friendship with Claudia. As she recounted their history, I was both amused and secretly horrified.

"Claudia and I were best friends at the University of Washington," Mother murmured as she ran the heavy brush through my hair. "We first met in the Home Economics building one freezing November afternoon in 1914. I had caught a cold and was suffering terribly. She was sitting at the table next to me, coughing and sneezing as badly as I. Soon we engaged a sneezing contest of sorts. Eventually we both fell into a fit of giggles and decided to go for a cup of hot tea. We were inseparable from that day on."

"But Mother, why does Lizzie have the same last name as her mother? Where's her father?" I asked. My mother shifted from one foot to the other and took a deep breath while knotting one of my rags rather tightly.

"Ouch," I complained. "That's too tight!"

"I'm sorry." She fumbled to untie the cloth, her slender fingers unaccustomed to this task. "I'm not quite sure how to tell you this. I guess the best way to put it is that after she left college, Claudia became the pariah of Capitol Hill."

"What's a pariah?" I asked. By the look on my mother's face, it wasn't very nice.

"An outcast. Poor Claudia was rejected by her family and neighbors. It all started in 1919, after the general strike. That's when she met Lizzie's father. Claudia was a true socialist, much to her parents' embarrassment. She was the one who first took me to Blanc's and introduced me to your father, who was a friend of Ole Hanson, our former mayor. Oh, your daddy was so dashing!" Mother clapped her hands with glee.

"But who was Blanc?" I asked eagerly.

"Blanc's was a wonderful cafe which was very popular back then, full of young artists, intellectuals and students. It was located in a smoky basement." Mother's eyes began to gleam with memory. "We spent many happy evenings there until things heated up. Claudia's boyfriend was a powerful Indian Wobblie. Tobi was quite a man."

Mother gazed out the window at the city lights. From the room's view, the street lamps glowed in long, tapered rows down to the heart of Seattle. Yesler Way and the Port of Seattle were visible in the distance and the large, round clock at the King Street Station shone like a painted moon. Nearby, Smith Tower windows were glimmering match flames. Staring at the scene, my mother's eyes glazed over. I waited, enraptured by her enchanting face made ageless by the lamplight's soft caress. I could image her back then as an independent young woman, charming and free-spirited during the roaring twenties, an exciting time compared to life now. I knew she had been a bit of a flapper, much to my grandparents' disapproval. I often wondered why my mother had become so complacent. Was it marriage, or ridiculous social conformity we must obey? Mother smiled wistfully and shook her head, reawakening to her life as a wife and mother.

"So what's a Wobblie?"

"Wobblie stands for Industrial Workers of the World. They were an organization that stood for workers rights. They had a lot of power in Seattle during that time. Let me tell you, your Papa wasn't fond of them at all, nor was Colonel Coomes. He forbidden Claudia from seeing Tobi, but she was stubborn. She continued to see him and eventually became pregnant shortly after your father and I got married."

So that's why Lizzie was so interested in my Indian doll! Her daddy was an Indian. "So what happened to them?" I felt heart-broken already.

"I'm not sure of all the details. I quit going to Blanc's after things got crazy down there. There was a lot of fighting between the socialists, labor and others. Tobi and Claudia became more involved in the movement. After a while Tobi left town. Some say old Coomes put the dogs after him. Claudia was alone with Lizzie and no job or home to go to. Her family refused to take her in. They were evil to her and I hated them for it." She paused, took a deep breath and shivered. I felt startled by her reaction. I'd never heard my mother speak of anyone that way in my entire life. "Anyway, that's enough of that. I know it's quite shocking. Please don't ever speak a word of this to Lizzie. It would only bring her pain."

Speechless, I rose from the satin-covered stool as my mother gathered me in her arms. "I'm very lucky. I almost got caught up in all of that madness. If your daddy hadn't asked me to marry him, I might have ended up like Claudia."

I shuddered. Why would Mother say that? I nestled my face into the crook of her neck. She was sweet and warm and I felt very safe with her. "Mama, Claudia is a sinner, isn't she? I mean, having a baby without being married and all?"

Mother pulled away and looked me squarely in the eye. "Claudia is my friend. I don't judge her for what she did. It is her life, not mine. I still accept her. Claudia is one of the truest people I know. You mustn't judge her either. You know, your grandmother nearly refused to allow them to move in. If Reverend Norpucker hadn't just preached his timely rhetoric of forgiveness and goodwill, I doubt Lizzie would be in your bed right now. Speaking of which, off to bed with you, too."

As I planted a kiss on my mother's cheek, my heart swelled. I loved my mother so very much. How *lucky* I was to have her.

Scooting downstairs, I searched out my father to kiss him goodnight. He was in his den, smoking a pipe and reading the *Seattle Times*. My father was a nocturnal man. When in search of comfort after a bad dream, I would find him in his den, reading legal briefs long after midnight. He slept only a few hours a night, rising before dawn to catch the first streetcar to the city. He was highly intelligent, and though reserved, he was a devoted and loving father. His greatest joy, besides his family, was his airplane. He had learned to fly during the war and had taken many risks in honor of our country. He had a drawer full of medals and a letter from President Wilson commending him for his courage. I was very proud of my father, not only for his accomplishments, but because of his patience. He often spent hours with me as I struggled to learn Latin and taught me everything there was to know about the stars. To top it all off, he was exceptionally handsome. As I crawled onto his lap, I whispered in his ear, "Thanks for letting Lizzie and her mother stay."

He chuckled softly. "I don't have much say about those types of things, Em. It was your grandparents' decision, but I'm glad, too." His blue eyes sparkled as he gave me a wink. I smoothed his salt and pepper hair with my hand, gazing admiringly into his eyes.

"I don't think it's going to be so bad without Eloise now. I was really angry this morning, and worried, too. I'm afraid for our friends, Daddy. Mother said she will help Eloise find another job, but what will Charlie and Robert do now?"

"President Roosevelt has just cut the New Deal," he stated in a tone that meant business. My family was wary of Roosevelt. They were Republicans in the strictest sense of the word. Yet I also knew my family was very worried about the Depression. We were hopeful that

President Roosevelt's leadership would make a difference. As the end of the First Hundred Days approached, we were pleased that many positive changes had taken place in our government.

"That means Charlie and Robert will get emergency relief, right?"

"Yes, they will. Now it's rather late, young lady. You must be on your way." He gave me a reassuring smile as I wrapped my arms around his neck. He smelled of spice and tobacco and his cheek was rough with stubble as I kissed him gently.

"Night Daddy! Sleep tight," I murmured, scampering out of the room.

When I reached my door, I could hear the faint sound of singing. Lizzie must be waiting for me, I thought, remembering once again of the little miracle who had entered my life. The door swung open and there was Lizzie, dressed an old gray petticoat, spinning around the room with my teddy bear in her arms. She stopped and gave me a playful smirk.

"Hi," I said a little awkwardly. I had never had a friend sleep over before. She seemed to notice my sudden shyness and reached out for my hand.

"Here," she said, tossing the bear on the bed. "Let's do the tango." Without warning, Lizzie pressed her willowy body to mine and clutched my hand, pushing our arms directly out in front of us. The shyness left me and I was filled with exaltation as she marched me across the floor and spun me around, humming a steady beat under her breath. She smelled of soap and honey and her body was warm. Her long black hair, damp from the bath, clung to my cheeks as we swayed to and fro. She lunged me back until my head nearly touched the ground and then, with a strength of a man, held my body prone as if I was suspended in thin air. A momentary rush swept through my veins as I became an ethereal being in the arms of an angel. She lifted me effortlessly with a delighted smile on her face. Lizzie pulled away and gave a deep bow.

"And now you know how to tango," she purred and climbed into bed. I stared at her, laughing.

"That was fun!" I replied, climbing in after her. I snapped off the lamp and giggled again in the darkness. "Where in heaven's name do you learn things like that?" I whispered, still dizzy with pleasure.

"My mama. Told ya we were partners."

"Oh, dear," I mumbled off-handedly. "I forgot to say my prayers.

Grandmother fell in love with Lizzie, despite her occasional blurting of ain't and her propensity to lick the glassware. She brought out the heart in the old woman, who always gave Lizzie a little pocket money after she'd baked a batch of Ginny's favorite anise cookies. Whatever Lizzie's secret, I was thrilled at the arrangement.

Lizzie's birthday was on July fourth. Every year, my family ferried to our cabin on Bainbridge Island to celebrate. As our departure grew closer, Mother rushed around, leaving luggage on bedroom thresholds. Meanwhile, I agonized over a gift for Lizzie, though I had already spent hours wandering through Mrs. Crepson's Toyshop. That morning as I packed, the answer came to me. The gift had been there in my room all along, but rather than risk taking the doll to the cabin, I decided to hide it in her room before we left for the island. Lizzie would return to find it there.

The week on Bainbridge Island was grand. The sun shone brightly for five days straight and the evenings were cool and breezy. My grandparents chose to stay in the city, which suited me just fine. Our summer place was nestled in a thicket of evergreens with the closest neighbor a quarter of a mile away. Located on a sandy beach where the chilly Puget Sound waters were shallow and rich with sea life, our log cabin was furnished with knotty pine, braided rugs, star quilts and pots of fuchsias and geraniums. The children slept on the screened-in porch while the adults enjoyed the solitude of the three loft bedrooms. We had running water in the kitchen and a small bathroom upstairs. Most of the cooking was done on a cast iron stove, which was fueled by driftwood and the rare bucket of coal.

We spent our days at the beach, digging clams, pulling mussels out of the rocks and chasing the sand crabs that scurried along the shore. My brothers followed us around, much to my irritation, but Lizzie adored them and was as patient as a lady-in-waiting. She treated them royally, giving Jack piggyback rides and secretly teaching Ernest how to play poker. I was never jealous, because I could tell how important it was to her to love and be loved.

In the evenings, Father built a bonfire on the beach and we huddled around it, singing songs and roasting marshmallows. The night before Lizzie's birthday, Charles Woodruff came to dinner. He was a bachelor friend of my father's. Charles was tall and skinny with a beak nose and a receding hairline. I thought he was positively ugly and Lizzie was certain he had abnormal genes. In our insufferable, adolescent wisdom, we thought it was obvious why he was still a bachelor, but evidently Claudia found him charming. Her laughter rang out in the night like the coo of a dove and she was more playful than usual. Silhouetted by the tangerine sunset, Claudia became a light-dappled belle of the ball. Her sheer cotton frock clung to her ample bosom and rounded hips and her thick black river of hair rippled down her back in luxurious waves. While sitting around the campfire, Charles's eyes glowed with admiration as she sang a delightful rendition of Gilbert and Sullivan's *Poor Wandering One*. I loved this inspiring woman, particularly for the relief she gave to my mother. Around Claudia, Mother discarded her modest blouses and calf-length skirts and donned camisoles and dungarees. In a piquant gesture of surrender, my father threw off his shoes *and* I caught him slapping my mother's bottom more than once during our stay.

While the adults remained on the beach, chatting about politics, art, and the latest jazz music, the moon rose in the indigo sky. Lizzie and I crouched on our cots, straining to hear their conversation. Watching Lizzie from the corner of my eye, I could see she greatly disapproved of Charles. In the dimming light, her black eyes flashed while her mouth narrowed into a thin line across her face.

"Can't stand him! Mama shouldn't be flirtin' with that buffoon!" Lizzie lamented. She nervously twisted her braids into a huge knot and chewed on her bottom lip.

"Maybe your mother is lonely. I mean, it's not like she has a husband or anything."

Lizzie drew up like a viper ready to strike. "You listen to me, Emily Strong," she hissed. "It ain't my mama's fault my daddy left, do you understand me?"

My heart tightened. I hadn't meant to hurt her. "Of course not, but is he going to come back?" I expected a sharp answer, but instead Lizzie just hung her head in defeat. I reached out and put my arm around her. "I'm so sorry. I shouldn't have said that." Her shoulders began to shake under my embrace. Though I hadn't known her long, I knew it was rare for Lizzie to cry. She was highly disciplined, controlling her emotions as easily as a chameleon changes colors. As I listened to her shallow sobs, it was obvious to me how she yearned for her absent father.

"Never mind. I'm sure he'll come back someday. You'll see him again," I assured her. I don't even know if he's alive! I thought, but my words seemed to soothe Lizzie. She looked up, her tear-streaked face now transformed into the eager features of a hopeful child and smiled.

"Yeah, I'll see him again."

Side by side on our quilt-covered cots, we watched the stars come out. In the distance, the snow-tipped Olympic Mountains peaked like fluffy meringue against the violet horizon. The waves lapped softly against the shore, lulling our minds to distraction. The adults were quiet, their conversations whispered. My brothers had long been asleep and snored contentedly nearby.

"Look, there's the Big Dipper. Do you see it?"

Lizzie squinted up at the stars. "What's the Big Dipper?" she asked in a faint voice. I smiled in the darkness. I supposed she hadn't seen too many constellations, living in the basement of the hotel.

"The Big Dipper is a constellation, a star shape. Here I'll teach you." Methodically I pointed out the various pictures in the sky. Lizzie was a quick study and immediately caught on. I was thrilled to share this mystery with someone other than Father, but my love for the heavens wasn't limited to the stars. Someday I would be a pilot and soar through the atmosphere like an eagle, but I hadn't yet shared that dream with anyone.

"Look, Emily … over there. What is that shape?" she eagerly asked. I stared up at the black velvet sky, studded with diamond stars, trying to get my bearings.

"That's the twins. See their heads and their arms and legs." I took Lizzie's hand in my own and used her index finger to trace the lines of the twinkling stars. She nodded as a blissful cry escaped her lips.

"That's us," she murmured. "We are twins, twin sisters in our hearts. Promise me you'll be my friend forever," she added in a whisper that spoke of ironclad loyalty and everlasting love.

"Forever, Lizzie," I replied and held her hand until we fell asleep.

July fourth was oven-hot. By midday we'd all grown crabby from the sultry heat. There was no breeze and the air had the dank smell of impending rain. Ernest and Lizzie were on the porch, shooting marbles, Mother and Father were on a walk and Jack was building a sand castle with Claudia's help. I was holding my book to my nose, totally absorbed in *The Great Gatsby* when I happened to see my folks approaching from the corner of my eye. My mother's hand was over her mouth and she was gagging. Father stood next to her, his arm wrapped around her waist to hold her up. He appeared worried and

Mother was as white as a bone. I ran down the porch steps and onto the beach.

"What is it, Mother? Are you all right?" I asked, unaccustomed to Father's furrowed brow. Before she could answer, she vomited her breakfast. Father gave me a distressed look and together we helped Mother to the porch. Claudia came up from the beach about the same time with a look of indulging pity on her face.

"Melanie, it'll pass, Love. I'll make you some peppermint tea. That should take away the nausea." My head rotated from Mother to Father to Claudia and back again like a mechanical doll. Lizzie burst into a fit of giggles.

"Don't you know nothin'?" she scoffed as the adults disappeared into the house. "Ya mama's with child, girl! as my nigger friends say." She smiled at me with that incorrigible grin of hers.

"I don't believe you!" I retorted, feeling both stupid and mystified.

"Go ask her yourself then," she quipped. "I know because I've seen it before. All the young maids at the Olympic looked like your mama and got sick too, when they was pregnant."

Crushed by my own ignorance, I ran into the house. My mother was seated at the large oak table, her head down, with a metal mixing bowl in her lap. Her retching continued as my father lovingly rubbed her shoulders.

"Oh, Melly, why didn't you tell me?" he murmured.

"I was afraid to, George, what with the money problems and all."

"Melanie, we're not in any trouble. Joseph is sure the economy is on its way up. We can afford another child, for Pete's sakes." He knelt down and held her small hands in his, looking deeply into her eyes. "Hey, my darling, this is good news!" he continued. "You mustn't ever be afraid to tell me anything ever again. And don't worry about your mother. I'll handle her." My mother nodded, her glistening eyes tinged with gratitude, and grabbed the metal bowl again. My father rose and saw me standing by the door.

"Hey, Emmy! Did you hear the good news? You're going to have another little brother or sister soon." With that, a flash of lightening lit up the sky as the others came scurrying into the cabin to avoid the first drops of rain.

That evening, we celebrated Lizzie's birthday with a tasty meal of fresh crab, steamed mussels and baked potatoes. Claudia had baked a chocolate devil's food cake, Lizzie's favorite, and she and I gorged ourselves. Claudia had precious little money, but her first relief check had finally arrived the week before, enabling her to buy Lizzie a small music box with a dancing ballerina. I gave Lizzie a card made from leftover doilies. My parents gave her a silver dollar and my brothers ceremoniously presented her with their most sacred marbles. Even back then, Lizzie was well loved in our family! As Lizzie paused to make her birthday wish, I wondered if she was asking for her father's return. Because I loved my own father so much, I was certain that her complete happiness relied upon this.

Later that night, as Lizzie and I snuggled in our sleeping bags, we began to discuss Mother's pregnancy. "I can't believe Mother can get pregnant. She seems too old," I mumbled, still awed by the news.

"Girl, she's only 36. I'm sure she still has her monthlies," Lizzie replied.

Instant humiliation swept through me again. Silence filled the space until Lizzie let out a heavy sigh. "Don't tell me ya don't know what I'm talkin' about. Geez, where ya been, Emily? Okay, take a deep breath and get ready to hear this." Lizzie was self-assured and totally in control, instructing me as though I was a child. I fumed, but kept my composure. By the time she was done explaining, I no longer fumed, but rather, was shaken to the core. Breasts and hairy armpits were bad enough!

I thought about it all the way home. Menstruation was a word I'd heard my mother use with my grandmother, but I'd never bothered to ask its meaning. Their conversations were always couched in sullen whispers. Gauging by the way they acted, it wasn't something I wanted to know about. Besides, Grandmother Ginny gave me the feeling it was none of my business. One withering look from her and I knew not to ask.

Upon our arrival at home, I'd accepted the traumatic realities of becoming a woman. More importantly, I was anxious for Lizzie to find the birthday gift I had left behind. I ran to my room to drop off my luggage. Lizzie trudged by, carrying her little canvas bag and a box full of beach souvenirs.

"Lizzie," I murmured as she passed. "Don't forget, your birthday present from me is in your room." Her face lit up at the suggestion as she hurried down the hall toward the tower stairs. As she turned the corner, she shot me a sly glance.

"Okay, I know you're dyin' to watch me open it. Come on then."

I let out a gleeful sigh and ran down the hall to catch up with her.

We tiptoed up the steps and opened the door to the tower room. Twenty feet in diameter, the bright, butter-yellow room was circular with large square windows skirting half the perimeter. Claudia had dressed it up the best she could. Mother had found some leftover blue and white gingham and Claudia, with her natural creative streak, had quickly whipped up a set of curtains and a matching bedspread for the full-size brass bed. Fresh flowers sweetened the room and rows of dried roses hung from the windows. A battered butler's table was heaped with copies of the *Seattle Call*, a small socialist weekly and *Women of Tomorrow*, a magazine with a feminist theme. I knew my grandfather would drop dead if he knew Claudia was an active socialist, but she was very discreet. Only my mother, Lizzie and I knew that she attended their weekly meetings.

Something caught my eye as I entered the room. On the vanity sat a shiny silver frame. I walked over and picked it up, gazing at the photograph of a tall, angular man with long black hair and serious eyes. Claudia stood next to him with a baby in her arms. I gasped in surprise.

"Leave that alone!" Lizzie's voice rang out in admonishment. I spun around to face her, the frame still in my hand. "I said put that down," she snarled. I stared at her, startled. Carefully I put down the photograph and began to walk toward the door.

"Where are you going?" she asked, her tone softening.

"You mustn't talk to me that way," I snapped, turning away. "I'm not a dog. You should ask me nicely." There was a moment of silence as if she hadn't heard me.

"Oh, goodie! Is this my present?" Her voice came out in a gasp. I spun around. She had found the Indian doll lying on the bed. She picked it up and cradled it like a baby. Slowly her body began to sway, as if she were rocking the doll to sleep.

"Yes," I replied, perplexed by her reactions. I started to work my way to the door, when I heard her whisper,

"Please don't go. I'm sorry I was rude."

"Okay," I answered. "But you mustn't shout at me like that. I want to be your friend, but sometimes I'm afraid of you. There is so much about you I don't understand."

"Me, too."

"Me, too, what?"

"There's lots about me I dunno either. That picture, it's my Daddy and Mama and me. I was two years old. Daddy left the day after that picture was taken. We've been alone ever since. I hid it from you for the longest time, always puttin' it away when I knew you were comin' up. I didn't want people to know my Daddy is an Indian. Lots of people hate Indians. I thought maybe you'd hate me, too."

I rushed over to Lizzie and threw my arms around her. "I'd never ever hate you, not in a million years. Oh, Lizzie, you're my best friend." I gurgled, my emotions thick in my throat. Lizzie leaned her head against my shoulder and sighed.

"I love my doll. I'll think of my daddy now, every time I see it. Thank you." We stood like that for a long time: my arms around Lizzie, her head on my shoulder with the Indian doll tucked into her arms. I felt like a big sister to her. She needed so much reassurance, though she was worldly and in many ways, much more confident than I. She had opened a little space in me that hadn't been there before. My life had always been so perfect, so easy and so full of plenty, I realized. I wanted her to have that; I wanted to share my good fortune.

3

During the Great Depression, every American city acquired desperate, poverty-ridden communities named after our highly inept and floundering President Hoover, who neglected the state of our country until people began to die of hunger. All across our nation, people who were bereft of jobs, homes and financial security were forced to live in these disease-ridden shantytowns. What the crash of '29 had put into motion, Hoover fueled by his inaction and indifference. Since my grandparents were diehard Republicans, they chose to ignore the horrors south of Skid Road. I'd been taught to believe that the unemployed were mere criminals and scoundrels who wouldn't work if they could. Yet after one visit to Seattle's Hooverville, I was never the same.

It was Lizzie's idea to go. She had a friend she often visited there during the summer, unbeknownst to me or any of my family. Initially I was terrified at the suggestion of such a risky adventure. I could only imagine disease-ridden rats, open sewers and men who would take advantage of adolescent girls in the most despicable ways. Therefore I was much relieved when I learned of Lizzie's chaperon, Big Ben, a giant of a man who worked as a shoeshiner at the Olympic Hotel. He was as black as tar, as gentle as a puppy and I loved him immediately. It was during the glorious Indian summer that we began our secret weekly ritual.

School started after Labor day that year and it was decided that Lizzie would attend Holy Names Academy with me, by the grace of my grandfather's wallet. Papa Joseph's endless labors had paid off with a new contract to build a luxury ship for the Prince of Wales. As a result, our household became a bit more jovial and considerably more relaxed. Papa Joseph celebrated our good fortune by purchasing a new Stromberg-Carlson radio for the parlor. Over the summer, we'd all grown very fond of listening to Arthur Godfrey's witty news programs and the evening serial, "The Goldbergs." Though Papa had a general dislike of Jews, or 'kykes' as he called them, his raucous laughter could be heard all over our great house as he listened to the tales of the hilarious Jewish family from New York City's Lower East Side. His second blessing upon our household was securing a decent education for Lizzie.

Lizzie was put off by my school at first. The elegant Romanesque structure with its pale exterior and Neo-classical angels peeking out from every nook and cranny was daunting compared to the drab public school she had attended. However, despite her initial misgivings, Lizzie eventually accepted the place. In less than three weeks after her arrival at Holy Names, she'd completely given up her slum slang, as I called it, and began to use proper grammar, at least in the presence of teachers and other adults. Additionally, Lizzie was an excellent student, so it didn't take long for the nuns to favor her.

Every morning at eight, we walked seven blocks to school and every afternoon we'd return promptly home at three, except for Thursdays. Claudia worked at the Third Avenue soup kitchen that day and so, with my mother's approval, Lizzie and I were allowed to take the streetcar there. Upon our arrival, Lizzie would eventually convince her mother to allow us to go to Bartell Drugstore for a soda. Claudia was busy with her work, so she'd always give in with the stipulation that we be back in time to catch the streetcar to Capitol Hill.

From then on, it was a race against time. We would fly down the street to the Olympic Hotel where Big Ben sat on the curb, his pancake-flat hands wrapped around a steaming cup of black coffee. He was so tall that his bent knees nearly touched his shoulders. His fleeced head was as round as Ernest's new basketball and his whitewashed smile was so bright, it could wake up a hibernating bear. Though his dinner break was his only time to rest, Big Ben never said no to Lizzie's requests to accompany us. Each of us would grab one of Big Ben's hands and we'd jump on the first streetcar heading south to the community of tin, tar paper and packing box shanties.

Our final destination was the East side of Hooverville through narrow, filthy alleys where beaten souls sat on stumps, their hollow eyes dulled by hunger and despair. On occasion a stranger's eyes rested hungrily on my breasts. Grateful for Big Ben, I clutched his hand tighter as we hurried past. I felt tremendously daring as we skipped through the hovels, but my compassion for these lost ones was enormous. Sometimes Lizzie and I would pack extra food in our school bags, handing out apples or biscuits to a few of the more familiar folks.

At the end of a long alley there was a *barabaras* where an old Indian lived. Though his body was emaciated, he still cared for himself with pride. A thick black braid trailed like a bull snake down his back and his dwelling was spotlessly clean. Lizzie said he was a mystic who could read people's minds. There was something unusual about the ancient fellow. His cloudy eyes glowed with wisdom and his grip was strong when his sinewy hand shook mine.

Little Bull's home was hollowed out of the rubble like a small cave with a rustic clay oven in one corner and a pile of wood in the other. A couple of crates served as chairs and a few animal skins adorn the walls. Little Bull slept on a black bear hide that was rolled up in one corner. On the wall hung a beautiful, leather-webbed ring covered with feathers, shells and beads. The old Indian called it a dream catcher. He said whenever he needed an answer to an important question, he would spin around the fire, dream catcher in hand. Soon the dream catcher caught the answer from the universe. Later, Little Bull would dream the answer he was seeking. I took quite a liking to the elder, though he was as foreign to me as snow to a Tahitian.

Once there, we'd seat ourselves down next to Little Bull on his colorful Indian blanket and listen to his exciting tales of life before the white man. Little Bull was once an interpreter for the Lummi and Samish tribes and had also worked in the lumber camps, but now he was too old and sick to do either. However, his storytelling had become famous in this part of the city where there was no other form of entertainment except a game of cards.

I'll never forget the visit during which I received my sacred tribal name. That afternoon Little Bull began by teaching us to mimic 13 different mountain birds. His strange, squeaky voice could sing the most beautiful arias from the bluebird's lilting song to the seagull's mournful cry. Inevitably our crew would dissolve into fits of laughter whenever Lizzie or I tried to copy him. Yet the language of animals was one of his simpler lessons and in his gentle way, Little Bull taught me more about life than anyone had before him.

"Emily, you shall have the name of White Dove from now on," he said after I'd made a pitiful attempt to imitate the pretty bird. Reaching forward, he tucked a white feather behind my ear. "Do you know why?"

"Not because I can sing like one, that's for sure!" I grinned as Lizzie giggled in affirmation. With an indulgent smile, he continued,

"In my culture we see the appearance of the dove as a good omen, for it is she who brings peace to the world. Lizzie has found peace in your friendship together. For that I am grateful, for then I may find peace." I nodded, thoroughly entranced by his eyes, burning like bolts of lightening into my own. With a deep drag on his pipe, Little Bull blew a billow of smoke in my direction.

Lizzie loved episodes such as this, believing Little Bull's revelations as easily as I believed in our Lord, Jesus Christ.

During one of the last sunny days of October, we made our final trip to Hooverville. The sky was a bright cornflower blue and in the distance, Mt. Rainier towered above the city as our holy citadel of hope. Red and gold maple leaves were sprinkled like confetti on the lawn of the Academy as we raced out its huge, paneled doors to catch the bus. Before long we arrived at the Third Avenue soup kitchen. Its decrepit doorway was tucked between two boarded-up windows on a section of the street that was desperate for commerce. Scraps of paper were stamped on the sidewalk from the recent rain shower and the air smelled of stale smoke and barley soup. Despondent merchants leaned against the buildings, yearning for a sale. Even the bleak business of panhandling had moved to Fifth and Pine where the elite still frequented the antique shops and fine restaurants. A line of hungry-looking people waited outside for their meager meal. We walked through the alley to the back door and entered the cooking area where we found Claudia. She was bustling about, stirring big pots of stew and tossing biscuits into tin bowls. Her pretty face was flushed and her blue eyes twinkled as she caught sight of us.

"Hello girls! How was your day?" she asked cheerfully.

"Great, Mama . I got an 'A' on my history exam," Lizzie gloated, her wide mouth turning up at the corners.

"Good girl, Lizzie! I knew you could do it. See, the Academy is doing you some good. I knew I'd made the right decision to accept Joseph's help. Remember what I've always said, an education is what makes the difference between a free woman and an enslaved one."

I smiled at Claudia. She was so smart! "May we go to Bartell's today, Claudia?" I asked.

Claudia sighed and wiped her hands on her greasy apron. "Okay, but behave yourselves."

Off we went, rushing out the door and down Third Avenue, crossing at Pine and up to Fourth where we stopped in front the decorous entrance of the Olympic Hotel. There we found Big Ben, waving his arm at us. The streetcar was nearly full when we jumped on at Fourth and Pine and headed down the street. The further south we traveled, the more dilapidated the city became. Several storefronts were boarded up and vacancy signs frequently appeared. The lumbering streetcar turned at Fortson Square, sometimes called Pigeon Square for all the birds that gathered there. Screeching pigeons cried for scraps, but there was little to be found. Signs advertising Turkey Red Cigarettes, Rainier Beer and posters relishing the joys of the 'Bump and Grind' houses were the only touch of color in this gray part of the world. We hopped off at Second and Yesler and scurried down Skid Road toward Little Bull's home. It was nearly four o'clock when we arrived. As usual, our stay would be less than a half an hour.

When we entered the dugout, we found Little Bull huddled up in a corner next to his makeshift stove, wrapped in his bearskin. He was coughing badly and his skin was yellow and pasty looking. A bottle full of a murky green substance was on the floor next to him. I wondered if it was one of his native medicines.

"Hello, my friends. I'm glad you are here," he whispered in a voice like sandpaper.

We shuffled in and sat on the crates, staring, tongue-tied, at Little Bull. It was disturbing to see our storyteller feeling so poorly. Big Ben reached into his coat and pulled out a couple of raw potatoes and a cabbage.

"This is for you," Big Ben muttered with difficulty. Clearly the kindhearted Negro felt as helpless as I did.

"Thank you, my son. You're very good to me, but this will be that last time you will need to help me. The Great Father has called to me and soon I shall return to the land of Grandfather Spirit."

Big Ben shook his head, his voice cracking. "Jesus be with you, man."

"But let us take you to the hospital," I blurted, avoiding Lizzie's slashing gaze.

"No, White Dove. There is nothing the white man's medicines can do for me. I need to return home. That's where I will find peace."

I wanted to interrupt, argue, persuade him to reconsider, but his eyes told me to remain silent and I obeyed. "I wish to give you something before I go, Singing Sparrow." He addressed Lizzie in the Indian name he'd given her long ago. I glanced over at her in the dim light. She was trembling as though gripped by the icy claws of winter. Her face was ashen with grief.

Lizzie knelt down next to Little Bull and placed her hand on his heart. Her ebony eyes glowed with tender affection as she spoke. "Little Bull, I wish you didn't have to go. I'll miss you terribly." Her voice was thick with emotion. She bowed her head as Little Bull shoved the tip of a sage stick into the fire to light it. He waved the stick's pungent smoke around Lizzie's body until she appeared to be suspended in a cloud. With great effort, he slowly reached his hand down and pulled a small leather bag from his pocket.

"This is my medicine bag, Singing Sparrow. It's filled with magical treasures and protective medicines. You'll need this in the days when the wrathful white warrior ravages our earth. Many lives will be shed, but yours will be spared if you keep this medicine bag with you." I stared at him, memorizing his haunting words as he placed the bag around Lizzie's neck. Immediately her face became peaceful as though the bag were a tonic for her sorrow. From her school bag, Lizzie pulled out a jar of amber liquid.

"I love you, Little Bull. I hope this firewater will ease the pain of your illness." She planted a kiss on his withered cheek and stepped away, motioning to Big Ben. He bent down next to Little Bull and took his frail hands into his own.

"Man, you been like a daddy to me. I was hopin' to get you outta here. Ain't der nothin' I can do for you?" his sonorous voice rumbled.

Little Bull's smile transformed his face into a sheet of crushed parchment. "Nothing you can do, big fella. Now off with you all, and get these young ladies back in time. Don't worry about me. The tribe will fetch me at dawn."

We stumbled out of the dugout, blinking in the pale autumn light. Lizzie seemed dazed, so Big Ben wrapped his great muscular arm around her shoulders, holding her close to him. Smiling down at me, he squeezed my hand. "You gonna be all right, Miss Emily?" he asked.

"I guess so. I feel sorry for Little Bull. We should do something, Big Ben."

"Ain't nothin we kin do. His family be comin' for him. I seen him out on the tidal flats before, his arms raised like a preacher. He calls to 'em."

"I don't understand. Why does he live in Hooverville if he could be with his tribe?"

Big Ben shrugged his broad, blue-uniformed shoulders. "Don't know, 'cept maybe he's some kinda teacher. He's been telling stories to them poor men down there for lotta years."

As we hurried back to the soup kitchen, I remembered to ask Lizzie what was in the bottle she'd given Little Bull.

"Old Overholt Whiskey, that's what," she replied casually as she gazed into Frederick and Nelson's picture window at a mink-draped mannequin.

"So where'd you get it?"

"I found it in the hidden cupboard on the west tower stairs. It belongs to Papa Joseph, but since he's always talking about the importance of caring for your fellow man, I didn't think he'd mind if I took some for Little Bull."

I clapped my hand over my mouth and giggled, "You've got guts! I'd never take a risk like that."

"Hey, you should see what else it up there! Your Papa's got some weird stuff. A flag with a strange sign on it, like a cross with sides, and two white robes with gold braid."

"That's probably his Mason stuff. Nobody's supposed to see it. He'd have a fit if he knew you'd been up there. You be careful!"

Her steady gaze told me that she would, indeed, be very, very careful.

❖   ❖   ❖

Autumn's remainder sped by and before we knew it, Santa's season had arrived. I woke up early on the Saturday morning before Christmas Eve. The house was quiet except for my dog's contented snoring rising from the carpet below me. Chippy was one of my best friends, a constant companion in good times and bad. Ironically, he had only one nemesis. Papa Joseph barely tolerated poor Chip, who was careful to stay out of the old man's way, even when outside in the garden.

Climbing out of bed, I knelt down, giving the dog a hug. He groaned with pleasure while his fluffy tail continued its happy thudding. I donned a dressing gown, ran downstairs to the front door where I grabbed the newspaper and let the dog out.

The newspaper was a sought-after commodity in our home. Beyond the borders of our country, the world was becoming an unpredictable place. I was intrigued by all that was happening, particularly because a dynamic new leader had gained power in my grandfather's native country of Germany. Adolf Hitler had become a household name, rekindling a sense of cultural pride I'd rarely witnessed in my family. Since Hitler's arrival in *Deutschland*, Papa Joseph had played German folk music on the phonograph nearly every day. Josephine was instructed to cook *sauerbraten, spatzle* and *strudel* for Sunday dinners. With my father's approval, my brothers were enrolled in German language classes and Papa's normal brooding was replaced with a gregarious appetite for celebration. Many evenings, friends from the German Society would visit, drinking pilsner until the wee hours of the morning. We all basked in Papa's newly acquired sense of fun. I grew fonder of my grandfather as time passed, inspired by his hopeful attitude for the old country. In retrospect, I shudder to think where we might have ended up if it hadn't been for Lizzie.

I'd have to scan the paper quickly before Papa arrived for breakfast. Scampering into the kitchen, I found Josephine hugging the side of the stove. Her obese body, round as a truck tire, jiggled as she briskly stirred a pot of oatmeal. Nearby Lizzie was busily kneading a batch of strudel dough. I poured myself a cup of coffee, a habit which I had kept secret from all but my kitchen cohorts and buried my nose in the paper. Lizzie glanced over at me.

"So what's the news today?" she mumbled, her arms elbow-deep in dough.

"Sounds like the isolationists are at it again, quibbling about Roosevelt. Rain is expected for Christmas and Frederick and Nelson's Santa Claus will be handing out gifts at the Children's Home tomorrow."

Lizzie yawned. "Santa ain't real. I don't know why they keep lying to the kids like that."

"I guess I don't see it as lying. I mean, if you believe in Santa Claus, you believe in hope and the goodness of giving. You know all about that, Lizzie."

"True. Hey, did you hear all the commotion last night? I could have sworn I heard a baby cryin' in the middle of the night." Lizzie paused as I stared at her.

"The baby!" I jumped up from the table and grabbed her arm. "Come on!"

Seconds later we sped up the staircase, three steps at a time and ran down the hallway to my parents' room. Quietly, I knocked on the door. "Mama," I whispered. "May I come in?" Father opened the door, dressed in his flannel robe and house slippers. His eyes had dark circles under them, but his face was full of joy. "You've got yourself another brother, Emmy. Come on in and take a look," he murmured.

Lizzie and I tiptoed into the room. My mother was sitting up in the bed. Her peach silk robe was draped over her shoulders and her right breast was slightly exposed. A blue bundle was tucked into the crook of her arm.

"When, how?" I stuttered, approaching the bed to look down at the shriveled little being in her arms. He reminded me of the newborn pigs I'd seen at the Ellensburg State Fair.

"Jonathan came so suddenly, we didn't have time to go to the hospital. Dr. Cruthers came to the house instead," my mother explained with a weary smile.

I looked around the room. There was a bedpan and a lump of towels on the floor next to the bed. Despite the cold, the window was open slightly ajar. My mother had the baby in her bed! Lizzie had an expression of amazed wonder on her face. She leaned closer and touched the baby's head.

"Oh, look, he's gonna have black hair," she cooed. "Can I hold him?"

"Of course, Lizzie. Why don't you sit down on the bed and get yourself settled." My mother handed Lizzie the bundle called Jonathan while I silently ruminated over the arrival of yet another brother. I had to admit the baby was sort of cute.

"You named him after Uncle Jonathan?" I asked, trying to sound casual. Mother gave the briefest of affirmations. Mention of Uncle Jonathan usually brought tears to Mother's eyes. He was her older brother who had died in the trenches of the Great War. Only two years apart in age, they were very close growing up. Mother always said that Johnny had protected her from Grandmother's wrath and she had protected him from the wide-eyed girls who swarmed him like flies.

Uncle Jonathan was missing in action for nearly five years after the war. As a result, I was born into a household mired in despair. As a young child, I recalled the hollow look that would appear on my grandfather's face whenever his son's name was mentioned. By the time Jack was born, all hope for Jonathan's return had dissolved. Eventually the suffocating cloak of gloom gradually lifted, but Jonathan was still a subject of great discontent. Papa Joseph could never accept that his own countrymen had killed his son.

My thoughts stopped with the sound of my mother's deep sigh.

She glanced over at my father and nodded. "Okay, young ladies, time to go. Mother needs her rest," he said.

Lizzie handed the dozing baby back to my father, who placed him into a little bassinet next to the bed. As we drifted out the door, Lizzie turned back to my mother and said,

"I love little Jonathan already. I hope you'll let me help you with him."

My parents shared an amused smile. "Thank you, Lizzie. We certainly will," Mother replied.

I wandered downstairs to the library, contemplating the miraculous, middle-of-the night event. I found Papa Joseph in the library, staring at Jonathan's medal of valor. It hung above the fireplace mantel.

"I couldn't find the newspaper this morning, *fraulein*," he grumbled. "I thought I warned you about that."

"I'm sorry," I apologized. Walking over to his bulky frame, I wrapped my arms around his waist and gave him a hug. "I love you, Papa."

He gazed down at me with a flicker of sadness in his eyes. "Why, Emily, what was the meaning of that?"

I blushed. "I don't know," I stuttered self-consciously. "I guess you looked like you needed a hug." Papa's silver, handlebar mustache twitched as his steel gray eyes peered down at me under a chunky hedge of eyebrows.

"You're quite a perceptive young lady." He turned away and looked back at the medal.

"Are you glad Mother and Father named the baby after Uncle Jonathan?"

Papa Joseph gave a nod. "Yes, I am."

The next comment slipped out of my mouth before I could stop it. I was as shocked as he was at my candor. "I'm sorry Jonathan died."

Papa heaved his body into the nearby armchair and put his hands over his eyes. Minutes passed in utter silence. He might punish me, I thought, remembering the last time I'd angered him after leaving my bicycle out on the curb. He wouldn't talk to me for almost a month. It was as though I was invisible to him, which for me was the most painful punishment of all.

"I'm sorry, too. The Germans were very wrong to start that damn war. Hopefully Adolf Hitler will be the answer to my old country's woes. I'm placing a lot of faith in him."

I leaned against his chair, noticing that his bald head gleamed with sweat, though the room was rather chilly. I crouched on the floor next to him and gingerly took his hand. "I hope so, too." We sat there quietly in the shadows, lost in thought, but imperceptibly connected to one another. "Please tell me the story of your mama again. It's my very favorite."

Papa Joseph chuckled, stroking his mustache thoughtfully. "*Sitzen Sie.*"

The library was the perfect setting for one of Papa's stories. Dark and splendidly appointed with walnut paneling and wall-to-wall bookcases stuffed with leather-bound classics, the room hinted of hidden treasures and exotic adventures. A Siberian tiger skin covered the gleaming parquet floor like a lump of vanilla ice cream adrift in a sea of chocolate sauce. A large globe sat on the monolithic oak desk, marked with lines indicating my grandfather's overseas travels. On various antique tables, Chinese jade carvings competed with African heads and Indonesian shadow puppets. Claudia had decorated the mantel with sprigs of fresh holly and red-ribboned baskets of pine cones sat on the brick hearth. Curling up on the tiger skin at my grandfather's feet, I peered into his pale eyes and waited. He cleared his voice and stared out across the room as though he could see a continent away.

"I was born in a castle in the heart of the Bavarian forest in 1874. My mother, Gerda Danglemeier, was a lady-in-waiting at the royal court of Kaiser Wilhelm Hohenzollern. Mother was only 22 when she discovered she was pregnant by a lover she had taken once during a moment of passion. Though my father was a handsome young buck, he was a mere foot soldier and not of her class. They weren't allowed to wed and eventually he was banished. Oh, my poor mother." He gazed off and shook his head as if to rid his mind of a momentary pain.

When Papa Joseph returned to the story, his voice had deepened as if memory itself had aged him. "After I was born, the presiding princess of the castle tried to force my mother to give me up, but she refused. Her only option was to leave the country to avoid further disgrace. In 1875 my mother and I boarded a luxury liner and set sail to New York City. Three years later, she met a well-to-do banker, Otto Danfrauer. He was like a father to me." Papa's eyes glistened with haunted thoughts as he said gruffly, "You know the rest of the story. I need some breakfast now."

Nodding dutifully, I started towards the door as he added, "You're a good girl, Emily. *Eine gute Deutsche fraulein.*"

After delivering his breakfast, I skipped upstairs to dress, my mind still dancing with inspiration. Papa's stories had an amazing way of raising my opinion of myself.

"Psst … ," a voice hissed. I turned around on the landing and squinted down the hall.

"Em, come here." A finger curled out from around the door of the big storage closet.

Traipsing to the closet, I pulled open the door. "Claudia, why are you hiding in here?"

"I have Lizzie's Santa Claus gift, but I need some help putting it together."

I hurriedly stepped in and shut the door. The large closet was more like a room than a storage space. In the corner was the most beautiful bike I'd ever laid eyes on. It was a gleaming cerulean blue with ribbons on the wheels and a little horn attached to the handlebars.

"Gosh, that's beautiful, but you have one problem, Claudia." I gave a half smile. "Lizzie doesn't believe in Santa Claus."

"Well, she will now, won't she?" Claudia's eyes sparkled with a childlike glee. "I've wanted to do this for her for so long," she cried as she handed me the tire pump.

I stood there uncomfortably, shifting from one foot to the other until Claudia caught my eye.

"Say it! You can't hurt my feelings. We were too damn poor. But because your wonderful family, I've been able to set some money aside from my job at the hospital. I don't know what I'd do without all of you." She gave me a sincere smile and patted my hand. "Now pump up those tires while I hold this thing still."

"Maybe it's not my place to ask, but I've always wondered," I said while pushing the pump handle up and down. "Why doesn't your family help you?" Claudia gave me a look of infinite sadness.

"It's a long story. I don't know if I have the courage or the heart to tell you."

I stood there, wishing I could disappear. "That's okay. It's none of my business anyway," I mumbled.

"You're right. It isn't," Claudia agreed as I breathed a sigh of relief. "But I think if you knew a little more, you might understand my Lizzie better. She's had a hard time of it. She has a scar on her right hand.

Have you seen it?" Claudia's face was grave as she searched mine. I nodded, flinching unconsciously as it came to mind. On the palm of Lizzie's hand was a deep, perfectly round purple scar about the size of a nickel. I'd often wondered about its cause. Once when I touched it, Lizzie pulled away as though I had bit her. I'd never mentioned it again.

"It happened when she was three years old. Tobi, her father, had left us and I was completely broke. I swallowed the measly bit of pride I had remaining and went to my father for help. I'll never forget that day as long as I live."

Claudia's face grew pale as she slipped into the memory. "I'd taken Lizzie with me to my parent's home on Millionaire's Row. Gosh, I was desperate. Neither of my parents had ever seen Lizzie. Oh, she was so adorable! Her black hair was cut in a bob and her smile was as sweet as could be. But my parents were not pleased. They knew her daddy was an Indian. My father pulled us into the library, locked the door and began screaming at me, accusing me of ruining his reputation in the city and shaming my mother beyond repair. Poor little Lizzie was so frightened by all the yelling. Eventually my father grew so angry he slapped me across the face. At that moment, Lizzie picked up his lit cigar from the ashtray on his desk and shoved it into the palm of her hand. I was so caught up in the argument, I didn't see what was happening until the smell of burning flesh began to fill the room. She held that cigar there without a whimper. How could a child do that? I still ask myself. Needless to say, Lizzie's action silenced my father. I think Lizzie wanted to stop him and that was the only way she could think of." Claudia gave a sudden tremble and closed her eyes tightly. When she opened them again, they were damp with the dew of tragedy. She reached out and placed her hands on my shoulders, murmuring, "Lizzie is a mystery to me. It's as though she's lived a thousand years."

I nodded, speechless, but understanding exactly what she meant. Lizzie had already become my window to the universe.

Christmas of 1933 was the most joyful Christmas I can remember until after the war. The gifts under the tree were not exotic, or plentiful, but the voice of a newborn child echoed throughout our festive home and the scents of mouth-watering meals filled our heads.

Claudia had decorated the Christmas tree with electric lights and the boys had strung miles of popcorn strands while Lizzie and Josephine had added gingerbread ornaments. Papa surprised us all with an overflowing bag of pecans and a gigantic box of chocolates—a rare treat even for our household. Even Grandmother Ginny fussed about, fastening mistletoe to the chandeliers and hanging colorful stockings from the mantels.

When I look back, I don't think we'd ever been happier. As the new year came upon us, the Danfrauer family had much to be grateful for. When I search my mind today, I still try to recall one clue, one small hint that might have prepared us for the years to come, but I can think of none.

4

"It's a shame you haven't seen David yet," I gushed, gazing out my bedroom window at the stately Georgian mansion where new neighbors had recently moved in.

Lizzie, who was sitting in my blue chintz chair feeding Jonathan, merely shrugged. "What's the big deal about boys anyway?" she grumbled. "I've never seen a ninth grade girl get so charged up about anything in my life. Ever since you started going to charm school, you've gone kooky in the head," Lizzie grinned, crossed her eyes and stuck out her tongue.

I regarded Lizzie with exaggerated disdain. "You know, a girl who makes a joke of everything pushes romance away from her."

Lizzie made a gagging sound as she rocked Jonathan to sleep. "Put your etiquette in the back seat. Once Johnny's asleep, let's visit Mr. Gerstein. He said he has a new book on birds for me."

"I can't figure out why you're so fascinated by birds, and you won't even take one short flight with Father. You know he's taking me flying tomorrow. Are you sure you don't want to come?"

Lizzie shook her head. "You'll never get my skinny ass in a plane."

I laughed as we left the room and walked down the hall to Mother's room where Lizzie put Johnny to bed.

"Come on!" she urged, racing down the stairs ahead of me. We skipped across the lawn to the shed where we grabbed our bicycles.

"Last one to Gerstein's is a rotten egg," I hollered as I sped ahead.

"Slow down, you! Hey, speaking of the devil," she shouted. "There's Tommy Mason, all spiffed up with nowhere to go." Sure enough, my old childhood friend was sauntering across the street in his Seattle Prep school uniform like a boot camp graduate in a parade.

I slowed down my bike to her pace. "He's not that bad, Lizzie. Besides, he's got a huge crush on you."

"Don't remind me! I doubledare you to kiss him!" she said flippantly.

I paused to think about my plan. "Okay, I'll tell you what, if I kiss Tommy Mason, you have to do something for me."

"There ain't nothin' you could think of that would scare me," she retorted playfully.

"Wanna bet? How about you have to go flying with Father tomorrow!"

Lizzie's skin blanched to a sickly mustard upon hearing my suggestion. Swallowing hard, she slowly climbed off her bike and leaned it against the wall of Gerstein's. "Okay," she whispered with closed eyes. "I'll do it."

That night after dinner, I telephoned Tommy, convincing him to climb up the oak tree and crawl through my window where he believed Lizzie would be hiding in the wardrobe, waiting for a kiss. It was a mean trick, but it was the only way to get Tommy to do it. I knew he wouldn't kiss me in a million years. Yet I was determined to get Lizzie up in a plane, so if this was what was required, so be it.

It was a pretty evening in late May. Surrounded by a silky sky, Mt. Rainier glowed in the waning sunlight like heaven's golden dome. The family had gathered on the back terrace to listen to the radio and lap up a batch of Papa's homemade vanilla ice cream. Papa made a big production over our tasty concoction. He sang a German folk song at top volume as he cranked the machine and dished out enormous portions to everyone. After our fill, we sat down to enjoy an evening of radio entertainment. A sense of comfort clutched my heart as I leaned back in the hammock with Lizzie, listening to the exciting pursuits of the glamorous chorus line sisters, Myrt and Marge. In the backyard, Ernest and Jack tossed a football while Mother, fresh-faced and glowing, rocked Jonathan in the lawn swing. Claudia and Grandmother sat side by side on the canvas-covered divan, knitting an afghan. Father and Papa relaxed at the picnic table. An antique Persian chessboard was sandwiched on the table between them, along with two crystal goblets filled with Drambuie. Papa fingered his mustache and Father gripped his pipe in studious concentration as each vied for his own make-believe kingdom.

As the melodramatic episode of Myrt and Marge came to an end, I motioned to Lizzie to follow me into the house. "And now, for our favorite Jewish family, the endearing, Goldbergs," the radio announcer said.

"Turn it off," Papa Joseph growled.

"Why, Papa?" Mother asked quietly. "It's our favorite program."

"I don't want to hear about those damn kykes. They're the scourge of the earth!"

"Joseph, please!" Father balked. "We don't believe that in our family."

41

"Do you mean to tell me you still haven't read *Mein Kampf?*"

"No, and I don't intend to," Mother replied firmly. I stood perfectly still, watching this suspenseful drama unfold. Claudia rose and walked toward me.

"Excuse me, Emily," she whispered as she slipped into the house. Claudia always left during family arguments, with Lizzie automatically in tow. I, however, stayed rooted to the spot. I wasn't going to miss this episode of the Danfrauer soap opera.

"Joseph, not everyone in this family embraces Hitler's philosophy," Father responded stiffly.

"Embrace it? You must live it, my man!" Papa Joseph shouted. His waxed mustache began to twitch frantically. His heavy jowls quivered like a bowl of jelly as spittle flew from his lips. "You mustn't put money in the Jews' pockets any longer," he raged. "Lord knows they've swindled us for far too long as it is! They contaminate our society! They should all be exterminated."

A dreadful silence filled the circle. The boys had drifted away, invisible in the bushes beyond the garden. For a moment, no one seemed to breathe, as though the tension in the air had caused an inescapable vacuum. All I could think of was kind Mr. Gerstein and his sweet wife, Edith. My grandfather certainly wasn't referring to them!

"The children enjoy this show. There's no reason to impose the Hitler's views on them, is there?" Father asked in a tense voice.

Papa Joseph's face grew dark as he sputtered, "It is most important that Hitler's views become our views. He is well-respected by many Germans and this family is a German family. It's about time we had someone to be proud of."

"He's defying the treaty, for heaven's sakes. How can you support a man who challenges the Versailles agreement?"

"I don't give a damn about the Versailles Treaty. After Britain and France's preposterous secret treaties to take over Germany, how can you take them seriously? Hitler is our true ally, not those corrupt Anglos!" Papa yelled.

His rage seemed to heat the atmosphere as he spoke. Mother's bright eyes were bulging with fear and her skin had become a ghastly white. With a pleading look, she stared at Ginny, but she just continued her knitting with icy-cold detachment.

"That was over 18 years ago. The world is a different place. Germany must regain its strength, like the rest of us, but not at the expense of the Jews or anyone else. Don't you think we've had enough war for one century? If Hitler continues to anger the rest of Europe, that will be the result, I'm certain," Father explained without a trace of trepidation. My father had lived with Papa for a long time. He was very adept at side-stepping my grandfather's unpredictable outbursts, but I could see the toll this took by the anguish in his eyes.

Papa rose up in his chair, his bulky frame towering over my father. "Just remember where you live, George. This is still my house. If you don't like Hitler, get out," he hissed as he shoved his index finger at my father's nose. Father didn't flinch.

Mother's trembling voice broke the tension. "Children, it's getting late. Time for bed. Ernest, Jackie, come in now," she called. I took that opportunity to disappear into the house, wondering what other harsh words might be said tonight.

I ran up the stairs to my room, entirely perplexed by the nasty scene on the patio. I pushed my tumultuous thoughts aside; it was nearly time for Tommy's arrival. Moving to the window, I looked down and saw the top of his baseball cap as he struggled to make the treacherous climb up the oak tree. He'll do anything for Lizzie, I thought with a touch of pity. Lizzie was already positioned outside my door, her eye peering in through the keyhole.

I had to hand it to him, Tommy was an enterprising young chap. He climbed through the window with a bundle of yellow daffodils clenched between his teeth. Glancing down, I saw an empty space in the middle of our pristine bulb garden. I laughed and gave him a slap on the head. "Tommy, what's the deal? You can't even pick them from your own garden?" As I yanked the flowers from his mouth, he produced a goofy smile.

"So where's Lizzie?" he asked in a squeaky voice. Adolescence had finally attacked his vocal chords.

"She'll only do it in the wardrobe. You have to close your eyes and put your nose in the corner of the room until you hear a knock on the wardrobe door. That will be your signal to enter. Then she'll kiss you and if you tell anyone, Tommy, I swear I'll cut your ears off," I threatened, forcing a stern frown. "Remember, *you owe me one*." Tommy nodded like a dog begging for a bone as I grabbed his shoulders and spun him around, shoving him into the opposite corner. "Now count," I ordered.

I crawled quietly into the closet while he counted, pressing myself against the armory of pinafores, pleated wool skirts and plaid jumpers. He climbed in moments later and whispered a ridiculous phrase, "Oh Lizzie, you are so beautiful" as his hands poked at my chin. I leaned forward and stuck my lips into the air. His landed on mine in a haphazard smash and then we froze as my grandmother's voice echoed in our ears.

"Emily!" My heart started to race. Where was Lizzie? Two voices mumbled as the sound of footsteps drifted down the hall. I held my breath, waiting for silence. Tommy released a little sigh.

"Geez, I guess I'd better get out of here, huh?" With that, he nearly flew from the closet and scrambled out of the window. The last thing he said was, "I love you, Lizzie."

It was nearly five minutes before I stopped laughing. Lizzie stepped into the room as I crawled out of the wardrobe.

"Where in the heck were you?" I giggled.

"Whew, that was a close call," she murmured, wiping invisible sweat from her brow. Your grandmother was looking for you. I couldn't just stand in front of your door, looking like some mobster. I acted as if I was looking for you too, said you wasn't in your room. So, how was Mr. Sausagebreath's kiss, then, Emily?" she scoffed, her lips curling into a sardonic grin.

"Shut up, Lizzie!"

She giggled so hard she collapsed on the bed, holding her crotch. "I'm goin' to pee my panties. I can't believe you kissed that moron!" she hooted with glee. I laughed, too, because I'd won the bet after all.

That night, I tossed and turned, riddled with questions. My grandfather's anger frightened me and his motives were a mystery. Why did he suddenly hate the Jews? What did Hitler have to do with it? Why was the world so complicated? If people could just learn to accept each other's differences, perhaps we could live in harmony. Apparently man's need to repress others had fueled a struggle for freedom all around the world. Japan had invaded Manchuria and now Hitler was challenging the peace treaty, which was supposed to prevent more world wars. What were we, the children of the future, to believe when we witnessed such pandemonium?

Early the next morning I dragged Lizzie out of bed in time to go flying as she'd promised. We were sitting in the back seat of my father's car, waiting to leave for Boeing field where Father kept his de Havilland Puss Moth. The sky was bluer than a robin's egg and the wind was at five knots per hour from the east. Anxious excitement filled me for it had been over nine months since our last excursion. Father was not a poor weather flyer, primarily due to Mother's insistence on safety. Though my brothers occasionally flew with him, I was the one who usually wanted to go. I loved it as much as my father. He had already begun to teach me the basics by the time Lizzie accompanied us that bright spring day.

"Wait until you experience the liftoff and the way your stomach rises in sync with the machine. You'll soar like the birds that you love so much, Lizzie!" I bubbled, bouncing up and down on the springy leather seats in anticipation.

Lizzie sat next to me, as tense as a trapped animal. Her face was pale and tiny beads of sweat covered her turned-up nose.

"You look scared pea green! It's not as bad as you think," I tried to convince her. Still, silence. "Look, I never pester you about this kind of stuff, but I've got to ask you. Why are you so afraid?" I pushed on, frustrated by ignorance.

Taking her chin in my hand, I turned her toward me and gazed into a face of pure terror. I whispered. "You don't have to do this, you know. Just forget the bet. I don't care about it."

"I never break a promise," she whispered without breaking our gaze. "So I'll tell you why, seeins' it's drivin' you crazy. When I was three years old, we went to visit my grandparents. Grandfather acted very friendly to me at first. He put me on his shoulders and bounced me around the house. Eventually he carried me upstairs to the library. There was a balcony up there. He was joking. Then suddenly his voice got very creepy. We were on the balcony when he lifted me off his shoulders and then he hung me over the edge. He called me a filthy Injun brat ... said he was going to drop me." Lizzie's shoulders started to shake as tears filled her eyes, but before she could continue, my father climbed into the car.

"Hey, girls! Are you ready to fly with the angels?" he asked cheerfully. Lizzie bit her lip and looked out the window.

Impulsively leaning over the back seat, I chirped, "We can't wait!" Father smiled, entirely oblivious to Lizzie's state of mind. He turned on the radio and began to whistle. I reached over and clutched Lizzie's hand, holding it all the way to the airstrip. When we arrived, Father went into the air traffic controller's office to sign into the logbook. Lizzie quietly climbed out of the car, her movements stiff.

"I said you don't have to go," I repeated. "You can wait for us in the terminal. I'm so sorry about what happened."

"Me, too, but I'm not going to let his meanness hurt me anymore. Thanks for letting me tell you that stuff. It feels better now that I've told someone. I'm going up in that plane. I'm going to get rid of this icky fear once and for all."

Minutes later we were strapping ourselves into the gleaming silver de Havilland. The engines roared and the propellers began to spin as Father checked the instruments. I sat in the front seat next to him, continuously looking back to check on Lizzie.

She gave me a determined smile. "It's okay, " she mouthed. "I can do this."

Soon we were taxing down the runway for takeoff. We lifted off the ground with a burst of power as Father pushed to full throttle. The shiny, metallic bird glided in a great curve to the southwest and then north until we were flying over the city. I felt the rush of bubbling joy in my veins. Lizzie was no longer huddled down in her seat. She was leaning over and staring out the window as we flew past the Smith Tower.

"Wow wee! This is great!" she screamed. "The buildings are like Jack's toy building blocks. Everybody looks like ants. Oh, Mr. Strong, this is wonderful!" she added with a giggle. I laughed in relief. Lizzie was as brave as they come. I still couldn't comprehend what she'd told me. My heart had felt crushed by the horror of it. What an evil, sadistic man her grandfather was! The intense hatred Lizzie had expressed toward her grandparents made sense to me now. Most importantly, Lizzie had shared her tragic secret. After all this time, she was finally beginning to trust me.

By the time we returned from our airborne odyssey, Lizzie was nearly as excited about flying as I was. She was transfixed by the instruments and begged to sit next to Father the next time we flew. "Flying is in our blood, Emily," Father often said. "Once you experience the magic of flight, you can never be completely happy earthbound." This was true for me. I was committed to piloting my first solo flight before school started in the fall.

The summer sped by. I spent most of it learning everything I could about the mechanics of flight including Morse Code and navigational techniques. The third Sunday of August was a turning point in my life. I waited on the tarmac, fidgeting like a toddler in church while my father convinced the air traffic controller I was ready for my first flight. When I learned I wasn't allowed to use the Seattle Flying Club's Piper Cub to solo, I was crestfallen. Solo wouldn't truly be solo because we were using the law firm's two-pilot plane instead. Father promised to turn the controls over to me and I was prepared.

Minutes later I strolled beside Father toward the plane, trying to match his long stride. The Seattle sky was clear and the weather, absolutely perfect for flight. Father was whistling as he grabbed my hand and squeezed it. "Are you ready for this?"

"As much as I'll ever be. You know, I have the strangest feeling. I know there are only a handful of women pilots, but I know I'm going to be an important pilot. Sometimes I imagine myself in huge military planes, shooting ammo and flying like an ace."

"I admire you, Emmy. You've worked very hard for the past three months to do this. I've never seen a child so darn determined. You've even given up gazing at David next door." He chuckled as he opened the plane's narrow door. "Now climb into the cockpit, Lady of the Sky."

I finally stopped blushing after I'd checked all the instruments and gone through takeoff protocol. Grabbing the throttle, I began to cruise down the runway, paying close attention to my instruments. The loud buzzing of the engines helped to drowned the agitation in my head as I went through the steps over and over. Father reached out and tapped the airspeed indicator.

"Watch this as you lift off," he mouthed.

"I know!" I nodded my head vigorously, hoping he wouldn't play back seat driver. I needed all of my concentration. About two-thirds of the way down the runway, I adjusted the flaps and the plane began to lift into the air. Within seconds we were airborne. The feeling was indescribable. I was all power, yet as giddy as a girl on her first date. Gliding in a sensuous world of liquid blue, we leveled out and began to head north toward the San Juan Islands. Thin powder-puff clouds peppered the sky as we passed over Lake Union and the University of Washington campus. Green Lake looked like a dot of turquoise and the Richmond Beach docks were surrounded by bathtub-sized boats. I turned the plane in a 90 degree arc and dipped toward Lopez Island.

47

We touched down an hour later, but it was evening before I was completely grounded. I floated away from the hanger, jabbering like an idiot about my next flight. I was eager to attempt stall and spin maneuvers as soon as possible. Father only indulged in the fancy tactics when the air currents were just right. Spinning the plane was the most thrilling, leaving my heart in my throat every time. Father would stall the plane by putting the nose straight up and kicking the rudder, forcing a nose-dive. Then the plane begins to spin in rapid circles, like a toy top, faster and faster as the ground swells up, and the world becomes a kaleidoscope of color. Recovery requires pulling the nose of the aircraft up and shoving the stick forward until the plane levels out again. It's an experience beyond compare.

By the time I climbed into bed that night, I realized a transformation had unfolded when that silver bird and I became one, when it succumbed to my hand and relinquished its roaring power to me. I was seduced by that power in a way I imagined few women had ever been seduced. My magnificent steel lover sent a screaming rush in my veins and a ticklish throb in my heart and I cried out for more. David might be cute, but during the summer of '34, I knew no other love than my mechanical companion.

"I had a dream about Little Bull last night. I was sitting in your Papa's car, all alone and I was crying really hard, but I didn't know why. Then Little Bull came to me from the sky. He had wings on his back, eagle's wings. He told me everything was going to be all right and then he flew away, right into the sun. Little Bull was sent by my daddy to keep an eye on me. Didn't you know that?" Lizzie's voice teased.

Startled, I swung around from my vanity table to stare at her. "What are you talking about?"

"I guess I forgot to tell you. Little Bull is my granddaddy. Tobi sent him to Seattle because it was too dangerous for him to stay here. There's some people in this town who didn't like my daddy so much after the General Strike."

Once again, Lizzie had caught me off-guard. How had I overlooked their relationship after visiting Little Bull with her so often? Shaking my head, I got up and walked over to my bed, offering her my hand.

"Hey, it's time to do your hair now," I said, pulling her up. Lizzie positioned herself in front of me so I could braid her hair. The silky ebony sheet had grown down to her bottom. I brushed and braided it for her every morning. Claudia worked the graveyard shift at the hospital now and she was too tired to do her daughter's hair. After five or six hours of sleep, Claudia would work for Grandmother. She was able to save a little money from her orderly job, but not enough to move out, though she wanted to get her own place as soon as possible. Papa's Nazi lectures grated on everyone's nerves, but Claudia's tolerance was diminishing the fastest. She was a socialist, but more than that, she despised prejudice of any kind. Recently, Papa Joseph's anti-Semitism had been exacerbated by Father Coughlin, the Detroit radio priest who preached that the Jews were conspiring to take over the world. My parents thought it was ridiculous the way my grandfather carried on, but they ignored him and encouraged us to do the same. However, poor Claudia was suffering from his contemptuous words. I was glad that she and Charles had recently become engaged. Soon she could leave this crazy house of ours.

"Okay, all done. Whew, that was a job! Your hair is so long now, it's getting hard to braid."

"I'm half Indian. I wear braids like my ancestors," she explained proudly.

I stood up and grabbed my rain slicker, sliding it on over my woolen sweater. "One of these days your hair will be dragging on the ground."

She gave me an impertinent grin, shoving me out the door and down the stairs to the front door. Pebbles of water pounded the ground as we stepped out. The rain had been drowning Seattle daily since Halloween. I was sick and tired of the damp cold, but as it was only mid-November, we still faced another four months of foul weather. As we turned onto Madison Avenue, a car horn honked loudly behind us.

"Would you ladies like a ride," a deep voice called from a shiny, black DeSoto.

"Would you look who it is! Lover Boy," Lizzie murmured. I stared through the steamy window. My heart quickened as I caught David's warm smile.

"Shh, Liz." Elbowing her, I smiled demurely. "Sure, we'd love one, David."

"Come around the other side. The door is unlocked."

I grabbed Lizzie's arm and sloshed through a huge, black puddle.

Shaking the water off my galoshes, I climbed into the elegant vehicle. David watched me with an amused look as I scooted across the front seat.

"How have you been?" he said cheerfully. Lizzie shot him a wide smile.

"Great, David, just great. Love this rain! The more the better," she replied facetiously.

Pushing back wet tendrils of hair from my forehead, I ignored Lizzie and smiled. "I'm great, too. Gosh, we didn't see you all summer. What have you been up to?"

"I was visiting my grandparents in San Francisco. How was your summer?"

"Good," we said in unison.

I waited for Lizzie to talk as he turned toward the academy, but she was silent. "I got my pilot's license," I said quietly.

David pulled the car over to the curb in front of Holy Names Academy. "You what?" he asked incredulously. His eyes grew wide with admiration.

"And she's damn good, too," Lizzie spurted as she climbed out of the car. "See ya, David. Thanks for the ride." As I slid toward the door, David grabbed my arm. His eyes glistened as he ran a hand through his hair in hesitation. "Wait, Emily. Listen, I know you've only met me a couple of times, but I was wondering if you'd like to go to the matinee with me on Saturday? There's a Garbo film playing at the Neptune."

"The Neptune? I'd love to, David." The winter chill instantly vanished as a flooding warmth ran through me.

"Okay, I'll pick you up at one."

"Thanks for the ride and the invitation. Bye." The bell rang as I ran toward the doors of the Academy. Looking back, I saw he was still watching me as I stepped into the building. My heart was racing. My first date! Would my parents let me go? He was even cuter than I remembered. Sitting so close to him, I could see he already shaved and he had his drivers license!

Saturday rolled around with the first sparkle of sunshine in weeks, a good omen in my opinion. My parents approved of David and had no qualms about our date. As I dressed for the occasion, Lizzie lounged on my bed, counting her baseball cards.

"Excited?" she mumbled, engrossed in her Babe Ruth stack.

"Of course! There's so much electricity between us. I felt it again the other day."

"Keep your wits about you!" I glanced up from the vanity to see Lizzie scowled furiously at me. I looked away. My feelings were now hurt. She seemed to notice, because she forced a smile and added, "Hey I'm glad for you. I know you really like David. Just make me one promise, okay?" Lizzie's eyes looked earnestly into mine. "Don't forget about me. Lots of girls get so busy with their boyfriends, they forget about their friends."

I sat down on the bed beside her and grabbed her hand. "Don't worry! You're my best friend in the whole world. That'll never happen," I assured her pressing her hand to my cheek as the doorbell rang announcing David's arrival.

By the time we'd parked on the University of Washington campus, I'd learned much about David's life before his arrival in Seattle. He was the youngest of three boys, but his two older brothers, Herbert and Dean, were in California attending Stanford University. As the youngest, he confessed to being pampered, but he never felt quite as intelligent as Herbert or as business-minded as Dean. His first love was basketball, though he also played a mean game of tennis. I'd seen him playing at the tennis club a few times before he'd returned to San Francisco for the summer. He also studied French and had a penchant for cooking. He admitted his secret wish was to be a chef, but his parents expected him to attend law school.

As we walked, David waved at a throng of noisy boys across the street. "Guys from Seattle Prep," he mentioned. "Kind of a rough crowd. Gerry Gordon in particular. He's a real slug." David shrugged and gave his cute, crinkle-eyed smile. "Hey, what do you think of the Huskies? Quite a team, huh? I can't wait for the next game."

"Great team. My father loves football, too."

Our discussion moved to our family's favorite sport. In my mind, I thanked my father for teaching me the rules of the game. I could see David was impressed with my ability to converse on the intricacies of football.

The autumn air was crisp. Multicolored leaves blanketed the sidewalk as we strolled along. The street was busy with youthful shoppers and vendors selling everything from purple and gold pennants to crisp pretzels hanging by purple ribbons, quirky reminders of the collegiate atmosphere. David paused near a vendor selling scarves.

"Do you want one," he asked boldly, scooping up a purple wool scarf with gold fringe.

"David, you're already paying for the cinema," I blushed. Undoubtedly my face was blazing red by now.

"That's okay. Last summer I worked for my grandparents." He gently wound the scarf around my neck and murmured to the vendor, "We'll take it."

As we turned away, he smiled at me. "You're lovely, you know?" I wanted to melt and sing and throw my arms around him, but I did none of those. I just gave him the best Mona Lisa smile.

"Why did you move to Seattle?" I asked. A floating sensation accompanied me as I kept in step with him, reminding me of how I felt after my first glass of sherry.

"My father was hired by Boeing as an aeronautics engineer, so you see why I was so surprised when I learned you could fly. That is really something. I've never met a woman pilot before."

As we walked down University Avenue, I gazed at the crowd of students who were lined up for *Queen Christina*. "Look at the line. Do you think we'll be able to get in?"

"Don't worry, I rode my bike over earlier this morning to buy our tickets. This is one film I didn't want to miss."

"Now I'm impressed. You must love the cinema."

"Love it. It's the best way to escape that I can think of. How about you?"

"I love movies, too, but flying is my favorite escape. When the weather is better, I'd really like to take you up, that is if you want to."

You're really amazing. How old are you anyway?"

I looked away. He didn't know? "Almost sixteen, but I thought you knew that."

"Sixteen. *Sweet* sixteen. I'd say that phrase is pretty accurate." He tossed his car keys in the air and laughed. "I was just wondering, is this your first date?"

I choked. How was I supposed to answer that? He grinned at me. "I was right! It is!" he chuckled. "I guess I should consider myself quite a lucky guy."

Stopping in the middle of the sidewalk, I glared at him testily. This boy was teasing me, but I knew how to handle teasing, particularly from the other gender.

"You listen to me, David Miller. I'm dating you for one reason," I started. I wasn't exactly angry, but I wasn't about to let him have the upper hand. "Because." I stopped.

"Because why?" David was very close to me now. His blue eyes searched mine, melting my line of defense with their innocent curiosity.

"Because I like you," I answered bluntly.

Blushing profusely, he gave me a grin, replying, "I like you, too, Emily. A lot."

We walked the rest of the way in silence. I think we were both trying to stop our hearts from pounding. The Neptune Theater on University Way was considered one of the finest in the city, rivaling the Egyptian and the Paramount. David took my hand and led me toward the auditorium. We stepped through the maroon velvet drapes where rows of scalloped light fixtures glowed, marking the way to well-padded chairs. An enormous screen loomed in front of us as the lights flickered off and music began to play. Sitting back with a sigh, I soon became bewitched by Greta Garbo's arresting, sensuous beauty. Lost in the romance, I nearly forgot David was by my side. A few times I stole a glance in his direction, but he seemed as captivated as I. Two hours later, the film's conclusion left me with a poignant, bittersweet feeling. Much to my chagrin, I felt tears rolling down my cheeks. David handed me his handkerchief and slipped his hand around mine, squeezing it tenderly.

"You're soft inside, Emily Strong," he whispered into my ear. "I like that in a woman." The hairs on the back of my neck stood up and shivers ran down my spine as he continued. "I never would have guessed it from someone who has the courage to fly above the clouds."

My face reddened, but the feel of my small hand securely held in his large one set my heart on fire. From that day forward, David was my guy and I was his girl.

5

The year of 1935 was riddled with unexpected challenges for the Danfrauer household, but I was so immersed in my own life, I often failed to react. By winter's end, I was completely in love with David in the all-or-nothing, gushing way only a teenager can be. We spent countless hours together, whether we were studying French, playing tennis or going to the movies. My parents were too distracted to pay attention to my adolescent preoccupation. Therefore, I avoided many of the emotional collisions of my clan.

Claudia was laid off from her hospital job in January. In response to their financial woes, Lizzie began working every Saturday at the drugstore. Her pert grin and no-nonsense manner made her a favorite with customers. Mrs. Gerstein planned to visit her mother in Dusseldorf during the summer so Lizzie's employment was well-timed.

Ginny found blood in her stool in mid-March and had to have surgery. Her colon had traces of cancer, but she refused treatment. The doctor concluded she was living on borrowed time, but she avoided any further discussion of the matter. The sense of impending doom continued.

Due to poor health, Josephine was fired. As a result, Claudia took full responsibility of the family meals in addition to her regular housekeeping duties. Mother and Father paid Claudia for her extra work. Yet despite the additional pay, I knew she and Lizzie wouldn't leave until the wedding, primarily due to Claudia's sense of duty to our family.

Every time our troubles bogged me down, David whisked me away from the family drama. There wasn't much I could do for the situation other than to continue as I was. Early summer brought roses and sunshine, but my home remained draped in lethargic despondency. My father lost a big legal case and Jonathan was sick with the measles throughout most of June. One particular Saturday in July, the house was empty except for myself and the baby. I was upstairs playing with Jonathan when the doorbell rang. Quickly I put Johnny in his crib. "I'll be back in a minute," I yelled, sprinting down the stairs. When I opened the door, David was on the doorstep.

"Hi," he whispered. His sparkling eyes cast a look of pleasure over me. "Where is everyone?"

"It's just Johnny and me this morning. What are you up to?"

"I came to give you something," he murmured. "Is this a good time?

"Sure, just let me check on Jonathan. Come on!" I skipped up the stairs to the baby's room with David close behind.

"Look, he's asleep," I murmured as I stood beside the crib. I could feel David's warm breath on my neck as he leaned over to gaze down at Johnny. The baby's ebony curls were damp with perspiration and his thumb was squeezed tightly into his little pink mouth. David reached out and patted his back.

"He's a cute little fella." When I turned and looked up at David, he was staring at me with an odd expression on his face.

"I've been waiting to do this for so long. I can't wait another day." David hesitated, as though gathering courage and then, to my surprise, he took me into his arms and kissed me. His lips pressed tenderly against mine and his tongue moved into my mouth as I opened my lips to him. Probing gently, he pulled me closer until my breasts rubbed against his chest. I slid my tongue into his mouth, marking territory, caressing the crevices, exploring this amazing new world of love. His soft lips became my center of gravity; to detach would be to plummet through the atmosphere, dangerously unrestrained. After a few seconds, David pulled away, panting softly, his eyes gleaming. My knees buckled with the pleasure of it all: the primal throbbing heat of my groin, the fluttering in my belly, the tingling erection of my nipples. Dazed, I grinned at him. He swallowed hard and licked his lips as though to linger on the aftertaste.

"This could get dangerous," I stuttered.

He nodded, suddenly bashful "Em, I'm crazy about you. I know we're so young and all, but I want you to be my steady. I want you to wear my ring." He slowly slipped his class ring from his tanned hand and pulled a piece of brown string from his pocket. "I know this won't fit you, so I brought this." David wove the string through the ring and tied a knot at the end. The chunky gold ring fell into the crack between my heaving breasts.

I reached up and wrapped my arms around his neck, placing my lips on his. This time our kiss was tender and timid, but I felt my blood rushing as though I'd kicked out all my emotional rudders. I had no choice but to soar.

55

"Come on," I whispered breathlessly, pulling away and taking him by the hand. "We'd better go downstairs." When we reached the foyer, the front door burst open and Lizzie skidded across the polished floor. When she came to a stop, she froze, staring from David to me.

"What the heck have you two been up to?" she demanded.

"David was just leaving," I explained as he scooted toward the door.

"I'll call you later," he said with a twisted smile, disappearing in a hasty escape.

"So this looks pretty damn suspicious. I hope you didn't do anything I wouldn't do." With a cocky tone, Lizzie put her hands on her hips and produced the meanest scowl she could muster.

"What David and I do together is none of your business. You act as though I'm some kind of a floozy." My tone was scathing, but I didn't care.

"Certainly not a floozy! *Not you, the mighty Miss Strong.* You're the little rich pilot girl with *gorgeous* hair and a *gorgeous* figure and a boyfriend that every girl in town wishes was hers." Lizzie threw me a taunting grimace and fled upstairs.

"Come on. Let's not fight," I called after her.

"Who's fighting?" I heard her reply. "I just don't know if I like you any more."

Shivering, I sat on the bottom stair with my head in my hands. I never wanted this to happen, I thought. Why was Lizzie so accusatory? Misery invaded my bones. Lizzie was my best friend, so I decided I'd better try to make amends. After Mother and Claudia returned, I'd take Lizzie to the cinema or to the new diner down the street.

I wandered back upstairs to check on Jonathan. He was still asleep so I trotted down to the kitchen for a cup of hot tea. As I stepped through the butler's door, the back door slammed. I ran into the kitchen and opened the door in time to see Lizzie rushing out the gate. As she glanced back at me, she flipped me a nasty look. She was mad, as mad as I'd ever seen her and I knew it was my fault.

By late afternoon, guilt had eclipsed the joy of my first kiss and Lizzie had still not returned. When Claudia asked where she was, I told her I assumed Lizzie had gone back to work. By dinner time, she still wasn't home, so Claudia asked that I call Mr. Gerstein at the store.

"Hello, Mr. Gerstein? This is Emily. Is Lizzie still there?" A deep shock shot through my system as he explained.

"Lizzie wasn't feeling well today, so she went home early," he replied.

I hung up the phone and ran back to the kitchen, skittish with worry. "Lizzie's not at work," I mumbled.

Claudia turned, eyeing me with suspicion. "Then where is she?" she asked tersely.

"I don't know," I stuttered. "We got into a little argument and she took off and I thought she went back to the store."

Claudia threw her hands into the air. "Where would she go?" she demanded.

"She might go to see Big Ben."

Claudia sighed heavily and sat down in a chair, shaking her head. "Big Ben's moved away. I hope she has sense enough to come home soon. It'll be dark in a couple of hours."

Dinner came and went and still no Lizzie. Even Grandmother began to pace as the evening wore on. When the sunset had turned the sky to a soft orange, my father grabbed Claudia's arm and said, "Let's go." As they walked out the front door, Father called over his shoulder, "Melanie, call Joseph at the German Society and tell him to start checking along Capital Avenue. Claudia and I will drive down to the Olympic Hotel and see what they know."

"Father, let me come with you, please!" I begged.

"No." His voice was firm. "You help Mother with the boys. We'll find her, don't worry."

The hall clock chimed nine o'clock as I tucked Jack into bed. At nine years old, he becoming a fine lad with a fantastic imagination and a love for the exotic. I truly enjoyed reading to him and tonight we were finishing the last chapter of *Call of the Wild*, but unfortunately my mind was elsewhere. Eventually Jack pulled the book from my hands.

"Hey Sis, I know you're worried about Lizzie. Why don't we finish this tomorrow?"

"Thanks, Jackie. You're a sweetheart. Give me a kiss." He pecked me on the cheek and wiped his own after I returned the gesture. I wandered out and down the hall to my room. When I stepped inside, there was Lizzie cowering on my bed. Black tears of rage streaked her cheeks, her red eyes were swollen and her checkered cotton dress was dirty and torn. The worse thing of all was her braids. They were gone.

My heart twisted into a hollow knot as I ran to the bed and knelt down beside her. "What happened to you?" I cried. "We've been scared to death! Oh, my poor Lizzie!" As I drew closer to her, I saw the raw terror in her eyes.

She shook her head and cried, "Damn Prep School jerks, Gerry and Dick were going to scalp me and then some!" She trembled with silent tears. Leaning forward, I pulled her into my arms, crushing her against me as though the pressure of my body would restore her defenses.

"I'm so sorry," I stuttered, fighting for the right words, so livid I couldn't see straight. "I'm going to get those boys!" I growled. She stopped crying and gazed at me in desperation.

"I was walking home from the Olympic hotel, missed the last trolley. Those boys drove up and asked if I wanted a ride. I was in a hurry so I said okay." She shuddered, swallowed hard and licked the saliva from her lips. "They went down Capital Hill toward Skid Road, laughing at me. The big one called me a damn Injun and then the other said, 'Do you know what the Indians did to my great-grandfather? Scalped him!' Then the other laughed and said, 'Gerry, it's pay-back time.'"

She stopped, wiping her dripping nose on her arm before she continued. "By that time we were close to the park so they pulled over and made me get out and walk over to some trees. The big one pulled out a knife while the other held me down. They sawed off my braids."

I shook my head as my eyes filled with tears. "Those animals!" My rage boiled up like seething lava as I recalled a time the two bullies beat up Ernest.

Lizzie continued to wrap her unsavory words around me like chains. "Then the little fat one said, "Let's get us some pussy." He grabbed my breasts and squeezed so hard, I screamed. Then he tried to touch me down there. It was so awful. I even wet my pants!" Her voice turned into a scratching whine.

I was so disgusted I didn't know how to react, though Lizzie was determined to continue, despite my dumb silence. She clenched her fists, adding, "But they didn't get me, Em. I had my keys, you see." She paused for impact, her eyes shining with the memory of her courage. "I slid the keys from my pocket and shoved them right in that little one's eye. He jumped away, screaming like a banshee and the big one yelled that a police car was coming. They both ran to their car and drove away. The policeman didn't even see me there on the ground without my hair."

"You're so brave! You stopped them!" I finally muttered in

amazement. Summoning myself to action, I said, "Let me help you clean up." Walking over to my sink, I turned on the water, rinsing a washcloth until it was warm and spongy with water. As I gently washed her tear-streaked face, an unexpected decision came to me. Lying next to the sink was a pair of scissors. Slipping back to the sink, I deliberately picked up the scissors, my mind intent on my next step. If my best friend had to suffer, so would I. Lifting my ponytail into the air, I snipped it completely off before Lizzie could say a word.

I heard a loud gasp from behind me as I turned around with a large clump of curly hair in my hand. "What in the heck did you do that for?" Lizzie exclaimed.

"Remember what you said once, about us being like the twin stars? I couldn't let that change, could I? Now come here and we'll tidy up our new hair styles."

After I'd turned Lizzie into a miniature Cleopatra, she transformed me into an older woman.

"David's going to love it," she whispered, obviously pleased with her handiwork.

"About that, Lizzie. I'm so sorry for everything I said." I rushed my words and threw my arms around her waist, hugging her close. "I'm so sorry."

Her hand stroked my head as she murmured, "I'm just jealous, that's all. I miss you."

Lizzie never told anyone else what had happened to her that night. Instead we made up another, far less threatening tale. Yet revenge is sweet and we were determined to have ours.

David was leaving the following Sunday, so we had to put our plan quickly into action. We also decided to invite Tommy Mason along. Though we never told the boys the reason for our retaliation, both of them happily agreed to help us. David couldn't stand the sight of Gerry Gordon and Dick Potter while Tommy admitted they'd plunged his head in the school toilets more times than he could count.

On Saturday nights, Gerry and Dick often drove down to Green Lake in Gerry's snazzy new silver Pontiac to drink beer and prey on innocent public school girls. Green Lake was a popular swimming hole by day and famous necking spot by night. Approximately two miles around, it harbored a small theater, a cluster of docks, a boat house and an ice cream stand. The lake was a convenient place for other nocturnal pastimes as well. A number of university students were arrested each year for illegal drinking and other lewd behaviors. Nevertheless, people from all over the city came to walk, play horseshoes, skate and socialize at the edge of the lulling green waters.

Our plan was simple. A movie with David and Tommy was our excuse to get out of the house. The evening was balmy and calm, despite our jitters. Giggling with excitement, we went over our plan for the umpteenth time as we headed for Green Lake, circling it until we spotted Gerry and Dick who were sitting in Gerry's automobile, lasciviously eyeing a group of college girls nearby.

We drove behind the boathouse and parked out of view. Trembling with anticipation and driven by a mutual sense of purpose, the four of us crept around the building and down to the spiny green reeds along the bank. From where we hid, I could see Gerry and Dick as they chugged down bottles of beer. The window on the driver's side was rolled all the way down and Gerry was yelling at a couple of scantily dressed girls who frolicked in the water.

The sun was beginning to set by the time David retrieved the old canoe he'd hidden in the brush the day before. Both Lizzie and I had become excellent swimmers during our time at the cabin, so we weren't the least bit afraid. The disguise we wore underneath our dresses came from a costume shop downtown. The sheer, skin-colored leotards appeared invisible from any distance beyond thirty feet, which suited us just fine. Skinny-dipping had become a popular activity for some.

"Okay," David murmured as he and Tommy crawled back to the bushes where we were hiding. "At nine o'clock, the girls will sneak down to the water and climb into the canoe. We're far enough away from those idiots that they won't recognize you. Lizzie, are you all right?" David asked tenderly, touching her arm. He seemed to understand that whatever had occurred between Lizzie and the two scoundrels had been horrible. I caught his eye and felt my heart swell. He was so kind! Meanwhile, Tommy was grinning from ear-to-ear. He was thrilled to have an opportunity for revenge. Clearly he hated Gerry and Dick for the cruelty he'd endured from the two bullies over the years.

"Yeah, Lizzie, are you all right?" Tommy whined.

"Of course, I've never been better. I can't wait to see the look on Gerry's face!"

"Listen to the two of them. What a couple of bums!" David said, shaking his head. We stopped to listen over the clamorous thudding of our anxious hearts. Across the lake, Gerry and Dick were hooting and

60

hollering as they became drunker. We waited quietly in the tall cat tales as the waning sunlight disappeared. David sat next to me, holding my hand. I searched myself for feelings of fear, but more than anything, I felt exalted. I was still seething over what those boys had done to Lizzie. Her braids were her symbolic umbilical cords, her spiritual link to her father's culture. No one had the right to take that away from her, not to mention the failed rape attempt.

When the time was right, David gave us the nod and Lizzie and I rose, two beatific sirens in the night. We climbed into the canoe and pushed off, grinning with confidence as we slowly paddled across the water. The straggling cadre of swimmers had vanished leaving only the occasional couple walking arm-in-arm along the water's lapping edge. I was exhilarated by our daring. Infallible avengers, Lizzie and I would treat these belligerent boys to something even they would never forget.

"Are you scared?" I asked Lizzie, moving my paddle up and down in the glassy water.

"Are you kidding? I can't hardly wait!" Lizzie confessed with a little giggle. As soon as we were within a 100 yards of the shore where Gerry's car was parked, I began to call.

"Is that Gerry Gordon in that car?" I cried, using my sassiest voice. "I do believe that's you, Gerry and your adorable friend, Dick Potter. Hey boys, why don't you come for a swim." I'd caught their attention. Gerry hung his head out the window.

"Who is that?" he yelled. His crewcut was as slick as freshly cut grass in the pallid light.

"You don't know us, but we know who you are. All the girls at Holy Names have mentioned you! I'm new in town. My name's Cassidy and this here is Penelope." I heard Lizzie groan.

"Couldn't you think of a better name than that?" she mumbled.

"You gals come on into shore. We'd like to take a better look at you," Dick hollered out his window.

"We were hoping you'd go skinny-dipping with us," I replied, slowly pulling my dress over my head. The leotard underneath clung to my skin. My breasts had grown quite a lot in the past year. I was now what people called voluptuous. Most of the time I found it embarrassing, but it certainly had its advantages tonight. At the sight of my 'nudity', Gerry and Dick leapt out of the car as though it was on fire. The night was growing darker by the minute and I was glad. I could see their faces fairly well and hoped they wouldn't recognize ours.

"How about you girls paddle over to that dock and we'll meet you?" Gerry suggested, followed by a sinister chuckle.

"Perfect," I whispered to Lizzie "That's just where we want them." Lizzie shot me a frightful smile.

"Yes sirree, it sure is," she giggled. Then she shouted her reply. "Can't wait, you hunk of manly flesh." One of our victims gave a loud groan of desire. On our right, David and Tommy crept slowly along the shoreline. Camouflaged by the brush, at a distance they appeared to be two stray dogs. Gerry and Dick continued toward us. Lizzie and I pretended to paddle, but only drifted slowly toward the long wooden pier.

"So, Gerry, I hear you're quite the lover boy," I called. In the sparse light, Gerry lifted his chin and grin. Dick slugged him on the arm and said something I couldn't hear. Lizzie called in her best boarding school accent, "Hello, boys. Are you ready for some fun? How do you like this?" She slipped her dress off seductively.

Gerry give a hoot, "Yeah, baby, I like that a lot." I began to get anxious now. The dock was looming and they began running toward us. I didn't want to turn around quite yet, unsure if David and Tommy had reached their destination. Then I heard it: a slow crunching of gravel, a swoosh and a final gurgling sigh. We'd done it!

My breath caught in my throat as I gestured to Lizzie. "Did you hear it?" I whispered, giddy with success.

"Yeah," she cried. "Now let's get the heck out of here."

Lizzie and I began to row backwards as fast as we could. "Sorry, boys. We have to go. I hear my father calling on the other side of the lake. If he finds us out here with you boys, he'll scalp your hides." I looked back to see the two of them holding their arms up in confusion. As they turned toward Gerry's car, their words echoed across the water.

"What the fuck?" Dick screamed, followed by, "Shit almighty." They'd seen it. The Pontiac was submerged. Only the top of the gleaming silver roof was visible. Hurriedly we made it to shore and pulled the canoe out of the water. Out of the darkness, Tommy appeared to help us pull it into the reeds. "Come on. David's waiting in the car. We did it!" He was choking with mirth.

All the way back to the theater, we roared with laughter. Undoubtedly those prep school boys had learned a lesson about chasing women. It can get you into a mess of trouble.

6

After David left for California, Lizzie and I were once again inseparable. She still worked the fountain at Gerstein's while I helped out around the store occasionally. Papa had vowed to cut ties to all Jews, but my folks supported my job wholeheartedly, refusing to discuss it with my grandfather any further. Fortunately he was rarely at home. In the evenings, he met his German cronies downtown to converse about the Third Reich. Call it silly, but I felt queasy whenever I thought about Hitler, though I couldn't exactly say why.

Grandmother Ginny had recovered from her surgery, but she'd become more agitated in the past few months. On more than one occasion, I caught her talking to herself. Though Mother was highly distressed by her mother's condition, Ginny refused to talked about it, so we all left it alone. In the meantime, Claudia had found another part-time job. Much to everyone's relief, her veil of depression lifted and she reclaimed her happy-go-lucky self. During our visits to the cabin, Charles often joined us. He absolutely adored Claudia, constantly bringing her gifts and wooing her with murmurs of undying love. Fortunately, Lizzie was less threatened by his presence and even made mention that if they got married, she could have her own bedroom for the first time in her life.

David came home from San Francisco at the end of August. I was overjoyed to see him. We were necking in his car one night shortly after his return when I noticed how intense our kissing and touching had become. As I felt his body's heat burning into mine, I knew it was only a matter of time until we went all the way. Then I thought of Claudia's predicament with Lizzie and my blood froze. How much longer could I hold onto my virginity and still keep David happy?

As his hand reached for my breast, I pulled away. He took my cue, asking, "How was Mrs. Gerstein's trip? I've heard some weird stories about Germany's chancellor."

"I don't know. She was supposed to return last week, but she sent a telegram a couple of days ago to say she needed to stay longer. I hope Mrs. Gerstein is safe," I replied as a shiver suddenly shot down my spine.

"You know, it's getting bad over there for Jews. Hitler has taken away their citizenship with the Nuremberg Racial Laws. Have you read *Mein Kampf?*"

"No, I guess I really don't want to. Why, have you?"

"Yes. Hitler has some crazy ideas about racial purity and stuff. I think he's nuts, but many Americans agree with him."

"Yeah, like Papa. Boy, is he strange lately. I just stay out of his way."

"Good plan. It's kind of like my dad and I. Whenever he drinks, I go into hiding." He gave a long sigh, conveying the misery he endured at home. I felt so sorry for him. His father could be a real jerk at times.

"Here we are." David pulled the car over. "I'd better see my folks for a while. I'll call you later, okay?"

"Sure thing!" I smiled brightly. "See you soon. I'm so glad you're home." But beneath my mantel of joy, troublesome worry brewed.

Mrs. Gerstein didn't return home in time for Christmas. By then, Mr. Gerstein was beside himself with worry. I began to feel the ache of impending doom in the pit of my stomach whenever he discussed her absence. One January afternoon as Lizzie and I were counting inventory, Mr. Gerstein came to us in tears.

"Edith is being held by the German Gestapo," he sobbed, stumbling over a shipping crate as he approached us. Lizzie and I looked at each other in shock. Our dear friend and employer wasn't the sort to cry. How could this have happened?

"Mr. Gerstein," Lizzie cried, rising up to help him. She wrapped her arms around his chubby, heaving shoulders. "I'm so sorry! This is terrible. What can we do to help?"

"I need to go to Germany as soon as possible. There is danger in Germany for her. Edith should've returned with her brother, but she wouldn't leave her mother. Mutti doesn't want to leave Europe. Oh, she can be so stubborn!" Mr. Gerstein explained through his tears.

"Mr. Gerstein, why have the Gestapo held your wife?" I asked in disbelief.

"Edith wants to bring Mutti out of the country, but my mother-in-law no longer has citizenship under German law. There was some trouble and my Edith had one of her tempers. Mutti's telegram said my Edith was arrested!"

Instant panic spread among the three of us like a contagious disease. I began to pace rapidly around the room, Lizzie squeezed her hands together until they turned blue and Mr. Gerstein's sobs increased.

"Hey, what's going on here?" David's voice asked from the doorway.

"David, I'm so glad you're here! The most awful thing has happened," I cried and began to explain.

Calm and rational thinking was David's forte in a crisis. "Okay, everyone, let's think about this. Mr. Gerstein, you need to go get her before it's too late."

Wringing his hands, Mr. Gerstein began to mutter to himself. *"Ich habe kein geld."*

"What did he say?" David asked me, his pale blue eyes gleaming like ice cubes.

"He has no money. This store is all he has." I shook my head. "We need to find someone to lend him some money."

"I begged Edith to get her citizenship," Mr. Gerstein mumbled. "She was always too busy with this store." He pounded his fist on a wooden pallet in fury, splintering the wood. Crumpling to the floor, he held his bruised hand against his chest and hung his head.

"It's too late to worry about that now, Mr. Gerstein," David said gently. "We will help you. While you're gone, we can run the store for you. We'll find the money for you, too. You must believe there's a way."

"Yes, I can trust you young people. Perhaps there is a way, after all." Mr. Gerstein's face lightened with our offers of support.

I squeezed my eyes shut, searching for answers. Though my parents were paying off their loans, Papa still had plenty of money. Did I have the guts to ask him for some of his hoard to rescue Mrs. Gerstein? No doubt he'd rather die than do such a thing, considering his attitude toward Jews. Yet regardless of his convictions, I had mine. Watching Mr. Gerstein rise off the floor, bravely shoving off the hard shell of hopeless, tempting possibility, I knew what I had to do.

"Mr. Gerstein, I think I can help. Papa has some money he could share with you."

Lizzie gave a guttural groan. "Come on, Em! You've got to be kidding. That old coot wouldn't part with a dime to help Jews," she warned.

I spun around, looking directly into her eyes. She recoiled slightly as though my eyes had the power to silence. "I've got to try at least. Well, don't I?" I demanded, my tone edgy.

"Yes, you do, Em," Lizzie said with a watchful eye. "It's the only hope we have."

❖　　❖　　❖

My opportunity came the following day. I had practiced my speech a half a dozen times and felt fairly confident. Though I had asked Father for the money the night before, the answer came as expected. He only had 200 dollars to contribute, not enough to buy the airplane ticket, much less pay off any possible bribes. He was willing to ask his law partners, while encouraging us to find other sources. When I suggested I ask Papa, Father's face belied success. Nevertheless, he promised to back me up all the way.

After our morning coffee, I gave my father a nod and the two of us headed for the library where Papa was reading the Sunday paper. Safe with Father at my side, I swallowed hard, dug my nails into my palms and stepped into the hallowed sanctum. In the corner of the library, Papa sat in his favorite leather chair, motionless, yet nevertheless domineering.

Shoving down my butterflies, I began, "Papa, I need to talk to you about something very, very important." With a grunt, he lowered the newspaper from his face, looking at me in that intimidating way of his. His eyebrows raised curiously upon seeing Father.

"What is it?" he griped. Obviously an interruption was not in my favor.

I gave my most solemn church face and stated, "It's about the Gersteins."

Less than two minutes into my explanation, Papa began to glower, his face turning crimson with repressed fury. Despite my initial determination, I was already faltering as I continued in pursuit of my cause.

"But Mr. Gerstein will pay you back. Won't you even consider a loan? After all, the Gersteins have given us credit at the store for years!" I scrunched up my face, looking to Father for encouragement. He gave me a hard glance, which said, "Go on, you can do it." Tears of frustration sprang to my eyes, but Papa simply wouldn't hear me. Instead, he threw down the paper, rose from his chair and began to stomp around the room like a charging bull.

"Kykes, damn kykes. I'm sick and tired of kykes and niggers and all the rest of the scum," he screamed with clenched fists and rigid limbs. His black rage swirled around me like a bitter fog. Stubbornly, I stood my ground, despite my trembling, but my words temporarily faded at the sight of his fury.

"See that flag, *see it*!" He pointed to the giant, red flag marked with a bold, black swastika, which was tacked to the wall. "This is the hope and future of Germany! How dare you ask me to save the scum of the earth, the Jew!" he bellowed.

"But Mrs. Gerstein isn't scum. You know that! She's a nice lady. Listen to me, Mrs. Gerstein is in danger," I beseeched, questioning my own sanity as I added, "Maybe the Gestapo made a mistake. Please help Mrs.Gerstein, *please*!"

My father and I watched as Papa suddenly began to rip books from the shelves. "Do you see these books?" he shrieked, shaking a thick, leather-bound text in each hand like a two-fisted drinker toasting to his own shame. "Hitler says burn them. Trash, this stuff, look here-we even have that asshole Freud in the pile. And that damn existentialist Jewish shit, Buber! Where in the hell did these books come from?"

With that, Papa took his Tiffany cigarette lighter and attempted to light the corner of Martin Buber's *Zwiesprache*. The Jewish classic fought the flame though the pungent smell of scorched cowhide permeated the room. "Listen to me, you little Jew-lover," he continued, his voice menacingly sweet. "For the Jews there is only *verhangnis*, do you understand? There is only doom." He tossed the books into the fireplace and wiped his hands angrily against his legs.

My father shook his head, his own face a storm of wrath. "That is quite enough, Joseph," he shouted.

"Papa, why do you hate the Jews so much?" I rattled uncontrollably, tears of hopelessness now streaming down my cheeks. "I thought you were a Christian. Christians believe in loving their neighbors. Have you forgotten that Jesus was a Jew?"

Before I could catch my breath, Papa stormed across the room toward me. Father couldn't react fast enough to stop him before he had grabbed a chunk of my hair and thrown me against a book-lined wall. Several books, knocked loose by impact, fell across my body like bricks. I shuddered and covered my head with my hands. Father grabbed Papa by the arms and held him firmly, growling, "Leave my daughter alone." More frightened than I'd ever been in my life, I waited for a fist fight to begin, but the men, heaving with anger, stayed motionless until Papa shook Father off.

"Joseph, that's enough. You'll never touch my daughter again!" I'd never seen my father so overwrought, yet he contained his anger with a trembling hand. "If you do," Father continued, choking back his rage, "I'll have you in court so fast, you won't know what hit you!"

Slowly Papa raised his palm as if to slap Father, but instead he ran his hand over his naked head and sighed. "I became careless with my temper, George. Forgive me. I'm not a man who loses his control." Papa's face was gray and his eyes watered.

"Don't ask for my forgiveness," Father hissed venomously. "Ask for Emily's."

I was still slumped on the floor, afraid to look into Papa's face. My scalp hurt where he'd pulled my hair and fallen books' corners jabbed me like pokers. With all of my heart, I wished I could disappear.

Papa came over to me and held out his hand. "Come on, young lady. I apologize, but you must understand what a terrible mistake you are making. You are too young, too immature to grasp our complicated world. Someday you will accept what I believe in. You will be proud to be a German."

I didn't take his hand, but shied away. Confused and hurt, I wanted to lash out at him like a wild creature, scratching and biting until he fell to the ground as I had done. Instead I whimpered, scrambling across the floor on my hands and knees until I reached the door. Then I fled, hightailing it to my room where I had a good cry.

I felt branded by his hatred, scarred by the disease called bigotry. Was there a core of humanity left in my grandfather? How could he believe in ethnic cleansing? The concept disgusted me. Though I no longer trusted Papa, I couldn't unleash my loyalty toward him. I'd always believed he was a man of substance. Hardworking, driven, intelligent and strong, he had held things together when times were hard. He was the sturdy ship sailing against the ferocity of life. To my peevish disappointment, my selective perception had deleted the bleaker aspects of his personality. Papa Joseph emulated those attributes, but he was also a zealous bigot whose destructive nature and vicious hatred placed others' lives in jeopardy. What had happened to the man I knew?

My home had become a sanctuary of lies. Grandmother's cold, callous criticisms and domineering stoicism, Papa's despicable beliefs and morose disposition, Father, loyal and reserved, who often kept silent to it all, as though invisibility was safety and my mother, who still cowered in the face of her parent's disapproval. Our house was a house of secrets, of personal betrayal and moral hypocrisy. Could the world outside these walls see how disturbed we really were?

A while later, Mother knocked on my bedroom door. "May I come in, Emmy?"

"Yes," I mumbled, still immersed in self-pity. She tiptoed to the bed and sat beside me, stroking my hair as I wept silently into my pillow.

"Father told me what happened, darling. I'm so sorry. Papa is a troubled man."

I gritted my teeth and turned to face her. "Why are you so afraid of him? What does he have on you?" I snapped. The question came out of the blue, surprising both of us with its accuracy.

Mother hung her head and sighed. Her furrowed brow was deeper than I remembered and she looked weary. "It's a long story that I've sworn to secrecy. If you knew, if Father knew, our life would never again be the same."

"Tell me," I pleaded. "Help me to understand this horrible hypocrisy you tolerate. Stop babying me! How do you think I will become a strong grown-up unless I'm treated like one. You're acting as if I'm stupid!"

Mother's eyes clouded with tears as she resisted my pleas. I watched as she transformed into a pitiful child and I wanted to shake her. Once again, I restrained my urge to take her hand and hold it in mine. "I'm all right. Papa didn't really hurt me. He just scared me, but I'm not going to bow to him anymore. I don't care what he thinks of me or my beliefs. You and Father always tolerate his garbage," I huffed.

"I'm proud of you," she whispered, stroking my cheek. "Your desire to help the Gersteins is very admirable. Both your father and I think so, but I can't fight Papa because ... I can't say why." Shaking her head with remorse, Mother rose to leave, but I pulled her back. With all the tenderness I could muster, I murmured,

"Someday, I'd like to hear about your secret with Papa. The one that keeps you a prisoner." Mother gave a self-effacing smile. "Maybe someday you shall."

As the weeks rolled by, David, Lizzie and I continued our commitment to help Mr. Gerstein, despite Papa's pathetic reaction.

His mother-in law had sent a telegram at Christmas to say that Edith had been released, but that her German passport had been confiscated. After a series of unsuccessful phone calls to the U.S. State Department, David reached Senator Wagner, known as a liberal advocate for labor and the protector of the downtrodden. Wagner promised to discuss the matter with the German Ambassador in Washington D.C. Meanwhile, Mr. Gerstein made arrangements to rescue his wife.

David rearranged his classes so that he could run the store during Mr. Gerstein's absence. After school, Lizzie and I would arrive and work until closing. With chins held high, the three of us were a sizzling Tour de' Force when it came to managing the Five and Dime. Friends of the Gersteins also helped out. Mr. Kaplan, a local clothing merchant, ordered the inventory and Peter Lantor, a certified accountant, took charge of the books. Father scrounged another 200 dollars from his law partners and Mother generously tucked into her rainy day account for another 100. Upon hearing of Mr. Gerstein's plight, many members of Seattle's Jewish community also lent financial support. Thus, with his livelihood securely intact, Mr. Gerstein left for Germany on February 27, just days before Hitler invaded the Rhineland.

We embraced the rosy months of spring with spirited vigor, believing that with our support, the Gersteins would arrive home safely. Yet as June crept into view, our faith began to tremble. We had managed the store on our own for nearly four months without a word from our beloved friends. Needless to say, we became increasingly worried.

One bright Saturday morning, David strutted into the drugstore, taking me completely by surprise. He whipped out a bouquet of daffodils from behind his back and bowed dramatically, "To the woman I love."

As there were no customers, I flung my arms around him, pressing myself to him and surging amorously at the feel of his warm embrace. "I miss you. What are you doing here? Don't you have to study today?"

"My last two finals were yesterday. Hurrah! World Literature during the Middle Ages and Calculus, to hell with you!" he proclaimed, triumphantly thrusting his fist in the air. "The fraternity is having a year-end bash tonight. I was hoping you'd come with me."

"I'd love to!" I giggled excitedly. We were still safely alone, so I leaned up for another kiss. We stood together, hesitating, our hearts racing. As his eyes burned into mine. I knew what he was thinking. It was an all out war between our weakening reason and burgeoning lust. I had to talk to someone and soon. Mother had once said if I ever found myself in such a predicament, she'd help me through it. Now I needed her womanly advice.

I broke the mood by messing his hair. "Come on, we're getting too hot for our own good and I think I see Mrs. Mansfield coming up the street in this direction."

It was a quiet day at the store. Only a few customers trickled in, so we relished the time we had alone. Lizzie arrived to work at two o'clock. Her eyes twinkled when she saw me.

"I hear you've got a big date tonight, gal. You'd better be getting on home and get yourself looking sexy."

"I know," I groaned, raking my hands through my hair. "I'm wrestling with my conscience about just that. I feel like I'm exploding inside whenever David touches me."

Lizzie shrugged. "That's not the worst thing there is. Just remember what happened to your mother and mine. Lucky for me I'm here, but what your mother went through. Not a pretty thing." She shook her head again and began to walk away, but I grabbed her arm, pulling her back.

"What are you talking about?" I demanded.

Lizzie's eyes became obsidian pebbles. "Uh oh! I thought you knew. Geez, I'm a dummy! Never mind."

"No way you're getting out of this one. I want to know what you're talking about." An overwhelming sense of betrayal shot through me like a bullet. I wanted to shake her, but stopped the impulse when David emerged from the back of the store.

"Bye. See you tonight," I exclaimed, stomping out in a huff. I was in a near frenzy by the time I got home. I hated secrets. Moreover, I hated being left out.

Racing into the house, I bounded up the stairs and down the hall to my parent's room, calling out my mother's name. She was sitting at her mahogany writing desk, composing a letter as I entered noisily.

"Shh, Jonathan's napping. How are you, Sweetheart?" She smiled. I plopped down on her damask bedspread and threw her a confused pout.

"Great and terrible and frustrated," I replied, searching for words.

Her oval face as flawless as a pearl, Mother turned her stool toward me, staring intently into my eyes. "What's bothering you?" She nodded at me expectantly.

"A lot," I admitted, my words spraying out in a jumble. "I want to talk to you about David and about sex and about you and Claudia, and what Lizzie said." I paused and took a deep breath. Concern crisscrossed Mother's delicate features. She came to the bed and sat down, taking my hand in hers.

"I've been waiting for this little talk, hoping you'd come to me. I've noticed how you look at David now. I know what that look means," she whispered. "Do you want to tell me about it?"

I bowed my head to her breast. I felt so vulnerable in her arms. "I want him to touch me. I want to learn about love. I know I'm too young, but when I'm with him, I feel like I'm on fire. What should I do?"

She stroked my hair and sighed deeply. "It all goes together, you know. Love and sex and what comes of that. I feel like my own life is passing before my eyes. When you first began dating David, I knew this time was not too far off. I've been thinking about this for a long while, since your incident with Papa. I guess it's time to tell you the truth." Her tone suddenly became soaked in deep sorrow. "I lost my first child, Emmy."

Pulling away, I stared into a face that had become a stranger's. "What do you mean, lost a baby?" I began to tremble from the inside out. Nothing made sense. I grabbed my mother's shoulders. "Tell me!"

She lifted her face, gazing at me with troubled eyes. "You *will* think less of me, but now you also might understand. Love is a strange thing. It bites you when you least expect it and mauls you until you think you've lost yourself. Before I met your father, I fell in love with a magnificent tiger, a man who devoured me with his love. He was a friend of Tobi's. Marcel was French Canadian, rugged and free-spirited and devilishly handsome. He was also a vagabond, a labor mercenary hired to help the Wobblies. I fell in love with him the first time we met. Oh, he was smooth! He asked me to dance and my body turned to jelly at his touch. We played cat and mouse for months. I dated him, felt confused by my feelings for him and broke it off, but I could never resist him completely." She paused, staring out the window dreamily before continuing.

"One weekend Claudia and I decided to go to our cabin with a few friends. At the last minute the other two girls couldn't go, so Claudia and I went alone. We were turning out the lights for bed when there was a knock on the door. We opened it to find Tobi and Marcel. I guess Claudia had told them we would be there. They'd been chased by a gang of angry strikebreakers and had left Seattle in Tobi's canoe. They needed a place to hide for a few days. In my idealistic way, I believed these men were heroes. They bedded down on the porch, but shortly after midnight, I heard Tobi go into Claudia's room. I laid in bed, waiting. I knew Marcel would come to me and when he did, I gave myself to him, loving him with every ounce of me."

Mother sighed, swept away by vivid memory, her eyes glassy with lust, but I shooed the thought away. Daughters weren't supposed to think of their mothers as lustful.

As if reading my mind, Mother threw me a furtive glance. I looked away, sensing my innocent intrusion on her private memory. In some ways, Mother was a mystery to me. Against the background of the Danfrauer regime, it was hard to believe she'd once been so free. I wanted to know every detail, but it was improper of me to ask, so instead I waited as she gathered herself again.

"The following week he left Seattle for Chicago to work with the Teamsters. I cried for weeks. A month passed and I began throwing up. Everything I put in my mouth made me sick, but I just thought it was my grief over Marcel. Thankfully Claudia was there for me. She was the one who figured out I was pregnant."

Her voice wound down like an old gramophone as she slumped over. Damp coils of auburn hair clung to her forehead and the underarms of her blue polkadot dress was dark with rings of perspiration. Her eyes closed painfully. As quickly as the blush had come, it was gone. Her face was no longer pearly white. It now had a greenish pallor to it. As I struggled to grasp this news, another tragic story stirred in my dormant memory. Mother had been so bitter when she'd told me about Claudia's illegitimate pregnancy and so quick to defend Claudia's decision to keep Lizzie. Then I recalled Lizzie's words: *but what your mother went through was not a pretty thing.* So this was my mother's secret: she was forced to give her baby up for adoption.

Paralyzing silence filled the room. Outside, the warm June air echoed with snoring lawn mowers, chirping birds and children's laughter, but Mother and I were locked in the distant past. I felt a nebulous cloud of humiliation rolling off my mother. Extending my arms toward her, she collapsed into me, weak and without support. I wasn't sure what to do next, but from within me, a deep geyser of compassion spilled to the surface. "It wasn't your fault, Mama. It's okay. I'm sure the baby got a very good home," I comforted as her tears broke free, trickling down her face.

She grimaced and shook her head violently. "Oh no, you've got it all wrong. Let me finish. At the time, I didn't know what to do. I was so afraid. Finally, I told your grandmother. What a mistake! She called me a "little tramp" and said I'd have to learn my lesson the hard way. I begged to keep the baby, but Papa raged that his mother's family had suffered from the humiliation of his own illegitimacy and he wasn't going to let that happen to our family. Then he forced me to go to Tacoma, to a doctor. He carved my baby out of me like a butcher carves a piece of meat. He took my baby. He killed my little girl," she sobbed uncontrollably.

My poor mother! *They* had killed her baby, I thought furiously. How they had shamed her! I recalled when my father had once asked her why she was so timid around her parents. She'd shaken her head and changed the subject. Suddenly I hated my mother's family and everything they stood for. I could no longer tolerate their arrogant hypocrisy. Their "holier than thou" attitude contradicted their own guilty truths. Like an invisible tumor, it grew inside of us, trapping us in our "proper" place by way of silent humiliation while, on the outside, we wore a cloak of pride, trimmed with the gaudy braid of self-importance. Hadn't I been taught that pride was one of the seven deadly sins? Yet my grandparents thrived on it, flaunting their wealth, turning their backs on our Jewish neighbors and even worse, forcing a back alley abortion on their daughter. At this awakening to my true legacy, I was outraged.

"I don't understand. Why do we live here? How can you stand it after what they did to you? Why don't we leave?" I cried in anger.

Mother heaved a sigh as if releasing her invisible poisons. "I never heard from Marcel again. I suppose I was just one of many women for him. Then I met your father and within six months we were engaged to be married. He was a young attorney with a solid future. I loved him, though differently than I'd loved Marcel. Marcel represented everything opposite to what I knew. He was the antithesis of my world:

adventurous, exotic, mysterious and therefore very enticing. Your father *was* my world: educated, sensible, socially acceptable and conservative. I loved George for his stability and his undying love for me. There was one hitch, though. Your father didn't have the money to buy a house. Gramma and Grampa Strong were not well off, so Papa offered to let us live here until we could save enough to move out. I went along with it because I felt so powerless and guilty about what had happen. Besides, Uncle Jonathan was still missing and my parents needed me to hang on to. One more time, they got their way. Then the Depression hit and we started having babies, ..." Mother shrugged in that "I give up" way of hers which only infuriated me more.

"They make me sick!" I spit out my words, consumed with hatred.

"It's a terrible thing, but that was the past. I told you only to help you decide on your own life. I know you love David, but you must remember the consequences of love. If he truly loves you, he'll wait; but more importantly, if you truly respect yourself, so will you." With that she left the room to tend to a bawling Jonathan.

That evening after I'd bathed, washed my hair and applied my lipstick, I slipped into Mother's emerald green crepe dress. The sleeveless gown had a sweetheart neckline and French darts that made my waist look more slender than it was. The full skirt flowed, falling just above my ankles, making a rustling sound as I walked. I'd also borrowed her matching green pumps and a pair of her gemstone drop earrings. I had to admit, I looked beautiful.

Yet the tragedy of my mother's youth was foremost in my mind. I shuddered when I recalled the stories I'd heard about the wharf girls who often lost their lives from botched abortions. I powdered my nose, although I was already pale from my mother's wrenching reality. As far as I was concerned, my grandparents were heretics. From now on, I would challenge their authority and speak my mind, even if it meant punishment or rejection. Because of them, my mother had lost a daughter. That was unforgivable.

By the time the doorbell rang, I was certain that no matter how much I wanted David, I wasn't going to risk my integrity. I couldn't bear to lose a child, or my parent's respect, or as in Claudia's case, my opportunity for financial independence. If David truly loved me, he could wait, and if I lost him in the process, I would endure.

Minutes later, David and I were on our way. Yet his joviality couldn't budge my morose mood. I had to tell him the truth about my family, about me. And so I asked him to park the car and I repeated my mother's story.

"And so you see, my mother has lived with this terrible secret. It's no wonder to me that Papa has so much control over our lives. Furthermore he's a bastard and a bigot and fraud. Ginny is an abusive, controlling old witch. She shames all of us into silence. My family is pathetic. Our family's history is a gigantic lie. We are a lie, David." The words rushed out of my mouth, as though a flood had finally crested. Abruptly I stopped with dry eyes and a heaving chest, aware an enormous burden had vanished. David reached to me with his hand and turned my face to his.

"It's okay, Emily. You needn't be ashamed. Don't you think all families have their secrets? Mine does. We don't tell. None of us tell. It would blow our cover. It would reduce us to insignificance." He paused, allowing the revelation to sink in.

I looked into his accepting eyes and knew he was right. His father was a brutal drunk and his mother was a weak hypochondriac. These were his secrets.

Yet I didn't quite understand. "What do you mean, reduce us to insignificance?" I asked haltingly. "Our secrets are not insignificant. They are the very reason my family acts as they do."

"You're right, but our secrets are only stories which we believe will somehow expose our dark sides. We can't accept our shadows for fear of condemnation. Some go to church and listen to what we are told: sinners, repent! We all strive for significance, Em. We want to be acknowledged, accepted, and most of all, loved. When our past is full of bad things, we feel less than everyone else, so what do we do? We pretend, we color the truth, hoping that no one will ever see the original."

He paused, his brow furrowed in concentration. "Do you know why my father has such high aspirations for my brothers and me? Because he has never believed his own life is significant."

"But David, he's a physics engineer at Boeing, building some of the most incredible flying machines the world has ever seen. How can that be insignificant?" I asked.

His eyes glowed with a blazing light as he said very softly, "I know why you've brought this up, Em. I know we both want to go all the way." His eyes burrowed into mine, sending a rush of passion through my belly. "I want to make love to you so badly, but now that I know what I do, I could never expect you to take such a risk. I want to marry you someday. I want you to have my children, but not yet. We can still love one another. We'll just have to keep things under control. I don't want you to have any regrets when it comes to us."

I smiled, out of relief, admiration and lastly, out of comradeship. "I love you."

David stared into my eyes and whispered, "I love you, too."

The Gersteins walked into the Five and Dime on August 26th, six months to the day of Mr. Gerstein's departure. When Mrs. Gerstein stepped over the store's threshold, she fell to her knees, kissing the black and white checked linoleum floor like a parishioner at the feet of a saint. Her plump, robin-breasted body was much thinner than I remembered and her short, black hair was now streaked with gray, but there was still a sparkle in her steady, black eyes. Mr.Gerstein followed her in, limping badly. I rushed over and threw my arms around him, shouting for Lizzie, who came racing over from the soda fountain. David, hearing the commotion, ran out of the storage room, hollering at the top of his lungs," Welcome home!" This was the day we'd all prayed for. Our friends had returned.

"Mr. and Mrs. Gerstein, you're home!" we sang as Lizzie rushed to Mr. Gerstein and buried her face in his flannel shirt. Our Jewish friend was like a father to Lizzie and their emotions at once got the better of them. Tears shone in both of their eyes when she pulled away.

"My precious children," Mrs. Gerstein cried, clutching Lizzie's hands and sweeping her around the store in a wanton waltz. "The store looks better than ever. I'm so happy to be home!" Her face unleashed an exaggerated series of emotions, from happiness and awe to a sudden flash of ancient fear and then quickly back to relieved joy.

Our beloved shopkeeper sighed happily and raised his hands to the sky. "Yahweh didn't forget the children of Israel, Edith. Look at our young messengers of God and what they have done for us!" He pointed to the three of us. "It's so good to be home."

"Why did it take you so long to return?" David urged. Mr. Gerstein shook his head as his wife trailed over to him. Taking his hand, she bowed demurely.

"He rescued me, children. The Gestapo had taken my passport, so

he had to smuggle me out of our old country. Oh, he was so brave!"
she explained. "You see! He was injured on the border of the Rhineland
before we escaped into France. My poor *liebchen* was shot by those
wicked, evil men. Thank God, a French priest rescued us. What an
awful ordeal!" I could see by Mr. Gerstein's face, he hadn't wanted her
to tell us the story. A deep sense of resignation burned in his eyes as he
shoved his fist into the palm of his hand. I'd never seen the Jew appear
so defeated.

"What about your mother?" I asked, instantly hoping I hadn't tore
open any emotional wounds.

"She's safe with our French friends. They will care for her now.
Mutti refused to leave Europe and we were afraid to leave her in
Germany." Mrs. Gerstein became momentarily still, but her face
showed terrible fear. "She will be safe, won't she, *liebchen*?" she
whimpered in a squeaky voice.

"Yes, she'll be safe," Mr.Gerstein assured her, his rosy cheeks at
full color. His aquiline nose quivered as he spoke and as his wife turned
away, I caught the despair in his heavy-lidded, sable eyes. There was no
doubt in my mind, his mother-in-law might not always be safe.

We spent the rest of the day in celebration. Mr. Gerstein offered
every customer a free soda while Lizzie and I handed out balloons to
the children. After closing, David, Lizzie and I left the Gersteins to
revel in their good fortune. Since February, the store had grossed over
8,000 dollars. When the neighborhood had learned of the Gersteins'
plight, the store's business had improved substantially. They would
have plenty of money to pay off their debts.

Despite their return to plenty, there was starving in their hearts.
The Gersteins had been forced to escape from the Nazis because they
were Jewish. After his wife had left for home to unpack and get
resettled, Mr. Gerstein took the three of us aside and told us things
that made my hair stand on end. What the Nazis were doing to the
Jewish people was simply unbelievable! Jews awoke to find their
businesses had been burned to the ground during the night. Their
children were harassed in the schools and their mothers were refused
goods and services by gentile merchants. Constant surveillance and
intimidation tactics were perpetrated upon them and many were
forced to endure severe public humiliation. Our Jewish friends had
witnessed a terrifying force in the land of my grandfather. I was now
convinced of the threat Hitler that posed to world peace. With turmoil

happening all over the globe, my faith in mankind was shrinking. Japan was occupying Manchuria and Mussolini had attacked the poor, defenseless African nation of Ethiopia. Dictators were on the rise and no one was doing anything to stop them. America was a land of pathetic isolationists.

Over the next few months our lives returned to normal, though family and school obligations were foremost on our minds. One day David called me with urgency in his voice, "Em, I need to talk to you. Can you meet me at the park?"

"Sure, but first I have to change Grandmother's sheets. She's not doing very well," I murmured flatly. It was a pale Saturday morning in late November and Grandmother was dying. I hadn't slept all night as it was my turn to look after her. Ginny's decrepit body was rotting away, but her stoic pride had doubled its efforts to maintain vitality. Cancer was a disgusting disease. This morning the sheets had been covered with feces and blood. Mother and I had carefully carried her tiny frame to the bath to wash her. She refused to look either of us in the eye, but we knew gratitude by her sighs when the warm water lapped her shriveled, chalky skin. The three of us women struggled against this disease like comrades in a perilous war against time. Grandmother Ginny hadn't much time left, but for the time there was, Mother and I were bound by duty to protect. Yet it was a tremendous relief to hear David's voice. He was the light for me when darkness encroached upon my field of hope and dreams.

"Is 20 minutes, okay?" David's voice sounded unusually tense.

"Sure." I hung up, pondering his urgency. Racing back upstairs, I rolled up the filthy sheets while gagging from the stench. After rinsing them in the utility sink, I tossed them in a bucket of bleach, grateful for the sharp but cleansing scent. Then I quietly excused myself and ran out the door. Jumping into the car, I drove down the drive, my worry mounting. Upon my arrival, I saw David standing in the front of the Seattle Art Museum under a Japanese maple. I parked the car and hurriedly ran toward him.

"Hi. How are you?" I panted as he pulled me to him, kissing me hungrily. I noticed his hair was combed differently. A thick piece fell over his forehead.

"Let's go to the pond," he suggested. "I have something to tell you."

We walked to the pond in silence. I couldn't think of a thing to say and I knew David well enough to wait with my questions. The sky was a milky white and the damp, autumn air smelled of burned leaves and decay. I shivered in my cardigan, wishing I'd worn an overcoat. David responded to my slight nuance and put his arm around me tightly. We clung together as he gathered his words.

"I'm leaving after Christmas," he murmured.

"What are you talking about?" I cried, feeling a cold panic sweep through me.

David pulled away and put his face in his hands. "He's worse than ever. I can't stand it anymore." I knew he was talking about his father. Arturo Miller's drinking problem had worsened to the point where David had endured numerous verbal and physical assaults. In September, he'd decided to live full-time at the fraternity to avoid his father, but he struggled with the costs. After his father refused to pay the fraternity's boarding fees, David began working as the Sigma Nu cook in order to pay his room and board. He had become increasingly despondent about school as time went on.

"What happened?" I asked softly, fearing his answer. David slowly pushed his hair away from his forehead to reveal a deep purple gash just above his right eyebrow.

"He hit me with his walking stick." He gritted his teeth, but his voice was full of tears.

"I'm so sorry. What a horrible thing!" I caressed his cheek. "Why? Why did he do this?"

"The same old thing. A 'B' average isn't good enough, especially for law school. I told him, I'm not an academic genius and I'm not cut out for law. He was angrier than I've ever seen him. Drunker, too. He stormed around, hollering that I had to become a lawyer. Finally I admitted I want to be a chef and that it wasn't his choice any more. That's when he hit me."

I clenched my fists, feeling a helpless sorrow shadowed by an aching desire for revenge. How dare Mr. Miller be so unyielding and cruel! I gazed at David with brimming compassion. He looked as though he hadn't shaved in days and his blue eyes had lost their sparkle. Feeling hopeless and frustrated, I wrapped my arms around his broad shoulders in a feeble attempt to cradle him.

"What are you going to do?"

"I spoke to my brother, Herbert. He's got a room for me at his house in San Francisco. I'm going down there to look for a job. I hope

I can get a cooking job in one of the big hotels. Besides, San Francisco has some excellent culinary schools I could attend." He peered into my eyes woefully. "I've got to get out on my own. He'll break me otherwise."

I shook my head and struggled for a brave face, but the dam burst and I began to weep. I couldn't imagine my life without David. "How long will you be gone?" I blubbered.

"I don't know. It's hard to say. If I can get some training, I'll return as soon as I can. Em, please try to understand. This is the best thing for me and for our future. I promise I'll write every day." He scooped me up into his arms and kissed me hard.

Three and a half weeks later, David left on the train for San Francisco and a part of me died. The first days of January were a soap opera vignette of lost love and tearful regrets. I hadn't realized how much I'd come to rely on his friendship. I cried, I moped, I slept a lot and generally became a pathetic nuisance, indulging in a mourning period that flourished without the slightest fight. Yet it was the beginning of 1937, the advent of many deaths. As I look back now, I wonder if David's departure might have been an omen for what was to come.

7

Ginny died on Valentine's Day. Her helpless moans had become hideous screams at night, stirring all of us from sleep. Jack and Jonathan, who slept in the room next to the makeshift infirmary, began to have nightmares. Shortly after the new year, Ginny fell into a morphine-induced coma. It was a wicked time as she disintegrated into a pile of bones and parchment. Her limbs had shriveled into dried, purplish stalks, like rhubarb gone to frost. Her breasts dangled like empty, worn stockings and her skin smelled of death. I prayed to God to let her go, seeing her slow demise as a metaphor for my loss of David. The day the death rattle began, I walked to the church to retrieve Reverend Norpucker. By the time he'd arrived, she was gone.

Papa Joseph was the hardest hit by her death. As we stood around the grave, watching the dirt cover her expensive coffin, I felt tremendous compassion for the old man. He was on his knees, blubbering like a baby, his pride all but gone. I hadn't realized my grandfather had the capacity for such sorrow.

After she died, our clan fell into a short-lived gloom and then, like a late spring snowmelt, our home's ambiance began to burst with new life. Mother didn't have Ginny's iron-fisted style, which for us children was a great cause for celebration. Jack was the most effected by our newfound freedom. He began to sing and whistle. His tuba now boomed from the parlor and his games of chase with Jonathan were no longer outlawed.

Ernest began to lend a hand in the kitchen. Except for Sunday morning snack raids, he'd never been permitted there. Grandmother had thought it unseemly for a young man. Now Ernest arose every morning to help Lizzie and Claudia. He kneaded bread dough, shucked corn and stuffed chickens like a professional. I later learned it was his love for Lizzie that drew him forth.

The ominous cloak of responsibility rose from my back like a black cloud of smoke after Ginny's death, but David's absence still played heavily on my heart. Fortunately, Lizzie eased that chafing wound with salves of encouragement and honesty. One Saturday morning in April, I awoke to find her in bed next to me, picking at her toenails with a pocket knife.

I rolled over, groaning like an old sow. "Don't pick your toenails in my bed," I muttered grumpily.

Lizzie laughed. "Why not? Today's your day to change the sheets since Mama's out shopping all day."

"Will she ever find the right dress?" I demanded. "I can't believe a wedding dress is so hard to find."

"It's got to be perfect. This is her first dress-up wedding. Besides, it has to match our bridesmaid dresses," she chattered brightly. Ignoring her, I rolled back over and shoved my fanny in her direction.

"Those dresses make us look like a couple of Little Bow Peeps. I can't believe your mother is so crazy about them. I hope David isn't too shocked when he sees me." Claudia had spent countless hours sewing our matching bridesmaid dresses and I loathed every inch of lace on them. I was certain I looked like a nincompoop in the *Gone with the Wind* imitation.

"Ah, come on. The dresses aren't that bad," Lizzie drawled. "Ernest says I look beautiful in mine."

"He would. He thinks you walk on water."

Lizzie gawked at me in surprise. "Ernest is a nice kid, but he's like a brother to me."

"I know. I just wish you'd consider dating a little. You're going on 17 and you've never had a date."

"I know," she said quietly. "I'm just not interested."

"I want you to know that wonderful floating feeling when you love someone." My voice wavered and tears rose up in my eyes. Lizzie reached down and wiped a random drop from my cheek.

"Hey, I know you miss David, but you've got to get a hold of yourself."

"But women and men are supposed to be together. It's natural to be in a partnership, even the Bible says so," I replied smugly, fully expecting one of our vigorous debates to unfold. I sat up in bed to watch Lizzie wind herself into a frenzy. She jumped off the window seat, her black eyes darting about as she wrung her hands. One strap of her dungarees hung off her shoulder and the sleeves of her old oxford shirt were rolled up to her elbows, exposing her smooth, brown arms.

"Let me ask you something. How many women do you see at the altar of your precious church? How many stories in the Bible tell of women who have power? How many pictures, stain glass windows and statues depict women? Doesn't that bother you? Even the hymns are *hims*." She shot me a tempestuous scowl. "I tell you, women need to get smart. You've got to live like the old Emily, full of spunk and fun. David will be back soon enough!"

Lizzie must have seen the confused look on my face, because she added gently, "Have you forgotten how much you love to fly? When was the last time you took to the skies?"

"I just don't feel like doing much of anything, lately. Even flying doesn't excite me anymore."

"I thought you were going to be the next Amelia Earhart. How pathetic! Look how David's absence has effected you. You've become a boring lump. You need to get out and have some fun. I have an idea that I think will cheer you up."

"What?" I asked in a flat voice.

"Your dad and I have been doing some talking. He has a client who lives on San Juan Island, remember?" I nodded. Father's new client was a very wealthy timber baron who was suing the state over a land right's issue.

"Your father needs some legal papers delivered to him as soon as possible. I offered to co-pilot the plane with you so we could deliver them today."

"And he said yes? I don't believe you!"

"Your father is as worried about you as I am. Besides, I took a few lessons from him last summer, remember? I've had my nose to the grindstone, reading those flight manuals. It won't be long until I get my license, too. Between the two of us, we can manage it."

The idea of flying took hold. I was tired of my self-imposed isolation and even more, my wallowing self-pity. Maybe a trip was just what I needed.

Later that morning, as we walked across the field to the plane, Father gave us the rundown. "Mr. Weyer is a very busy man. He'll have a driver waiting at the runway to pick you up. You will be taken to his estate where he'll sign the papers. If you would like to stop for lunch on the way back, there are a couple of nice cafes not far from the airstrip. Grab a bite to eat and then hightail it home, agreed?"

I smiled with my mind more on the glistening silver bird than his words. Taking a deliberate breath, I pried my eyes from the plane and replied, "Of course, Father."

Minutes later, we were airborne. Admittedly, the joy of flying erased any lingering doubts. I'd forgotten how healing a break from gravity could be. Lizzie was doing very well as my co-pilot, checking the readings, keeping her eyes on the landmarks and singing, *Love for Sale*, her favorite song. The sky was as blue as a sapphire and the tail winds increased our time. In less than an hour we were back on the ground, taxiing toward a long, gray limousine that had looked like a silver bullet from the air.

"Now this is exciting," Lizzie chirped. "I used to see limousines drive up in front of the Olympic Hotel sometimes, but I've never had the chance to ride in one."

"Let's just get this over with," I insisted. "There are a couple of shops in Friday Harbor that are worth visiting. What time is it now?"

"One o'clock."

"Good. The weather should hold if we want to dally a bit."

As we trotted toward the car, a stout man in a tailored uniform and gold braid cap jumped out of the limousine and saluted us, casting a baleful eye from Lizzie to me and back again. Apparently he wasn't expecting two high school girls. After introducing ourselves to Calvin the chauffeur, we climbed into the limousine's back seat and began our journey along the narrow, bumpy, coastline road.

I gazed out the windows at the rugged wilderness. The island was sparsely populated. Groves of Douglas fir dotted the landscape as we turned down a dirt road and approached a large building that appeared to be a hunting lodge. Twin totem poles supported a high-pitched, shingled roof. At the end of a stone walkway, there was a set of double oak doors with heavy iron handles. Thick rhododendron bushes blanketed the grounds around the lodge and overflowing pots of fuschias and day lilies skirted the portico. It was breathtaking in a rustic sort of way. Both Lizzie and I gasped at the sight of it, despite our wish to appear unimpressed.

"Young ladies, we have arrived," Calvin announced in a nasally British accent. He parked the vehicle as the front doors of the lodge swung open. There stood the famous Mr. Weyer, a man known for his strong business acumen and notorious eccentricity. He gave the two of us a quick glance and barked, "The papers."

I fumbled around in Father's heavy leather briefcase, yanking out a handful of carefully typed sheets of legal paper. Mr. Weyer took them from me without so much as a nod of thanks and marched back into the house. Lizzie and I stood awkwardly next to the limousine while Calvin watched us like a hawk.

The afternoon sun was scorching and there was no breeze to cut the heat so when I saw a small bench under a shady maple tree, I asked, "You don't mind if we wait over there, do you, Mr. Calvin?" He grunted in approval as we trudged to the bench a few yards away.

As we sat down, Lizzie whispered, "I'm glad I have my medicine bag. There's something strange about this place."

"What are you talking about?" I grumbled.

"I don't know how to explain it, but I get a weird, ghostly feeling here."

"For an atheist, you certainly have a superstitious mind. There are no ghosts. If you think so, I dare you to ask Calvin about it."

"No sweat, Emily!" She jumped off the bench and loped toward Calvin, who looked utterly dismayed at her approach. His squinting, pig-like eyes fixed on her suspiciously. His jowls hung in loose folds upon his short neck and his pug nose was flat against his face. Their conversation was muted, but Lizzie skipped back over to me minutes later.

"See, I was right," she said gleefully. "The mansion was built on ancient Indian burial grounds. Bad news for Mr. Weyer."

"Mr. Calvin explained it to you just like that?" I marveled, wondering how anyone could get information from such a peevish old coot.

"Not exactly. I hinted around as if I knew the place was haunted and before long, he admitted it."

"You've got a knack, Liz. People always confide in you."

"Yep, it's because I take them by surprise with my gutsy attitude," she nodded with a sly grin. "But now I can't wait to get out of here. This place makes my hair stand on end."

Another 10 minutes had passed when Mr. Weyer came out of the house, thrusting the papers into Calvin's hands and promptly disappearing inside. When we approached the car, the chauffeur held the papers out at me with a satisfied snort. I shrugged and slid them back into the briefcase. Climbing in, we told him to return us to Friday Harbor and that we would find a ride to the airport from there. He grunted, but agreed to drop us in front of Pilagrees's Cafe.

By the time Calvin dropped us off, a snappy breeze was blowing and an ominous bank of black clouds had appeared to the north. Stepping out of the limousine, we were greeted by the screeching cries of gulls mingling with the rumble of marine engines and shouts of fishermen. Yet once inside the cafe, we stepped back into time. Fishing nets hung from the low wooden rafters, strung with petrified starfish and Japanese floats. The dusty, cramped dining room held 10 crudely constructed wooden tables that were covered with newsprint and topped with hurricane lamps. The kitchen was hidden behind a bamboo screen. A faded mermaid was painted on one wall and a lascivious, eye-popping sailor was on the other.

The restaurant looked the same as it did nearly seven years ago, when my father had brought me here for lunch after one of our first flights to the island. Though I'd only been a youngster, I'd revealed to him my desire to become a pilot. There had been a storm moving through, so we had sat on the rough wooden benches and talked until nightfall. I'd shivered, the scrawny little thing that I was, so he'd held me close while the tempest had rattled the windows and the lightening had crashed outside, telling me everything he loved about flight and comparing it to a human spirit's evolution through life.

"First, you are launched into the world," he'd explained in his soothing baritone. "Just like when you left your mama's womb, you take off like a bird leaving the nest. With wings of courage and curiosity and a rudder of temperance and reason, you glide through life, hitting an air pocket now and then, taking a few bumps along the way. There are tail winds to push you along, encouraging you toward greater freedom and growth and then there are the head winds."

Anxiously I'd placed my small hand over his large one. "What are head winds, Daddy?" I'd demanded, eager for all the knowledge he could give.

"Head winds hold you back. They resist your thrust for growth and keep you from moving as fast as you'd like. Throughout life, you will meet the head winds, whether it be on the ground or in the air. Watch out for them, for they can fool you. Sometimes their strength will appear greater than your own. Perseverance and wisdom are produced by encounters with life's head winds." I've never forgotten his wisdom, I realized as Lizzie nudged me, breaking my reverie.

"Wake up, you! The waitress is ready to seat us. By the way, we'd better head home right after lunch. It's nearly two o'clock and the weather isn't looking too good," she warned.

"Don't worry! The weather on the islands is always a bit drippy. We'll be out of here by four."

We ordered a lunch of crab sandwiches and iced tea. As we ate, my mind drifted back to my father's words.

"Penny for your thoughts," she asked, slurping the last drop of ice tea.

"Father's in my head, giving me some wise advice."

"I hope he's telling you to get on with it, without the adorable David," she whined, drawing out his name with an Italian twist.

"As a matter of fact he was." I laughed at her accuracy, but Lizzie didn't think my response was funny. She gave a little shudder and glanced at her watch again.

"Just relax, would you? The airstrip is just down the road!"

Lizzie frowned. "I just have bad feeling about this. That storm's about to hit any minute."

"What's the alternative?" I asked, while paying for lunch.

"I don't know! You tell me," she demanded.

"Leave, of course! The storm is moving through. Look!" As we stepped out the door, I pointed to the north. There was a low band of light on the horizon, indicating a clearing. "By the time we reach the airplane, this storm should be about over."

Boy, I was wrong! The rain seemed to fall harder as we stumbled through the puddles toward the airstrip. It seemed to take forever to reach our destination, particularly as Lizzie was cursing me all the way, reminding me how it was my fault we were in this predicament! We were both dripping wet by the time we climbed into the plane. As there wasn't a control tower on the island yet, just a marked landing strip, it was up to each pilot to use their best judgment on flying conditions.

"We're in trouble now," Lizzie exclaimed, giving me a nasty glare.

"Shush," I demanded. "Look, if we don't take off soon, it'll be dark and I'm not landing in the dark. If we take off, we may hit some turbulence, but we can manage. I flew with Father once in a storm. It was rough, but we made it okay."

Lizzie drew her medicine bag over her head and opened it. Pulling out a small pebble, she held it tightly in her hand over her heart and began a strange chant.

"What in the heck are you doing?"

"Calling to the spirits to protect us. Now be quiet!" Lizzie continued for a few more minutes, but to me it seemed like hours. Finally she opened her eyes and nodded. "Okay, we'll be safe."

"Holy cow!" I wanted to say she was nuts, but the aggravation wouldn't help, so I started the engines and checked the instruments carefully. The rain had slowed and there were some bright spots on the horizon, but we'd be flying into the heaviest clouds.

We took off immediately. I resisted the urge to overuse the throttle, but I had to get above the clouds. Dark, billowy vapors swallowed the plane, blinding us to direction. Pounding like bullets against the windshield, long rivets of water obscured our vision. I fought back anxiety as an eerie claustrophobia overtook me.

The head winds were strong, pushing hard against the light plane. As I struggled to maintain speed, an invisible hand suddenly slapped the starboard side, throwing Lizzie against me and tilting the aircraft at a sharp angle momentarily. A cramp of panic swept through my gut as the engulfing wind tossed us from side to side. Then I fell into utter terror as reality hit me. I could no longer control this situation. The hand of fate was upon us. We could crash! The trembling came so hard that I clutched the wheel until my hands hurt. My throat became a vat of acid as nausea bubbled and burned. I thought about dying, our young bodies plunging to oblivion, our families discovering us, mangled and torn beyond recognition. "No, God, I'm not ready," my brain wailed, but I bit my lip to stop from crying out. If Lizzie could hold it together, so could I.

The plane felt like a paper toy in the wind now. I had no control for long seconds at a time. The wind lifted and plunged the aircraft until I thought the wings would snap. For a moment I considered jumping out, preferring the icy Puget Sound waters to this horror. Even Lizzie paled under the small cockpit light. Her stark black hair fell around her face in dripping strings and her skin looked translucent. One of her hands white-knuckled the medicine bag. When the plane hit an air pocket, we were thrown forward by the impact. Lizzie hit her head on the instrument panels and I bit my tongue so hard it began to bleed. I fought to hold the plane steady, crying out a nonsensical prayer.

"I don't know what to do. It won't stay up!" I screamed.

The plane veered to the right and then left, losing altitude with each thrust. I thought of the Indian ghosts and burial grounds and my friend's superstitious leanings.

"Down there, land down there. It will be okay," Lizzie insisted, pointing down while shaking her fist. "There's a reservation down there. Get below the clouds so we can find a place to land." There was no time to argue. I had to trust her; there was no other choice. I pushed the control stick downward. The plane had lost enough elevation to bring us out of the cloud bank in seconds. Below, the world was a foggy brown mass, but I could see a open meadow that looked flat from above. Sheets of rain prohibited any clear indications of the terrain, so I crossed my fingers and prayed. The ground seemed to jump up to meet us as we hit hard. The wheels bounced across the meadow like rubber balls on tarmac. I pulled the throttle down as a grove of trees appeared in front of us, careful not to nose-dive in the slippery dirt. As the plane came to a fitful stop, my breath returned, along with a pounding head and a bursting gratitude.

We didn't speak for a long moment, but held each other, squeezing tight to quell the final shudders of fear that swept our trembling bodies. "We made it!" I whispered. "Thank God, we made it."

Lizzie nodded as tears formed in her eyes. She brushed them away and held onto me again.

"What do we do now?" I sputtered, as we climbed from the plane. "It's almost dark and we're in the middle of nowhere. Our family's going to be scared out of their wits. We've got to get home somehow."

Pulling her rain slicker tightly around her, she said, "Follow me."

She led me through the trees as though she knew exactly where she was going. Jabbering like an idiot from nerves, I repeatedly asked Lizzie where she was taking us. Ignoring me, she continued confidently forward. Just when panic laid its lecherous hand again on my heart, a small log cabin came into view.

"How did you know this was here?"

"Hush!" she warned as she walked up to the low, planked door and knocked. We stood there for a few minutes, but no one answered. I squinted to see into a tiny, curtained window. To my surprise, Lizzie opened the door and walked in.

"What are you doing?" I hissed, looking over my shoulder anxiously.

"Come on in. It's safe. You must believe me," she insisted. We stepped into a simple one-room cabin. A stone fireplace hugged one wall along with a welcome sight- a neatly stacked pile of logs. The dirt floor was bare, but cleanly swept. Two narrow cots, piled with deer skins, rested against the adjacent walls. A stool and a few log stumps served as chairs. In the middle of the room, I spied a rough wooden table, piled with strips of dried meat, a leather pouch and a can of beans.

"Good, he left some food," Lizzie murmured, more to herself than me. She picked up a piece of meat and ripped off a bite.

"What do you mean, 'he'?" I shouted, suddenly overcome with the shakes. I couldn't stand her secrecy, especially not now.

"Relax. This cabin belongs to a friend of my mother's." She smiled and took a soft deerskin from the bed, wrapping it around me. "I'll make a fire," she added. "You look like you're still in shock."

I was too tired and frightened to argue. We were safe and there was nothing we could do until morning. Nightfall had arrived and I had no idea where we were. Peeling off my wet clothes, I climbed onto one of the cots and wrapped myself snugly in the musty-smelling deerskin. I remember watching the fire burn for a while, but soon after, I fell into a deep sleep.

I awoke the next morning to the sound of Lizzie's voice singing *Love for Sale*. As I sat up, the animal skin fell away, revealing my nakedness. Lizzie heard my movements because she looked over at me, her eyes growing wide. We'd dressed and undressed around each other hundreds of times, shyly, always covering ourselves and turning away. She was staring at my breasts with a curious expression on her face.

"You have beautiful breasts, Emmy. I've always wanted to see your breasts," she announced boldly. She walked up to me and kneeled down. "Do you want to see mine?"

"Okay," I answered shyly.

Lizzie pulled off her sweater and brassiere to reveal two perfectly round, peach-size breasts. Her nipples were much darker than mine and very large in comparison. Time was lost as we stared at one another.

"Ever touched yourself, Emily?" she asked. There was a gleam in her eye, a challenge for the truth.

"I want to sometimes, when I think of David. Do you?"

Lizzie jumped up and danced to the window to avoid my gaze. Over her shoulder she replied, "Plenty. Especially when I think about sex. I do it like this." Suddenly she turned around and leaned back against the wall. I knew immediately what she was about to do. I felt both nervous and thrilled as I watched. Closing her eyes, she rubbed herself slowly with her fingers until her body began to shake against her hand and she moaned softly. "See, that's all you have to do. It's easy and it feels real good. You should do it after you've been with David," she murmured with a heavy sigh of pleasure. My heart fluttered as I considered the consequences had we been caught like this. I quickly reached for my clothes.

"Lizzie?"

"Yes?"

"I feel kind of weird about this."

She laughed aloud as she skipped over and wrapped her arms around me. Her spongy breasts felt warm against my own. "Oh, Emmy, don't worry. We've got to learn about this stuff somehow," she whispered, hugging me gently. "We're two teenage girls, remember? I just taught you something important, that's all. Don't worry, girl. Nothing has changed between us."

With that, she pulled away to put on her clothes. "Look what I found," she said brightly, pointing to the table. "A pan for our beans."

After we gobbled down the beans, we headed back to the plane. The day was sunny and clear as though the prior night's storm had been a figment of our imaginations. After checking out the plane, we climbed aboard and took off, both of us singing *Love for Sale*. Needless to say, my family had called out the police and the Coast Guard in full force. We were greeted like lost war heroes and our story was told for weeks after, but not all of it, of course.

8

It was the morning of Claudia and Charles's wedding. Lizzie and I were in my room, giggling and gasping our way through the heaps of clothing: corsets, camisoles, hoops, petticoats, dresses, sashes, shoes, and the wide-brimmed straw hats trimmed with clumps of white and yellow daisies tied with gaudy yellow bows.

"I guess I should be glad David got that promotion at the St. Francis Hotel. I couldn't stand to have him see me as Scarlet O'Hara," I grumbled as I struggled with my hat.

Lizzie laughed as she waddled to the dressing table, her hoop swaying like a bell. "Yeah, I'm beginning to agree with you. Tie this thing for me, will you?"

When we finally finished dressing, we helped my brothers with their bow ties and corsages. The noisy excitement increased as we rushed around in preparation, but soon enough the family piled into the cars to drive to the Seattle Yacht Club where the wedding was to be held.

Perched on eastern edge of Portage Bay, the famous club overlooked the Montlake Cut and the University of Washington campus. Surrounded by elegant ships and dozens of sailboats, the stately white building with porthole windows and a rooftop captain's deck emitted an aura of leisure and old wealth. The gardens surrounding the club were immaculate and bursting with towering striped tiger lilies, clusters of indigo hyacinth and fragrant lilac bushes. Well-tended rose gardens bordered the waterfront. The club's semi-circular balcony was ideal for viewing the Olympic Mountains to the west and Mt. Rainier to the south.

Claudia had dressed by the time Lizzie and I waddled into the club's dressing room. She was the prettiest bride I'd ever seen. She'd sewn her romantic, ivory satin dress. Studded with tiny pearl beads, the tapered bodice showed off her generous bosom and small waist. The long sleeves were sheer lace and the full skirt was nearly as wide as our hoop ones. A pleated, six-foot satin train trailed behind. Claudia had gathered her wavy, black hair into a bun upon which lay a gardenia wreath. She was glowing with cheeks blushed pink and wide-set, sapphire eyes. Chattering like a monkey when we entered, she fussed with her train one minute and pinched her cheeks the next. Nervous anxiety wasn't a customary state for Claudia and I found myself quite amused by her agitated twittering.

Mother looked stunning in her matron of honor's buttercup chiffon gown. My heart sang with pride as I admired her. She was doing her best to calm Claudia down, though anxiety hadn't been lost on her either.

"We have 20 minutes before the wedding starts, Claudia. Now take a deep breath and calm down. That's right, breath, breath," Mother instructed, raising her hand up and down in front of her chest with each exaggerated breath.

Claudia's face became redder as the two of them huffed and puffed.

"Hey, what about us? Don't we look great?" Lizzie blurted with a wild spin around the room. In the three foot diameter hoop, she reminded me of a bright yellow top.

"Of course you look absolutely gorgeous. Don't the girls look wonderful, Melanie?"

Mother nodded, smiling broadly. "Claudia, let's open a bottle of champagne for the four of us."

With great anticipation, we toasted our glowing bride, wishing her happiness and a long life with Charles. As we held up our glasses, I could have sworn a flicker of doubt shadowed Claudia's eyes, but the brief sadness was quickly replaced by an ebullient smile as we drank to life.

Soon Ernest knocked on the door, "It's time," he announced and we were off!

A short time later, as I stood in the bridal procession next to Lizzie waiting for our cue, I looked over at the murmuring guests. Over 100 people were seated in rows of folding chairs on the club's perfectly manicured lawn. Claudia and Charles had many friends from all walks of life. On Claudia's side of the gathering, artsy-looking men in wire-rimmed glasses and baggy linen blazers sat next to primly dressed ladies with stiff spines and pursed lips. Several esteemed physician colleagues of Charles's sat on the right side of the aisle along with his aged mother, Agnes, University Alumni and Seattle Tennis Club friends. Neighbors such as the Gersteins, the Masons and the Millers mingled on both sides of the cluster. A few of the downtrodden from the soup kitchen had also arrived, dressed shabbily, but welcomed without hesitation by the beautiful bride's genuine smile.

As the wedding march began, I glanced over at Lizzie. She beamed proudly as her mother appeared on my father's arm. I wondered again why Claudia's family had refused to attend this special event. Then, from the corner of my eye, I caught sight of a Rolls Royce pulling into the driveway at the edge of the grass behind us. As Claudia floated down the grassy aisle, with her eyes rapturously glued on her attentive groom, an elderly couple stepped out of the car. Lizzie gasped and I knew immediately her grandparents had just arrived.

Claudia's parents took a seat in the back row. Mr. Coomes was a very large man, with a barrel chest and long arms. In his black tuxedo, he reminded me of a gigantic penguin. His salt and pepper hair was thin and scrappy and his pudgy face avoided the slightest expression of joy. Mrs. Coomes was a wizened woman who was completely gray from her hair and skin to her well-tailored silk suit. She looked drained as though she'd taken a lifelong beating. I felt a surge of pity for her. Certainly she must miss her daughter! Just then I felt Lizzie's hand drop from her bouquet and touch the side of my dress, so I lowered my hand to hold hers. Her skin was cold and clammy and her hand grasped mine as though for dear life.

It seemed only seconds and the ceremony was complete. The wedding march boomed out from the four-piece band on the balcony, awakening me from my mental wanderings. With beatific smiles, Claudia and Charles trotted back down the aisle as the guests tossed handfuls of rice through the air. When her turn came, Lizzie continued to clutch my hand, though Charles's younger brother, Frederick, held out his arm to accompany her. Meanwhile, Jack bobbed up and down, blocking our way as he released wads of rice from his jacket pockets. Ernest caught sight of Lizzie's expression and looked at me questioningly. I mouthed, "her grandparents are here."

Lizzie was frozen to the spot, though Frederick began to pull on her arm. "Go on, Liz, Father won't let your grandparents bother you," I encouraged. Claudia paused at the end of the aisle, obviously seeing her parents as well. She swung around anxiously, her face as pale as the gardenias in her hair.

"Lizzie, come to me," she called through the crowd. Lizzie tore away from my father, running awkwardly to her mother. Together, Charles, Claudia and Lizzie advanced forward as an invincible team, strong and undaunted, arm-in-arm. In seconds they were climbing the balcony steps to form their receiving line from above. Claudia lifted her chin with pride as she paused above us. By the time I reached the end of the walk, the elderly Coomes were edging toward their car just a few feet away. They'd stayed long enough, I guessed, but my heart hurt for Claudia and Lizzie.

Suddenly a strange thing happened. Glancing down at me from the top of the stairs with a sly grin, Claudia prepared to throw her bridal bouquet. I was alert to her implied signal. To catch the bountiful cluster of yellow rosebuds and white gardenias would be a good omen for me. Other young women in the crowd jostled one another, each hopeful as superstition became their impetus. As she tossed the flowers in my direction, a sudden gust blew over from the cut, sweeping the bouquet to my left. I reached out to grab it, but it continued passed me, floating like a balloon until it landed at Mrs. Coomes's feet. Her perfectly-plucked eyebrows arched quizzically as she bent down to pick it up. The crowd hushed as she gazed down at her daughter's symbol of new life. Raising her face, Mrs. Coomes stared up at Claudia and mouthed, "Thank you." Claudia gave her a twisted little smile, like that of a bashful child. The tension between them was so intense, I could have cut it with a knife. In my opinion, Claudia would have liked nothing better than to fly into her mother's arms, but social decorum inhibited such gestures. Besides, her father appeared malevolent, with his dark scowl and impatient tugging of his wife's arm. The giant of a man even ignored Papa's wave as the two of them climbed into the car and disappeared from sight.

A tentative moment passed before Claudia donned a carefree smile. Soon the reception was bubbling with champagne, laughter, music and good spirits. As the lovers kissed for the crowd, I trembled with tender romance. The joy of their love imbued all of us with a sense of hope and promise.

The last guests left around seven that evening. Since Claudia and Charles weren't leaving for their honeymoon immediately, Papa offered an evening cruise on his yacht. Gathering the few remaining bottles of the champagne, the men and boys hustled down the dock to the *Starlight*, Papa's forty-foot cruiser while the women scurried back inside the yacht club to change from our wedding attire. Though Lizzie and I had neglected to bring other clothing, we removed the hoops and as many layers of petticoats as possible.

Papa's yacht was the epitome of elegance and good taste. The gleaming teak interior was studded with brass fixtures and comfortable, overstuffed couches and chairs. Marine art graced the gleaming, curved walls and the fully fitted galley could serve a meal to a king.

Both decks sported mahogany railings though the lower deck had cording between each anchored post. The lower deck was also outfitted with wicker deck chairs and a card table. A bar and an RCA phonograph completed the entertainment area. Without a doubt, the *Starlight* was one of the finest yachts in the greater Puget Sound. Papa wouldn't have it any other way.

By the time we cast off, the sun was beginning to set. Papa turned on the cruising lights and honked his horn, announcing our departure. We cruised through the Montlake Cut toward Lake Washington. On the upper deck, Papa, Charles and Father puffed on Cuban cigars. I could hear their boasting and good humor, despite the wind in my ears. Meanwhile, the boys had found warmth and solitude in the cabin. They busied themselves with a game of Chinese checkers.

Mother, Claudia, Lizzie and I stood on the lower deck, watching the sun fade behind the Olympic mountains. How I missed my David! As though reading my mind, Claudia walked over to me and placed her arm around my waist. She sighed deeply, emitting a happiness that wrapped itself around me like a cocoon. I echoed her sigh and she turned toward me.

"Emily, don't worry about David. He'll come home and you'll have your wedding day, too. Now I want you to promise me, you'll always watch out for my crazy Lizzie. One of these days, she's going to leave my sight, but when she does, I know you'll be there."

"Of course I will," I murmured, hugging her warmly.

We were floating in the middle of the lake when Jonathan suddenly ran out of the cabin.

"The big boys are cheating," he whined, pulling on his ebony curls in frustration.

"Come here, Johnny," Claudia called, hoisting the sticky, cake-covered toddler into her arms and whispering soothing phrases into his ear.

What happened next was so swift and terrifying, that it still buckles my knees to recall it. Without warning, Papa began to shout, first in German, and then again in English.

"Watch out," he hollered. "We're going to hit." Though I couldn't see what he was talking about, I quickly braced myself against the wooden railing just in case. Claudia was still whispering to Jonathan and evidently didn't hear him.

"Claudia!" I warned her, but the jolt that shook the yacht was so powerful, I was flung across the deck like a tossed penny. Plates and glasses hurled across the deck, breaking all around me. Groans from the bowels of the ship competed with splintering glass as the *Starlight* lurched like a teeter-totter out of control. Crashing objects and cracking wood filled my awareness while screams and shouts echoed into the night.

When I eventually pulled myself up, my arms and legs were as heavy as lead pipes. I wobbled to the card table while the boat rocked recklessly. Jerking my head toward the ship's stern, I only saw swirling darkness. Lizzie was against the outer cabin wall, braced on all fours and clinging to a large metal cleat. Mother had hit her head and was sitting near Lizzie, moaning as she rubbed out the pain.

"Where are Claudia and Jonathan?" I shouted. Lizzie scrambled up off the deck before I could say another word, pointing wildly at something out of my line of vision. Her eyes grew wide as she ran to the starboard side of the boat. Lizzie released a blood-curdling cry and disappeared into the water, her yellow gown ballooning like a parachute. It was then that I saw the broken railing and realized Claudia and Jonathan had been flung overboard.

I struggled to the railing and looked down. The inky water below looked like the monstrous black mouth of a shark that had just ate a school of Parrot fish. I watched the frightening shapes squirm and fight as the waves swallowed my loved ones. In reaction, I grabbed a life ring and threw it overboard, glimpsing Jonathan's panicked face just before he went underwater. Fortunately, Lizzie grabbed his jacket before it was too late.

The dense waters around them churned, but Jonathan was able to wrap his arms around Lizzie's neck, clinging helplessly as she grabbed the ring. With superhuman strength, I dragged them up to the ship's deck as Father and Charles appeared at my side. My head whipped back and forth, but to my horror, I saw no sign of Claudia. Enormous objects, sticking out of the water at sharp angles, appeared and were thrust against the side of the boat by the raging current. Gigantic logs imprisoned the boat like medieval spears.

Diving in, Charles swam around in circles, barely avoiding the bobbing logs as he called out his beloved's name. Ripping off his jacket, Ernest prepared to dive in, though Mother had him tethered with a rope before he jumped. Praying with heart-wrenching desire, clutching one another, breathless, crying, beseeching God while time stretched into eternity, we waited, but it was no use. Our darling, precious Claudia was gone.

After her drowning, I hid in my room for days. My mind swam around in a fog while the horrible scene played over and over again. From a remote place inside my brain, a voice of denigration called out, blaming and accusatory. I was a good swimmer. Why didn't I jump in to save her? Then it became my turn to blame. I defiled Papa. The incompetent idiot had run into a logjam! And my father ... he should've been able to save her! Not to mention that pathetic Charles! He'd had a hold of her for a moment, didn't he? How could he have let her go? I became bitterly angry with God. It wasn't fair. Claudia, sweet Claudia, who had loved us all unconditionally, who'd brought music and laughter into our tamed, repressed, predictable household. Our Claudia, who helped the sick and poor, who sang to the birds and cradled me like a baby when I was feeling sad. "How could you, God?" I shouted over and over. "How dare you do this!"

Claudia's body was found three days later, entangled in the logjam that the *Starlight* had collided with. Her body was submerged between two enormous firs, but her glittering diamond wedding ring had caught the attention of some early morning fishermen.

Charles wouldn't allow Lizzie to see her mother's body, as she was bloated beyond recognition. Lizzie was furious, locking herself in the tower for days, refusing to come out. I delivered food to her door, begging her to talk to me, but a raw, threatening growl told me not to push her. I couldn't imagine what she might be feeling. I wondered if she blamed herself. My heart cried out for her, but I was useless to help.

Nobody in our home spoke for days. Mother disappeared into her room, Father took the boys to the cabin to 'explain' and Papa escaped to work. Charles was arranging the funeral. We were all too worthless to be of assistance to him.

The night before the funeral, I arose at midnight, agitated and suffering from insomnia. Though Mother didn't respond to my knock, I could hear her quiet sobs. Her cold, unexpected avoidance stabbed at me like an ice pick and loneliness crawled under my skin like shingles, irritating every cell of my body.

Lizzie! The thought of her grieving alone was unbearably tragic, but I needed her comfort, too. Tiptoeing up the tower stairs, I heard a voice coming from her room. To my relief, her door was slightly ajar. I pushed it open and looked into the shadowy space. Lizzie was on her knees at the side of her bed, whispering faintly. Straining, I heard her desperate words.

"Now I lay me down to sleep. I pray to God, my soul to keep. I will not die before I wake, but bring Mama home and my soul you *must* take," she beseeched. I flew across the room, knelt down and wrapped my body around hers, holding her until she convulsed into wracking sobs.

"Oh, Lizzie, it wasn't your fault," I repeated, my own tears unstoppable. When she drew away from me, her eyes glittered with a touch of madness.

"God has visited me, Emmy. He sent the angels and they promised Mama will be safe. They promised me. Do you believe me? Tell me you believe me!" she cried hysterically.

"I believe you," I pulled her close again. Sensing a presence, I turned, and saw my mother standing at the door, peering in. In her white nightgown, she looked like a visiting apparition, without solid body or form.

She whispered timidly, "May I come in, Elizabeth?"

Lizzie drew away from me and reached out her hand. Mother ran to her and they embraced, their bodies melting together in a symbiotic gesture of survival. Our sandbags of stoicism caved in and a powerful tidal wave of grief washed over us. Clinging to one another, we surrendered to our grief, cursing and crying without restraint, a trembling clump of women, lost in the dark.

9

The final days of autumn became a simile for our family's suffering. As the leaves of summer turned from green to yellow to red and fell from the trees, we also withered. I joined the Kappa Kappa Gamma sorority a few weeks later. I drifted through rush week with a placating, plastic smile, making small talk without engaging anyone. Frankly, I was surprised I'd been invited at all. Afterwards, I decided to continue to live at home rather than the sorority house, needing to be with Lizzie as much as possible.

David continued to write, but his encouraging words seemed shallow now. After all that I had been through, his letters didn't have much of an impact. Nothing could cheer me up. Thrashing about in my own murky waters, I could have cared less about what was going on around me.

Nineteen thirty-eight heralded much activity on the planet. Fascism was rapidly replacing democracy. While Japan tightly grasped China's throat, King Carol squashed Rumania under his thumb and Mussolini's fist continued to pound at Spain's back door. Treaties were ripped in two, as dictators became more popular than diplomats. On March 12th, Austria crumbled into the palm of Hitler's hand like a dead leaf underfoot. Papa was jubilant at Germany's relentless ambitions. He spent more and more time at his 'meetings', irrefutably funneling more than just emotional energy to Hitler's cause. His den had become a living museum for Third Reich memorabilia and we were now forbidden to go in there. Mother insisted the door stay locked when Papa was away.

Seattle had an early spring that year. Yellow-headed daffodils danced in the soft, breezy skies and the crimson tulips' sensuality stirred something inside me for the first time in ages. I began to enjoy my classes and the campus life. In April I joined the journalism staff of the student paper, *The Daily*. Covering stories of campus politics became a major impetus for reviving my social life. I was less likely to go to gatherings for a drink and a good time than to interview a student union delegate, but at least I was out and about again.

One afternoon, I was frolicking through the commons, admiring the flowering cherry trees when I heard a voice.

"I've been watching you for weeks and I do believe this is the first time I've seen you smile," a raspy voice resonated from nearby. Standing under the canopy of buzzing blossoms, looking up at the glorious pink flowers, I was reluctant to shift my gaze. A man stepped into my periphery, his bearded face tilted up, and his eyes wide with indulgent preoccupation.

"Beautiful, aren't they?" he murmured.

"Yes, like cotton candy clouds," I replied absently.

"Do you like to fly?"

Now I looked over at the encroaching apparition, consciously taking him in. The young man next to me was no taller than I. His frame was slight and his bushy black hair was nearly to his shoulders. I caught his smoldering eyes and blushed. He seemed to look right through me, piercing my very soul. Nodding in response, I fumbled with my books, suddenly self-conscious.

"Pardon me," he said. "I must introduce myself. My name is Rossolitti Marquez, but you may call me Ross."

"Hello, Ross," I stuttered, staring at his stark white teeth that appeared through a jungle of facial hair. "I'm Emily Strong." I took his outstretched hand. His warm, delicate fingers wrapped themselves around mine as a slight shiver ran through me.

"I've often seen you at the Students for Socialism meetings."

"I'm sorry, I don't recall meeting you."

"No need to apologize. Why would an attractive woman like you take notice of me?" he retorted with a touch of mirth in his long-lashed eyes.

I giggled uncomfortably.

"Why do you laugh? Do you not appreciate my flattery?" His face was whimsical and yet haughty. "I guess my mother was right then. She always said flattery will get you nowhere," he chuckled.

"Your mother was quite wrong. I'm happy to accept your complement. I haven't felt beautiful in months."

"What wicked thing stole your beauty then, my lady?" He cocked his head and bent closer to me, awaiting my secret. I could smell the faint scent of cigarettes and coffee on his breath. He quickly moved back, hesitating. "Forgive me! What was I thinking? I have no right!" he admonished himself.

"No, it's okay. I had a dear friend recently pass away. Her death has had a profound effect on me for months. I'm just now starting to feel better."

His eyes looked deeply into mine. "I'm so very sorry for you, Emily." I blushed again. Who was this man? My heart had sped up, but I had to ask myself why. He wasn't even my type. Ross responded to my awkwardness by saying, "A cup of coffee for your troubles?"

I shrugged, attempting nonchalance. "Okay."

He offered his arm in a gesture of sincere courtesy and I took it. He limped as we walked toward the cafeteria, but he gave no indication of pain.

Once settled with coffee and sandwiches, Ross and I talked until dark. The cafeteria janitor eventually began to mop around our feet in an obvious attempt to oust us. I glanced at my watch, startled to see it was nearly nine o'clock. We'd talked for over five hours about everything from Ella Fitzgerald to the Stalin's merciless annihilation of the Bolshevik Party. One minute he was bursting with laughter at one of my silly jokes, the next minute, his eyes sweetened solemnly as my tears appeared from painful memories. Without a second thought, I had poured my heart out to him.

Ross shared that he was born in Barcelona to an American-born mother and Spanish Duke. Because Ross was their only child, he was swiftly exiled to America on the eve of General Franco's revolution. He had been at the University for two years and was studying law. Active in student politics, he was also a musician, occasionally playing the flute in a jazz band downtown. I found him oddly diffident and utterly charming.

"I've got to go, Ross. I had no idea it was so late," I insisted.

"May I walk you home?"

I nodded. "As a matter of fact, I'm staying at the sorority house tonight."

We strolled down Memorial Way in the moonlight, past Parrington Hall and the observatory, laughing and teasing one another as though we'd been friends for years. As we trudged along, his limp was more pronounced than before. I couldn't conceal my curiosity any longer. "So how did it happen?"

"You must be talking about this," he winced, pointing to his leg. "I was injured during a game of polo. My horse and I fell. I fared far better than he, however."

"I'm sorry. Did you break your leg?"

"Yes and his, too, was broken. Unfortunately a horse's leg doesn't mend. I had to shoot him," he paused, swallowing his tears. His lips

103

trembled and he looked down. "I guess Amelia was right. *Courage is the price that life exacts for granting peace.*"

I stopped walking and gazed into his dark face. He had repeated the quote I'd often used as my solace when grief became too much to bear. Amelia Earhart's words were my creed after Claudia's death.

To my surprise, I became overwhelmed with the desire to kiss Ross. I'd never kissed anyone except David. Certainly in the closet with Tommy Mason didn't count. I leaned toward him and closed my eyes. My lips met his while his arms wrapped around me, sweeping me into a sensuous river of desire. His mouth was tender and his mustache tickled my upper lip as his tongue probed my mouth. I felt woozy and out of control, but I pulled away abruptly as David's face came into my mind.

Ross almost purred as he looked into my eyes. "Oh, Emily, you're something else."

"Need to stop," I whispered as guilt crept up my neck. This kiss was unnerving. My body had had melted into his. Under the street lamp, I could see a large bulge in his pants.

"I've got to go," I muttered and ran toward the Kappa house, a giant, red-bricked shadow across the street.

"I hope to see you soon, Emily," he called, but I kept running.

I didn't see Ross for many weeks afterwards, yet whatever had happened between us had left a mark upon my heart. His words echoed in my head and his smoky scent lingered on my wool blazer for days. I couldn't understand my reaction to him. As hard as I tried to banish him from my thoughts, Ross would not leave my mind. I knew my relationship with David would be at risk if I spent another moment with Ross. Furthermore his long dark hair, heavy beard and Trotsky spectacles would drive my family around the bend.

Spent cherry blossoms covered the campus grounds like confetti and the sun shone bravely through roaming clouds. My last class was over and summer beckoned. I had great plans for myself. After meeting with a couple of reporters from the *Seattle Times*, I'd landed myself a part-time job at the paper as a mail clerk. I was skipping down to Frosh Pond, freed from the encumbrances of academia when I spotted Ross. He lounged languidly on the edge of the shimmering pool, feeding bread to a gaggle of honking geese as though he hadn't a care in the world. His slender body was clothed in knee-length trousers, an open crewneck shirt and sandals. His overgrown beard had shrunk to a goatee and his mustache had vanished. His hair was combed back in a tangled mass of curls. I was about to retreat, but he'd spotted me, and was calling my name. Thrilled that he remembered me and giddy beyond reason, I scurried over to him like a wiggling pup.

"You've been avoiding me, Miss Strong. May I be so bold as to ask why?" Ross gazed up at me, his eyes teasing.

How dare he make me feel so … how did he make me feel? My heart was pounding and that familiar tingle of desire stirred in my groin. Apparently sensing my passion, Ross gave a deep, throaty chuckle and patted a place on the wall next to him. "Come over here, Emily. I've missed you," he said huskily, never taking his eyes from mine. Swallowing hard, I sat down.

Silence wedged between us for a few moments, but his gaze never left me. The lusty heat in my body rose as his eyes peeled off my light cotton dress, then my slip, eventually my brassiere and panties. My skin tingled and my nipples hardened to attention, but the rest of me was jelly. I should have gotten up and run until I couldn't go any farther, but I didn't. One of his fingers moved to my face, sliding down my cheek softly. Then he cupped his hand around my neck and pulled me to him. His kiss was like a torch, lighting me from head to toe.

"Stop!" I cried, yanking myself from his grasp. He chuckled again, his eyes adoring me.

"We're hot together, Lady. Just don't let me get you alone. I might not be able to control myself," he murmured seductively, his voice like velvet.

Me neither! Yet I managed to recapture my poise. Giving a convincing smile, I said, "I need to get going. I wish I could stay, but … "

"You wish you could stay and then again, you don't. Perhaps you're afraid of me. By the way, who does that ring belong to?" He reached up and quickly slipped his finger through David's class ring that I wore around my neck. The chunky piece of gold hung like a lead weight on his slim finger. "Is this why you've been avoiding me?"

"As a matter of fact, I do have a beau. He lives in San Francisco," I blurted out.

"Oh," he replied. Ross looked sincerely hurt. His eyes grew misty as he rubbed his beard. "I guess I'm the fool then, huh?"

"I should have told you. How could you have known? After all I didn't say anything about David."

He held up his hand to silence me. "No need to explain. There hasn't been a day I haven't thought about you since we first met and that's my fault. Didn't you get my messages at the Kappa house?"

"No, but I haven't been to the sorority in weeks. I've been staying at home. It's easier to study for finals there."

"So you don't want to see me again?" he implored, his wide eyes begging to the contrary.

"Ross, I don't know."

"Is your boyfriend coming back?"

"I don't know. He, well, maybe this summer."

"What is it? Am I not good enough for a sorority lass?" he teased, running his finger seductively up my arm. With a self-effacing smirk, he added, "Doesn't my royal blood count for anything?"

"No, of course you're good enough for me! Listen, I have an idea. Why don't you come by the house tonight, for dinner. Say about six?" I anxiously suggested, my words racing far ahead of my reason.

His face lit up as he replied, "Okay! I'd love to."

I scribbled my address on a piece of notebook paper and got up to leave. As I was about to step away, he grabbed my hand, looking up at me. "Thanks," he said lightly and squeezed my hand.

"He's just a friend," I told myself as I hurried away, but I didn't have any idea what that meant anymore.

When I arrived home, there was a bouquet of flowers waiting for me in the foyer: six pink roses and a card from David. Flowers had become his weekly ritual in the past few months as we drifted farther away from one another. I hadn't seen him in a year and a half. How long should I hang on to our long distance relationship?

"Emily, is that you?" Mother's voice called from the parlor. "Come in here, Dear. There's someone here to see you." I threw my books on the oak halltree and paused in front of the mirror. My ponytail was loose, dipping to one side and my silk dress was wrinkled. My cheeks were flushed bright red from my bike ride home. "To hell with it," I whispered and stepped into the parlor. My heart stopped. There, framed against the picture windows, stood David.

"Em," he cried and rushed to me, wrapping his arms around me.

"I'll take my leave," Mother said sweetly as she slipped from the room.

"Oh, God, I've missed you," he murmured. Holding my face in his broad hands, he kissed me gently. I blushed with guilt as Ross's face came to mind. I felt helpless, caught between the crashing tide and the jagged rocks.

"What are you doing home?" I gasped.

"I wanted to surprise you. I'm here on holiday, but I'm going to find a job if it's the last thing I do," he announced, grinning from ear-to-ear.

I inspected him carefully: his blonde wavy hair, cut short, his square jaw and wide mouth, his crinkling blue eyes. I still loved him deeply, of that there was no doubt. I kissed him again and felt the kindling ignite. Clinging to him, I pressed myself against his hard chest as his hands timidly ran down my hips, cupping my bottom, squeezing it softly, and then quickly moving back up to my waist.

"Don't do this," he whispered. "I'll go crazy." All of a sudden, I froze with an icy realization. Certainly David had been invited to dinner. My mother wouldn't miss that opportunity. But I'd invited Ross! I didn't even have his telephone number to cancel.

"So tell me about yourself," David insisted, pulling me to the sofa.

My head pounded as I tried to respond. "Are you staying for dinner?"

"Of course! You know your mother. I was hoping that afterwards you and I could go for a drive. My new car is outside. Did you see it?" he said proudly.

I hadn't even noticed. Images of Ross had wiped out my vision. "Well, yes. Listen, I have something I need to say." I fumbled with my words. "I've invited a friend for dinner, too. His name is Ross. He's from Spain. You'll really like him."

David's face clouded over. "You should see your face, Em," he mumbled.

"What do you mean?" I sputtered as a subtle fear strangled me.

"You look like a little kid caught stealing a candy bar. Why don't you tell me what you mean by 'friend'?"

"For heavens sakes, David. Don't interrogate me. I hardly know him really. We met after he saw me at a Students for Socialism meeting."

"Students for Socialism? I didn't realize you were so politically motivated."

"I told you, I'm reporting for *The Daily* now," I retorted, indignation fueling my words.

"Hey, I'm sorry. Don't get mad." David's eyes looked longingly into mine. "I know I deserve it, being gone so long. I couldn't expect you to wear the proverbial chastity belt now could I?"

"It's not like that. We're friends and that's that. In fact, I was hoping Lizzie would find him attractive," I added, stretching the truth. What perfect timing! At that moment, Lizzie bounded into the room.

"What do you know! If it isn't the long-lost lover?" she spurted gaily.

David smiled. "Hey, Lizzie girl, how are you?" He jumped up and gave her a bear hug. Lizzie winked at me from around his broad shoulder.

"Holy moly, he's home," she mouthed.

"So how's the gourmet world?" she asked as they sat down.

"Great. Hey, Liz, I'm so sorry about your mom," David said tenderly. "I wish I could have been here for you." His eyes watered, but Lizzie shrugged.

"I'm a lot better now, but thanks anyway. I knew you were thinking of me," she quipped.

"So, it sounds like we're going to have a reunion of sorts tonight. Emily just mentioned a friend she's invited to dinner. A guy named Ross."

Lizzie sent me a surreptitious glance.

"Just a friend from the socialism group. I've only known him a short while, but I thought you'd enjoy his company, Liz." I smiled ingenuously.

At six o'clock sharp, Ross arrived, looking very dapper in a European-styled silk suit. I caught my breath as he stepped inside. "Wow, you look *magnifico*!" he whistled.

Before I could answer, Lizzie careened down the stairs, chasing after Jonathan who carried one of her shoes in his hand. Lizzie wore a clinging purple dress that had belonged to Claudia. Her hair fell loosely around her shoulders and she'd even put on lipstick. She looked stunning.

Ross's eyes left me, amused by the race. Jonathan ducked behind me to hide and Lizzie, in heated pursuit, skidded into Ross so that he had to reach out to catch her. Their eyes locked in surprise, and his face froze in a look of delight.

"Hi," he murmured.

"Hi," Lizzie replied. I laughed uncomfortably as Jonathan shoved her shoe into my face.

"Take it, Sis," he hollered, "And promise not to give it to Lizzie. She won't give me back my favorite marble."

"Listen, short stuff, I won that marble fair and square," Lizzie replied, putting her hands firmly on her narrow hips and looking at Jonathan with shrewd indifference. Ross continued his fascinated stare. Any fire he and I had sparked was quickly spreading.

To add to the confusion, David appeared. Ross turned toward him and their eyes met. Ross turned back, his face curious while Lizzie wrestled with Jonathan for her shoe. David lifted his chin and stepped through the door, offering his hand to Ross.

"Hello, I'm David Miller," he said in a friendly voice.

Ross took his hand coolly, shook it and quickly released it.

"Ross Marquez," he replied with a mocking grin. "Looks like you're having a party tonight, Emily. Thank you for the honor of your invitation."

Fortunately at that moment, Lizzie jumped in. "Ross, isn't it wonderful that David is finally home? I'm sure Emily has told you all about him. Why don't we go out to the patio so we can all get acquainted," she suggested amiably.

We followed her out to the backyard. Ross stepped in front of me and David followed behind, grabbing my hand and holding it firmly. Mother and Father were out on the patio with refreshments. Soon introductions were made. Father raised his eyebrows at me, questioning Ross's presence. Oddly, I was beginning to wonder myself. Though Ross had been invited as my 'date', David was my boyfriend. Lizzie assumed I'd invited Ross on her account, a situation that would normally produce rebellion from my chaste little friend. Yet her eyes hadn't left Ross since he arrived. She'd transformed into Cinderella at the ball. It was obvious to me who was the Prince.

The rest of the evening was a blur. At dinner, I giggled too much, spilled my water and forgot to help clear the table. Lizzie sat next to Ross, having the time of her life, while I tried my best to appear cheerful. David was irritatingly attentive, ogling me nonstop. I couldn't tell if I was more excited by Ross's elusive sensuality or David's secret stroking of my thigh under the table.

Papa Joseph came in after the main course, ranting and raving about Roosevelt's latest indecencies with regards to the new tax bill.

He stomped around the dining room for a few moments, refused dinner and left. Moments later, we heard the German national anthem booming from the library.

"You're of German descent?" Ross asked politely.

My father shifted uncomfortably in his seat and Mother began to play with her peach torte, making stabbing motions with her fork. "My grandfather is German," I responded in a flat monotone.

"Do you know what the Germans did at Guernica?" he asked tersely. "I don't believe there's ever been a worse atrocity in my country."

"I agree," David replied, nodding his head emphatically. "Hitler is threatening world peace at this very moment. I wish America would do something about this. I'm sick of reading about Hitler's conquests."

"I'm with you, but don't say that to Papa Joseph," Lizzie added. "We don't talk politics in this house any more, do we?" She looked challengingly at my parents, but they refused to meet her steady gaze. Father pushed his chair away from the table and mumbled something about legal briefs while Mother suggested the "young folks" have a glass of sherry in the parlor. I was exhausted and feigned a headache. Lizzie and Ross retreated to the parlor, sharing a private joke as they left.

"If you're going up to bed, I guess I'll go home," David said. As we walked toward the front door, I stalled, searching for the right words.

"David, I'm sorry if this evening has been strange."

David held up his hand and gave a shrug. "Stop. I don't need an explanation. It's pretty clear to me what might have happened between you and Mr. Marquez if I hadn't returned home, but I can live with that, Em. Considering how long I've been gone, I can't expect much else." He gave me an endearing smile. "I'll call you tomorrow."

I reached over to kiss him. "I'm so glad you're back, my love," I whispered.

"Me, too, Emily. Me, too."

10

The following morning David phoned, asking to take me for a ride in his new car. As I bathed and dressed, I recounted the evening while my internal struggle grew. Fantasies of Ross sparred with memories of David. In the mirror I saw an attractive, curvaceous young woman, but in my heart, I was a tormented soul begging for answers.

When David arrived, I realized he'd become more handsome during his absence. His new masculinity was obvious as he jumped out of his shiny, silver car and sauntered toward me. I stood on the porch, smiling and hopeful.

"Hey Babe, you look great!" David remarked as he approached the house. Scooping me into his arms, he kissed me.

"What would Father say if he saw you kiss me like that!" I giggled self-consciously.

"You're a big girl. I think he'd understand." David's eyes crinkled up in the adorable way I remembered.

We drove along Madison Avenue, chatting cheerfully. Not surprisingly, after a few hours together, David and I picked up where we'd left off over a year ago. Our love was as deep and enduring as an ancient riverbed. Though our conversation flowed, during the silences, we continued to communicate. In a way, David and I had grown up together, learning each other's nuances until they'd become second nature. He didn't mention the prior evening other than to say he had enjoyed it. Unfortunately for me, in the back of my mind Ross was clamoring for attention.

David dropped me off at home after our drive, planning to spend the remainder of the afternoon searching for work. As I waved good-bye, I had no idea what the future would bring. There was no doubt I had feelings for both David and Ross: a complex prospect at best. Good or bad, Ross was the most seductive man I'd ever met.

As I stepped into my house, Lizzie skipped out of the parlor with a face lit up like a firecracker.

"I'm so glad you're here, Emily. I need a ride to the University District. Will you take me?"

"Sure. I've got to stop at the sorority for some of my things. Where are you going?" I asked casually.

"Ross just called. He wants to meet me for coffee at Day's restaurant," she sang. My heart sank to my toes. So this was his form of punishment. Nodding, I grabbed my keys and motioned for her to follow. As we climbed into the car, her soliloquy on the virtues of Ross began.

"I'm so glad you invited Ross last night. He is wonderful and so gorgeous," she bubbled, her eyes shiny with joy. Gorgeous! I'd never heard her use that word for a man before! I fumed in silence, so angry I couldn't speak. By the time we reached the Montlake Bridge, I wanted to strangle Lizzie. She wouldn't stop talking about Ross.

"You know, for the first time in my life, I think I could actually enjoy dating. I've never felt so excited before. Last night when he said good-bye, he kissed my hand! I thought I'd melt on the spot. You know what I mean, don't you? He's out of this world! By the way, don't worry about picking me up. Ross said he'd give me a ride home," she added as I dropped her off.

I drove away, sick with dismay. When I arrived at the Kappa house a few minutes later, I was nearly in tears. One of my 'sisters' was manning the phones when I walked in.

"Hi, Joan," I mumbled, fishing for my mail in the boxes on the wall above her.

"Hi, Emily. A guy stopped by here this morning. Left a letter, but had me pull another one he'd brought by a few weeks ago. Strange little fellow, kinda cute in a gypsy sort of way. He insisted the second letter was better than the first. I almost kept both for you, but he was waiting around, so I thought I'd better get rid of it like he'd asked. Really though, I can't imagine what you'd want with a skinny little Spaniard." As usual, she blabbed non-stop. I'd forgotten how annoying Joan could be.

"He's just a friend, Joan. Where's the letter?" Winking, she handed me a pale blue envelope with a raised gold crest. "Thanks," I replied and hurried upstairs to clear out my bureau.

As soon as I finished at the house, I drove to Green Lake and walked down to the beach with the letter grasped tightly in hand. With trembling anxiety, I tore open the elegant envelope and began to read,

Dearest Emily,

How love the limb-loosener sweeps me away. Since our evening together, I haven't been the same man. You're the most enchanting young woman I've ever known. Had I a magic carpet, I would whisk you away

with me. I long to take you into my arms, into my bed. The fire within me burns hard and hot for you. Until we meet again, I shall dream. With love, Ross.

David had written me some romantic poetry, but nothing as steamy as this. There was a sudden dampness between my thighs as I stared out at the placid lake. Then it occurred to me. Now he was with Lizzie. That didn't make sense, unless he was hoping to create an ally. The letter wasn't dated, but Joan wouldn't have thrown the wrong one away?

❖   ❖   ❖

The next few weeks zipped by. I started my new job at the *Seattle Times*. David visited me nearly every night. We sat in the garden, drove to our family's property on Magnolia to admire the beautiful skyline or walked around Volunteer Park. In the meantime, David had pounded the pavement, delivering resumes to every restaurant in the city. His vacation was drawing to an end and he still hadn't found a job, but my man was infallibly optimistic.

On David's last night in Seattle, we decided to invite Lizzie out with us. We picked her up at the Five and Dime around five o'clock. She ducked into the Pontiac, yanking off her apron and smoothing back her hair.

"Gosh, I'm pooped. Thanks for inviting me. Where are we going tonight?"

David jumped in, "Since it's my last night home, I thought I'd take you two gals to the Four Seasons for dinner."

Lizzie and I gasped simultaneously. "That's far too expensive!" I replied.

"I have an ulterior motive. I'd like to see the chef. Perhaps the third time will be the charm."

"You and Ross are the two most determined men I know," Lizzie remarked with admiration. Before I could stop myself, my head whipped around and my mouth fell open.

"You look surprised, Emily," she smugly replied. "Ross is very ambitious. You should see him run the socialist meetings. He has superb leadership skills. Memberships have doubled now that Ivan Zomaskus left and Ross has taken charge."

David scoffed good-naturedly. "Shut your mouth before the flies come in, Em. You obviously don't know Ross Rossolitti very well."

"His name is Rossolitti Marquez," I retorted darkly. "And you're right, I don't know him well at all." What Lizzie and David didn't realize was that Ross's leadership didn't surprise me in the least. It was Lizzie's casual mention of Ross that had me undone. I'd visited with her over the breakfast table numerous times in the past three weeks and never once did she mention she'd been seeing Ross. I felt duped. His letter had spoken of amorous intentions, yet he hadn't called me once. Furthermore, the note I'd left in his mailbox had never been acknowledged.

Our elegant evening should have been enjoyable, but I was not as relaxed as I might have been. The Olympic Hotel's restaurant was richly appointed with dark paneling, swirling floral carpets, white linen tablecloths and well-polished silver. David left the table for a period of time, searching out the pastry chef. Lizzie was preoccupied, and how I wished I could read her mind. Though the Caesar salad was delectable and the Chateaubriand melted in my mouth, I had little appetite. My mind was too preoccupied with questions of Ross. Moments later I received some unexpected news.

"I have something exciting to share," she began. Not Ross again! I thought.

"Really? And what's that?" I tried to sound kind, but my tone came out rather condescending.

Unabashed, she continued, "Remember when your father had to go to Friday Harbor last week? Since you were working at the paper, I accompanied him as his co-pilot. When we arrived, the most wonderful thing happened. Do you remember Mr. Weyer?"

"What about Weirdo Weyer?" I asked, leaning forward with interest.

"He invited us into the house for lunch. He had Indian art all over the place. He really admires my people's culture. We got along like a house on fire. Later when I mentioned that I was a certified pilot, he offered me a job."

"He did *what*?"

"He's just bought a new plane, a Lockheed 14, just like Howard Hughes's. He wants me to be the co-pilot. I'll only fly a few hours a week, but he's going to pay me $150 a month! Can you believe my luck?"

This was fabulous news! She'd graduated with excellent grades, but she had no money for college. My parents had offered to help her, but she'd refused their assistance. "That's incredible. I'm so pleased for you!" I replied enthusiastically.

By the time David returned to the table, we were hugging and laughing. He looked relieved by my ebullient smile. "Listen to Lizzie's good news, David," I prompted. She repeated her story with my encouragement.

David took her hands in his and squeezed them warmly. "Liz, this is a great new beginning for you. Who knows where it will lead! And ladies, I'm pleased to impart some good news as well. I'll be home sooner than I thought. Chef Bergeron has just put the icing on the cake, as we say in the pastry business. I've got a new job beginning September first. I'll be home for good in less than two months!"

I was happy and stunned and secretly sad all at the same time. I'd banked on a little more time to sort out the David vs. Ross predicament. Lizzie wasn't the only one to throw in a ringer tonight.

Work kept me busy for the summer's remainder. Though I waited for a telephone call from Ross, I never heard a word. My long hours prohibited me from attending the socialist meetings, though Lizzie didn't miss one. She bragged that she and Ross often went for coffee afterwards, which sent my jealousy meter sky-high. Eventually, I wondered if he had lost interest in me completely. Nevertheless whenever I thought of him, I tingled from head to toe.

One evening after work I drove to the University District to hunt for an apartment for David. I hadn't found anything reasonable on Queen Anne and the only apartments he could afford downtown were dilapidated and filthy. I parked my car and wandered up Brooklyn Avenue until I found myself standing in front of the Tudor apartments where Ross lived. As luck would have it, there was a vacancy sign posted in front. Without thinking, I wandered toward Ross's door. As I reached it, I could hear a radio playing inside. I knocked a few times, but there was no answer. Giving up, I walked over to the vacancy sign and scribbled down the landlady's phone number. As I paused to leave, my curiosity got the better of me. The evening was darkening, but the alley looked safe enough so I hurried down the narrow pathway and found his bedroom window.

Peeking in where the curtain had been left open, I could make out a figure. As my eyes adjusted to the dim light, I realized it was Ross, completely naked! My heart quickened as I looked at his slender body. He had thick, curly black hair on his chest and groin and his penis was very engorged. Fascinated, I stared at it and imagined holding it. I was just about to turn away, ashamed by my voyeurism, when I heard him call out. Pausing, I watched in shock as Lizzie stepped into the room, wearing one of my lace slips. Ross walked over to her and began to nuzzle her neck. She leaned her head back with her eyes closed as he pulled down the slip's straps. The flimsy fabric slid down her brown skin and fell to the floor. She was naked underneath. Ross fondled and sucked her breasts while his hand slid down to her bush of hair. I could see the ecstasy in her face and felt the heat in my own body as he played with her. Drenched with sweat, I fought to breathe. Though I knew it was terribly, terribly wrong to watch, I couldn't pull myself away.

Ross laid Lizzie on the bed and opened her legs, entering her with a deep groan of pleasure. They were a perfect pair: slender, small and dark as their bodies undulating in the primal rhythm of love. Lizzie looked beautiful as she clung to him, hungry and intense, raising her hips to meet his. I thought I might be sick as they moved faster, his hard penis sliding in and out of her as she cried out lustily. Finally I couldn't take anymore! Turning, I ran away as torrents of angry tears streamed down my face.

I drove around Seattle for hours in a complete daze as the scene repeated itself in my mind. Though horrified and deeply hurt, I was still so aroused, I nearly cried for sexual release. Eventually I returned home, thankful that the house was quiet and everyone was asleep. I went directly to bed, but I tossed and turned, unable to resist my body's demands. My mind swirled with erotic impressions of Lizzie and Ross until I came, shuddering with a twisted mixture of pleasure and pain. How I wished David was home! I wanted him to take me like a bull, pounding and thrusting until my body was swollen and bruised by our coupling. The situation wasn't fair, another voice shouted. I want Ross!

It was the shameful, selfish truth. I still wanted Ross. I'd wanted him from the first day I met him and I couldn't deny it any longer. It had been impossible to get him out of my system and now it would be even harder. Ross was hungry in his lovemaking. His moves were deft and his body was nimble and sleek. David was a beefy boxer in comparison. Would I ever feel this way with David again?

I was beginning to doze off when I heard a faint, repetitive tapping sound outside my window. I climbed out of bed and looked out. To my astonishment, a figure was stealthily climbing up the winding trellis of the east tower.

When the figure's face turned toward the moon, I saw that it was Lizzie, sneaking into the house. That did it. I was furious. How dare she make love to Ross until all hours and then sneak back into her room under all of our noses! I grabbed my bathrobe, flew out of my room and raced down the hall to the tower stairs, opening her door just as the top of her head appeared at the windowsill. Slipping into the rocking chair, I tried to calm my churning stomach as she lifted her leg over the sill and crawled inside. The room was dark except for a spill of moonlight. I was barely visible and the old rocker was the only sound as it creaked an ominous warning. Frightened at my intrusion, she gasped, whispering, "What are you doing here?"

"I should ask you the same thing, Elizabeth Coomes. Why are you climbing through the window like a thief in the night?" I interrogated haughtily.

"You know our curfew is 11 o'clock. I didn't want to disturb your parents," she confessed.

"That's baloney. You're a liar!" I spit back. "Where do little communists go on Tuesday nights until midnight?"

"I was visiting Ross."

"You mean, screwing Ross!"

Now it was Lizzie's turn to get defensive. Her words came out like razors, slicing me with their accuracy. "What I do with Ross is none of your damn business."

"So you're admitting it. You're sleeping with him."

Lizzie gave a cynical little bark. "You're jealous."

"No, I'm not. I just thought you were smarter than that. You're going to end up just like your mother, pregnant, poverty-stricken and without a husband."

Lizzie lurched toward me as swift as a cat, slapping me so hard across the face that the rocker nearly tipped to the floor. "Get out now, before I tear every bit of the hair from your prissy little head."

As I stood up, I tasted blood in my mouth. Turning away, I slunk to the door. Pausing, I whispered, "I'm sorry. I shouldn't have said that."

"Get out," she hissed. With that, I hurried away, holding my stinging cheek as tears burned my eyes.

❖   ❖   ❖

I woke up late the next morning. When I shuffled downstairs at 11, Mother was in the kitchen, baking cherry pies. Jonathan sat at her feet on the floor, playing tiddledee-winks.

"Good morning, darling," she greeted. "You look exhausted. Did you sleep poorly?"

I smiled, feeling my swollen lip crack, and trudged over to get a cup of coffee. "Hi, small fry," I mumbled, ruffling Jonathan's mop of curls.

"It's a lovely day," Mother continued. "I'm going to take Jack and Jonathan to Madison Park for a swim. Do you want to come along before work?"

"No thanks. I need to talk to Lizzie when she comes down."

"Sweetheart, didn't you know? She's flown the coop!" Mother's eyes sparkled merrily as her hand swept through the air, imitating a bird's wings. "I'm quite proud of her, though I'm a little worried, letting her go like this. She's not yet 18, but she's been saving and planning for this, so I had to give her my blessing."

"What are you talking about?" I asked, now wide awake. A chill swept through me suddenly and I shivered.

"Lizzie is moving into an apartment on Brooklyn Avenue in the University District. Apparently there was a vacant one-bedroom for only 18 dollars a month. She can afford that now with her new job. She'll even be able to buy a car and still save up for college."

"Where is she now?" I stuttered, shaken by this unexpected turn of events.

"She moved most of her things yesterday while you were at work. Apparently she and Ross have borrowed a truck and will be back this afternoon for the rocking chair, her bed and the dresser. I thought I might give her a few pieces of Ginny's sitting room furniture, too."

"Mother, that furniture is ours! You can't give it to Lizzie!" I shrieked, certain that Lizzie was moving in with Ross. Why did she need furniture?

She looked at me cautiously. "What's gotten into you? We don't need that old furniture any more. Lizzie doesn't have anything of her own. Why are you acting like this?"

I averted my eyes, trying to ignore her blistering gaze. Jonathan piped up, "Mommy, is Lizzie a big girl now?"

"Yes, she is," Mother replied. If you only knew, Mother, I thought, itching with spite.

Mother eyed me again, suspiciously this time. "Jonathan, why don't you run along. I think Jack is outside in the tree house."

Jonathan obeyed, sprinting out the back door on his wiry little legs.

Mother poured herself a cup of coffee and sat down, looking directly at me.

"This is about Ross, isn't it?" she stated.

I nodded, tears filling my eyes with dread. I covered my face with my hands to avoid her gaze.

"I could tell you had feelings for him at dinner that night. He's an extremely handsome fellow and as sexy as they get. I saw the red flag within minutes," Mother sighed and stroked my arm. "He reminded me of Marcel."

"I feel horrible. Lizzie loves him, too, and I'm sure he loves her, but I can't wipe him from my mind. I think about him constantly," I whimpered.

The dam inside me broke, and I wept until there was nothing left but dry heaves. "Hush, now, my angel," Mother soothed, caressing my head. "I understand. I really do. Sometimes what appears to be the most appetizing can be the most poisonous. Ross is not your type of man. Lizzie, on the other hand, can handle him. She's got more spit and vinegar than you do, my love. Remember what happened to me when I played with fire."

Searing anger rose again in my chest, but I knew Mother was right. Ross was dangerous for a girl like me. Lizzie was different, wilier, more self-possessed and driven by deep currents of her own. She'd been granted a lifetime of experiences which taught her how to bargain. In the face of calamity, she was a champion. Her heart had matured in a way that mine never would. It had to do with her pain, her losses, and her true grit. It had to do with her insistence for life.

II

One rainy afternoon after David's return, I was leaving the campus when I ran into Gerry Gordon. Though I knew Gerry attended the University, I'd never bumped into him before now. Gerry was known as a campus troublemaker. I hadn't actually spoken to him since the incident at Green Lake, but I had seen him from afar at several Husky football games. Usually intoxicated, his obnoxious mouth constantly put him in harm's way.

As I stepped onto the brick pathway outside the ivy-covered building, Gerry and his friends suddenly appeared. He sauntered toward me, purposely blocking my passage. With a nasty sneer, he hung his thumbs in his trouser belt loops and crowed, "If it ain't the tightest piece of ass on campus! Hey, boys, do you know Emily Strong? Winking at his buddies, he added, "I hear poor old David Miller still ain't become a man on account of her." With a unanimous chuckle, the four boys gazed up and down my body as though I was an item for purchase.

My face burned with embarrassed outrage. "Get out of my way," I said hotly. "I don't have time for jerks like you." I tried to walk around them, but the four cads surrounded me, preventing my escape.

"You know what else I know," Gerry snarled, moving so close I could feel the heat of his breath on my face. "Your idiot friend Tommy Mason got drunk the other night and opened his big mouth a little too much. Started boasting about a car he rolled into Green Lake a few years ago. My car!"

I tried to avoid his eyes, but the rage in his voice sent shivers up my spine. He grabbed me by the shoulders and yanked me closer, whispering, "Your Papa told me some things about you, too, Bitch. You're a Nazi-hater and good Germans don't like Nazi-haters. Let me warn you, you'd better watch your step. If you fuck with me again, you'll pay."

To my surprise, my own anger lifted me out of fear and I stared fiercely back at him. "Get your hands off me now, or I'll expose your father's bribe to admissions faster than you can say 'boo'," I snarled back, recalling this dirty piece of gossip just in time. Of course at the time, I had no reason to think he'd hurt me. Papa was his local idol after all.

I continued to stare into his cold, hateful eyes, unwilling to shrink from his gaze. He gave an evil chuckle and clapped his hands. "Let's go, men. We've got better things to do than waste our time with this fuckin' bitch."

The four of them turned and walked away, their hands shoved deep into their trouser pockets, the sound of their voices menacingly low. I'd heard rumors that a number of students had joined a secret society, which supported the Nazi cause, but it hadn't crossed my mind that Gerry was one of them. Now I was certain of it. I hurried away, glad to be rid of them. Gerry Gordon gave me the creeps.

Later that night, David and I met at his new apartment for dinner. The small, simply furnished studio space was lit with glowing candles and a romantic ballad played on the phonograph as I walked in. I was still upset by my encounter with Gerry, so when David hugged me, I bristled unintentionally. Sensitive to my moods, he released me and took my hand, leading me to the sofa.

"What is it, Em?" he asked as we sat down.

"I ran into Gerry Gordon today," I replied hesitantly, not entirely certain I wanted to repeat our conversation to David.

David's eyes searched my face for clues. "What did he say to you? Come on, Emmy, tell me."

I released a heavy sigh. "I guess Tommy blew our cover and mentioned Gerry's car drowning at a party. Wow, was he mad!"

David's face became drawn. "I was afraid of that. Tommy's got a mouth on him. I thought it was just a matter of time until he bragged about our little act of revenge. What did Gordon say to you?"

I looked away, humiliated. "Nothing, really."

"Come on. I can tell he upset you. What did he say?"

"Basically, that I'm a prude."

"Oh, for Pete's sakes!" David replied, jumping up and pacing the floor. "That sonofabitch!"

"David, stop. Who cares what he thinks? Besides, I'm not a prude. In fact, I've been waiting for this night for a long time." I shot him a seductive little smile.

"What are you talking about?" A question mark crossed his handsome features.

I didn't reply, but instead deliberately unbuttoned my blouse and let it fall to the floor. David gave a little gasp as I unhook my bra and pulled it off. I could feel the heat in my body rise as my nipples hardened to erection. "Sit down, David," I instructed and reached out, pulling him to the couch. He was speechless as I stood up and moved to the center of the room. With a seductive sway of my hips, I slid off my skirt and slip, revealing my garter belt, stockings and a pair of pale pink buttocks. David had never seen me completely naked before, and only rarely had he seen my breasts in the dim of night. He was motionless as I walked over to him, my high heels clicking in time to the music's percussion beat. I could see the large bulge in his pants as I bent over, my breasts swaying as I unzipped his zipper. I toyed with his member as David shivered involuntarily and moaned, kissing my breasts.

"Em, you're so beautiful," he whispered, running his hands over my body.

After a few moments I murmured, "I'm ready now." My voice sounded different to me, husky and sexier, and my body felt swollen and wanting.

"I'm ready, David. I want you inside of me."

We made love for the rest of the night, on the couch, on the braided rug, on the bed and later in his tiny shower. I fell asleep in David's arms for the first time in our life together and never had another doubt about my love for him. Despite Lizzie's unintentional betrayal with Ross, her act of sexual independence opened the door for me to do the same. It was a decision I didn't regret. I also didn't regret any lost opportunities. Though Ross Marquez was sexually alluring, he was definitely not for me. David was my man, through and through.

With the consummation of our love, David became more loving and protective of me and I of him. He was concerned that I enjoy our lovemaking so I happily shared my body's secrets, delighting in his eagerness for knowledge. We were daring and playful and as horny as newlyweds. We became engaged on my 20th birthday in October.

Although the subject of Ross and I was never discussed, David was troubled by our estrangement from Lizzie. I hadn't spoken to her since that terrible night in the tower, but I had left many notes in her mailbox at the Brooklyn apartment. I was deeply hurt by her rejection, but I also felt relieved that I didn't have to see Ross. The wound was still too fresh. Lizzie sent a card on my birthday, enclosing an eagle feather, which she mentioned she'd found at Weyer's estate. The message in the card read: *Long years apart can make no breach a second cannot fill.* It was a quote from Emily Dickinson that I had read at

Claudia's funeral. Perhaps for the time being, Lizzie, too, was content to leave well enough alone.

Yet, I missed her friendship sorely. She'd always been my confidante and ally, my playmate and sister. A part of me was dead without her in my life and I often became tearful from missing her.

As 1938 drew to a close, I immersed myself in my classes and my budding writing career. I was one of the lead writers for *The Daily*, covering a variety of subjects from the arts to alumni activities, but I asked to have campus politics reassigned. The further I stayed from that topic, the better. Through the grapevine, there was talk of the lovers. Ross and Lizzie were becoming famous in the student body as spokespersons against world tyranny. She could only afford to take one class on campus, but that was enough for her to be elected to the student government. Before long, she and Ross had recruited a large constituency of pro-war proletariat. In their view, the only way to stop the insurrection of despotism was to fight back with words and political action. I remained a staunch member of America's Neutrality Party until one night in November when *Kristalnacht* changed the world forever.

Kristalnacht is German for 'Night of Crystal'. That night of tragedy between a minor German diplomat and a Jewish student ripped many belief systems to shreds and designated the Jews to the Final Solution. Distraught over the despicable treatment of his parents, Grynszpan killed Ernst vom Rath in the Parisian German Embassy, shattering the lives of the European Jews forever. Within 24 hours of the random murder, Jews' businesses, homes and synagogues were destroyed by Nazi storm troopers. In just one day, 91 Jews had been murdered and 30,000 were arrested. The news of this horror ended my apathy and I began to protest, primarily through my journalism.

I also refused to listen to Papa's Nazi hogwash and encouraged my family to do the same. Yet in hindsight, the estrangement between my grandfather and me had happened long before. Since our disagreement over the Gersteins, Papa and I had developed an understanding. You leave me alone and I'll leave you alone. His fitful rages had decreased since Ginny's death, but his emotional swings were as high as they were low. After one of his meetings at the German Society, Papa was jubilant. Other times, he stomped through the house, yelling about the injustices of the Roosevelt government. I was so embarrassed by his unpredictable behavior that I rarely invited friends to the house.

The last time I brought friends to our old home was in mid-March. My sorority sisters, Madeleine and Janice, and I had just finished winter quarter finals. We were in dire need of relaxation and pampering, so Mother invited us over for dinner.

That evening, after cocktails and conversation, I helped Mother to serve the meal in the dining room as my friends were seated. Soon Papa came in from his den for dinner. Father was away on a business trip, Ernest was out with friends, and Mother had sent the younger boys upstairs, so it was the four women and Papa Joseph at the table. I could see he was immediately taken with Madeleine, a voluptuous redhead.

"So, Madeleine, what is your favorite subject at school?" Papa asked, walking around the table to pour an expensive bottle of Chardonnay.

"I'd have to say my favorite subject is boys," she giggled, exuding the bubbly optimism that was the key to her popularity on campus.

Papa's laughter boomed throughout the dining room. "The boys must enjoy that! You know, I've always told Emily, college is the best place to find a decent husband nowadays."

In response to their ridiculous banter, Janice choked on her wine, muffling her groan of disbelief into her napkin. A scholar at heart, boys were the last thing on her mind. Fortunately, the awkward moment passed. Papa winked good-naturedly at Janice and continued joking with my friends. With a sigh of relief, I began to relax as the conversation continued.

"I'm so relieved finals are over! I feel like I've been living in prison for weeks now!" Madeleine sighed, rolling her eyes dramatically.

"Speaking of prison, can you believe what's just happened in Czechoslovakia?" Janice grimaced. "I still have relatives over there. I can't believe that despicable Hitler. He's putting everyone in danger!"

I cringed, waiting for the reprisal. Papa Joseph sputtered through a mouthful of rice, his beefy face shriveling like he was sucking a lemon.

"I beg your pardon, young lady," he began, his voice on edge. "Hitler is an exceptional leader. When Hitler went into Czechoslovakia, he did so to assist and protect his people. It is our destiny, you see."

"No, Sir, I don't see," Janice replied quietly, brushing her bangs from her eyes. I tried to catch her eye to warn her to keep silent, but was unsuccessful. "All I see, Sir, is the carnage and destruction by the

Third Reich. Pardon me if I disagree, but he hasn't protected anyone. As far as I'm concerned, Hitler is a monster."

Papa slammed his fist on the table so hard glasses tumbled in every direction. He stood up and spat out his food. A gooey brown mass landed on Janice's salad plate. "That's what I think of you and your ignorant insolence," he growled.

Without so much as a quiver of hesitation, I stood up and began to speak in an acidic monotone. "Papa, stop your rude and vicious behavior right now. You've humiliated me in front of my friends. Please leave before you upset them any further."

Papa's bulbous head began to weave back and forth as his body shook with rage. I braced myself for his assault, willing to take my punishment in the name of justice. With a sharp gaze, my eyes bore into him. I maintained my defenses with a contained fury so great that its power shriveled him before our very eyes. Like a dog suddenly made wet, Papa gave an odd shake of his body, turned and stomped out of the dining room.

Mother began to mumble incoherent apologies of embarrassment as she wiped up his mess.

Madeleine reached over and took my hand. "Oh, poor Emily," she consoled. "How horrible for you to have to live with him." Then she looked at my mother, her eyes widening as she clapped her hand over her mouth. "Oh, Mrs. Strong, I'm so sorry. I didn't mean to offend you!"

My mother held up a trembling hand. "There's no need for you to apologize. His behavior is unforgivable. We tolerate him because he's an old man, but even old men shouldn't act like that. You girls don't have to stay."

"No, Mrs. Strong," Janice insisted. "Of course we will stay." Madeleine nodded in agreement as I walked over to the liquor cabinet.

"I need a glass of whiskey," I stated numbly. "Anyone else?"

My parents began building their own home on the Magnolia plot soon after the dinner incident. In fact, Mother became so distraught after Papa's outburst that evening, she spent a week alone at the cabin. Upon her return, it was evident to all of us, she'd somehow broken free of his emotional bondage. Her statement to me was concise and unwavering: I have to leave this house and *him*, before it's too late for all of *us*.

Meanwhile the *Seattle Times* offered me a summer internship writing the historical chronicles of Bainbridge Island. Clearly my solution to a summer home lie in our family's property there. Fortunately, Papa had stopped visiting our cabin shortly after Ginny's death, so I felt safe from his intrusion.

On the last day of classes, I called my mother to discuss my imminent move to the island. She and Father were taking the boys there for a few days before I moved in, and it was just my luck that Papa would be out of town on business during part of that time. I was eager to spend a long-awaited night in my own bed.

On the night my folks left for the cabin, I drove by the house to drop off some of my things. As I approached, it was obvious some of Papa's German cronies were visiting. Rowdy German folk music boomed out from the open windows and a crowd of men stood on the front porch. In the middle of their circle stood Gerry Gordon. Shuddering, I continued on, praying he didn't see me. I wouldn't exposed myself to that snake if it was my last day on earth. As I drove away, I caught sight of Chippy in the rearview mirror. He was hiding in the bushes. Poor Chippy, I thought regretfully. My dog was forced to tolerate those nasty intruders. I would take him on a long walk in the park tomorrow, I decided. According to Mother, Papa was scheduled to fly out at 11 o'clock the next morning.

I left the sorority at noon the following day with my bags packed for the weekend. When I arrived at the house, Chippy hobbled out from his doghouse to greet me. His tail thumped listlessly against my leg as I unlocked the house and stepped in. The house was pleasantly quiet. Mother had left a note, wishing me a nice stay at home. As I started up the stairs to my room, Chip began to whine.

"Oh, Chippy, you can't make it up the stairs any more, can you, old boy?" I cooed. "Here, let me carry you."

As I picked him up, his whining increased. I wondered if his hips were bothering him again. As I carried him up, I whispered soothing phrases in his ear, but his cries grew louder the closer we approached my bedroom. A cold dart of dread shot up my spine. Was someone else in the house? I swallowed hard and set Chip down in front of my bedroom door. He pushed his wet nose against my legs, wedging himself between me and the door.

"For heaven sakes, Chip. What's the matter with you?" I grumbled as I opened my bedroom door. My knees buckled and I grabbed the door jamb as I scanned the frightening sight before me. My room had been transformed into a revolting freak show. My curtains, canopy and bedspread glowed like enormous devil eyes, taunting me with their diabolic symbolism. They were now Nazi flags. My perfume bottles, glass knickknacks, photographs and school memorabilia were scattered on the floor, unrecognizable in shattered shards of splintered glass. On my bulletin board a grinning face leered at me. Beneath the face, the poster read: *Der Deutsche Student: Kampft Fur Fuhrer Und Volk*, roughly translated: The German Student: Mind for Hitler and the people. My dresser was littered with Nazi literature; I recognized the bold script and the German declarations of power. Even more hideous was the large photograph sitting on my bedside table. Hitler, with his sadistic demeanor, reduced me to tears. Finally, my eyes moved to my most precious keepsake, the doll collection. All of the dolls were in various states of undress, their limbs bent at unnatural angles. On the floor in front of my cabinet, lay my Palestinian doll. His turban-covered head was shoved into the oven of my toy cast-iron stove. As I took a single step into the room, I saw a visitor lying on my bed. Cut out of cardboard was a life-size effigy of the Jewish student, Grynszpan, with a hunting knife plunged through his heart.

Screaming, I spun around and ran down the stairs away from the feces of my grandfather's passion. Whining sympathetically, Chippy followed me as I flew down the stairs to call David. As I dialed the phone, I watched in frozen horror as my feeble, beloved dog tripped on the stairs and tumbled down, landing at the bottom in a motionless heap.

"Chippy," I cried, dropping the phone and running to his side. My dog wouldn't get up. He lay on his right side, limp and not breathing. I moved my face to his, breathing air into his mouth and nose. "Come on, Chip, wake up," I begged hysterically.

As my hand moved down the dog's soft, familiar torso, I felt a patch of rough skin beneath my hand. His left hip was red as though matted with blood. I leaned closer and pulled back the thick fur to reveal a grotesque series of shapes burned into his skin. My precious dog had been branded with the sign of the Nazi swastika.

When David found me, I was curled up on the floor with Chip's head in my lap, sobbing uncontrollably. I wouldn't let David touch me or the dog, though I continued to rock Chip, begging him to get up, trying to lift his lifeless body.

David grabbed me by the shoulders and gave me a hard shake. "Come out of it, Emily. Chip is dead!" he shouted. His voice tugged at my mind, but the fog of denial was very thick.

Acknowledging David for the first time, I screamed, "Get it out of my room!" I heard my voice, but it didn't sound like me. David quickly sprinted up the stairs, but I didn't care anymore. I just wanted my dog alive. I held Chip and sobbed until his thick golden coat was drenched. Soon David ran back downstairs, his face twisted into an ugly grimace. He dialed the phone and spoke to someone, but I was crying too hard to hear him. The next thing I knew, Lizzie was beside me. Her arms wrapped around me, stroking my dog and crying with me. As I buried my face into her neck, I saw two pairs of men's shoes go up the stairs. I smelled Lizzie again, a subtle, windswept smell and heard her voice calling my name. Minutes must have passed, but it felt like days when David and Ross came back down the stairs. The red tip of a flag swept by my cheek as their steps faded away. Eventually Lizzie began to speak,

"Emmy, should I call the doctor? Are you all right?" I raised my face from Chip's chest and stared at her. I couldn't think or feel. My body was completely numb.

Lizzie brought a blanket and instructed me to help her lift Chip onto it. He felt lighter, as though his spirit, now gone, had been his true substance. We wrapped him like a baby and carried him into the parlor, placing him on the sofa where I curled up next to him, mumbling the same phrase over and over again. "It's my fault."

She shook her head and said quietly. "Your grandfather and his friends are very evil men. This is the work of a true Nazi, Emmy."

David and Ross entered the parlor, smelling of a campfire. Lizzie explained that they had burned everything in my room that belonged to the Nazis. My friends convinced me to bury Chip in the garden under the maple tree where, as a puppy, he'd chewed on the trunk. I sat on the grass with Chip's head in my lap while Ross and David dug a large hole. Lizzie went to the shed and found a pair of two by fours. She nailed them into a cross and found some dark blue paint, which she knew was my favorite color. Crouching down beside me, she whispered softly, "Emmy, love, what should we write on his cross?"

"Start at the far end of the board." I pointed shakily. "Write, "To my beloved Chippy. *Courage is the price that life extracts for granting peace.* I love you, Emily."

Lizzie's script was beautiful: curled, round and evenly-spaced. When the lettering was finished, I sighed deeply, a shuddering sigh of repressed despair. The men, solemn and devout in their task, carefully lifted Chippy from my arms and laid him in the cool, musty earth. Ross held the cross while David pounded it in with a hammer. Then we covered my dog with dirt. No one moved for a long time. Then David came to me and held me in his arms.

"Come on, Sweetheart. Let's go," he encouraged. I let him help me to his car. Ross and Lizzie followed us out to the driveway.

As they climbed into Ross's little roadster, Lizzie called, "I love you, Em. I'll call you soon." It was the first time Lizzie had ever told me she loved me.

For the remainder of the weekend, I tried to cool my scorched heart and calm my raving mind. I stayed at David's apartment. My lover called in sick to work the next day, refusing to leave my side. My days were full of irrational ranting for revenge while my nights contained unnerving nightmares that tore me from sleep in a desperate panic. I refused to accept what had happened! How could anyone torture an animal like that? I was willing to bet that Gerry Gordon was responsible for Chippy's hideous tattoo. I conjured up a series of punitive retribution in my mind. Yet life works in strange ways and I wonder if my own evil thoughts played a part in Gerry's subsequent fate. Two weeks after the incident with Chippy, Gerry Gordon was killed late one night in a car accident when he was racing down the wrong side of Aurora Avenue.

I decided not to tell my family about Chip's accident. I chose to create a complete cover-up, rather than explaining the shocking events of that day. The following Tuesday, I simply explained that our old dog had succumb to a natural death while they were away. It was less of a betrayal to myself to keep quiet than to tell my folks about the dog or the state of my room.

A few weeks after Chip's death, Lizzie, Ross, David and I met for dinner at Blanc's where we became reacquainted. Ross was so upset by Papa's Nazi activities that he wanted to report him to the authorities. Fortunately, Lizzie urged him to reconsider. Joseph Danfrauer hadn't committed a crime and my family's name was at stake, she patiently explained.

My mother had been quite right about Lizzie. My best friend knew how to handle Ross. He acted like a harmless kitten around her. I was pleased to discover I no longer had strong feelings for Mr. Marquez. David had washed those away over time with his enduring love. Once, when Lizzie was in the rest room and David was retrieving drinks, I mentioned Ross's letter of months before. Ross answered as I had expected. Shoving his unruly hair back with the palm of his hand, his eyes playful, he replied, "I'm glad you understood. I was wild over Lizzie after I met her at your house. The next morning, I rushed to the Kappa house to get the other letter I'd written right after I'd met you. I'm glad you didn't get that first one! I'd had a crush on you for so long from afar, I'd written some really sappy stuff. When I saw you and David together, I could tell there could never be anything between you and me."

I didn't tell Ross that my dumb sorority sister, Joan, had evidently made a mistake by tossing away the wrong letter. Yet I didn't care anymore. I'd forgiven myself for my impetuous immaturity while forgiving Ross for his.

❖　　　❖　　　❖

With David's subsequent return to Seattle, I felt the happiest I'd been in a long time. I wasn't alone in my sentiments. After years of economic and social restraint, America was becoming energized. The country had finally overcome the Depression's strangling hold and people were ready for action. By the time the new year rolled around, I was experiencing a personal emancipation of sorts. The *Times* editors were so pleased with the public's response to my work that they hired me to do occasional articles for the Sunday edition. Not only did this offer me a clear sense of identity, but it also defined my future career goals. Though I'd once longed to be a pilot, the airlines were still refusing to hire women, so I learned to be satisfied with flying as a hobby. Journalism was the direction in which I was headed.

Happily, Lizzie and I were close friends again. She and Ross often joined David and me for dinner and weekends at the cabin. After New Year's, I moved out of the Kappa house into her apartment. Since she usually spent her nights at Ross's place, I had enough space to myself to work and relax. I was still covering the arts for *The Daily*, so I attended every movie that played in Seattle.

It was the year of the final curtain call, however. The world beyond America continued to become less stable as countries were gobbled up by the Axis powers at a pace too swift to digest. After Hitler ignited World War II by his invasion of Poland, we all sat up a little straighter as a subtle fear tugged at our minds and hearts, but overall, I believe the citizens of our great land lived in sheer ignorance, unwilling to step forward in support of our neighbors' liberty. Stupidly, most of us still believed we could avoid the conflicts by ignoring the global tragedies. Yet it wasn't long before the Danfrauer clan's tenacious resistance to reality gave way to a new breed of drama regarding the world at large.

In April, Ross made plans to return to Spain. He'd been to Barcelona to participate in a clandestine effort to undermine Franco's military regime. Ross had a fervency that hadn't been tapped during his American exile and he was ready for action, but Lizzie didn't take the news very well. She'd lost too many people in her life and she'd come to depend on Ross more than she'd anticipated. He adored Lizzie and almost convinced her to come with him, but in her heart, she was certain he would eventually grow weary of her. My dear friend had learned a lot from Ross, just as her mother had from Tobi, but her roots were in Seattle.

Ross was leaving for Spain on May 28th after his last day of classes. We had a going-away party for him at the apartments, inviting many of his friends from the Students for Socialism organization as well as a smattering of older intellectuals who hung out at Blanc's. David had borrowed a huge, open-pit barbecue from the Four Seasons and Lizzie had hired Jack's combo band to play jazz.

At the party, we danced, ate fresh crab, drank martinis and delved into deep conversations about the world's state of affairs. I was enjoying the festivities immensely until I caught sight of Ross, standing in the corner of the yard against a lamppost. His dark brow was drawn over his eyes and he was scowling ferociously. Ross had just finished a conversation with a man named Howard, of whom I knew very little except that he was an avid socialist. Howard left the party shortly thereafter, upon which Ross and Lizzie disappeared into the bedroom. At first I thought they were enjoying a final lover's farewell, but when my friend returned, she was paler than I'd seen her since her mother's death. In the back of my mind, Ross's apparently upsetting conversation with Howard left a lingering impression.

When the party was over, David, Lizzie and I drove Ross to the

Seattle train station. After tears, hugs and promises, Ross pulled me aside, whispering, "You must promise me one thing, Em. Make sure Lizzie doesn't interfere with your family, whatever happens. She could be in grave danger. Another thing, stay away from your family home for the next few weeks. It'll be better that way."

Before I could respond, Lizzie was in his arms. I was silent on the way home, ruminating on Ross's elusive warning. I'd never known her to interfere with my family. What was Ross worried about?

Two weeks later, Lizzie began asking me deliberate questions that, in retrospect, should have been my clues. We were lying on our twin beds, drinking coffee and chatting. The weather was hot and humid and we were content to lie beneath the ceiling fan.

"So, are your folks moving this weekend?" Lizzie asked while kicking her shapely legs in the air.

"Yep. Papa told Mother she can take whatever she wants. He's so upset about their leaving, he isn't even putting up a fight."

"Does Papa Joseph still use the west tower for an office?"

"Yes. Mother made him keep all his Nazi stuff up there. She got fed up with having it displayed all over the house. I suppose once my folks are gone, he'll make a Third Reich museum out of the castle."

"What about his shipyard office? Does he have anything in there?"

"I doubt it," I replied. "Why?"

"No reason. Just curious." She flung her shapely legs down and rolled off the bed. "Time for something fun anyway," she added casually. "Now that Ross is gone and school's out for the summer, I don't know what to do with myself. Weyer only needs me a couple of days a week."

"Sometimes I can't believe all that has happened to us since we met by the church gates over seven years ago," I said, considering how she'd come to work for the old timber baron. "We've learned so much together." She shot me an odd look as she headed into the bathroom.

"Yeah," she agreed, turning on the shower. "Too bad Papa hasn't." It was deliberate comment, but she was in the shower before I could ask her about it.

I climbed out of bed and walked outside in my housecoat. Grabbing our copy of the newspaper from the doorstep, I read the latest news from Europe. Hitler's troops had crossed the Seine and were heading for Paris. Mussolini's patience had been stretched to the breaking point. The night before, he had declared war on Germany. I wasn't surprised and pondered on how long we could refrain from war. As long as we weren't fighting on our own soil, we were able to distance ourselves from the annihilation of our friends abroad. It sickened me.

On the same page as one of my articles, I spied a small blurb on the FBI's investigation of Axis supporters in America. Apparently, there'd been a number of Americans under investigation for subversive activities up and down the East Coast. In the west, the Japanese, in particular, were highly suspect.

Lizzie came out of the bathroom a few minutes later. "Your turn. There's still enough hot water," she quipped. "So how about going to the cabin tonight?"

"Won't work. I've got to be at the paper for a staff meeting tomorrow morning. Let's go tomorrow night. We can still have two nights before you have to fly on Friday."

Lizzie's brow furrowed, but she nodded. "Okay, I guess that will do."

❖ ❖ ❖

On Wednesday afternoon at two, we rendezvoused at our apartment. Lizzie was standing on the sidewalk, tapping her foot impatiently as I drove up.

"What's up?" I hollered.

"I'll have to meet you later. Weyer called. He needs me to fly some papers to Friday Harbor this afternoon. I'll meet you at the cabin tonight instead."

"I can wait for you," I suggested, climbing out of the car.

"No," she stated in an abrupt voice. "I'll meet you there later."

"Okay," I agreed, wondering why she was in such a tizzy. She sped away in Ross's Plymouth roadster, his farewell gift to her.

I gathered my things and called David to let him know I'd be gone for a few days. Once on the ferry to Bainbridge, I climbed the stairs to the top deck to view the Olympic Mountains before the clouds obscured them. Lizzie's attitude still puzzled me, but her mood swings had been frequent since Ross's departure. Still our family cabin was my haven of peace and I always enjoyed time alone, so I wasn't upset she would be arriving later.

Upon my arrival at the cabin, I unpacked my car and immediately took a walk along the beach in the drizzle. The heat wave had finally broken and the rain fell mercifully. Later, I broiled the cod and vegetables and sat by the window, waiting for Lizzie. When she hadn't arrived by 10, I decided she'd missed the last ferry for Bainbridge Island, so I went to bed.

The sun was just beginning to rise when I was awakened by the sound of a propeller. At first, I thought I was dreaming, but the sound was so persistent, I got up to look out the window. There, at the end of the spit, sat a two-seat bi-plane! I was barely awake, but already in shock as I yanked on a pair of dungarees and my sneakers. Grabbing a sweater, I ran out of the cabin and down the beach toward the plane. Lizzie cut the engines just as I got there.

"What in the heck are you doing?" I screamed.

Lizzie pulled off her goggles and gave a dull laugh. "I need your help. Get in and when I tell you, begin to drop those little red bags at your feet out of the plane and into the water. Don't ask any questions until we're done. Do you understand me?" Her eyes were cold slits of steel and her mouth was tightly pursed. I knew better than to argue with her. She threw me a leather jacket, a scarf and a pair of goggles. I climbed in the back of the plane and strapped myself in. I couldn't believe she'd landed on the spit. The sand was very soft! Before I could yawn, she had us up in the air and flying over the island.

The wind whipped in my ears through the scarf and my stomach rose into my chest each time we hit an air pocket. We were headed north toward the San Juan Islands. I was looking down over the water when Lizzie suddenly reached back and whacked my shoulder.

"Now," she hollered over the noise. "Throw those things."

Surrounding my feet were about a dozen knotted bundles of red cloth, each about half the size of a basketball and as heavy as a can of vegetables. I lifted the first bundle and tossed it over the side of the plane. It sailed down like a miniature missile and disappeared into the Puget Sound. I continued with my task, watching out for ships below. By the time I was done, we were nearly to Friday Harbor. Soon Lizzie landed on the airstrip next to Weyer's beastly Lockheed 14.

As we climbed out of the bi-plane, I asked, "What in the heck was that all about?"

"Shut up and switch planes," she snapped with ruthless determination. We took off into the sky within minutes, landing at Boeing Field about an hour later.

Lizzie's roadster was in the parking lot nearby. Her tense state told me to stay quiet until after she'd checked in with the tower, completed her flight log and we'd turned north toward Seattle. "Now we'll catch the ferry," Lizzie stated. "We're just in time for the eight o'clock."

We boarded the ferry and settled ourselves on an upper deck bench. Lizzie took a deep breath. "We're safe," she mumbled, looking around like a sleuth from a Dashiell Hammett detective thriller. "I'll explain now."

"Finally!" I retorted sarcastically. She shot me a sideways glare.

"Look, I probably saved your Papa from a few years in the slammer, not to mention your family's reputation, your father's career and even possibly yours, so don't give me any guff."

"For heaven's sakes. Tell me!" I beseeched.

"Remember the night of Ross's going-away party?" she began furtively. "Remember towards the end of the evening when he was talking to Howard?"

"Yes, I remember. Go on."

"He told Ross that the FBI planned to begin to search houses of people in the community who were suspected Axis supporters. Apparently your grandfather was on their list. I had to get that crap out of your house. So last night after I flew Weyer's beast to Friday Harbor, I borrowed his bi-plane. I got to the house by dark and climbed up the tower trellis into the house. I didn't want anyone to hear me, so I scooted through the tunnel until I got to the west tower. God, you should have seen that place. It was wall-to-wall Nazi." She paused as a middle-aged man passed by.

"I gathered everything I could. Everything that even smelled like the Third Reich. Since there was so much, I bundled it up in his flag and used a cut curtain cord to lower it out the window down to the lawn. Shit, I was scared!" She shivered slightly. "I kept thinking the FBI would show up any minute and I'd be the one going to Alcatraz. Then I drove to Holy Names Academy and sneaked into the girls' locker rooms with that junk and spent the next hour cutting up the flag and bundling his crap. Then I went back to the airport and flew to the cabin with all of it!" Taking another deep breath, she swallowed hard and closed her eyes. "I just hope I didn't miss anything."

I looked out at the churning water, overwhelmed by her courage. Despite her revilement of my grandfather's ludicrous beliefs, she had risked her life for us, for my family. Taking her hands in mine, I looked deeply into her eyes and murmured, "Thank you, Lizzie."

The following day we returned to Seattle. I wanted to warn my parents, but I knew I couldn't. Mother would never leave her family home if she believed Papa was in trouble. It was fate that I decided to spend Friday night there for the last time. God always provides, as Ginny used to say.

On the following Saturday about eight o'clock, I was up and dressed, helping Mother in the kitchen. On the radio, Count Basie's orchestra played a tune from *Porgy and Bess* while outside the rain fell in steady gray lines. I'd helped my parents move all the boxes to their new home the day before. There were only a few more loads of furniture and they'd been done with it. As I scanned the newspaper for some good news, there was a loud knock at the front door.

"Emily, would you get that please?" Mother asked as she flipped the rasher of bacon.

"Sure," I replied, shuffling to the front door in my slippers. When I opened it, five men stood there. Two were dressed in stiff, black suits. The other three wore navy blue uniforms. The labels on their broad chests read: "US Security". One of the men, a tall, skinny fellow, flipped out a badge.

"FBI, Ma'am," he stated in a flat voice. "May we come in?"

I swallowed hard as my legs turned to jelly. Lizzie had saved us by two days!

The next two hours were the longest, most frightening hours I'd ever spent in my life. The men began their search in the parlor. Ignoring my muffled outcries, they tore cushions from the sofas and shoved books to the floor. By the time Mother had retrieved Father from the shower, they had confiscated the family Bible. Mother stood white-faced and silent while Father began to speak in a rumbling courtroom timbre.

"Gentlemen, I'll have you know I'm an attorney. I'd like to know the meaning of this outrage?" His voice was measured, but a tiny spot of blood on his chin jiggled when he talked.

The other FBI officer, the short, squat, dour bulldog, replied, "We have reason to believe you have items in this home which may lead to criminal charges against your father-in-law, Mr. Joseph Danfrauer, by the United States government. We have been given information by a reliable source that Mr. Danfrauer is supporting the Nazi party."

Gasping, my mother's eyes grew wide and she collapsed. Father reached out and grabbed her, effortlessly lifting her to the sofa. Meanwhile, the imperturbable FBI looked on without a touch of concern. Then the Bulldog pointed to the door. "Let's move," he growled. Father looked up in exasperation and then quickly glanced over at me.

Mother's fainting was a perfect distraction. "Father, I'll take them through the house on a little tour so you can care for Mother," I stated firmly. As I ushered the men out of the parlor, I shot Father a quick wink.

Meanwhile in the back of my mind, I was dreaming up ways to avoid Papa's bedroom. I had no idea what he kept in there. On a hunch, after they'd ransacked the library, I led the men to my parent's bedroom. I'd helped Mother move all her clothes the day before, so only Father's clothing was left in the closets. To give them the idea the room was Papa's, I said, "Certainly if you have any suspicions, it isn't with the Strongs. My parents have no association with the German Society. In fact, my mother abhors Hitler." Then I shoved open the bedroom door and held out my hand and smiled, "There you are."

After they'd dug through closets and turned over the mattress, I led them up the stairs to the west tower. Entering Papa's private domain, I noticed how barren the room looked.

"My grandfather is rarely up here anymore, gentlemen," I explained, trying to keep my voice steady. "His knees are quite bad, so it's almost impossible for him to climb the stairs. Nevertheless, they rummaged through the room, yanking out the desk drawers and removing pictures from the wall. I sat down in a leather chair and leaned back warily. As I did so, I spied a piece of paper that was stuck in the corner behind the back cushion. Slyly, I slipped my hands around it and tucked it in my skirt pocket. Meanwhile, the three uniformed fellows, who looked like a trio of Papa's shipyard workers, grunted and groaned as they turned over Papa's desk.

Eventually Father arrived at the door, his face drawn and pale. "Are you gentlemen satisfied with the desecration you've created in our home?" he spit furiously as Ernest peered over his shoulder. I noticed with a start that he now matched Father's height. Except for the results of aging, Ernest resembled Father more than any of us. He had the same solid body, compact facial features and square jaw. Together, he and Father looked very intimidating. Jack trotted up the stairs and stood next to Ernest, his blonde hair tousled, his frame slighter in both height and breadth. Compared to his older brother, Jack was still a child. He had a feather of peach fuzz across his upper lip, but his cheeks were still full and rosy.

Yet it was Jack, the middle son of ripe ambitions and sometimes heedless judgment, who stepped into the room and gave a little bow. To my utter surprise and Father's, judging by the look on his face, Jack began an oratory that, to this very day, repeats itself like a presidential address in my mind.

"Excuse me, Father, there's something I need to say to the gentlemen," Jack began, looking directly at the two suited agents with a sincere smile. "I just want you to know how grateful we are for your protection. Any inaccurate statements made against my grandfather were undoubtedly due to the jealousy from which many of his competitors suffer. Agreed, Joseph Danfrauer is an active member of the German Society. He, like many of our great Americans, takes pride in his humble roots, but he's a loyal citizen who's currently in Washington D.C., hammering out a contract to build additional ships in the event we must fight the evil fascist, Adolf Hitler."

With that, Jack approached each of them and eagerly pumped their arms, as they stood, their mouths hanging open. Jack then led the men downstairs and out the front door, continuing his laudatory speech on their courageous service. By the time the FBI had driven away in their black sedans, my father was howling with laughter. He slapped Jack on the back proudly. "Son, you are as good as they get! You'll make a damn fine courtroom attorney."

Stepping back into the house, I reached into my skirt pocket and pulled out the piece of paper I'd found in the chair. As I turned it over, I saw it was a small, personally-signed photograph of Adolf Hitler.

12

Jack claimed a well-deserved stint as our family hero. He beamed with pride while we breathed a huge sigh of relief. The threat to our lives had been frightening and shameful. Due to my grandfather's incorrigible ideology and our passive tolerance, we had nearly lost our dignity to public exposure and misplaced scapegoating. He deserved to pay for his sins, but not us. We had faithfully followed the rules we'd been taught about life: respect your elders, keep unsavory secrets to yourself, protect the family as best you can. Why had none of us taken a stand against Joseph Danfrauer's pathological attitudes? My parents had tried to ignore my grandfather's disgraceful passions and my brothers had learned long ago it was safer to keep your mouth shut. Though I was as bitter as old coffee toward Papa, I'd also allowed my opinions to go unvoiced. Ironically, if Papa had known his 'Aryan boy' had led the FBI out of our home by the proverbial nose, he would have been as proud as the *Fuhrer* himself upon the occupation of Paris. Yet Jack swore all of us to secrecy, stating, "Papa must realize he's wrong. Dead wrong. Let him suffer with the belief his junk was confiscated and the FBI might arrest him any day."

Our pretty new house was the center of our attentions that summer. The modern ranch-styled home sprawled across an acre on Magnolia Boulevard overlooking Elliot Bay. Mother was thrilled with the roomy kitchen while Father was content to sit on the porch every evening and watch the breathtaking sunsets. Ernest spent countless hours in the yard, designing the landscaping with David and Jack's help. Little Jonathan, now five, was always underfoot, wanting so badly to be like the 'big boys'.

Tensions in America heightened as the last of the Indian summer faded away. The Allies were being beaten mercilessly by the Germans and the devils' Blitzkrieg had destroyed much of Britain. Every night we listened to Edward Murrow's war updates as he brought the latest news from the rooftops of London. His velvet tongue and cultivated diction described blackouts stretching from Birmingham to Bethlehem, of rations and displaced children and the heroic deeds of everyday folk. It was torture to live vicariously through other's anguish. Guilt and helplessness crept through me like leprosy, eating away my spirit piece by piece.

Christmas was a grueling time for America. It was difficult to be merry when the rest of the world was suffering. Instead of buying gifts, we sent care packages to family friends in England and France. Mother invited the Gersteins for Christmas dinner. She honored them by providing an eight-candled menorah at the table, along with our own nativity scene. After a simple meal of corned beef, potatoes and cabbage rolls, I played the piano and we all sang Christmas carols. I missed the sound of Papa's sonorous voice in the chorus. His absence was obvious and despite our disdain for his ideals, I believe we all hoped he'd turn up eventually.

One shining memory remains with me during that time of self-imposed austerity: the vision of Ernest and Lizzie dancing by candlelight on Christmas Eve. Everyone else had gone to bed save David, Lizzie, Ernest and myself. The four of us were in the living room, an expansive, wooden-beamed area with wall-to-floor windows. Because of our magnificent view of the Puget Sound, Mother hadn't put up curtains. Outside the night was clear and dark. The sky and sea seemed to melt together in an endless black pool. The twinkling stars and lights of the ships on the bay were indistinguishable.

The boys had pushed back the furniture so we could dance. At midnight, the radio began to play a medley of Christmas songs sung by Frank Sinatra. His sensuous voice soothed me as I swayed in David's arms, my half-closed eyes drifting to Lizzie and Ernest nearby. Ernest's chiseled face glowed as he held her tightly in his arms. His broad shoulders towered over her willowy frame so that their bodies appeared to have converged into one. As they spun around, Lizzie's face came into view. In the candlelight, I saw glimmering drops of light reflecting off her cheeks. I realized with a start that the lights were tears. After the song ended, David and I fell into the couch to snuggle. When I looked up, Ernest was kissing Lizzie so passionately that I averted my eyes in embarrassment. Why it came as such a surprise I'll never know. In reflection, Ernest had adored my friend for as long as I could remember, but I didn't realize she felt anything other than brotherly love for him. David elbowed me, an enormous, satisfied grin on his face. Leaning closer, he whispered, "It's about time he kissed her."

Despite the tragedy in the world, Ernest and Lizzie's love

blossomed. For Lizzie, her love affair with Ernest was different than her affair with Ross. She was quietly amused by it all. Her desire for blazing passion had faded into a wish for pastel tenderness. With our sweet, shy Ernest, she had found the stability, warmth and enduring loyalty that she needed. That security alone had a profound effect on her well-being.

Ernest was thrilled that he'd finally won his Madonna's love. He blushed constantly and was sometimes perplexed by this woman whom he'd worshipped for nearly seven years. Yet he persevered and by that summer, on the day of our wedding in fact, Ernest asked Lizzie for her hand in marriage.

In the meantime, David and I had a quiet ceremony of our own in the summer of 1941. With war looming, we kept it simple. Sadly Papa didn't come to the ceremonies, though he touched our love with a true gift. To my utter surprise and delight, he deeded the Bainbridge Island cabin to David and me.

David and I moved into the cabin the week after the wedding. We ferried to our jobs in the city every morning and returned home to our blissful, newlywed solitude. We painted, refinished and hammered, repaired torn screens and replaced rotting porch boards, planted milk crates with geraniums, hauled in an array of over-stuffed thrift store furniture and hung a few modern paintings from Mother's collection. We couldn't have been happier, particularly considering the circumstances.

However at a subconscious level, we were all terrified. It was only a matter of time before America became involved in the global warfare we were trying so hard to avoid. Both David and Ernest had been required to register for the Selective Service as they were over 18.

By autumn, Seattle was percolating with anxious energy. The increase in war munitions production caused a flurry of activity in the shipyards and along the waterfront, business flourished. Battle-ready fleets of navy vessels left the Puget Sound for places such as Hawaii, California and Midway Island. On Aug. 12th, Roosevelt and Prime Minister Churchill signed the Atlantic Charter. Since the Lend-Lease Act, we as a nation had virtually abandoned our neutrality stance. The American motto was "aid short of war' and we were totally involved in the war except for the commitment of troops.

Our little home's first Christmas party was on Dec. 7th. David and I lined the front porch with luminaries and put our tree up early for the festivities. Lizzie and I baked endless batches of cookies, fudge and divinity and Ernest and David prepared exotic hors d'oeuvres. We loaded up on coffee and biscuits for breakfast. We collected every sleeping bag we could find so our guests could stay over if they wished.

The evening was damp and overcast, but unseasonably warm. We dressed in red and green tartan wool and David wore a Santa Claus hat. Our friends arrived on the seven o'clock ferry, laughing, joyful and prepared to have a festive evening. Lizzie brought little bottles of her own Yuletide elixir, which she called Lizzie's Loaded Libation. I had no idea what she made it out of, but by midnight we were all giggling and dancing like gypsies after a carnival. We sang Christmas carols and stood on the porch to watch Venus flirt with the moon. It was a magical night, the last one we'd have for a long, long time.

The next morning, I awoke spoon-style in David's arms. I murmured, "Love me" as his hands cupped my breasts and his body found mine. After we made love, I pulled on my housecoat, ran a brush through my hair and trotted to the bathroom, leaving my lover to doze. Quietly I slipped downstairs, tiptoeing past the slumbering sighs of our holiday hedonists. As I turned on the radio, their chorus of snores nearly drowned out the news broadcast, but the sheer and frantic horror in the announcer's voice caught my immediate attention. His message shot up my spine like an electric current, invisible, but as lethal as poison. Japan had bombed Pearl Harbor. America was now at war.

I turned up the radio and screamed for everyone to wake up. David was the first to race down the stairs, his face a white mask in the morning light. "It's started," he stated solemnly.

"I repeat, this morning at 7:35 a.m. Hawaiian time, the Japanese Air Force and Navy began a vicious torpedo attack on the American base at Pearl Harbor, Oahu. At this time, hundreds of American soldiers are known to be dead and the battleship Oklahoma is afire," the newscaster announced.

One by one, our guests came straggling out of their beds, looks of confused disbelief in their eyes. We huddled around our small radio and listened dumbly. I glanced around the room. My fellow reporters, Rob, Grant, Simon and Jeffrey were all enlisted in the Selective Service as was David. Madeleine and her husband, Joe's baby birth was just a few months away. Fortunately, Joe worked for Boeing Aircraft Company. Perhaps he wouldn't have to fight. Janice and Tommy Mason had just become engaged. Lizzie and Ernest were planning their April wedding. What would become of us? The youth of our nation, America's future?

As I looked around at my dearest friends, slumped over with fear, it dawned on me. This would be the last time we would ever be together like this. After today, we would all, in one way or another, never be the same again. A prickly realization swept me away, like a rip tide that sucks away the strongest of crustaceans, tearing them from their firm hold on life. Our enemy's victorious, premeditated attack was a testimony to America's sluggish illusions and tunnel-vision idealism. The same denial, which emotionally paralyzed my family, was the very affliction poisoning my nation. Now to live required the ability to anticipate, act, even embrace tragedy before it sucked you down. My mouth became parched with dread as I looked at the youthful, innocent faces around me, their features juxtaposed: a yearning for yesterday's memory of protection, taunt with today's brazen admonition of war. I wanted to warn them, parcel out the devastating news in digestible bits. The terrible truth was that. Some of us would die before this war was over.

The next two weeks were a blur. I was at the *Times* 14 hours a day, trying to sort out the mountains of news that arrived. At first there were less than 100 casualties at Pearl Harbor, with thousands missing, then the numbers rose. The final death toll was 2,403, with another 1,178 injured. We lost the core of our Pacific Fleet including 8 battleships as well as countless destroyers and cruisers. One hundred and fifty U.S. planes were destroyed. On Dec. 8th, Congress declared war on Japan. Three days later, when the Axis powers backed Japan, we formally declared war on them as well. We were in the war for good.

David was called to service on Feb. 20th. Within the week, he was scheduled to leave for New Jersey by train. Once there, he'd be hustled through an intensified boot camp to be followed by a cruise across the Atlantic to join his American army brothers on the plains of Europe. He and I wrapped ourselves around each other and cried for days when we got the news. I begged him to use his culinary skills to stay off the battlefield, but David was no coward. He would fight as hard as any other man. I just couldn't imagine David crawling along the ground with a machine gun, taking human life, crying out for God's protection, salting the earth with his tears. The thought of his injury or death put me into an internal hysteria. My stomach ached constantly and I cried for no apparent reason.

In the meantime, Ernest joined the U.S. Air Corp. After a speedy preparation in San Diego, Ernest's division departed on the aircraft carrier, Enterprise, heading for American-owned Midway Island. His departure was on April 11th, two weeks before their planned wedding and just days after the Japanese captured Bataan and massacred 15,000 of our boys. We all breathed an enormous sigh of relief that Ernest hadn't been called earlier. Our neighbors weren't so lucky. Two doors down from my parents' home, the Jackson's front window now displayed a gold star instead of the fighting boy's blue one. We all knew what that signified. Harry Jackson had been aboard the Oklahoma the morning of Dec. 7th.

Lizzie kept her cool. She refused to elope, insisting she and my brother would have a proper wedding when this was all over. Standing on the train station platform with the rest of us, Lizzie appeared as stalwart and stoic as a nun receiving her chastity vows. Placing a specially made medicine bag around Ernest's neck, she kissed him passionately good-bye and waved him onto the train without a mere sniffle. I marveled at how well she hid her grief, but never envied her. She paid a heavy emotional price for such composure.

In his first letter upon his arrival in Great Britain, David wrote about the chilly British weather, the dismal living conditions, the tasteless barrack food and the frugal British rations. He talked of the recent devastation of York and Norwich, the temporal beauty of the budding English countryside and the raw determination of the Anglos to win this war. He hinted at possible attacks in North Africa and questioned the rumors of massive Jewish genocide.

At the end of April I discovered I was pregnant. I hadn't felt any different than normal, but I'd been so caught up in the drama of our lives, I hadn't the wherewithal to notice. Though I was thrilled about the baby, I told no one except Lizzie, trusting her to keep a secret. I didn't even write to David about it. I didn't want him to worry about me and the baby. He had enough to think about as it was. For good measure, I went to church every Sunday and negotiated in my prayers. God had to watch out for David now that we had a child on the way! That type of quixotic, make-believe bargaining was the only way I had to make sense of the insanity around me.

The persistent news of German U-boats on the east coast awakened a dormant cell in all of us. The audacity of those evil belligerents, how dare they threat our homeland! In the first six months of 1942, the Axis Powers destroyed hundreds of merchants ships and thousands of dollars of supplies. Their slithering tubes of steel were seemingly undetectable as they slunk like snails along our tidal waters. On the west coast, there was slight comfort in the fact that the Battle of Midway had eliminated the Japanese threat to Hawaii and the mainland. Ernest had been part of that mission, though we were unaware of his role until nearly a week later. We were horrified to learn that his aircraft carrier was at the scene of the battle, but we couldn't be sure of his assignment. There was so much we didn't know, though working at the *Times* gave me more information than the average citizen. As it turned out, Ernest had been a member of a B-25 bomber team who were successful in the destruction of four Japanese aircraft carriers plus numerous planes. We were so proud of him!

One evening in June, Lizzie and I were sitting contentedly on the porch, listening to the radio and admiring the view. From the porch, the beach glittered in the waning light as a cadre of rose-colored crabs marched down the shore. In the distance, a family of porpoise played in the indigo breakers. At that moment, I felt my baby stir for the first time, just a microsecond of motion, what my mother had once called 'the quickening'.

"Lizzie, feel this. It moved. I'm sure of it," I squealed in delight. Placing her hand over my belly, I held my breath, becoming very still. She waited, but Baby Miller had gone back to sleep. Yet the feeling, which remained within me, was so joyous and profound, the experience defied description. I closed my eyes and sighed.

"It's time to tell David now. I feel it's right. I made it past the first three months, so it's okay," I murmured.

"It's about time you tell David, you mean! I can't believe it's taken you this long. I'd have been blabbing it all over town by now if it were me. People need to hear some good news," she blurted insistently.

"Okay, tomorrow morning, I'll announce it to the family and the Millers. Now, I'm dying for some vanilla ice cream with chocolate sauce. Is there any sugar left in the larder?"

"The sugar is nearly gone. This rationing thing is a real pain. Before you know it, we'll be rationing like Britain. Coffee, gasoline, meat!" she complained, standing up and stretching. "I think there's enough for the sauce. I'll make it, little mom." She walked into the cabin as Glen Miller's *Chattanooga Choo-Choo* suddenly halted and an ominous voice echoed over the bay.

"Attention all citizens. News has just arrived from Canada that Vancouver Island has been attacked by what is presumed to be Japanese submarines. As a result, a coastal dim-out will be in effect as of 11 p.m. Pacific Standard Time. Repeat, Vancouver Island has been attacked. All communities are immediately placed in dim-out status."

Lizzie skidded back out the door, hollering, "Get your ass in here, Emily!" I stood up and scurried inside where we began to flip off lamps as fast as we could.

I ran upstairs in a panic, my heart pounding. What if they decided to torpedo us? We weren't that far from the Bremerton, the naval shipyard! Fear took my breath away as I raced to the only remaining light in the upstairs bedroom. Hurriedly, I turned it off and clambered back toward the stairs. Just as I reached the first step, I tripped on a throw rug and fell, bouncing down the stairs like a basketball. The wrenching pain of impact shot through me as my spine slammed against each stair. When I landed at the bottom, I laid there, the wind knocked out of me. My mind went back to the scene of Chip's fall and the bottom fell out of my emotional basket. Though I wasn't hurt, I began to weep uncontrollably.

By now, the cabin was completely dark, except for the darting reflection of the moon on the water. Lizzie called out from the direction of the kitchen. I heard her scuttle around furniture, bumping into this and that as I moved each of my limbs. She found me seconds later and tried to scoop me up in her arms, knocking me in the nose in the process.

"Ouch," I cried.

"Sorry, Honey. Is anything was broken?"

"Nothing's broken. I'm fine," I blubbered. "I just thought of poor Chippy, that's all." Hugging me, Lizzie gasped and drew away, but I couldn't see her face.

"What is it?" I asked, noticing I felt a little bruised. Thank God the steps to the loft were so few! I heard her as she stumbled through the darkness and returned with a candle. When she lit the match, I noticed my legs felt heavy and warm. She cupped her hand around the candle flame and moved it down to my dress.

"Oh, Emmy!" she cried in horror. I glanced down in the flickering light and saw what had caused her so much alarm. My dress was soaked with blood.

"The baby!" I screamed as I realized what had happened. "No, not my baby!" I spewed a bloodcurdling wail. Lizzie yanked the candle back and took a deep breath. I glanced up to see shadow demons laughing on the walls. They bobbed and danced, chuckling with silent glee. "Noooo," ranted the raging hysteria, my voice no longer my own.

"Emily, calm down. Don't worsen it," Lizzie begged, stroking my cheek. "Let me help you upstairs. You might just have a slight tear or something." I barely heard her coaxing words, but yet I followed. My tears fell in rivers as she helped me upstairs to the bathroom, pull off my housecoat and nightie and wipe the sticky blood from my legs and crotch. The ugly mess told the truth. Downstairs, somewhere in a black pool of darkness, the sequestered life inside me had slipped from my womb, shivered and died. It was gone; it's pitiful remains left to be seen in the light of day. A great yawning hole in my spirit fixed itself firmly to my heart and I acquiesced to the horrible reality. I had lost my piece of hope, my secret treasure, my wish-upon-a-star. Now all that was left was war.

When I awoke the next morning, I was neatly tucked into bed. The blankets were tight around my flattened body and Lizzie was asleep beside me. Laying my hand on my belly, I felt a part of me collapse. The baby had only been a figment of my imagination, I tried to convince myself.

Crawling painfully out of bed, I hobbled downstairs to see if my convictions were true. There was no blood nor body on the landing. I got down on my hands and knees to be sure. Pressing my nose to the wooden floor, I smelled for my baby. Was there a whiff of her? No. Lizzie had done a good job cleaning up. I heard footsteps and glanced up. She was standing at the top of the stairs in her nightgown, staring down at me.

"I cleaned it up. I put it in a little box and buried it. I'll show you," Lizzie said gently. She took my hand and led me outside.

The still morning air gave attentive dignity to my mission. Even the rolling waves seemed to pause, breeding a different silence on shore. No birds, no sea creatures, no sign of human life interfered with nature's plan. Near the watermark, a small mound appeared in the sand. I knelt down and began to dig in the wet mush, faster and faster. Chunks of sand flew in every direction as my blood pumped furiously through my veins. I felt crazed, but I had to see it. I had to be sure. When I got to the box, Lizzie began to sing, an eerie, dissonant Indian chant. I fumbled with the box, trying to pry off the lid that was now damp and stuck with mud. My hands shook as I finally opened it and peered inside. I saw what was left of my hope, a murky pale cocoon amidst a pool of dried blood. The little hooded being had eyes and stubby arms and legs. To my surprise, I didn't cry. My stale tears, like the blood, lacked the moisture of response. I replaced the box in the hole, covered it firmly, whispered a prayer and stiffly rose, returning to the house with Lizzie close behind. I would bury my grief, out of sight and out of mind.

I refused to tell anyone about the baby. I just couldn't deal with my feelings. It was easy enough to do amidst all of the upheaval and trembling farewells. Jack sensed something had happened to me, but he'd become strangely quiet after the exodus of his older brother. I was grateful he was too young to be called to war. Jack was the artist of the family. He was the last person I could see surviving the battlefields of Europe.

The family hadn't yet accepted Ernest's departure when Jack left from a football match in September. When Jack was reported missing by the head master on Monday morning, Mother fell into a state of paralyzing panic while Father combed the army recruiters and navy depots. They could find neither hide nor hair of him. The boy wanted so desperately to prove himself a man with or without my parents' blessings. It took nearly two weeks before we heard from Jack. By then, he was on a navy ship, headed for Hawaii. He apologized profusely to each of us as the telephone was passed from hand to hand.

"Sis, I'm sorry I had to do this, but you know Mom and Pop would never have let me go. I have to do this. There's all these guys out there, fighting for our country and I want to be one of them. Please don't be mad at me, please!" he begged in his sweet tenor voice.

"Stop your backpedaling. You don't need to do that with me. I was young once, too, remember? I'm proud of you, but I'm also scared to death. You've had 8 lives already," I said, reminding him of our family's joke. "You're our cat with one left. Use it wisely."

He chuckled over the crackling static line. "You're right. I'm going to be the best damn Navy man you've ever seen, Sis. I promise. Now pray for me, will you?"

"Of course I'll pray for you, Jackie. Keep your head on straight. I love you."

"I love you, too, Em. Bye."

I didn't say good-bye to Jack, though if the truth was to be known, I knew it might be the last chance I'd have.

13

In November, Lizzie began working for the Boeing Aircraft Company on an assembly line, riveting the wings of B-17 Flying Fortress bombers. To be perfectly frank, she hated it, but work for Weyer was scarce due to fuel rationing. Fortunately for me, my position at the newspaper had expanded to assistant editor of the Arts and Entertainment section. With my new position came a substantial pay increase that I began to put aside for David's return. He'd written often throughout the summer, but he never mentioned maneuvers or assignments. General Montgomery and his British Eighth Army had stopped Rommel at El Alamein just days prior to the arrival of his last letter. I read between the lines, wondering if his next mission would be to assist the British in trapping Rommel, the Desert Fox. After the American forces landed in French Morocco, David's letters ceased and I began to pray more than I ever had in my life.

Ernest was stationed in India where our bombers successfully attacked the docks at Rangoon, Burma. His rare letters from the land of the many-headed gods arrived weeks past their postmark. Ernest was fighting more than just the Japanese. The aircraft had been suffering from the dust, sweltering heat and humidity. There had been a few planes that had gone down in practice flights, crashing upon landing. I knew enough about engines to deduce the level of danger he encountered each time he went up.

Jack's fate was more uncertain. He had been transferred to submarine duty after his initial training and we had no contact with him after that. The idea of our carefree Jack cloistered aboard a claustrophobic submarine defied imagination. In all honesty, I prayed for him the most.

❖   ❖   ❖

A few weeks after Thanksgiving, Lizzie burst through the door of the *Times*. It was a quiet Saturday afternoon and I was catching up at my desk. The room in which I worked was typical of a newspaper office: long, narrow, colorless and cluttered with a few dozen desks. I'd stationed myself with my back to the daily hubbub, studying the latest *New York Times* piece on the film, *Casablanca*, which had recently been released in New York on Thanksgiving Day to rave reviews.

"Hi! I had to get over here as fast as possible," she cried as she tore off her rain slicker.

"Don't you have an umbrella?" I groaned as plummeting drops of rain landed all over my desk.

"I forgot it. Anyway, I could hardly wait to get here. We got the most fabulous telephone call after you left this morning!"

I glared up at her, appalled by the mess she'd delivered. My latest edition of the *New York Times Book Review* was so wet that the corners had begun to curl. The cover photo of C. S. Lewis was now ruined. Yet the look on her face shifted my attentions. Her split-toothed smile was broader than I'd seen in a long time.

Paying no attention to my obvious annoyance, she asked, "Have you ever heard of Jackie Cochran?"

I searched my brain. "Of course, the famous aviatrix!"

"Right. Well, remember a few days ago when we were talking about the WAFS? Nancy Love's women flyers? It has to do with them, sort of. Jackie actually called us to say she's in charge of a new program for women in the Army Air Forces. Can you believe our luck? She's looking for a few good female pilots to help with the cause. They're training down in Texas somewhere. Because we're both already licensed, she wants to know if we want to join up!"

I gave a loud whistle. "Wow! That's amazing!"

"I knew you'd want to give it some thought, but I told her I was ready for action. The class starts right after New Year's, but there are more classes beginning in February or March. We need to be interviewed and take the Army 64. I guess it's a pretty tough physical. Lucky for us we've been swimming at the YWCA. Anyway I'm going as soon as possible. What about you?"

"I have a good job, remember? And so do you!" I cried plaintively.

"Give me a chance to fly again and you're giving me the stars, Em. You should know that! I'm nothing but a human machine over there at Boeing. You have no idea how boring riveting can be! But you're right, why should you pass up an opportunity to fly B-25 bombers, Mustangs, Thunderbolts or an AT-6? You get to write the 'word' every day and spend hours upon hours in dark theaters," she mused sarcastically. "Now that's a contribution to the war effort!"

"Okay, I get your point, but this job is one I'll have for a long time. I'm giving up more than you are," I countered.

"Right, Emily!" Her voice curled with sarcasm. "As soon as Hal Douglas or Matt Sibs returns from overseas, you're history around here. There's no way Pilsby will let you stay in this job when one of them gets home. Get it, girl!"

As I began to contemplate her words, my lower lip jutted out. My pout of frustration was a direct result of the realization that Lizzie was correct. My editor, Gerald Pilsby, had made it quite clear that he didn't believe women belonged at the assistant editor's desk. Pilsby had often reminded me I was just a substitute in a tone that left no room for doubt. I let out a heavy sigh.

"All right, but I wouldn't want to leave until March. I've got the series on RKO I want to finish up. The last piece is scheduled for the third Sunday in February. I guess I could go right after that."

"Are you saying you're in?" Lizzie cried, grabbing my shoulders and shaking me.

I laughed at her enthusiasm. "Yes, I guess so."

On Feb. 24th, 1943, Elizabeth Tobi Coomes and I climbed aboard the three o'clock train destined for Texas. After saying our farewells on the platform, I gazed out of the compartment window, observing the remains of my family. Our small, perceptive Jonathan, with hair as black as a raven's wing, was a rather spoiled, but happy nine-year-old. He stood smugly between my parents, holding each of their hands as the train pulled away from the station. For the time being, he appeared to enjoy being an only child.

My mother, on the other hand, looked indelibly sad. Her dark auburn hair, now sprinkled with strands of white, was pulled tightly back from her face, emphasizing the sharpness of her high cheekbones while her eyelids drooped with weariness. I felt her tears in my chest as we smiled at one another, sharing a final breath drawn with a bittersweet shudder. Mother was proud of me, but she was also in need of me. My departure signified the loss she'd so dreaded, for I was her only remaining bastion of female support. Father, though still handsome, looked wan and dejected as I waved back at him. He and I had developed a very close relationship, particularly since David and

Ernest had left. I knew he'd miss me terribly. Yet despite my guilt for leaving, I had a purpose and a vision now which I hoped would sustain me through whatever this war could dish out.

Lizzie was bouncing off the seat with excitement as she waved farewell. Her sense of adventure was at an all-time high. Such enthusiasm had its advantages! My mood elevated with each mile as the train continued its rumbling departure through the outskirts of Seattle. The train was a flurry of activity. Burgeoning with service men of every variety, the crowded cars roared with ear-splitting noise. Though Lizzie was engaged to Ernest, she couldn't help but flirt and before too long, she had us sitting in the smoking car, swapping stories with boys in uniform from places like Tukwila and Bellingham.

The next three days were traveling torture in the crowded, smoky train. Looking back, I should have figured a way to fly us there. By the time we arrived in Dallas, I didn't have a spare breath of patience. Exhausted and grimy with travel, we crawled onto the bus to Sweetwater, wishing for a hot bath and a comfortable bed.

When we disembarked from the bus a half a day later, we were shocked by the austerity of our new home. Sweetwater was the bleakest place I'd ever seen. Surveying the dry, dusty town upon the treeless prairie of western Texas, it was as though we'd just landed on the moon. As a hot wind blew dust devils through the empty street in front of the bus station, a tough-looking cowboy, complete with a Texas hat, boots, spurs and a pistol on his hips, strode by, giving us the once over. He was a tall, lanky blonde with a mean, thin-lipped smile. I felt naked as he stared at me. Finally Lizzie snarled, "What are you staring at?" Her compact features were poised for combat with one eyebrow slightly raised and a sneer on the curl of her lip.

The cowboy didn't answer with words, but graced our presence by spitting a large brown loogie at our feet. Then he spun around and walked silently down the street. Just like a scene from a John Wayne movie, I thought in amusement.

Outside the bus station, we waited an eternity for a ride to the base. Finally we herded onto the cattle wagon, a primitive bus which bounced and bumped us on hard wooden benches for the three miles to Avenger Field. In some ways, the place was as I imagined it. Rows and rows of weathered barracks, a guard station, a control tower, airplane hangars and dozens of silver-winged planes zooming overhead.

We hustled into the administration building where we were

fingerprinted. Then we began a march to Rec Hall. With my first glimpse of the male cadets came a rush of reality. As the uniformed, stiff-spined troops paraded by, shouting "hup, two, three, four" in deep masculine voices, I swallowed hard and glanced back at Lizzie. "I can't believe we're really doing this," I whispered over my shoulder.

She grinned and winked at me. "We're doin' it, sister! And it's coed to boot!"

Soon we were sitting cross-legged on the Rec Hall floor filling out mountains of paperwork. Once completing that task, we shuffled to Hangar Two where we picked up our flight gear: goggles, helmets, flying suits and overalls. Though we didn't have proper uniforms, we were expected to wear "zootsuits," poorly fitting G.I. mechanic's overalls that were sinfully ugly. Made from putrid green twill, the size 44 suits had ape-like sleeves and baggy-bottomed trousers. Apparently sexiness was not an option in the military.

As we were escorted to our barracks, I squinted up to observe a pilot practicing stalls. The plane dipped to one side, pointing its nose down toward us, spinning faster and faster toward the earth. Just as the BT-13 appeared to be out of control, the metal creature recovered and lifted back up into the sky. I winced at the knowledge we would have to perform that feat solo in order to graduate.

After we were assigned to our barracks in alphabetical order, we were all called to order. Standing in the inescapable sun, trembling with exhaustion, I glanced at Lizzie as a stout man of about 40 years surveyed our motley crew.

"Attention!" Major Blithe barked. The 50 or so young women from all over America attempted a soldier's stance without much success. He paraded back and forth in front of us with a sour look on his sun-creased face. Dust blew into my nose and eyes as he passed me slowly, sizing me up.

"Do you have any idea how disgusting you all look?" he shouted grimly. "In the few weeks, there will only be a few of you losers left. Wash outs, most of you. How many of you think you can make it in this hellhole?"

A few of the women murmured softly as the weasel-faced man grimaced. "Look at the guy on either side of you," he grinned. "They'll be gone, I promise."

I shivered and glanced over at Lizzie. She stood erect with the same face I'd seen at the churchyard nearly ten years ago. I could only imagine the thoughts going through her tough little head. In retrospect, I probably wouldn't have made it without her tenacious grit.

In addition to the regular army requirements, we pilots were also required to study maps, plot wind drift and ground speed, display perfect aerobatics maneuvers and learn radio beam and cross-country navigation. Eventually, we'd have instrumentation instruction inside the suffocating Link Trainers. By the time we were finished, we'd be as well trained as any male cadet.

Life at Avenger Field continued for the next 16 weeks. Our daily schedule was relentlessly tiring. Every morning we awoke at 6:15 a.m. to the bugle-blasted reveille. We had to keep our bays spotlessly clean, despite the unnerving, ever-shifting Texas sand. The six-person bays were divided by shower and toilet stalls. The army cots had to be made so tight that a quarter could bounce off them and the regulation footlockers were spic and span for daily inspection. On the road across from our barracks lived the British cadets. We had to be careful during various stages of undress. On more than one occasion, a chorus of wolf whistles was heard from their direction. I had grown up with brothers and had little time for their bulging eyes.

Early on, we learned to check our shoes before we put them on. Twice my mate, Matilda, found scorpions in hers and once I discovered a lizard in mine. Rattlesnakes were plentiful, as were the blinding heat and smothering dust storms.

Every morning after we dressed and tidied the barracks, we were marched to breakfast by our flight lieutenant, a skinny, beak-nosed girl from Newark who had the most nasally accent I'd ever heard. After a simple fare of oatmeal, toast and coffee, half of us went to calisthenics and ground school while the other half reported to the flight line. The planes varied from primary Fairchilds and basic Vultees to advanced twin-engine machines. After lunch, we'd switch schedules. Because of the high numbers of trainees, there was a great demand for aircraft.

To my horror, the disagreeable cowboy we'd seen in town turned out to be my flight instructor. Mr. James Curtis Williams was a tough and heartless man who enjoyed making our lives miserable. During the first week of flying instruction, my knees were covered in black and blue bruises from his childish abuse. In a dual control aircraft when the instructor moves his control stick back and forth rapidly, the stick on the student's cockpit will knock the inside of the student's knees. I was so sore from Williams's assaults after that first week I could hardly walk. Perhaps I should have told the guy off, but I was so afraid of washing out, I held my tongue. Naturally, Lizzie wouldn't have withstood that type of treatment for a minute. I was glad her instructor had a penchant for dark-haired beauties with courage. Lizzie won Captain Hawkins's heart immediately.

Though the isolation of Avenger cushioned me to some degree, doing my part to put an end to the despicable war raised my confidence level and tossed my sense of aimlessness into oblivion. With regards to piloting, I was better prepared than most cadets because of my extensive navigational training. Lizzie, on the other hand, was well versed in flying techniques, showing up the rest of us with her fancy acrobatics. We both passed our basic-level training in the Fairchild PT-19 with glory. Before the training was over, I could roll, spin, loop and take that baby through the paces without so much as a hiccup. Next we moved to the BT-13. As a result of her exceptional skills, Lizzie was the first of us to solo the heavy, low-wing monoplane that we call the 'Vultee Vibrator' because of its inevitable shuddering when it reached takeoff speed.

Whenever one of the cadets had finished a solo in a new aircraft, the rest of us quickly rallied around, celebrating their success by giving the 'hot pilot, the one in the hot seat' a cool down in Avenger's wishing well. Filled with good-luck coins, the wishing well was a shallow reflecting pool that provided a place for our rite of passage. However, many of those penny-flung wishes never came true. After the first month, nearly 20 gals had washed-out. Another dozen followed in April, most of who were victims of indiscriminate chauvinism and malicious pranks. A few planes crashed, the pilots escaping by the skin of their teeth, only to discover later there had been an oil rag left in their carburetor!

One unfortunate Friday in May, I came close to my own wash out with Mr. Williams. I hadn't seen the tobacco-spitting tyrant since my preliminary training in the Fairchild. As a civilian pilot, he had been assigned to the entering trainees of each class, but he had the reputation for showing up unexpectedly to work with our team.

The weather was blisteringly hot and there was a heavy haze on the horizon. Inside my flightsuit, trickles of sweat ran down my belly. Standing impatiently inside Hangar Three, I was waiting for the mechanic to finish preparing the AT-6. Although I was excited to try my hand at the AT-6, my nerves were jittery with anxiety every time I attempted to fly a new plane.

Waiting for my call, I was daydreaming about David when I felt a stinging slap on my bottom. "Well, if it ain't Miss Miller, the lady with the tight ass," a voice snapped. Seething with embarrassment, I spun around to see James Curtis Williams.

"Please keep your hands to yourself, Mr. Williams."

Snickering, his icy-blue eyes grew cold as he looked me over, resting on my breasts, groin and thighs. Slowly he rocked back on his boot heels with his thumbs hitched in his dirty jean pockets and let out a loud belch that echoed through the hollow, corrugated steel hangar like a backfiring car. "One of these days, you's gonna fall off your high horse, Miss Miller. I'll be glad if I git to see it," he retorted with a sneer. "Maybe yous one of them gals that just needs a good ride from time to time." His laughter bounced sharply off the walls, causing my nerve endings to scrape against my skin like metal against metal.

I knew what Williams was referring to. I wasn't the first cadet to whom he'd made sexual insinuations, but I wasn't about to let his remarks shake me. Ignoring him, I turned away and grabbed the cable to pull the readied plane from the hangar. I wanted to get this task over with as quickly as possible.

Within minutes Williams and I were airborne, flying over a gully of blue bonnets. I relaxed a notch as the brilliant sunlight teased my face, viewing the ephemeral beauty that kept reality at bay. From above, the world and its complexities suddenly seemed insignificant. I relished that feeling of peace long enough to close my eyes. Then, without warning, Williams flipped the plane into a maneuver so violent that I was thrown to the right and forward like a ball on a string. My entire head filled with red as I left my world. Gasping for breath, I entered a black pit, drowning in an abyss of no return. I don't know how long I was out, but when I awoke, blood dripped from my nose and eye sockets. When I saw the mess, a new terror sank to the pit of my stomach. Would this be my wash out?

"What in the hell happened to you, Miller?" I heard his voice scream over my earphones. "You forget to tuck your chin, idiot?" A deep chuckle followed.

"You did that on purpose," I choked. "What kind of an instructor are you?"

"A hard-nosed one, filly. Now maybe you'll learn to mind your manners." I kept quiet, swallowing back my breakfast as it bubbled up my throat. I was too distraught to comment. My head pounded and I felt dizzy. Nevertheless, I wiped myself up the best I could, forcing my concentration to return. I wouldn't wash out on account of him.

Williams forced me to circle the field three more times before giving me the signal to land. Once grounded, he jumped out of the plane, as pleased as punch and strutted away, hollering over his shoulder, "Write it up, Miller."

I was seething with hatred by the time I returned to the hangar, but I was also terrified of reporting Williams. Despite the fact his maneuver was vicious and unnecessary, I had lost my concentration. I should have been paying closer attention to my co-pilot. Therefore, technically I was in the wrong. Misery zapped my strength as I plodded away, engorged with defeat.

As luck would have it, Lizzie was walking toward the hangar as I approached.

"Jesus in heaven, what happened to you!" she cried, running up to me.

"Sometimes I wonder why I'm doing this, Liz," I wheezed, still breathless from the experience. "Williams did an inverted spin without warning me. I had a red-out up there and went completely unconscious for a few seconds. Geez, it was scarier than hell! I'm glad we've only got a month to go. I want to kill that guy."

"What a horse's ass!" Lizzie cried, offering me a hug. "You look like you need a drink. I've still got that bottle of rockgut gin buried outside my barrack window. Go tell the flight lieutenant you're sick. You look a cot case! Then sneak over there and dig it up. Mine's marked by the third rock out from the window," she added, shoving me in the right direction.

As I limped away, a group of neophyte pilots marched by, singing a bawdy cadence called "Blood on the Cockpit". How appropriate, I thought.

Minutes later, I was squatting on my haunches in the boiling sand, nursing a bottle of gin while considering the situation. I was sick of everything that had to do with the war, though there was no separation from it. The war had swallowed my family, friends and my country. The war was the reason for my miscarriage, my runaway brother and my estranged grandfather. The war caused the terror in my dreams and the heartache of my longing and the sadness in the noble faces of strangers who had lost a loved one. The war was all evil men like Hitler and Williams who hadn't found a way to earn their honor, so they persecuted those who had found theirs. Above all else, it was the war's contagious hatred that really got to me.

❖ ❖ ❖

My experience with Mr. Williams was only one of the many obstacles along the path of the military pilot. Without question, I now knew the code: only the fittest survived. One gale of a night I was preparing to go up when my orders were changed. The male cadets had taken a half dozen more planes than they'd been assigned, so six of us were off the roster. Lizzie trotted over to me on the runaway to say hello.

"I'm off the roster," I shouted over the roar of engines and the howling wind.

"What a bugaboo! I can't wait to get up there. The moon is as full as a kangaroo's pouch. I'll see you tomorrow." Lizzie hustled off in the direction of her plane as I waved goodbye.

I trotted over to the Rec Hall to join my fellow cadets. We relaxed by playing cards or dancing the jitterbug to Count Basie's orchestra that was piped in from an ancient radio with poor reception. Nevertheless, we had fun! For those of us who had made it thus far, we could see the light at the end of the tunnel. Over the course of the past few months, lifelong friendship had formed as our group of determined young women fought against the odds to succeed. Now we were as tough as any male cadet and in many ways, a heck of a lot stronger. With graduation only days away, we were very close to achieving our ultimate goal.

I'd just won my second hand of gin rummy when the bad news filtered in. A squadron of planes had become lost on their way back from Lubbock. I knew from the acid churning in my gut that my best friend was one of them. Flinging my hand of cards on the table, I raced outside to the tarmac. The wind was a screaming tempest as I stepped out in the storm. Rushing toward the control tower, I looked up to see a blurry circle of lights on the blackening horizon. As the planes drew closer, I counted five sets of lights. There had been six planes in Lizzie's group. I leapt up the stairs of the tower, three at a time in haste. The young Texan controller, a more rugged version of my brother Jack, was at the controls when I entered the octagonal room. His face was as dark and fearful as the cloaked sky.

"Do something, Kevin. You must make contact!" I hollered, grabbing his arm and shaking it.

He lifted his hands in a gesture of surrender. "I've tried, but there's no answer. What do you want me to do?" As though I'd been slugged in the stomach, I hunched over in pain, sensing a disaster in the making. One by one the planes landed in the fog of grit and the pilots emerged, but Lizzie wasn't one of them. I left the tower and raced up to each woman, asking about her. Matilda was the last to land. I chased her plane as she taxied in.

"What happened to Lizzie?" I screamed as she jumped off the wing. She was shaking and her face was ashen.

"Her lights, they just disappeared," she replied, her voice in staccato. Tears burned my eyes as I begged for answers, firing question after question until the base commander arrived. A giant of a man, Major Urban gripped my shoulders and directed me back to the hangar.

"Calm down, Miller. Lizzie's a smart pilot. She wouldn't go down with her plane. That's what the parachutes are for, remember?"

"Yes, but she could be injured. This wind will kill her if the rattlers don't," I screamed at him. "We have to find her."

"Listen to me," the Major barked. "Don't be such a namby pamby. What do you think our boys are doing now? They're fighting in a bloody war, that's what. You're here because you want to help fight this damn war, too. This is it, the real thing. We're going to lose pilots, *female pilots*, in this war. Pull yourself together. We'll send out reconnaissance at dawn. We'll find Coomes, I promise you."

The next thing I knew, I'd been ushered to my barracks and put to bed. I was so numb that I didn't resist. After popping a tranquilizer in my mouth, Matilda tucked me in and stayed by my side all night. Heavy-headed, I opened my eyes as she shook me awake at the first crack of light.

"Emily, wake up. The reconnaissance plane has just radioed that they found the wreckage and the Sarge swears he saw a parachute pitched like a tent nearby. Lizzie must be all right!" she said excitedly. "Come on! We need to leave immediately."

Tentative relief soothed me as I quickly dressed and splashed cold water on my face. The unit jeep was revved up and ready to go when we stepped out of the barracks. The wind had died down and the humid smell of rain saturated my nostrils, a cleansing change from the night before. Flight Lieutenant Jacobs, Matilda and I rode in the jeep, heading on the main highway to Lubbock. We had driven about 15 miles as close to the flight path as possible when I caught sight of a bright red spot in the beige desert landscape. "Over there," I shouted, pointing to the speck of color.

Lt. Jacobs drove the jeep off the road and headed across a rough expanse of sagebrush and rubble, closing in on the red marker. When we reached it, I saw a red brassiere hanging on a leafless tree. Giddy laughter broke loose when we realized it belonged to Lizzie. That gaudy piece of satin and lace was a lifesaver that day! When Lizzie appeared, draped in her parachute and smiling like a cat who'd just swallowed the mouse, an indescribable joy overtook me.

"Lizzie," I cried, leaping from the jeep and running to her. "What happened?"

She pulled away and pointed to a mass of twisted steel in the distance. "Looks like this one's headed for the cemetery," she joked. "The plane just went out of control all of a sudden, shortly after I passed over Snyder. I barely had time to parachute out. Scarier than shit, Em. Anyway, I'm a little bruised and I think I sprained my ankle when I landed, but I'm okay otherwise. Thank Little Bull, I had my medicine bag."

"Yes," I muttered, looking into my dearest friend's eyes. "Thank God."

Two days later, after the investigation of the crash was complete, the news raced through the camp like a brush fire: Lizzie's AT-6 had been sabotaged; the rudder cables had been spliced. I can't explain the volcano of rage we all felt upon learning this. The cadets, fueled by disbelief, stomped through the barracks, ranting and raving, or conversely, smoldering with fierce disillusionment. It took days before our team felt safe enough to fly again. Most likely the sabotage had been executed by an Axis sympathizer-an American who found solace in becoming the proverbial Judas. Yet such a betrayal was utterly reprehensible to me. As with Papa Joseph, my dreams of ubiquitous American patriotism were once again shattered.

14

"We'll fight to the finish" became our class motto after Lizzie's crash. After our cavalier co-patriot's brush with death, those of us left became tougher and more determined for whatever came next. Not another trainee washed out. On June 13th, Jackie Cochran herself arrived from the Pentagon to award our courage and success. I still remember it as one of the most thrilling, but bittersweet moments in my life. After the graduation ceremony, our small, but gallant class celebrated with a party in the Rec Hall. Our laughter bubbled, as did the spiked punch, but soon enough our tears flowed with quiet longing. Nearly every woman in our group had a lover, brother or dear friend somewhere in the world with gun in hand. It was a bite of truth about our lives which we were forced to swallow. The patriotism and pride we shared with our beloved men was undeniable. Though our lives were incomparable to theirs in most terms, we had fought a rigorous battle against dangerous weather, demoralizing chauvinism and nerve-riveting sabotage and had won.

After graduation, I was sent to Love Field in Dallas with the Fifth Ferrying Group while Lizzie was sent to the Sixth Ferrying Group in Long Beach, California. At first, I was disheartened by the discovery we would be separated. As fate would have it, I hadn't received a letter from David in over a month. He had been part of the regiment of steady Samson Allies who had beaten the Axis Goliath in Tunisia, culminating in the fall of Tunis on May 7th. His letters told of the doomed Italians as they fled the city by land and sea and the heroic efforts of American and British soldiers as they lay siege to the enemy, capturing over 350,000 German and Italian prisoners. Though I hadn't heard from him since, I was certain by the further news on the Sicilian attacks that my courageous husband was part of the crew of men who were successful in occupying that Mediterranean island. The lack of communication was torturous as the numbers of deaths in the world war rose in number. The latest word on Ernest was thankfully positive. He'd flown over 60 missions without a scratch. Lizzie believed he was born under a protective star. With regards to my youngest of fighting brothers, much like him, we were all in the dark. As far as we knew,

"Submarine Jack" was still lurking in the turbulent waters of the Pacific, patrolling for Japanese subs. His last letter, now over four months old, was crammed with news of an amorous young Hawaiian girl whom he'd met while on leave.

I was kept very busy during the first few months at Love Field, ferrying B-17s from Washington D.C. to California and everywhere in between. We flew seven days a week, sometimes for 12 to 14 hours a day. They wanted us to use every bit of daylight available. I often found myself stuck in some hick town with no place to stay. Names like Bakersfield, Merced and Victorville became as familiar as old school chums' and sleeping on hotel lobby floors became a regular habit for many of us. We bedded down on grubby carpets, the smell of cigarettes and coffee still on our breath. My zootsuit became my coat of armor, protecting me from roaming hands in the night. I'd wake up at first daylight with a kink in my neck and a male pilot's arm slung across my back. The shifty predicaments didn't sway me from nun-like chastity, though I experienced some temptation and plenty of lonely nights. The long flights were the worst of it. Many led to incredibly grueling moments filled with blinding sandstorms, hail, and rain. Our return planes offered little comforts-open cockpits were often par for the course.

Two days before Christmas I was lying on my quilt-covered cot in my sheetrocked cubicle, growing increasingly weepy. Originally I'd banked on a ferrying assignment to Seattle, but on the last minute, it fell through. David had been on my mind non-stop for over a week. I longed for his voice, a kiss, anything that would connect me to my sweetheart.

Lizzie had telephoned earlier in the day. She was lonely, too, though it would have taken a pointed gun to get her to admit it. Gossip in the WASP circles suggested there were opportunities to relocate to the Northwest, specifically in Boise, Idaho. I asked her what she knew about a program developed for target-towing. Lizzie confirmed she'd heard of an additional training program in Dodge City, Kansas which had just begun two months before. The advanced training was to fly the fast and heavy bomber, the B-26. The ship was so beautifully designed, it had a name to fame: the Flying Torpedo. Knowing it may be our way to reunite, we promised one another further investigation.

From my steamed-up window, I watched the syrupy rain drip from the sky, clutching a dog-eared postcard from David now nearly 12 weeks old. He'd written it from the Sicilian capital once the Germans had surrendered. After an heroic escape from behind enemy lines, David was hit by exploding shrapnel from a mine, but his injuries weren't too severe. For his bravery, he'd received a purple heart and a promotion. He was now Lieutenant Miller, first class. I was so proud of him; reading his card again brought tears to my eyes. Just as the violin of despair began to play in my head, Sally Rogers, one of my barrack mates and a Dallas local, fluttered through my door.

"Hi ya'll. I've got a delivery. Somebody wants you to have some readin' material, I guess," she quipped, a broad smile on her rosy-red, freckled face.

"Anything to give me the Christmas spirit. I regret refusing my parents' offer to fly home," I lamented, taking the manila envelope from her.

"Now honey," she drawled in her creamy southern accent. "You promised to come on over to my house for Christmas. My folks and seven brothers and sisters will show you some true southern hospitality."

"Oh, Sal, I'm sorry. How rude of me! I can't wait to meet your family. I'm just a little worried about my own. My mother has been a nervous wreck since all of us left home."

"Of course, darlin', but I promise you we'll do our best to cheer you up. Just wait until you taste my mother's Christmas punch. Ooowee!"

"I can't wait. See you," I replied as she waved and trotted away.

But I'd spoke too soon. Inside the package I found a Pan American airline ticket to Seattle and a brief note. *See you soon for a Merry Christmas, Love Mr. and Mrs. Arturo Miller.* I couldn't believe it. I was on my way home!

I arrived in Seattle at 1900 hours the next evening. The Millers were there to pick me up. Mrs. Miller looked more frail than I remembered. Her thin hair was cut short and her glasses seemed to swallow her narrow face. Little did I know they'd intended my visit to be a surprise to my parents. On the way home from the airport, Mrs. Miller told me that she and Mother had become close friends in the past month. A tragic situation had brought them together. "Tommy Mason was killed during the Italian land campaign," Mrs. Miller explained with a tired sigh. "Your dear mother and I helped Mrs. Mason with the funeral arrangements."

I can still remember today how I felt at hearing the news of our first loved one's death. Tommy had been one of my best friends. The more I thought about him, the more my stomach caved in. Noticing my pain, Mrs. Miller patted my arm gently and said, "No matter what happens in this terrible war, we will always stand by you, Dear."

I knew what she meant: if David dies. If David dies. If David dies. The words began a demonic chant in my head as my face puckered and the tears flowed.

"I'm sorry," I gushed, my face in my hands. "I'm just so scared. I miss David so much." In truth we were all scared. The whole country was scared to death and all we talked about was bravery and battles won and campaigns still to fight. What about our losses, our pain and death?

Mother and Father didn't seem to notice our sorry state upon arrival. Before two words could be said, Mother was bursting with joy at the sight of me. We embraced as though we'd been apart for decades. Father ushered us into the house, offering glasses of champagne before I could take off my coat. Lizzie rushed in from the kitchen and threw her arms around me. She smelled of yeast and French perfume. I squeezed her so tight I thought she'd pop. Soon Johnny galloped in, lanky and grinning. His boisterous hug almost knocked me over. As Father handed me an overflowing glass of bubbly, I slipped in to see who else was visiting. There, on the leather sofa, behind which sparkled an ornate Christmas tree, sat Mrs.Gerstein. At the piano was Mr. Gerstein, grinning from ear to ear as he plunked out a simple rendition of *White Christmas*.

"Good evening, lovely lady. How smart you look in your uniform!" Mr. Gerstein greeted as I skipped over to the sofa and covered Mrs. Gerstein in kisses.

"I can't believe I'm home. It seems like it's been forever," I cried.

"Yes, it does," a voice murmured from behind me. It was a voice I knew so well, but was unwilling to believe. I told my mind to stop teasing me, but the voice spoke again. "Aren't you going to give your husband a kiss?"

I spun around and faced my David. He was dressed in his Army best, leaning on a pair of crutches, his radiant eyes sparkling with love and joy. My throat closed and I thought I might faint, but in seconds he was at my side, leaning on me for support as he kissed me hard and deep. He smelled of tobacco and mint and I breathed him in as if my life depended on it.

I can't explain how I felt at that moment. Maybe all of my life I'd wondered, just a tiny bit, if God really existed. I had prayed and gone to church and lived like normal folks, always believing the right path was the road of faith. Now something was different. Now, at this moment, I *knew*. I knew from the first insistent signals that had began over a week ago: David, David, David. God had heard my prayers, prayers of devotion that had spanned the universe for almost two years since my love's departure for boot camp. I'd wished for my man's safety and my man's return. I wasn't ignored by my Lord, but required to learn enduring patience, steadfast faith and the belief in miracles. These were lessons I would never forget.

About an hour later, after we'd caught up with each other's news, the doorbell rang. Mother glanced over at Father and shook her head as if to say, "Who could it be?" The conversations came to a halt as an odd premonition settled over the room. I snuggled closer to David on the couch and held my breath as Johnny raced to the door and opened it. I could hear his squeal and a deep rumble of an old man's voice from the other end of the living room.

"Papa's here!" he cried, dragging my grandfather in by the hand. We all froze, particularly the Gersteins as Papa shuffled in behind my brother. He looked terrible. Great gray circles surrounded his eyes and his body slumped over dejectedly. Compassion filled me as I watched his reaction.

His stony eyes flitted from person to person until they came to rest on Mr. Gerstein. In an uncharacteristic act, Papa trudged over the Jew and held out his hand.

"Happy Hanukkah, Gerstein," he mumbled, whereby he pulled one of the thickest cigars I've ever seen out of his coat pocket and handed it to the surprised man. Speechless, Otto simply accepted the gift with a child-like smile.

Then Papa turned and faced the rest of us. In a slightly pleading tone, he said, "I'm a very lonely man, folks. I know I've done a lot of damage to you in the past. I ask for your forgiveness so that I may share Christ's birth with you today." His mustache quivered and his eyes filled with tears as he spoke.

Mother stood up and flung herself at her father, almost tipping him over in her fervor to accept his apology. Father followed, shaking the old man's hand warmly. Though there were tears in all of our eyes as we hugged Papa, one by one, it was Mrs. Gerstein's words which settled in my heart that evening.

Through the din of professed familial love, Edith's tinny voice came through loud and clear.

"Joseph, you are a very lucky man," she said with shining eyes. "I haven't been with my entire family since I was 17 when I left Germany with Otto. We have no children to carry on our name. We are terribly afraid for our family in Europe, as you can probably guess. I can't tell you how grateful we are that your lovely daughter and son-in-law have included us now during this frightening time. It means more to us than we can say."

Papa nodded and replied, "War is a terrible thing, Edith. I'm sorry for your family." This time I truly believed him.

After a succulent Christmas dinner, we all plopped our over-stuffed frames onto the sofas to watch the stars come out. The sky was black velvet and studded with diamonds. Lizzie quizzed Jonathan on the constellations, their glossy ebony heads tilted toward one another as they cross-examined the Milky Way. In the leather armchairs, Mrs. Gerstein and Papa sat side by side, discussing their favorite Wagner operas. Mother and Father snuggled on the settee like newlyweds while Mr. Gerstein and I played around with *White Christmas* until we'd created a pretty little duet. As Mr. and Mrs. Miller boasted proud praises as to their youngest son's heroic feats aboard, David sang to the piano in his rich tenor voice, mimicking Bing Crosby quite well, I might add.

That night, Ernest telephoned from Calcutta. He was on leave for Christmas, but wasn't able to come home. He and Lizzie spoke for a long while, murmuring love talk before my mother begged for a word. Despite the distance between us, I could feel my brother's presence. Ernest and I had always been close, but in some ways the war and his relationship with Lizzie had deepened our sibling love. Though I could barely get a word in edgewise, I grabbed the phone long enough to wish him a merry Christmas. At midnight a telegram arrived from Jack which read: *Merry Christmas to all. Spending Christmas with my girl, Kanui, on Waikiki. Madly in love. Will write soon, Love and hugs, Jackie boy.*

I don't believe the bird of happiness had ever perched so surely on my shoulder as that night. It was difficult knowing my brothers were all alone in foreign lands, but the beauty of sparkling lights, the smell of cinnamon and pine, the rich notes of the music moved me to the moment. I truly enjoyed the holiday. All was quiet on our western front.

The day after Christmas, David called my base commander and requested additional leave. Then with shopping bags in hand, we caught a cab to the ferry terminal to make our first ride home. Sitting in the ferry lounge, David reached across the Formica table and took my hand.

"Gosh, you look ravishing," he whispered. "Do you have any idea how much I've fantasized about you in the past two years? Honestly, I thought I'd explode sometimes for my wanting."

I giggled, flirting for the first time in ages. "Why Mr. Miller, what about all those gorgeous pin-up girls you had plastered all over your tent?"

"Those pin-up girls can't hold a torch to you, Em. I can't wait to take your clothes off and kiss every inch of you," he whispered lustily. My face grew hot and I suddenly felt ashamed.

"David, there's something I need to tell you," I murmured.

To my horror, he responded with, "Oh, God, is there someone else?" His eyes pleaded with desperation.

"No, *never, ever.* I just had, well, after you left, I found out and then, she, it died." My words were so jumbled it was no surprise he didn't have a clue as to what I was talking about.

I took a laborious breath and forced myself to calm down. "I lost our baby. The night the Japanese attacked Vancouver Island. I fell down the stairs and I lost her. I was almost four months along."

"Oh, Sweetheart, I'm so sorry," he replied tenderly. I moved around the table and sat next to him, dropping my head to his shoulder as he held me close. We were silent, but listening to the other's thoughts of regret, of fear, of sorrow for all that had been lost and for the losses still to come. We would have more babies, a distant voice assured me, but friends like Tommy would never again step inside our cabin door, shouting, "Hello young lovers, wherever you are!" Never again would we listen to his jokes for the fourth time and laugh, or tease him about his funny ears. It was over, he was gone and memories didn't suffice. I thought of Janice, awkward, gangly Janice, who loved Tommy with every bit of her. She would never have the life she once dreamed of. All of this pain and disappointment because of what? Because of greed and arrogance and insane pursuits. Was it worth it? Would Hitler otherwise become our master?

The next two weeks were a whirlwind of activity. Between Lizzie and Jackie Cochran, we secured reassignment for Liz and me to Dodge City, Kansas for B-26 training as of Feb. 20th. For the next month, taking care of David was my entire focus, from bathing him, and cooking meals to catching up on delayed lovemaking. We found some rather interesting positions in coping with his cast, which made it all the more fun.

We spent hours at the cabin, watching the waves and working out the tight knots of battle fatigue in his mind and heart. He told me war stories that froze the deepest parts of me and his nightmares never ceased. I often awoke in the middle of the night to the cries of a terrified man.

In mid-January, his cast came off and we began his rehabilitation by walking for miles along the balmy coastline. Though David's initial comeback would be a desk job in England, he was slated to be back in action by May, providing his strength had returned. A few weeks later we said our good-byes one more time. As I waved to him from the airport landing, I had a new hope, a fresh wish-upon-a-star. One simple wish: he return home again safe and sound. Nothing else mattered. At the time, his unwavering conviction to return to Europe didn't phase me. I had as much lust for winning as the next guy. I had watched the simplest of folk working diligently in their Victory Gardens, school children as they trotted to the post offices to buy war stamps with their meager allowances, black-cloaked, tear-stained families huddled in cemeteries in the rain. I wanted to weep a thousand tears for all of them, but I knew the meaningful questions I had asked myself were beyond one child, one family, one town, or one country. The sum was so much greater than its parts. Freedom had a factor of many, an exponential lean on life that was unfathomable. We lived for freedom from the first time we crawled out of the cradle, turned our faces from our mother's bosom and took our first rough and tumble steps in the world. We pressed toward it as though it was instinct. Like a salmon swimming upstream to lay its eggs, we fought the rough waters, starved and overcame dangerous predators with one thought, one drive in mind: to remain unto ourselves. Ask me now, with all the death, misery and heartache that was to be my future and I would say it again. I would say, "Let's fight!"

15

After a three-month training spree on the B-26 in Dodge City, Lizzie and I were reassigned to Boise, Idaho. I loved Idaho the minute we entered mountain country. The fat sun glowed on the rolling forested slopes for as far as the eye could see and the sky was as blue as a mountain lupine. In the Midwest, the sun always seemed to be cloaked in a dirty brown haze. In Idaho, it boldly dominated the sky. Below us from the windows of the transport plane, I could see the blue-black rivers, snaking through the pristine landscape like squiggle lines on a child's drawing.

I was excited and confident now. The rigorous B-26 training had prepared me for anything and I was willing to take a gamble on the tow-target missions that awaited us. We'd heard a few horror stories already. Apparently one guy had his foot shot off when a gunner's stray bullet hit the plane instead of the target. There was also rumors of more sabotaged ships, but we were assured the maintenance crew at Gowen field was superb and well equipped.

One Saturday evening about a month after our arrival, Lizzie and I were in the barracks, dressing up for a night out on the town. The Ramblin' Inn Cafe was having a jitterbug contest and we had entered with a couple of our pilot friends, Tom Shay and Calvin Timmons. Lizzie decided to wear the only dress-up gown I'd brought from Seattle. I loved the shapely little number which followed the government's fabric-restricting regulations with one shoulder bare, a big bow on the slanting neckline and short skirt. After adding pads in her bra and an extra baste stitch here and there, the dress fit perfectly. While I searched for something to wear, there was hard knock at the door.

Cathy Wilson, our second-in-command flight officer, peeked in. "Emily, there's an urgent call for you," she stated in a serious tone. Without hesitation, I stormed out the door, half-dressed. The phone was at the end of the hall, dangling from the receiver like a life raft lost at sea. The analogy was closer to the truth than I wanted to admit. Somebody: Jack, Ernest or David, somebody had been hurt or the other! I grabbed the phone and held it to my ear.

"Hello," I gasped as Lizzie skidded after me.

"Emily, it's Jack. Our Jackie boy is gone," my father choked. His explanation garbled like a phonograph on high speed as I sank to the floor, the life draining out of me. Lizzie ripped the receiver from my hands, but I took no notice. Though I could hear her cries, my mind was otherwise consumed by an accusatory mantra. Not my little brother Jackie! The boy who never believed he was good enough, who secretly wondered if his Aryan blood was somehow suspect. Please God, not our happy-go-lucky Jackie who sang and joked and loved life intensely. I should have stopped him from going!

I lost track of time after that. I vaguely remember Lizzie escorting me home to Seattle. My family was devastated, unable to give comfort to one another. I stopped eating for days while sleep became a forgotten pleasure. Looking back, I am grateful for Lizzie and the Gersteins. Without them, none of us would have emotionally survived.

The memorial service didn't have an impact on my deadened nerves. I had a sense of the goings-on, but little true reaction. There wasn't a crowd as most would imagine based on Jack's popular personality. Most of his school friends were fighting overseas A trail of old girlfriends filed through, as did a few of the priests from Seattle Prep. Jackie was the only non-Catholic in his class. Nevertheless, Jackie's music teacher, Father Rosemond, gave a moving speech about my brother's contribution to the school, citing his musical talent, leadership prowess and his knack for harmless pranks. It was very touching, but my heart refused to budge. Denial was a perfect tonic for my ailment. After all, Jackie was our family's mystic, our amazing grace! Maybe our magician could return from Poseidon's murky domain, like Houdini from the Hudson, unchained and alive! Standing in the churchyard, surrounded by summer fog, I waited with baited breath, hoping he'd appear and we'd all clap at his incredible show. A macabre drama performed among the tipped tombstones and fingers of mist, it would be the coup de grace of illusion!

It wasn't until after Reverend Norpucker closed his bible and we bowed our heads, our tears dropping like rain, that I finally realized it wasn't going to happen. We were just like the other families in America's cemeteries whom I'd gaped at and wondered about. Who was wondering about us now as the cars rolled by, their passengers surreptitiously peeping out their half-rolled windows at us like we were freaks in a circus? "Another one gone," they'd say. "This damn war!"

"That other *one* was Jack Strong," I wanted to shout. "One of us!" But my voice was silenced by the grim truth. One of my dreams was razed and I lingered like smoke after a fire, fanned by empty promises and fragile tomorrows.

We returned to Boise and kept on dragging targets and being shot at and laughing fate in the face. Only once did a bullet actually enter the cockpit when I was flying. I welcomed it for a minute and then swallowed hard while thanking God I was still alive. After a while, Lizzie became angry. She said they shouldn't use some of the boys who thought target-shooting was a big joke. I just wanted life to go back to before the war. I'd live on Skid Road in a cardboard crate before I'd wish for this again.

On Oct. 4th, the *New York Times* ran an article stating the WASPS would be disbanded on Dec. 20th. We were simultaneously disappointed and thrilled. That could only mean the end was in sight. The fighting in Europe was at an all-time high now with the Allies moving over the continent like ants on a garbage pile. U.S. bombers had set Germany ablaze and as Churchhill had predicted, World War II had become an air war. All anyone talked about was the incredible world of fighting flight. The media's focus on the air didn't lessen my fears for David and only heighten those for Ernest. I secretly bargained in my mind, fool that I was, believing by losing our blessed Jack, the Strong family had paid their devil's dues. I was convinced the war would soon end, and we would be "ollie, ollie, oxen free!"

One afternoon in mid-November, the first snow began to fall. Dry, fluffy flakes filled the sky and padded the ground with a soft blanket of white. I was returning from a short B-24 ferrying expedition to Mountain Home when a few of my brothers in Thunderbolts gave me another little scare. In a playful game of tag, they chased me back to base in their swift pursuits without thought to the head winds that kept my old slug at slower speeds. I wasn't very happy about it and upon landing, marched over to the first pursuit I came to and screamed, "What in the hell did you think you were doing?" A dark-haired pilot climbed out and pulled off his goggles, smiling at me with a sideways grin.

"You must be Emily Strong. And I thought Lizzie was the feisty one!"

I gaped at the stranger. "Pardon me, but I don't think we've met," I stuttered, feeling the red rise in my cheeks as snowflakes dotted my lashes and face.

171

"Does the name Ross Marquez ring a bell?"

"Why yes, of course."

"I'm Ross's younger brother, Tye. Pleased to have your acquaintance!" he grinned and reached out his hand, his handsome features breaking my streak of self-consciousness. He was taller than Ross and more sturdy, but easily as charming.

"Hey, I'm sorry about that up there. I shouldn't have scared you." He gently brushed the snowflakes from my cheek. Blushing, I pulled off my itchy wool cap and shook out my hair. I could feel his admiring eyes on me as I fought to assume composure.

"So what are you doing here, Mr. Marquez?" I asked casually.

"Call me Tye," he insisted. He leaned toward me, his broad shoulders sheltering me from the snowfall. "Are you free now?"

"Are you asking me to dinner?" I quipped. "After that chase, you could do at least that!"

"I am asking you to dinner," he replied graciously, studying my face. "I just arrived yesterday, so you'll have to come up with the place. I'll find us a car. Let's get out of this snow, huh?"

As we stood silently side-by-side, filling out our flight logs, I felt the heat of attraction. As I turned to leave, he reached out and touched my arm. "See you in a half an hour then?"

"Okay. I want to hear all about you and your crazy brother!" I smiled coyly, at the same time wanting to slap myself for such flagrant flirting. As I wandered back to the barracks, my mind in a spin, I came across Lizzie. She was dressed in her Santiago blue uniform, her hair twisted up in a chignon under her starched cap.

"Hi!" she hollered from the mess hall door, jogging over to me.

"You'll never believe who I just met!" I cried, running beside her.

"Go on," she encouraged as we stepped into the warm building.

"Ross Marquez's brother, Tye."

"You what?" Her eyes grew wide and she bit her bottom lip. I could tell her feelings for Rossolitti Marquez were as ripe as they'd ever been.

"You should see him. I think he may be better-looking than Ross."

"It's the sex appeal that got me about Ross."

I frowned slightly as I changed into a fresh blouse. "I hate to admit it, but Tye may take the cake on that, too."

"If that's the case, we'll both be in trouble," Lizzie giggled. "So what are you getting all dressed up for?"

172

"We're going out to dinner and for safety's sake, I'd like you to come along." I could tell by the mischievous grin that spread across her face, she could hardly wait.

We climbed into the jeep with Tye a few minutes later. Introductions were made and he gave Liz a long look, whistling under his breath. "My brother told me you were beautiful, Elizabeth, but I'm stunned."

While we headed down the highway to town, both Liz and I began our friendly interrogation.

"So is Ross okay?" Lizzie began.

"He's great, still in Casablanca doing his rebel thing. He's living with a French buddy in the casbah at the moment. Knowing Ross, I'm sure they're up to no good. He sends his regards. After I learned I was being transferred to Boise, he told me to look you up." I glanced over at Liz, raising my eyebrows in question. I was surprised to learn she'd stayed in touch with Ross. She shrugged, getting my drift.

"So tell us the truth. Are you guys really from royalty?" she asked.

Tye gave us a cute sideways grin, showing a row of perfectly straight teeth. "Absolutely! Half Spanish royalty and half Jew." He paused and looked rather solemn. Now I finally understood Ross's strong loyalty to the Jews.

"How come Ross never mentioned you?" Lizzie demanded.

"We had a falling out the summer before he moved to Seattle. I went to visit him in Spain, just before the war broke out. We got into a fight over a girl and parted ways with more than a little anger between us."

"So who got the girl?" Lizzie asked, ignoring my elbow in her side.

"I guess you'd say I got the girl. She was a lovely thing, but she wasn't worth fighting my brother for. In the end, it turned out she had played us both for fools. Anyway, before Ross left for Casablanca, he came home and we made amends."

"Sorry guys, but I need to interrupt. Pull in here," I directed as the Ramblin' Inn came into sight. The Ramblin' Inn was built in the style of a Bavarian lodge, forested with multicolored Christmas lights. The sparkling sight struck me as a scene from a German fairy tale. I could hear the Andrew Sisters's "*Boogey Woogey Bugle Boy*" as we climbed from the jeep and ran inside.

The T-bone steaks were delicious, but spending three hours with Tye were far more so. He wined and dined and danced with the two of us until we were giddy. By the time we all said goodnight and went our separate ways, I knew my sheets wouldn't be the only damp ones by morning. I hadn't been with my man in nearly a year and poor Lizzie had waited for over two. Tipped off by the gorgeous man named Tye, we'd be dreaming of romance and hot kisses. Sex was like chocolate. Once you'd had it, it was a damn hard thing to give up.

After that delightful evening, Tye became another form of entertainment, but as it turned out, one of us entertained his company more than she should have.

❖   ❖   ❖

On Nov. 16th, my parents telephoned with more ghastly news. Ernest's plane had been shot down by the Japanese over Burma. His navigator had escaped, but Ernest was unable to because of a leg wound. From the mangroves, Randy Stotfelder had watched as Ernest had been dragged away by enemy soldiers. Ernest's last screaming words were: "Tell my family I'll be all right."

I believed him. What other choice did I have? Lizzie, on the other hand, turned to stone. For the first few days, she refused to speak to anyone. Therefore, the flight commander grounded her until further notice. By choice she remained confined to her room. By the end of the week, she'd become a walking shell, talking in monotones, blurry-eyed and gaunt from lack of food and sleep. Five days after the phone call, Cathy Wilson and I forced her to the infirmary where she was given some tranquilizers. After a 24-hour nap, she began to eat again. I spent hours with her every day, trying to comfort her, but she pushed me away. I pled with her to believe in Ernest, to have faith he would survive, but she ignored me. I couldn't reach her, no matter what I did.

The following week was Thanksgiving. She refused to come home for the holiday, though Cathy arranged a ferrying mission that would get us as far as Everett. When I begged her to come with me, Lizzie became as vicious as a starving dog with a bone, so I left to Seattle without her. My parents needed me as well, but I was distressed over leaving her in such a sorry state. The entire three days I was there, the Strong family spent in prayer. Jonathan had been shipped off to California to stay with my grandparents for the holiday. My parents felt it was best, considering their state of minds. Papa was very sick again, so they'd moved him to our house. Mother was at his side constantly and Father was as remote as a monk in meditation. None of us had any strength left. I cooked Thanksgiving dinner for the three of us. It was pitiful and I could hardly wait to get back to Boise.

Upon my return, I raced to Lizzie's room, hoping she'd survived all right. She was slow to answer the door and when she did, she looked flushed and in disarray. That's when I saw Tye sitting on the bed.

"What's going on here?" I snapped.

Lizzie gave a deep sigh and wandered back to the unmade bed, plopping down next to him. I noticed her blouse was only half-buttoned and her bra was on the floor. Tye's face had traces of lipstick on it. "Lizzie, what are you doing? Have you forgotten about Ernest, for God's sakes? I can't believe this!"

"Shut up, Emily. You're not my mother," she said flatly. "I can't be expected to be a nun to a dead man."

I ran to her and began to shake her shoulders violently. "You shut up! How dare you doubt Ernest. What's the matter with you?" I continued to shake her until Tye carefully peeled me off her.

"Leave her alone, Em. She didn't sleep with me. We were just messing around, but she's probably right, you know. Do you really think your brother has a chance in one of those gook camps? They're full of snakes, spiders and disease. Those Japs are known to torture their victims. If he's injured, it's even more dangerous. Wounds don't heal well in the tropics."

I spun around and spit in Tye's face, "How in the hell would you know what my brother is capable of? You're still stateside, fanning your lily white coward's ass." Fury raged through my veins, but I forced myself to quiet down.

"You listen to me, Elizabeth Coomes," I growled. "You tell Tye to leave now and you promise to never, ever see him again or I'll tell Ernest when he returns what a two-timing little tramp you've been. I understand how scared you are, but it's time to get smart. I'm warning you."

Hollow-eyed, Lizzie looked at Tye and nodded. He bent over and kissed her cheek, gave me a searing glance and stomped out. When I looked back at Liz, her head was in her hands and she was weeping. At that point, her tears were meaningless. I couldn't stand the sight of her, so I left.

As I bolted out the door and down the hallway, my anger boiled. I was ready to pounce on the biggest man who might get in my way.

Wretched, murderous thoughts filtered through the sludge in my head. "How dare she betray my brother!" Yet deep within from a hollow frightened place, I knew why she had. I knew the culprits by heart. Loneliness and fear were the strongest adversaries in the fight for home front survival. Loneliness fed upon us like ticks on a dog while fear bloated us with parasitic poisons. Lizzie was wrong, but for the first time, I realized she was also weak. I'd never thought of her that way, so it came as quite a shock.

I refused to speak to her for a few days, hoping time apart would soothe my repulsion. Nevertheless, I paid attention to her actions from a distance, continuously watchful of her movements, just in case she decided to challenge my admonition. To my relief, Lizzie dutifully avoided Tye under my alert eagle's eye. By the time Friday rolled around, I began to miss her company. I woke up in a cheerful mood and made a firm decision. It was time to resolve our differences.

After my morning assignment I returned to base and immediately began looking for her. I hadn't seen her at breakfast and her room was empty when I got there. After scribbling a note of appeal, I trotted down to the hangars to check the flight log. I was disappointed to see her name on the ferrying roster. She'd been assigned to fly to Pendleton to pick up some officers. We had less than two weeks to go and they'd chosen her for that assignment! Minutes later I heard my name over the outdoor intercom. I raced to my flight lieutenant's office.

Cathy Wilson was standing at her desk, her hand still on the base intercom, as I entered.

"What's going on?" I asked.

"There you are!" Cathy cried, her brown eyes were dark pools of desperation. "I think we'd better talk."

My stomach lurched as I followed her in and shut the door. I knew it; Ernest was dead. I began to tremble as she spoke. "Lizzie left this morning on a flight to Pendleton."

"I know," I interrupted impatiently. Thank God it wasn't Ernest.

"Emily, there's a problem. Apparently she got off course. She was about one hundred and fifty miles to the northwest of Pendleton, in Washington state near a town called Yakima, when her plane was last seen. Another civilian pilot picked up her SOS call. She'd lost both engines and was about to parachute out. The plane crashed into a barn," she said slowly. She looked down and fiddled with a pile of papers on her desk. Hesitancy lingered in the air like an old perfume.

I leaned forward, wanting to crawl over the desk. "And what?" I urged frantically.

Cathy glanced back up, her face gray with worry. "Her parachute was found at the edge of a river, but she was gone. There are search parties looking for her now. Our fear is that after she got out of the chute, she drowned."

I couldn't move or speak. I imagined Lizzie calling, "Em, help me!" and the vision of her in Lake Washington, trying to save Johnny and Claudia came to me. Racing to her room, I slung open the door and began to dig through her drawers, looking for her medicine bag. My superstitious mind began to work overtime. It would be all right if she had her bag.

In seconds, I had turned the room upside down, had searched her locker, her dressing table and as hysteria consumed me, began to rip apart her neatly-made bed. "For God sakes, Emily, stop!" Cathy demanded, grabbing my arms and holding me against her stout frame. "Why are you doing this?"

"If she has her bag, she'll be all right!" I screamed, struggling against her firm hold. "I'm looking for her medicine bag!"

"You mean that leather thing she wears around her neck when she flies?" Cathy let go of me and straightened her cap, her plump cheeks bright with color.

"Yeah, it's her protection."

Cathy sighed and shook her head. "She left it at the hangar, Em. She said you'd be needing it now. The mechanic brought it to me shortly after she took off."

So that was it. My best friend had given up. She'd left me, left Ernest, left the WASPS. I couldn't grasp it. Instead I waited for good news as the search parties trampled through the Cascade forests in search of my best friend. Unlike her accident in the Texan desert, I didn't charge out to find her. Washington was at least a day's drive away and my flight commander wouldn't let me fly. Besides, I refused to believe she was dead. At the same time, I didn't know what to believe. Had she done this on purpose? Was she planning some weird escape, or had she gone nuts over the Ernest thing, thinking she could fly across the world to find him?

I hung around the mess hall, walked in the foothills around the base, picked at my spaghetti while we waited for news. Anxious agitation keep me on the edge of my seat. By 9 o'clock there was still no word except that the search parties had retired for the night. I stayed in the mess and played a few hands of pinochle, but my mind wasn't on the game. It was after 11 when I wandered back to my room and fell across the bed. The tears didn't come, but the sadness did. The loneliness and disbelief were so oppressive, I felt like I'd been shut into a coffin. As I rolled over onto my pillow, I heard a crunching sound. Under the pillow was letter. I tore it open and began to read.

Dearest Emily,

I can't tell you how much I hurt right now. There are no words except to say that to experience your rejection has been harder than anything since my mother's death. I can't always be strong like you. You forget how different I am. I was born into hatred and abandonment and poverty. I am ashamed of my existence. Had I not arrived, my mother would have finished college and married someone of her own station. Tobi would have been a sweet memory and nothing more. But my birth changed everything for her and her family. I am a misfit and always have been. Even my actions with Tye prove it! I have no faith, no real beliefs and certainly now, no hope. I have lost my beloved Ernest, the most solid, true person I've ever known and then you, my best friend, defile me with your words. You say I am a tramp. Isn't that what you've always believed? If you're honest, you have always thought of me as less, as someone to be pitied. I can't stand that. I can't gain my freedom; I can't fight the head winds, if pity is my only tool. Please forgive me, but I must go. I must find my place in the world on a road less traveled. The medicine bag is yours, so you won't forget me.

I love you, dear friend, Lizzie.

The tears came like rain. I poured out my grief, my despair and my own shame. How could I be so punitive and so judgmental? Lizzie was right. I did believe I was holier than she was. I'd condemned her for being human. In error, I'd become the self-appointed accuser, searching for a crime that didn't exist. I was wrong, not wronged. I was the guilty one, not her and now I faced my sentencing: I had lost my best friend.

After a week, the search party gave up. I began to receive numerous phone calls from other pilots across the nation. Floods of support came via telegrams, cards and official memos. There was no one else to receive them. I was acknowledged as her only family. She had no one but myself and the Strong family and I had let her down. Yet I believed that she was still alive and though it may take time, I was determined to find her. There were plenty of places she might hide. It was just a matter of finding which one.

On Dec. 21st, I returned to Seattle. All Christmas celebrations were placed on hold. Teary and exhausted from caring for Papa, Mother was of little support to any of us. Jonathan and I put up a straggly, lopsided pine tree and draped it with strings of popcorn and tinsel while Father spent all his extra time at the shipyards, trying to keep Papa's business afloat. After Christmas, Mother and I finally had a chance to talk. She and I had a long conversation about Lizzie's whereabouts. Like me, Mother didn't want to believe she was dead, but in hiding until the war was over. We discussed places she might go: Papa's house, our cabin, the University district and the hovels of Skid Row. I decided to check everywhere I could think of, returning to our cabin first. The briny smell of the sea and the rhythm of the waves were calming, but the empty house did nothing for my sense of resolve. Next I checked with her co-workers at Boeing, her old friends at the Olympic Hotel, the bohemian crowd downtown.

My father, the cautious realist, tried to soften the blow from another angle. He was certain Lizzie was truly gone. He sited the weather, wild animals and hypothermia as plausible explanations for my inability to find her. He sat with me on the porch swing, watching the steel-gray sky dump water on the city one dreary February evening. His melodious voice offered little consolation, but his intentions were sincere.

"Emily, you've got to be reasonable. Lizzie's chances for survival in the Cascade forests in winter are about as slim as Ernest's. Maybe God has another plan for them," he suggested quietly.

"You mean in heaven. Oh, how sweet! Just think, Ernest and Lizzie and Jack are having a ball without us. They even know the outcome of this blasted war. Now that's a soothing thought, Father." The satire in my voice oozed like coagulated blood. "I feel a lot better knowing that!"

"No, I'm sure you don't, but there's no reason to tease yourself with unrealistic hope."

I turned to him, studying his lambent blue eyes in the fragmented light. "Then what now? What do I do? An endangered husband, one dead brother, another imprisoned, and a vanished best friend. Where do I go from here, Father? How do I pick up the pieces?" Falling against his shoulder, I began to cry. Silent, steady tears formed watery trails down his soft flannel shirt. When I looked up, he was trembling. His face sagged with well-contained sorrow. Losing his eldest sons had to be devastating, yet he so rarely let on. I hugged him to me, whispering, "You're a good man, Father. A very, very good man. Thank you for trying to help me." He reached up and gently stroked my head.

"I don't really know how to help you, nor myself or your mother. Thank goodness she has Joseph to tend to. It keeps her mind occupied. But me? There isn't a day that goes by that I don't think of Jack and Ernest and now Lizzie. This war has been hell for us. I despise this damn war. I despise it." He hung his head and wept.

I don't know how long Father and I sat out there, but the tips of my fingers were like icicles by the time we went in. Jonathan was sitting in the living room, looking out of the telescope when I stepped in to warm up by the fire. "Johnny, how can you see anything through that drizzle?" I mumbled, plopping down on the leather hassock near the hearth.

"Can't see the stars, if that's what you mean, but when I look into the scope, I see Ernest. He's okay, Sis. He's in this little hut, with vines all around it. He's eating some kind of fruit from a wooden bowl. There's a couple of gooks outside with guns, but they're nearly asleep. Ernest's got a map. He's going to escape soon."

I stared over at my little brother, aghast at such nonsense. I got up and walked over to him. "May I see?" I asked slowly, eyeing him with caution.

"You won't see it, Sis. You don't know about me, but I see stuff all the time. Mrs. Gerstein says I have a special gift. I saw David the other day. He'd just shot up a bunch of Nazis."

I cringed and grabbed Jonathan firmly by the shoulders. How dare he tease me like this! His crystal blue eyes mocked me as I gazed at him. "Stop that this minute, do you hear me? That is enough of that. You're going to hurt people if you keep this up."

"You just think I'm a mollycoddled little brat, Emily. You haven't a clue what else I know. I would have shared it, too, but not now. You're a nonbeliever."

"I am not!" My voice rose in outrage. "I believe in God just like you do!"

"You're not like Lizzie, though. She taught me to listen to the trees and the ocean. She taught me to believe in nature and things you can't always see. I miss Lizzie. I can't wait until she comes home."

I wanted to scream at Jonathan. His attitude was unforgivable at a time like this. I gave him the dirtiest look I could muster. "You listen to me, Squirt. You keep your queer thoughts to yourself. I'm trying to accept that Lizzie is gone!"

"But she's not, Emily. That's the whole point. She's not." With that Jonathan slipped out of the room without another word.

Living without Lizzie was like trying to navigate in a dense fog. I was timid with my own feelings, afraid that any minute the blanket of pain would suffocate me. I wrote letters to David nearly every day, though I doubt he received a third of them. I poured out my grief in poetry and rhyme and pounded on the piano until my fingers were callused, yet internally, I continued to wilt. To keep my mind occupied, Mother insisted we redecorate the cabin. She called in a plumber to fix the leaky faucets and replace the kitchen sink. We bought new windows and hired a crew of carpenters to shore up the porch. After scrubbing, painting and varnishing, I took my last hundred dollars and purchased pretty tartan cloth for drapes, an overstuffed sofa and love seat of dark green brushed wool upholstery, and a pair of Eastlake end tables and matching coffee table. On the walls, I hung a series of Post-Impressionist prints from a Pioneer Square second-hand store. It felt good to be productive again. Thank God for my mother.

One afternoon in late March, I was alone at the cabin. I'd attempted to clear out the memories of Lizzie, temporarily tucking her various gifts of paper-mache boxes, Indian baskets and her collection of primitive paintings into attic storage. Yet as I surveyed the living room, my eyes rested on a hook on the far side of the room next to the stone fireplace. I'd forgotten the medicine bag, which hung there. I shuddered with an involuntary reminder of my loss and walked over to the bag, yanking it from its resting place.

I'd never opened the bag, feeling it would be an intrusion of Lizzie's privacy. The bag was a gift from the great Indian, Little Bull. I'd often wondered about the mysterious treasures inside the bag. Standing in the dim room, lit only by the pearly sky, I made an unusual decision. After all, Lizzie had given me this bag for a reason. Lifting the bag off the hook, I grabbed matches from the coffee table and scurried into the kitchen for a cup of cornmeal. With my hands full, I shoved open the screen door with my foot and walked toward the beach.

The landscape's brooding palette was ideal for my mood. The insipid blue waters brushed the sand in smooth strokes while soiled foam sketched a jagged line as far as the eye could see. The sky was as white and flat as an untouched canvas. The water changed to deepening variations of gray as it stretched to infinity. In the distance, the sound of a foghorn gave an eerie groan. I commiserated with a couple of screeching seagulls as they searched for their dinner. The pickings are scarce for all of us, I thought while staring up at the soaring birds.

There wasn't a soul in sight as I settled onto an enormous seaweed-laced log hauled inland by the ferocious Puget Sound currents. To the northwest, the tips of the Olympics rose up like rows of shark's teeth. To the south, a patch of deep green cedars sheltered me from the prevailing winds. Phantom mists rose from the leaden spit like graveyard spirits. It was a haunting scene in which to induce magic. Shivering from the chill, I hastily got to work. Carefully placing my odd assortment on a flat section of the log, I glanced around for some tools. Finding a long stick, I drew a large circle in the sand and stepped into it with my items. After gathering a handful of dry twigs, I started a small fire in the center of the circle.

Soon a feathery blue flame danced and coiled against the air currents. Sprinkling the corn meal into the four directions, I bowed solemnly toward each. I was a novice at this, but I'd participate in Indian rituals with Lizzie enough times to know the significance of these mystical ceremonies. Every time she and I had enacted one, inexplicable occurrences happened. Today my wish was to bring forth knowledge.

I looked up into the sky and cried, "Great Spirit, please hear me now. I offer you gifts from the earth. I ask for secret knowledge. Please tell me if Lizzie is still alive so that I may move forward in my life!"

My voice was thick with stubborn tears, tears I had tried to leave behind a hundred times over. Suddenly I halted to gaze down at the bag, which hung around my neck. Slipping it over my head, I prepared a small bowl in the middle of my wool skirt to contain the bag's contents. Just as I was about to open the bag, a voice shouted my name. Cursing under my breath, I leaped up, shaken by the interruption. Attaining my bearings was almost impossible for a few minutes. I stood stalk-still, watching as a bobbing figure approached me. Breathing deeply, I stepped outside the circle as Chuck Adams, the telegram delivery boy, jogged up to me.

"Hello, Mrs. Miller. Sorry to bother you, but I have a telegram," he puffed, his skinny frame twisting as he spoke. I smiled politely and took the envelope from him.

"Thanks, Chuck," I replied blankly. Gathering my wits, I added, "Follow me up to the house. I have a batch of cookies for your family." He nodded eagerly, his pimply face beaming as we walked toward the house. He jabbered about this and that, but I didn't hear a word of it. I was still too upset to comment. I stepped into the cabin to get my purse and the cookies while he waited at the door.

"Thank you, Mrs. Miller," he mumbled shyly as I handed him the money. By the time I returned to the yard, the telephone was ringing. I slipped the telegram into my cardigan pocket and ran through the door. My mother was on the phone. Her breathy voice was edgy and sharp.

"Emily, where have you been?" she barked.

"Down at the beach. Why?"

"I've been trying to reach you for over three hours. Are you okay?" she asked nervously.

"Yes, I'm fine. You sound so worried. What is it?"

"Oh, Emmy, I'm so concerned about you. Every time I can't reach you, I think you've done something silly."

"Mother, you must trust me. I'm not going off the deep end, okay?"

"Okay, sweetheart. Will you call me later tonight?"

"Sure. I love you, Mom."

"I love you, too," she whispered with a sigh of relief. Hanging up the telephone, I squeezed my eyes tightly to block the tears. The war had worn on Mother. A merciless plague of heartache and fear had caused her gentle nature to take a dramatic shift. Once a stable, yet sensitive woman, she was now prone to hysteria and exhaustion. I was glad it was nearly over. With the enemies almost in our hands, she would soon be free.

Nevertheless, my prolonged visit to limbo was over. For my mother's sake, it was essential I act as normal as possible. By week's end I'd approached both the *Seattle Times* and the *Seattle Post Intelligencer* looking for work. The *Times* was fully staffed, but the *P.I.* was interested in hiring me. Within two weeks I was writing short pieces on art and theater again. I enjoyed getting back into the fast-paced hustle of journalism, particularly as the final dominoes of the global drama began to fall.

Every week, the world rocked with change. Roosevelt died on April 12th, bringing an end to one of the most applauded presidencies in our country's history. America's citizens wept, but our mourning was quickly pacified by the Allies' triumphant battle cries of success. The Third Army was making headway into the Czechoslovak border while the Ninth Army crossed the Elbe in force, striking eastward toward Berlin. The fascists' armies crumbled under the Allies' feet. On May 2nd, Hitler and Eva Braun took their own lives and were subsequently burned, along with piles of Nazi documents. On the same day, Mussolini and his mistress were executed and buried in paupers' graves in Milan. Shortly thereafter, the Germans began their evacuation of Denmark and Norway. We rejoiced with hope and relief as the Western Front was secured, acre by acre, city by city. For the Strong family, the best news of all was the liberation of over 400 starved and naked Ally prisoners of war by the British in Burma. On May 4th we got a phone call from the United States Air Force. Ernest had been rescued!

Contagious giddiness began to sweep through the populace. On May 8th, the war in Europe was declared officially over. The surrender was unconditional. We had won! The streets of Seattle sang with victory slogans and bright banners flew in honor of our success. People partied on every corner and the cafes and bars bulged with outrageous frivolity. I ran up and down the avenues and wove through the throngs, pen in hand, entirely thrilled to be part of such glorious celebration.

On May 12th, David called to tell me he was safe. His measured voice of jubilation was tempered by serious overtones. For him, the battle for emotional survival continued. In fact, in many ways, it had just begun. As I hung up the telephone, my stomach crawled up my throat, wanting to spew with the wickedness of life. David had called from an indescribably evil place. His platoon had just arrived at a concentration camp called Bergen Belsen.

16

Over three weeks had passed since David's telephone call from Bergen Belsen, but his unsavory predicament preyed on my mind like a horror movie with no ending, repeating the grisly scenes I imagined he must be encountering. From the desks of the *P. I.*, I'd learned that the number of Jews and other 'undesirables' who had died in the concentration camps was simply unbelievable. Some reports estimated the deaths at one million! The AP wire service sent photographs of the death camps: steel bars and barbed wire and human corpses stacked as high as a barn. Photos of emaciated, naked, hollow-eyed survivors stared out from the pages of the paper like grim reapers on Halloween. I visualized my compassionate David, courageously walking through cities of piled dead, stepping over rotting corpses and skirting wagons of bones.

On June 16th, I was at home when the phone rang. More and more often now, a ringing telephone meant good news: prisoners of war rescued, soldiers returning home, another battle in the Pacific won. As I scurried to answer the call, I glanced out of the front window. A double rainbow arched in a dazzling shower of color over Elliott Bay.

"Hello, Miller's residence."

"Hello, this is Mr. Miller," David sang.

"Oh, Darling, when are you coming home?"

"My duty doesn't end until August 28th," he replied, his tone disheartened.

I sighed heavily, disappointed by his reply. "That's weeks from now! I miss you so much."

"It's not long now, Emmy. Try to stay strong. Any word from Lizzie?"

"No, but,"

"The line's getting bad, so listen to me carefully," he shouted from the other side of the world. "There's someone who desperately needs our help. I've found Georgina Gerstein."

I gasped. Mr. and Mrs. Gerstein's niece! Otto's brother and his family's safety hadn't been a concern when the Nazis first began their victimization of Jews. They had been living in Rotterdam far from the threat of danger. Later, when the Germans invaded the Netherlands, we were worried, but the Gersteins were assured in a letter from Georgina's parents that the family had found safety by hiding with a Dutch Christian family.

"Georgina is the only one in their family who survived the camp. Both her folks died in the gas chambers and her older brother died of pneumonia. Gosh, Em, she's only 13 and barely alive. She's here at the hospital with me now. The Red Cross doctors are pumping her full of penicillin and food. You need to get your father on this immediately. We can bring her home as a refugee if we can get the proper documentation and money. I've got to go now, but I'm counting on you. I'll call you in a couple of days." With that, the line went dead, leaving me churning with an explosive mixture of exaltation and anxiety.

I immediately telephoned Father, explaining what David had told me. Luckily Father knew someone in the U.S. Immigration office who could secure Georgina's refugee visa. Next I called the Gersteins. They'd been living in ignorance as to fate of their relatives, clinging to the possibility that they were still alive. Mr. Gerstein's younger brother, Wolfgang, had been his only sibling. As my friend's tears made conversation impossible, I paused, struggling to think. Overcome by grief, Mr. Gerstein was too distraught to respond to my suggestions for a plan of action. Clearly, he hadn't the physical or emotional strength to visit the graveyard of his people. Nevertheless Georgina needed to get out of Germany as soon as possible and David couldn't bring her home until late August.

I searched my brain for solutions. If Lizzie were here, she would fetch Georgina without a bat of an eye. Listening to Mr. Gerstein's sobs, I considered my responsibility to my precious friends. The Gersteins had been part of my childhood. They had given me a strong sense of justice, a "fight for the underdog" mentality while loving me as one of their own. The scales of my love had teetered in their direction when Papa had shoved bigotry down my throat. Should I retrieve their niece?

The very thought shook me to the core. In truth, I was terrified to go to the land of my forefathers. Yet the irony almost caused me to laugh aloud. "I'm a journalist, for heaven sakes!" I chided silently as Mr. Gerstein's cries grew louder. "Journalists are supposed to go to their stories!"

"No, Emily, you're the cowardly lion," Grandmother Ginny's voice admonished from the recesses of my memory. In my mind's eye, the old woman appeared like a demon. She stood over me, the mocking gleam in her eye unbearable to watch, her clenched jaw as hard and unforgiving as granite. Suddenly I was six years old again, standing near the foamy lip of the Madison Beach shoreline. The summer day was dreary and overcast I was afraid to go into the pitch-black water, believing hideous monsters lurked in the depths of Lake Washington. "You are such a pathetic child," Ginny had sneered, shaking her head disapprovingly. I had stood on the beach with my head sinking into my torso like a frightened turtle as shame filled my pores. Mother had come to my rescue, patting my back and stating, "It's okay. Emily doesn't have swim today." But Mother's words didn't erase the scarlet letter of my grandmother's disgust. I had hated Ginny then, for her condemnation, her cynicism, her destruction of my spirit. Would I let her memory beat me again?

The question was there, lingering in the shadows, as Lizzie appeared in the corner of my mind. Standing with her hands on her hips, her black eyes flashing defiantly, she called out, "Remember what Amelia said about courage. This is your chance to find peace. You can do this, Emily. You must retrieve Georgina. You *must!*"

I squirmed, sullied by the fear of the unknown. Was I emotionally equipped to witness the atrocities of the Third Reich? Mrs. Gerstein came to the telephone and began asking about the location of the family's bodies and circumstances of their death. Her words became the background music to Lizzie's silent commands. Her presence felt so real, it was as though she was standing next to me. Though my stomach curdled when I contemplated the dreadful realities to come, I told Mrs. Gerstein that I would fetch Georgina.

Papa was asleep in his easy chair when I arrived at my folks' house. Carrying a cup of sweet, milky tea in my hand, I nudged him awake. "Here, Papa, drink this," I coaxed. After his eyes opened and his fitful coughing subsided, I began the speech I'd prepared on the ferry ride over to Seattle. With a deep breath, I said, "Papa, I have a favor to ask of you. I need 1,000 dollars."

His veined, yellowed eyes grew wide and he began to chuckle. "I don't know how your mother managed to produce such an impertinent young lady. You never cease to amaze me."

"It's to save the Otto Gerstein's niece. You had the chance to help them once before, when they were trying to bring Mrs. Gerstein's mother out, but you refused. Now she's dead." I paused briefly for effect before continuing, not yet daring to look directly at him.

"Papa, we don't get many second chances in life. What do you say?" I leaned forward and placed my hand on his shoulder. "I'll pay you back as soon as I can. Besides, you'll redeem yourself if you do this." The silence that followed my words felt like an arctic chill. Nevertheless I waited with baited breath, trying not to stare at his tired face.

"*Mein Gott,*" he eventually replied, closing his eyes and rubbing his day-old stubble. "Redeem myself? I suppose you would like me to redeem the whole of Germany next. I suppose it's my fault Hitler annihilated all those people." He was very old and frail, but his voice was strong, hinting of anger.

I sat up straight and cleared my voice. "No, of course I don't believe that," I said firmly. "But if there is one thing you've taught me, it's to take care of business. I'm going to help save a child's life. For me, that *is* taking care of business. It is so very, very important for me to do this." Placing my hand on his and softening my voice, I continued. "Dear Papa, remember my wedding day? You were so sick, but you fought to stay alive. You said it yourself; you had business to take care of with me. That desire restored your health. Now I'm asking for your help in carrying on that legacy. I want to tell my children that their great-grandfather Joseph was a hero."

Once again I waited, tense and hopeful, watching his thinning mustache quiver and twitch. My grandfather's broad shoulders drooped as he sat back in his chair and gave a deep sigh. Tears came, but he brushed them away.

Then, pointing toward the hall, he said, "My checkbook's in the desk. Go get it for me!"

On June 29th, I boarded a Boeing clipper plane for Europe with my passport, a refugee visa and two return airplane tickets in my hand. Father drove me to the airport. Mother was absolutely beside herself with worry, begging me not to go, but this time I couldn't bend. Fortunately Ernest was returning home in two days after his convalescence on Oahu. The Air Force had warned us about his condition. Emaciated and covered with sores, his leg still very fragile, he would require Mother's constant attention for a while. Still, she feared for my safety. Jonathan simply stated, "This'll be a tough fish to swallow, Emily."

Nearly 24 hours after my departure from Seattle, I arrived in Paris. The Le Bourget airport was crawling with hundreds of war-weary soldiers and civilians. Tattered, exhausted people pushed and shoved their way through the masses, looking for lost relatives, preparing for flights out of the country, or digging through piles of luggage. Some travelers were returning exiles, others sought refugee status. Scattered among the frenetic crowd were uniformed American and British soldiers, guns slung over their shoulders like extra limbs.

The smell of war was pervasive. A pretty girl, her head wrapped in dirty bandages, rushed to greet her limping lover while a black-cloaked, sobbing mother wrapped her arms around her small son. A legless man, his stumps wrapped in blood-soaked rags, scooted through the throngs on a wagon, his skinny arms pushing him forward like paddling oars. The cacophony of a dozen languages added to my confusion while the rancid odor of unwashed bodies engulfed me.

As I took in the pulsating pain of those around me, I felt I might burst with an excruciating sense of tragedy. I wanted to take strangers into my arms, wipe their tears and soothe their wounds, but I was a well-dressed, healthy and rosy-cheeked anomaly. Awkwardly, I reached into my bag and found a colorless scarf to cover my hair. In self-conscious haste, I wiped off my lipstick and removed my pearl earrings.

Waiting for my luggage, I noticed a number of flight tags were stamped Casablanca. For an instant I thought of Ross, but then brushed him aside. He wasn't returning to France. Spain was his home. Without warning, I felt a hand on my arm. "I'm here to help you reach Lieutenant Miller," the voice said, rich with resonance and familiarity. I spun around and looked into the face of a friend.

"Ross, I was just thinking of you!" I murmured, swept away by emotion. He stood there, smiling bewitchingly.

"And I, you, lovely Mrs. Miller. How good it is to see you again." He planted a breathy kiss on my right cheek. I wanted to fall into his arms, not for the sake of passion, but rather for protection.

"Thank God, you're here. I wasn't sure I could bear the train ride alone."

"David wouldn't have let you take the train alone. There are still quite a few Axis rebels who find it a juicy bit of fun to harass elegant young ladies like yourself. We wouldn't put you in harm's way." I looked at Ross carefully now. He was still astonishingly handsome, but his eyes were hardened by suffering, injustice and torn loyalties. In that moment I knew Ross had been the one to find Georgina Gerstein.

"Come," Ross replied. "The train leaves in one hour. We must hurry. I'll tell you what you want to know on the way to the train station."

He hustled me out of the airport and into a taxi. The roads teemed with battle-worn people. Nevertheless, an occasional beam of hope filtered through the shadows of despair. A small child fingered her hair and gave me a tender smile as the taxi wound through the narrow, cobblestone streets. A young woman strode by, carrying a French flag, its bright colors waving, her face lifted to the sun with pride. For a brief juncture our eyes locked, two omnipotent young women, each in her own way.

Traveling through the countryside toward Paris, the roads were lined with crumbling, charred houses and blackened churches with gothic spires which poked up like antennas in a sea of broken bricks. Factories, once prosperous, now stood as skeletons of another time while scores of demolished automobiles littered the landscape like enormous black beetles. Huddles of survivors raked through the debris, searching for a piece of luck, a memento of a life before war, a treasure with which to buy a loaf of bread. Malnourished children tried to keep up with their resourceful mothers as the women loaded their aprons with chipped teacups, filthy blankets or a rare piece of silver. On the street corners, shivering men stood in circles of three or four, hungrily sharing a single cigarette. I pulled out my notebook and began to scribble my observations while Ross gave a moving soliloquy on recent events.

"I was working for the Jewish resistance in Spain, helping to move Jews through, relocating them whenever possible, seeking out hiding places in their home locales as a last alternative. During that time, I learned of the Gerstein's relatives. We found them the Christian family in Rotterdam. Unfortunately, hiding places were never the best choice. The Gestapo found Mr. Gerstein's brother and his family about six months after they were placed. There was nothing I could do after that, but even now if I could just get my hands on one of those Nazis." Ross clenched his fists, his dark eyes gleaming fiercely with pain and renegade passion.

"Ross, the Gestapo are no longer. You talk as if you're still fighting them."

"You are so naive! The Nazis won't just disappear, never to be heard from again. They're everywhere, just a lot quieter now. They'll rear their ugly heads again. It's only a matter of time." His tone was prickly. I felt my own armor rise in defense.

"For heaven sakes, don't be so antagonistic. We won. The war is over!" I cried emphatically.

He sighed begrudgingly like an old man forced to arise from the comfort of his rocking chair. "There are all kinds of wars. Many are fought without bullets. Instilling fear is easy enough to do, even without weapons. Threats can be just as fatal to the human psyche. Wait until you see the Germans. They act as if they haven't done a thing wrong. I suppose arrogance is the only way they can live with themselves."

I grunted, impatient with his patronizing. He just shook his head and shot me a look of sympathy. Climbing out of the taxi, I insisted on paying my fare. Ross grabbed my bags and hustled through the converging crowd as I stumbled behind. When we stepped onto the dirty, littered platform, the loudspeaker boomed, announcing that the train destined for Hanover was pulling in.

As we moved toward our car, the doors opened and a group of people spilled out. Men, no older than I, shuffled toward me like old parishioners. Most of the men's hair was missing or had turned white. Shabbily dressed, scrawny women passed with vacant eyes and bony faces, shrinking from my presence though I stepped out of their way. The face, which struck me the most, belonged to a skinny girl of about 13 years of age. When we passed, I nodded and she smiled meekly in return. Her large dark eyes were rich with expression, but her smile disturbed me. I leaned over and tugged at Ross's sleeve.

"There was something strange about that girl," I whispered as we climbed aboard the train.

"No teeth," Ross answered as he tossed my suitcase onto the luggage shelf.

"You're right. How strange. Poor child!"

We settled down in our seats. The grimy train reeked of perspiration and diesel. I was emotionally exhausted and extremely fatigued, but at the same time, I felt a familiar excitement with Ross. I was anxious to have a good long chat. "So why would a young girl lose all of her teeth?" I asked casually.

"The Germans," Ross replied, his voice gruff.

I gave him a quizzical look. "I don't understand."

"Christ, you Americans have been in denial!" he groaned, running his hands through his thick black hair. Taking a deep breath, he threw me a look of exasperation. "Let me explain, Emily. At the beginning, the Jewish families often melted down their gold and put it in their teeth so the Germans wouldn't confiscate it. Later, when these Jews were sent to the camps, the Germans retaliated by pulling out their teeth, before exterminating most of them. I would guess that young girl survived by selling sex."

My skin began to crawl. "By doing *what*?"

Ross faced me and gazed deeply into my eyes. A subtle shift occurred at that moment. The energy between us softened and I experienced a tenderness from him I'd never known. Ross, the invincible patriot, became a doting big brother. Gently taking my hand, he began to speak in a very deliberate tone. "Emmy, it was like this. If the little Jewish girls were pretty *and* smart, they survived by selling their bodies for food and privileges. They fornicated with the soldiers to avoid the gas chamber, traded oral sex for a piece of bread, engaged in orgies on command rather than digging mass graves. All in a day's work."

"No way, Ross. The Germans didn't do that," I shouted, suddenly made hysterical by his shocking suggestion. "They starved the Jews and worked them too hard. That's all they did. The Germans didn't rape children, for heavens sakes! I don't believe you. It's not true. Germans are decent people at heart!"

"Please, keep your voice down," he growled, jerking his head around anxiously. "There are people on this train who understand English!" His voice dropped to a menacing hiss. "I can't believe you can say that the Germans are decent people. They raped, they murdered, they tortured and sent millions of babies and mothers and old folks to gas chambers. Wake up, Emily, wake up to the truth! We are talking about massive genocide of unbelievable proportions!" Ross could hardly contain his fury. His face was purple with rage and his eyes felt like knives as he glowered at me.

I felt my innards shrink. The space around me contracted, squeezing me until I couldn't breath anymore. My guts turned to jelly and I needed to get to a lavatory immediately. "I'm sorry, please excuse me," I mumbled to Ross as I stood up and walked shakily toward the toilets. I had barely sat down on the stool when my bowels let loose and tart yellow vomit covered my knees.

❖   ❖   ❖

The train was scheduled to arrive in Hanover at four the next morning. It was a long haul, nearly 16 hours with stops in several small towns along the way. I was glad our return airplane tickets would take us directly out of Hanover. I didn't want Georgina to be forced to endure this depressing journey.

We traveled through the battered French countryside all day. As if watching a film, we viewed the devastated villages, rapidly shuttling by our window. After awhile, I became disgusted by the war's legacies. Years of reparation were required before the return of the quaint, pastoral Europe I had once envisioned. Van Gogh's rich landscapes and Monet's peaceful pastels had become muddy remnants of desolation: a cluster of abandoned, burned-out tanks, ropes of coiled barb wire, scattered plane wreckage, stockpiles of wasted army rations, all in dull greens, browns, grays and blacks. I saw only ugly colors for ugly memories. Finally numbed to the scenes of destruction, I turned away from the window and talked with Ross, sharing my recent history and the truth about Lizzie. He was saddened by her disappearance, but hopeful.

"Lizzie is the toughest woman I've ever met. Believe me, after working for the Resistance, I've met quite a few. I can't imagine our fierce little friend succumbing to death. Not yet anyway." Ross shook his head and looked away. Speaking more to himself than to me, he added, "I miss that woman. She's quite a beauty and as smart as they come. I'm certain she's safe. I feel it in my gut. She won't come home until she's good and ready."

I hoped he was right, more than I could say. Lizzie was still in my blood, in my dreams, in my head and I missed her terribly.

Ross sat back and closed his eyes with a contented smile. I wondered if he was fantasizing about Lizzie. Nudging him, I murmured, "Do you still love her?" He was silent for a few moments, but eventually he opened his eyes, gazing in my direction. His ebony pupils seemed to bore right through me as if through me, he saw another time, a time before war had replaced rhetoric, a time when romantic ideals eclipsed pain.

"Love is a tough word for me, Emily. I don't know much about love. Not the kind of love you and David share. I'll never forget when I found your husband at the Haufbrau Haus last month. God, the man was missing you! Talked about you for over an hour. I thought I'd never have the chance to tell him about Georgina!" Ross chuckled and patted my hand in a brotherly fashion.

"I fell for you once, too," he continued, "but I couldn't have been the kind of man he is to you. I can't devote myself to anyone. I'm a nomad. I'll drift my entire life, but not aimlessly. Give me a cause and I'll rouse an army. Give me a heart and I'll collapse under its weight. Lizzie and I were once as hot as they come, but the fire eventually went out. It was time for me to move on. I know I hurt her, but I had no choice. Without the fire, I'm a dead man."

I nodded, warmed by his hand covering mine, feeling satisfied, disarmed by his truth. By late afternoon my eyelids began to droop. I dozed until we arrived at the French-Luxembourg border. British and French patrols came aboard and spent over two hours searching our train for Nazis who were escaping by the dozens into neutral Luxembourg. War criminal wasn't yet a legal term, so finding refuge was the closest road to freedom for many of the Axis mongrels.

The rolling emerald hills and lush vineyards of the Rhine River Valley passed by our windows in the early evening. I tried to enjoy the country's natural beauty, despite the boisterous vigilance of soldiers and guards. We dined on *bier, wurst* and *pommes frites* from a greasy cart in a nameless train station near Frankfurt. Images of the Grimm Brothers' haunted forests taunted me by nightfall. I fell into a dream-laden sleep around midnight. Grotesque visions of Hansel and Gretel starving in concentration camps and evil witches with loaded machine guns chasing me as I tried to rescue a group of school children. When the train pulled into Hanover station, I was wide awake and agitated though it was only three in the morning.

Ross found us a taxi. His High German was impeccable as he gave the sleepy driver directions to our lodgings. Hanover was dark and shadowy, all chiseled stone, oily asphalt and hard brick. Familiar sounds: a car passing, a dog barking, voices echoing through the quiet streets, all became cause for my hypervigilance. Between the fatigue and my overactive imagination, I fully expected a cadre of S.S. officers to surround us at any moment. Most of the street lamps had been destroyed during the war, but as the taxi's lights swung through the rubble-ridden streets, I caught glimpses of soldiers on night patrols. When I clutched Ross's arm in fear, he squeezed my hand and said, "Don't worry. They're the good guys. The Allies are taking no chances."

The Wengbauer Pension was lit by one small kerosene lamp as we stepped inside a few minutes later. I smelled a peculiar combination of a wet dog and apple cider odors. The sitting room furniture was sparse, but made of huge, chunky pieces of wood, like medieval castle memorabilia. The fireplace mantel was lined with colorful ceramic steins, gleaming in the dim light. Ross rang a bell and within seconds, a little old man in a nightcap and stained dressing gown stumbled through the doorway.

"*Guten Morgen, Mein Herr und Frau,*" he grumbled. Digging into a cubbyhole on the large oak desk in the corner, he handed Ross one key and pointed to the stairway to the left. I looked at Ross and tipped my head quizzically, awakened by an unwanted tickle in my groin. Would my silly fantasy never go away?

"Same room?" I asked, so demurely that my skin rippled with chagrin.

Ross chuckled, a low, sexy sound. "Don't I wish! No, Emily. I think your husband will be waiting for you."

I gasped joyfully. "David? Oh, why didn't you tell me!"

Ross shrugged. "I thought you liked surprises." I ran up the stairs ahead of him, Ross's quiet laughter following. When we reached the top of the stairway, Ross pointed to the first door on the left.

"Knock softly and Prince Charming will appear," he said wryly as he disappeared into the darkness.

"Emily, you're here!" David cried as he opened the door.

My husband was naked except for boxer shorts, his coiled blonde chest hair reflecting the room's candlelight, his beautiful face alit with love. I pressed myself to him, feeling his muscular body against mine, crushing him to me, his lips on my neck, his tongue in my mouth. He began to undress me before we'd shut the door, had me naked in minutes, his mouth everywhere on my body as I groaned and swooned. Dizzy with lust, I pulled out his penis. It seemed enormous, a thrusting machine which pounded into me, hard and demanding. I was sweet with pleasure, spreading my legs, wrapping them around his back, holding onto the brass headboard. Our lovemaking was over quickly, but our fire didn't recede, so we made love again as the hopeful sun began to rise on the smoky, remorseless city of Hanover.

David and I awoke in each other's arms. After a quick shower of cold water and lye soap, we were on the way to the Red Cross hospital. I stared out the window, my nose pressed to the greasy glass like a curious child. Ross and David were chatting amicably, making plans for our return to Seattle. Georgina and I were scheduled to fly home in three days. Like royalty, we were to be escorted to the airport by American soldiers.

We drove through many bombed areas where the black soot and piles of debris were neatly swept from the ancient cobblestone streets. Further on we passed a surviving church, once regal in its religiousness, now only a futile symbol of a nation who couldn't blush. On the streets of downtown, tidy queues of disgruntled people waited for bread, their noses slightly to the wind as Ally soldiers marched by. The Germans acted as if they couldn't stand the smell of our boys.

At first, I decided that Ross was right. The Germans didn't seem to understand the meaning of the word "guilty". Then my mind flashed on Papa's assault in the library so long ago. Despite his rage at my request to assist the Gersteins, in his smoky eyes I had seen a glimmer of hope and belief in the struggle for goodness. In Joseph Danfrauer's mind, the pursuit of perfection was the holiest goal of man. I knew these Germans were ashamed by what they had done, though their arrogant demeanor refused to acknowledge their humiliation. They had failed at the hands of an evil leader, had succumbed to Hitler's power in their own idealistic pursuit of perfection. Now this culture would do what Germans do best: disguise their disillusionment and despair. After reconsideration, I felt no angst for Papa or his people, only simple pity.

The Red Cross hospital was a rundown medieval building. Gray stone walls, dusted with lingering gun powder and pockmarked by broken windows, didn't have the sterile ambiance one would expect from a house of healing. I shivered as I climbed from the cab, glancing at the crowd of people who milled around the hospital's entrance. Weeping mothers tried to make their way into the building, but guards pushed them back. However when David, dressed in his decorated military uniform, nodded sharply, the wall of security men parted, allowing us to enter.

The three of us walked down a dim, narrow hallway and stepped into a bustling ward where black-gown nuns scurried by, serving parallel walls lined with bedridden, breathing skeletons. Some of the cots were encompassed by flimsy white curtains, others were not. The smell of antiseptic was so overpowering, I had to cover my nose. We walked down a long row of beds until we reached a curtained area. David murmured, *"Entshultigen Sie, bitte."* There was a mumbling response as he pulled back the curtain where she sat, an angel in white.

Georgina was unforgettably beautiful: raw, yearning and deathly pale. She stared at me with her wide, blue eyes, their irises like fragmented kaleidoscope glass. She seemed a thousand years old, her translucent face etched with experience, yet her gestures were childlike. As I walked toward her bed, she giggled and clasped her hands with embarrassed joy. Her thick, wavy hair had been hacked to her chin. The chocolate-colored strands were tangled into corkscrew curls. Her face was small and heart-shaped with high, arched eyebrows which suggested surprise. I was relieved to see that she still had all her teeth. Though she appeared to be fairly tall, Georgina couldn't have weighed more than 70 pounds.

I shook her hand and then without a second thought, bent over and wrapped my arms around her skinny torso, hugging her tightly. Georgina responded by holding on as if for dear life. I blinked back the flood of tears that threatened to erupt and sniffed loudly. Then I began to speak to her in simple German phrases. In seconds, my rusty German and her virgin English solicited a running start on friendship and I actually coaxed a laugh from her.

The makeshift hospital was unbearably crowded and rank with the smells of blood and death. Though David had been promised that Georgina would be released the following day, I became insistent that she be discharged immediately. In response to my urgency, my ancestral tongue came back like a lost puppy, full of vigor and high-voiced excitement. I raced from doctor to nurse, asking for proper medical advice and securing the papers for her release. While Ross stepped out for a cigarette, David just stood by and smiled. He always seemed to know when to let me take the lead.

I had brought three dresses for Georgina. Mrs. Gerstein had made two of them: a plaid Pendleton wool jumper with a matching beret and a blue cotton pinafore dress with simple white smocking. I'd added a delightful Frederick and Nelsen gown just for fun: a gorgeous emerald green taffeta party dress with a dropped waist. A big velvet bow hugged the right hip and the short sleeves were full. I'd purchased a pair of black tights and patent leather Mary Janes for good measure. To my delight, the precious little creature chose the taffeta dress.

In minutes I had helped her to wash and dress and had tied her hair back in a black satin ribbon. Self-consciousness gave way to giddy excitement as Georgina stepped around the curtain and stood in front of a cracked wall mirror that Ross had found in a nearby lavatory. At first she simply stared into the patchy glass, as uncertain and vaguely forgetful as twins meeting after years of separation. Running her hand timidly across the skirt of the dress, Georgina felt the fabric as though it might disappear, an expectant Cinderella at the stroke of midnight. Then her hand rose to her face, touching her mouth, cheeks and hair as a lover caresses the object of his desire. The cadaverous woman in the cot next to hers began to ooh and ahh as Georgina broke away and danced around her bed. Soon the whole ward awakened with interest at the young girl's antics. Georgina flitted and floated from bed to bed, swelling with pride, an apparition of youthful joy. She curtsied for the old Jewish priest who had lost both legs, bringing a smile to the gaffer's tortured face, spun in delicate circles for the young boy scarred from too many beatings, and kissed the blind mother and her newborn. Where her confidence came from, I'll never know, but Georgina walked out of that grim hospital with her head held high, as proud as a bride on her wedding day.

The four of us stepped onto the dour streets of Hanover and jumped into the nearest cab. Inside, I held Georgina close to me as we sat in the back of the battered Volkswagen, watching her from the corner of my eye as we traveled through the tired metropolis. With a heavy sigh, she smiled and closed her eyes as if in recall. Then, to my complete surprise, Georgina began to ask about Lizzie. I was so startled I didn't respond at first. "Fraulein Lizzie go to American trees?" she asked boldly in broken English. I stared at her, misunderstanding.

David piped up, "I've told Georgina all about your family, Lizzie and the Gersteins, of course. A few days after I mentioned Lizzie's disappearance, Georgina shared a dream she'd had. She dreamed Lizzie was living in the woods in an old cabin. Weird, huh?" His eyebrow drew up into a questioning arch and he shrugged. "Maybe you're a mystic, Georgina." He winked playfully.

She tilted her head to one side with curls bobbing, "Mystic?"

I shivered from a slight chill, wrapping my cardigan tighter around me. As I did, an envelope dropped out of the sweater pocket and fluttered onto the floor of the taxi. Georgina reached down and slowly picked it up, handing it to me with a timid smile. I realized in an instant it was the telegram I'd received a few weeks back after the beach ceremony, the telegram I'd never read.

"Here's the telegram you sent, David," I said, shaking my head in surprise. "I've never had a chance to read it until now."

Turning, David leaned over the front seat with a look of confusion. "I didn't send any telegrams to you, Sweetheart." The hair on the back of my neck rose while Georgina looked at me curiously.

"Go on, read it!" Ross quipped. Nodding, I opened the tattered note. It was only three lines, but those three lines caused my chin to quiver and my heart to pound. "Listen to this," I cried to my attentive audience.

My dear Emily,

Always remember: "Long years apart can make no breach a second cannot fill."

Yours always, Lizzie.

With tears streaming down my face, I hugged a bewildered Georgina while David and Ross whooped and hollered. Lizzie was alive! I was euphorically reborn by one promise: someday my best friend would come home.

"She's alive, just as I thought," Ross cried with a smug grin after our clamor had been quelled by the crotchety cab driver. We were in the mood to celebrate, so Ross suggested we stop at a *bierstuben* for a meal.

The *Edelweiss* was a cozy restaurant adorned with cookie cutter Bavarian furniture and brightly-colored embroidered tablecloths. I was amused to see the maitre' de wore *lederhosen* and the waitresses were dressed in dirndl skirts and stiffly starched aprons. The room was dark and smoky and somewhere from the rear of the establishment rose the whining nasal hum of an accordion.

Ross ordered a round of pilsners and a glass of lemonade. While we read the menu, I scouted the place. There were several German families among the American, French and English soldiers. Soon the waitress brought plates upon plates of *sauerbraten, pomme frittes* and *wiener schnitzel*. After the tasty meal, Georgina asked to use the ladies room. As we stood, I noticed the tattooed number on her wrist.

She grasped my hand tightly as we left the small dining area and entered the bar to find the *toilette*. The wheezing accordion music became louder as we wove our way through the jostling, inebriated crowd. At first I didn't notice the two stocky men sitting at the bar. When Georgina started to pass the second man, he swung his stool around and stuck out his leg just in time to cause her to trip and fly headfirst onto a nearby table. I watched in anguish, unable to save her as food and drink flew in every direction. Immediately diving to her rescue, I quickly wrapped apologies around the table of stunned and dripping soldiers as I wrung out her dress and wiped her tears. Then I spun around and glared at the ugly German who had tripped her. His acne-scarred face had the look of a hunter after a clean kill.

"*Dumm Jude*," he hissed, a glimmer of a smile passing over his beefy lips.

Suddenly a voracious fury erupted from the depths of my being. With its emergence came rabid hatred, hatred for everything that Germany stood for: the poisonous prejudice and murderous scapegoating of all degenerates who had maimed, tortured and killed in the name of my ancestry. In my frothing, snarling madness, I threw myself against him, pinning him to the bar. I was so close to him, I could smell his sweat and sour beer breath, feel the heat of his own hatred on my neck. He swore violently and attempted to right himself, but I drove on, shoving my fingers into his eye sockets as he screamed for mercy. His hands flew to his face, trying to shield himself, so I went for his groin, squeezing his scrotum until I felt finger meet finger. He howled and shoved me back by the force of his hysteria, but I wasn't done yet. I grabbed his hair and pulled it out by the handfuls and then with a final thrust, I tipped his stool and sent him reeling. Just as his friend rose to retaliate, David and Ross appeared. Before I could jump on the German's prone body, Ross had me firmly by the shoulders and was steering me out, scolding, "*Du bist ein nagel zu unsere sarg*,", which translated means, you are the nail in our coffin. David followed with Georgina, who by now was wide-eyed with astonished awe.

In seconds we were speeding away from the scene of my crime without pursuit. Needless to say, Ross hounded me all the way home. I didn't give a damn, though I knew we were lucky to escape unharmed. Nevertheless, the purging of my rage felt so good, it was transformational in its effect. Unaware of how angry I had become, the release detonated a new power within me. The exhilaration I felt by that one cruel act swept through me like a fire in a parched forest, roasting my innards with a tingling madness, winging from limb to limb, voracious and undeniable, setting my very arteries alight with a ravenous will to protect Georgina at all costs. At that moment in time, I wouldn't have traded that feeling for anything in the world.

By the time we returned to the pension, it was late evening. I nudged David out of our room, sending him off to Ross. Then I gently ushered Georgina into our room.

Once alone together, Georgina was extremely shy with me. Her eyes darted apprehensively around the small space we would be sharing. I wasn't sure how to calm her, so, without much conscious thought, I began to sing an old Polish lullaby my dear nanny Eloise had taught me. I took her hand and drew her to the bed. Ever so slowly, I began to brush her hair in long, smooth strokes, careful not to yank through the knots. As I hummed and brushed, her frail body began to relax. Her narrow shoulders slumped forward and her breathing slowed.

After a few moments Georgina fell back into my arms, weeping muffled, heaving sobs that rocked my soul and murmuring, "*Dankeschon*, Emily. *Dankeschon*." If I had ever questioned the sanctity of God, it was now as I comforted one of his *kinder*. "Why God, why? Are the Jews so different than us that you would allow this to happen?" I asked silently while rocking Georgina, her tears seeping into my skin. "How could you betray this innocent? After all, your son was a Jew."

Georgina cried herself to sleep in my arms. With whispering movements, I slipped off her shoes and mine and my crumpled wool skirt and cardigan. After reaching up to switch off the lamp, I scooted back down next to her on the bed. Carefully, I stroked Georgina's pale cheek, touched by her luminous beauty. Her face was at once peaceful and yet taut with secrets, the face of an innocent child forced to become an old soul. As I watched her, I asked God for help to know the right things to say to this young traveler of life. A quiet stir in my heart told me, as always, to have faith in myself. Then Lizzie's voice came to me, saying, "Remember Amelia Earhart's words, '*Courage is the price that life extracts for granting peace*'."

With a deep sigh of contentment, I pulled the goose down quilt over Georgina and me. As I did, I made a solemn vow. I would befriend, protect and teach this young girl all I knew about acceptance, forgiveness and love. Snuggling next to her, I smiled to myself and listened to the lulling rhythm of her breath until slumber.

17

Two days later, Georgina and I said goodbye to the men who had united us. David, dressed in his crisp uniform, his grin contagious, and Ross, dark and mysterious in his long black overcoat, his eyes flashing with triumph, waved goodbye from the Hanover airport landing as we scurried up the stairs of the huge aircraft. Though David would be home in another month, I knew I would never see Ross again. He was on his way to Palestine, to assist in the resettlement of the Jews there. Years later, I would read about him in *Time* magazine, but I would never again feel his warm breath on my skin nor hear his melodic poet's voice in my ears.

The Gersteins greeted us at the Seattle airport when we arrived. Georgina held my hand tightly as we stepped off the plane, her bright eyes wide with wonder. Mrs. Gerstein rushed up and immediately threw her arms around the girl. She had grown plump again with time and her spongy, robust body seemed to be the comfort Georgina was looking for.

"*Mein liebchen!*" Mrs. Gerstein cried as she held Georgina to her breast while tears ran down her cheeks in furious streams. The trembling child held onto her gushing aunt as though she'd never let go. Otto Gerstein stood by, awkwardly shifting from one foot to the other, with a bouquet of daisies in one hand and a pretty porcelain doll in the other. His bald head glistened with sweat as he bit his cheek, waiting patiently for his turn. Eventually Georgina drew away from Edith Gerstein and curtsied politely in his direction. Otto threw down the gifts to cradle her in his arms. Soon, I too, was overcome by their affections as they thanked me over and over again. Mr. Gerstein patted my head dotingly, as if uncertain as to the appropriate affection he should show a 25-year-old woman. Meanwhile, Edith Gerstein smothered me with kisses, dotting my face with red lipstick. Words like courage, honor and devotion fell out of their mouths, filling me with affirmation.

As we turned to leave, Papa Joseph, in his wheelchair, pushed by a very thin, limping Ernest, rambled down the terminal corridor toward us. Once I got my bearings, I ran to them, plunging myself at Ernest.

He held me tightly, his brotherly embrace comforting, his whispers of joy reassuring. To my relief, my brother seemed much the same, though his skin was mottled with scabs and his body felt smaller in my arms. When I looked into his eyes, I saw such pain that I gasped. Not only had my brother endured indescribable torture, but Ernest also believed his beloved was dead.

Frantically, I reached into my purse, searching until I found Lizzie's telegram. I thrust it into Ernest's hand, watching as he read, the floodlight of recognition crossing his features.

"Sis, is this a joke?" he sputtered, his face growing even paler.

"No joke! And I've been thinking about it, ever since Georgina told me her dream." I paused, gazing into his longing eyes. "It's a complicated story, but trust me, I think I know where she is."

He nodded emphatically, his fear quelled by hope. I turned and watched as the Gersteins, Papa and Georgina approached us. Georgina was sitting on Papa's lap, her bright face splashed by childish adventure, but it was Papa's grin that tipped my heart from its pedestal. He appeared more alive than he'd been in months. His wizened face was painted with unfamiliar lines: tender love and paternal devotion. Otto stopped pushing the chair as they approached, deep laughter rumbling from his chest. "Emily, you should see your face. You look like you just saw a Martian!" Papa boomed.

"Papa, I … ah," I stuttered, laughing self-consciously.

My grandfather shook his head and began to cough. As he did so, Georgina patted his back in a touching gesture of concern. "This chair is handy sometimes. Transportation for two," Papa joked and sputtered, donning a docile smile. After all of the trauma that Georgina had endured, there appeared to be plenty of love in this extended family to soothe her wounds.

I was determined to keep my promise to Ernest. The following morning, Mother and I took a leisurely walk down to the beach. Now that Ernest and I were safely home, she was returning to her old self. She laughed more, teased my father and dressed fashionably again. We wandered along the shore, watching the waves roll in and talking happily.

"Emily, I'm so happy you brought Georgina home after all. I

apologize for my worry regarding all of that, but I was so afraid for your safety. I didn't want my own little girl to see all that horror," she murmured, clutching my arm as we walked. "Still, fetching Georgina was very brave and I'm very, very proud of you."

"In some ways, Georgina reminds me of Lizzie. Gosh, I miss Liz." Sniffing, I closed my eyes and thought of her happy face.

"It's been a terrible few years. That damn war took its toll on all of us," she whispered.

I nodded and opened my eyes, now observing Mother as she sat down on a washed-up log, made brittle by salt and weather. She had aged. Her auburn tresses were streaked with gray and her eyes had feathery lines around them, but her figure was lovely and her skin still glowed.

She turned to face the sea as a gull passed overhead, crying out a mournful song. Her voice caught as she gasped, "I've lost my Jackie. I'll never get over his death. Never! He was my spirit in so many ways. Why in God's name did he have to die? Why?" Tears began to roll down her cheeks as I sat next to her, taking her hands in my own.

"Jackie was a sweet boy who didn't deserve to die. Losing Claudia and Jack will always be a mark on our hearts. Yet we have so much to be happy for, too. We must look to the sky, smile at the sun, you know?" I whispered, forcing myself to shake off my cumbersome mantle of sadness. I stared at my mother with silent encouragement, wanting desperately to hear her say it was okay, to be the mother I remembered: the mother of laughter and bare feet and song. Kneeling down, I began to unlaced her sandals.

"What are you doing?" she asked, giggling.

I took off my shoes, too and then said, "Smiling at the sun." She cocked her head, but I didn't give up the element of surprise. Grabbing her hand, I yanked her up and began to run toward the water, dragging her behind.

She screamed, "No!" but before she could slow us down, I had her knee-deep in the icy Puget Sound waters, splashing and hollering as I took her in. It was then I heard it, the laughter of the past, the unflappable, never-give-up laughter which had been part of my childhood.

We lied down on the silky sand, spreading our cotton circle skirts behind our heads. The sky was as blue as Wedgwood china and in the distance, the cry of gulls kept us company. As the bold July sun warmed our faces, I began humming the Polish lullaby.

"Eloise used to sing that song to you a long time ago," Mother commented wistfully. "It was your favorite."

"I know. It still is."

"Father said you want to use the plane this afternoon," she murmured in a singsong voice as though giving words to my tune.

"Yep, I'm taking Ernest up."

"You might not find her, you know."

"I know, but I can't bear the look of his eyes for another day. We have to try."

"Yes, you must. After all, it's what she'd do for you."

"I know. That's why I love Lizzie so much."

That afternoon, Ernest and I drove to Boeing field to board Father's new Cessna 180, a gift from Mr. Weyer who had died while I was away in Europe. As the executor of the millionaire's estate, Father was still sorting out the old man's will. He'd hinted at something very important in it, mentioning it had to do with Lizzie, but he refused to give me any more information. In the past few days since my return, I had spent some time in planning today's search. There was only one place left that I could think of where Lizzie might be, a place that had never before crossed my mind. Georgina's dream had jogged my memory. I'd even consulted with Jonathan who, at age 12, and unbeknownst to my parents, had begun to study the esoteric arts. At my request, he had done a tea leaf reading the night before. Though I thought it somewhat ridiculous, my hunch had been confirmed.

I hadn't exactly told Ernest my plans, afraid of getting his hopes too high. With Father in cahoots with me, I'd created a sufficient alibi. At breakfast, Father asked Ernest and me to collect some papers at Weyer's Friday Harbor estate. We convinced Ernest the trip would do him good. His time at home had only produced boredom and despondency.

The weather was perfect for flying. After leaving word at the tower, Ernest and I climbed into the snazzy little ship. Ernest agreed to co-pilot, admitting his last flight hadn't left him with positive memories. This was his first reference to Burma, but I had read enough to imagine the traumatic memories, which lurked in the minds of the

Bataan Death March survivors. Ernest wouldn't fully recover from that horrible experience until he had reunited with Lizzie. Only she had the power to heal him. In my heart, I prayed we'd be successful today.

"So, off to the most beautiful lodge in the world, Ernest?" I asked, toying with the instruments before starting the engine.

"I'm looking forward to it." Despite his words, his voice was flat and emotionless. Concentration consumed me while we prepared for take off. My nerves were on edge. This was my last shot at finding Lizzie.

Soon we were up in the powder blue sky, soaring west over the prettiest city in America. I tipped the plane to the north, veering toward Friday Harbor, considering how to explain my intentions to Ernest. Besides the chance I was dead wrong about finding Liz, there could be hazards. The landing field could be muddy or choked with weeds. Fortunately it hadn't rained for a week. As I fully expected, Ernest began to catch on as Friday Harbor appeared below us.

"Hey, where are you going?" he shouted over the roaring engine, his freckled face marked with confusion.

"Sorry I hadn't mentioned it, but there's a stop I need to make."

"What stop? We're over Friday Harbor now. Descend!"

"Don't worry. We're going to Lopez first. I want to show you something."

Ernest gave me a cutting look, but kept silent, his displeasure etched in the profile of his furrowed brow, bowed head and hunched shoulders. I would do anything to bring him happiness again! I flew over the southern tip of Lopez Island, keeping my eyes glued to the topography. It had been a stormy night during the last visit over 10 years ago.

Soon I caught a glimpse of an open expanse between the rolling cedar forests. I dipped down to take a closer look and sure enough, I spied a meadow below, blue with flowering larkspur. I crossed my fingers and began our descent, taking a level approach from the west. From that direction, the head winds offered the necessary resistance we needed in order to land quickly. The strip wasn't much more than 300 yards long by my guess. I held my breath and prepared for landing. It had been a long time since I'd done any grasshopper flying. Open field landings were popular at Avenger because the flat desert landscape, but we'd never dared such a landing in the rugged mountains of Idaho.

"Enough, Emily! What in the heck are you doing? There's no landing strip down there. What in the hell's going on?" My brother's voice was a brittle staccato, like metal scratching on stone.

"Don't worry!" I shouted. "I've landed here before in much worse conditions. The meadow is very flat." Within seconds we were on the ground, bouncing across a sea of indigo flowers. As I slowly pulled back the throttle, we came to a stop just a few yards clear of some dense undergrowth. Ernest had beads of sweat on his forehead and his jaw was ridged with anger, but he didn't say a word.

"Okay, let's go," I said, shoving open the cockpit door. After we climbed out, I stood still, trying to get my bearings. Scanning the edge of the woods, my eyes caught sight of an enormous fallen Douglas fir at the perimeter of the meadow. I motioned to Ernest to follow me.

"This way," I murmured, my heart pounding with anticipation.

"That's it! I can't stand it any more. Tell me where you're taking me, *now*, or I'm back to the plane," Ernest barked. I slowed my pace as we walked by the old fir and pointed into the woods.

"All right, here goes," I answered upon a deep breath of courage. "About 50 yards further on is a cabin. Remember the time Lizzie and I got lost on our way back from Friday Harbor and Mother and Father had the Coast Guard out looking for us? I'm taking you to the cabin we stayed in that night. According to Lizzie, it belongs to an old friend of her mother's. Maybe, just maybe we'll get lucky."

Ernest's eyes lit up and a warm smile spread across his face. "She told me about this place. She said it belonged to a guy named Little Bull. I've always wanted to see it."

I grabbed his arm and said, "Little Bull? That can't be right! He's dead."

"That's what she told me. Apparently she visited him a few times when she was dating Ross. You two weren't speaking much in those days, remember?"

As I nodded in surprise, I felt the enchantment of the forest encompass us. The firs were spaced to let rays of sunshine filter through. The padded forest floor was emerald green with moss and feathery ferns. Blue-gray patches of mushrooms and cherry red fungus added color to the natural beauty. Somewhere in the distance I heard the music of a gurgling brook, accompanied by the occasional flutter of a bird's wings. I'd forgotten how mystical this place was. I expected nymphs and elves to appear, bearing magic and illusion. I paused, taking

Ernest's hand in my own and squeezing it tightly.

"Thanks for coming with me, Ernie."

My brother smiled down at me, his eyes misty with affection. "Some day I'll tell you about my experience in the war. I don't think I would have survived it without my Lizzie's pretty face in my mind, encouraging me to go on. We've got to find her, Em."

I had no answer to that. What if she wasn't here? What if we had to accept that our Lizzie might never be found? What good are the memories then? Yet, there was life in our memories. They were the fabric of our lives, the tapestry of our dreams and the warp and weft of our tomorrow. Sighing, I reached over and hugged my brother, comforting him as best I could. The forest seemed to wrap herself around us like an old quilt. Without another word, we turned, synchronized to each other's movements and continued our walk.

We'd almost reached the outcropping when a man stepped out of the bushes. Ernest quickly moved to my side, putting his arm around me protectively as we stared at the man. He looked to be near Father's age. His square face was molded with good humor and his long, straight hair was gray, but his eyes and skin were a walnut brown. He was my height, lean in his blue jeans and plaid flannel shirt. In his muscular arms, he held a bundle of split logs.

Swallowing hard, I mumbled, "Excuse me, Sir, we don't mean to trespass. It's just that we were looking for that cabin over there." I pointed in the direction of the dwelling. "It used to belong to some friends of ours." Then I took the final plunge. "Do you know a young woman named Lizzie Coomes?"

A row of white teeth flashed as he began to chuckle, a warm, throaty sound that gave me reason to relax. He dumped the firewood to the ground and reached out to shake my hand. "My name is Tobi Irons," he said with a friendly smile. "You must be Emily." He turned to Ernest. "And if I'm not mistaken, young man, you are Ernest."

I was meeting Lizzie's father? I was stupid with shock, but my brother was his congenial self. He reached out his arm and pumped Tobi's arm happily. "Gosh, Sir, it's great to meet you. It's about time, too."

"I was right!" I hollered, gushing with joy as Lizzie stepped out of the cabin. Ernest dropped Tobi's hand and ran to her, lifting her into his arms with a rapturous cry. I don't think I'd ever seen Lizzie sob with happiness before, but there she was, crying unashamedly.

She was tinier than I remembered, as though life in the forest had pared away the extra layers of the Caucasian world. She wore a soft blue dress with a wide circle skirt which fluttered like butterfly wings in the warm breeze. She was barefoot and browned by the sun. A band of multicolored beads hung around her neck and her hair was long and free, hanging to her waist like a black velvet cape. She was a stunning apparition, the fairy I was hoping to see.

Then another surprise as Little Bull appeared at the cabin door behind Lizzie. I knew him the minute I saw him, though his ancient face was an accordion of bronzed parchment. Wrinkles rippled over wrinkles; only the shine of his eyes and a glimpse of a tooth broke the pattern. Reaching up, I unconsciously grabbed the medicine bag around my neck. I was wearing his magic.

"I see you have traveled the circle," Little Bull murmured as I reached for his outstretched hands. "You've become a woman since our last visit. How are you, White Dove?"

I gulped, remembering the precious name he'd given me so long ago. I was a mere child back in the days when Lizzie and I had sneaked down to the hovels of Skid Road in search of this dear one. In Little Bull's shriveled face, I saw the enduring tenderness and unconditional love I recalled from those earlier times. Leaning into him, I hugged his bony frame.

"I can't believe you're alive, Little Bull. You were so sick."

"That was why I had to return to my people. I couldn't serve the white man any longer. We of Turtle Island are hardy folks, my dear. You see how nature brings us good health."

I felt a light touch on my shoulder and released Little Bull, turning to find Lizzie standing before me. Slowly she reached up and stroked my cheek, gazing into my eyes. When she reached out her arms, I folded myself into her.

"Oh, Emmy, I've missed you, my dearest friend," she cried, hugging me tightly. Against my chest, Lizzie felt strong and lithe, like the girl I had always known. How I had missed her!

"Lizzie," I began as my tears wet her neck and cheeks. "I'm so sorry for what I did! I forced you into disappearing. I know that and I'm so grateful you are alive. You can't imagine how frightened I've been."

"But I sent you a telegram. I wanted you to know I was safe. Didn't you get the message?" Her small, spidery hands gripped my shoulders firmly as she stared into my eyes, searching for confirmation.

"No, I didn't get it until weeks later and even then, I didn't have a chance to read it. It's such a long, long story," I began, feeble with emotion. The rigor of maintaining courage had finally taken its toll and I felt as though my bones were crumbling from hardship of waiting. Lizzie's strong grip held me up and I became aware of how much she was an integral part of my life, of my very existence. She was my sister, my soulmate, the keeper of my secrets and the mentor of my womanhood.

After our blissful greetings, the five of us sat down on stumps in front of the cabin and talked while Tobi served us mint tea, wild berries and cornbread.

"So how did you get here, Liz?" I asked.

She leaned against Ernest, his broad body nestling hers and said with a drawn-out sigh, "Hitchhiked. I caught a ride with a trucker outside of Cle Elum that took me all the way to Anacortes. That's where I sent the telegram to Idaho, assuming you would receive it before your tour of duty ended. Then I hopped on an oil freighter. It was a lot easier than you might think!" She offered her old, familiar, gap-toothed smile.

"But why did you disappear?" Ernest asked, his face no longer harassed by grief.

Lizzie turned to face him, her voice quivering as she replied. "I thought you were dead. I had nowhere else to go. The WASPS were relieved of duty, Emily had a family to return to, but where did I fit in? I also blamed myself for your death. It was the one thing I couldn't grasp. Little Bull has told me all along you were alive, but I was too afraid to find out. I believed it was my fault, that you joined the Air Force because of me. Remember our talk, when I was adamant about defending our rights, freedom and so on. You enlisted the next day, Ernie. Then you were missing in action and presumed dead. I couldn't live with myself. I knew Tobi was staying here on Lopez, caring for Little Bull. What choice did I have? I felt my only future was here with my people."

"Have you known of your father's whereabouts all this time?" I asked incredulously. Her eyes flashed in that playful way of hers, mysterious and yet certain. She nodded to her father.

"We always communicate, though in other ways: through rituals, omens, messages from the stars. I have always known my daughter's whereabouts, even if I wasn't speaking or writing to her," Tobi explained.

"And truthfully, I've always known my father's whereabouts. Remember all of the rituals I used to do at the summer cabin? I guess you'd say they were my telephones to Tobi. Papa could have been in South Africa, but he'd still have heard me, so to speak." Lizzie gave me a wink. "I'd tried to tell you many times, Em, but you just didn't get it."

"Obviously not!" I agreed.

"I'll tell you who does," Ernest added. "Jonathan. You taught him well, Liz."

Little Bull cleared his throat. "Now that boy is very gifted," he stated matter-of-factly. Once again, I was utterly confused. To my knowledge, Little Bull had never met my little brother.

"Not in person, but in spirit, White Dove," the elder offered in response to my thoughts.

The sun began to disappear behind the forest wall and the sky above paled. Shadows erased light from our faces and a damp chill invaded the atmosphere. Ernest nodded in my direction, summoning my attention. "Em, we need to get back soon. The folks will be worried." He leaned over and whispered into Lizzie's ear. She nodded as Ernest pulled away from her and stood up. Solemnly, he walked over to Tobi and bent down on one knee, his open features glowing with expectation.

"Sir, I'd like to take your daughter back with me tonight." Poor Ernest's face turned poppy red as he sputtered, "Sir, I guess I should have mentioned it before now, but I'd like to ask for your approval for your daughter's hand in marriage, if that's all right with you, Sir."

Tobi gave a boisterous laugh and slapped Ernest on the back. "You're like the young beaver who swallowed too much water. Catch your breath, Son. You have my blessings."

18

Just after dawn on Aug. 6th, 1945, American forces dropped the atom bomb on Japan. The "fat boy" was huge, equaling 20,000 tons of TNT. The explosion destroyed the entire city of Hiroshima. Part of that bomb was made in our own state in a remote place on the Columbia River called Richland Village. Four days later, a second atom bomb was dropped on Nagasaki, another annihilation to save the world. Finally, on Aug. 15th, the Japanese surrendered. The war was over. Still that didn't stop them from one last dirty deed. The American cruiser, Indianapolis, was sunk in the sea, killing every man aboard, 1,196 in all, the day before their surrender.

David returned from Europe two weeks later, wearing seven military decorations including a Congressional Medal of Honor. My husband was exhausted and yet jubilant, as were all of our brave boys. Welcome-home parties for our heroes were as common as Jefferson-head nickels. With global conflict no longer our focus and our deliverance from evil secured, our world was again safe from the ravages of insatiable greed and tempestuous foreign power. *America the Beautiful* was sung with the fervency of youthful idealism and triumphant pride. The citizens of Seattle celebrated for the remainder of the Indian summer with backyard parties, church potlucks, neighborhood parades and all-city picnics. As a nation, we were natural optimists. "Put your tears on the back burner and get on with it," Grandmother Ginny would say, and we did.

David and I had a special reason to celebrate. I was pregnant. Our lusty reunion in Hanover had produced a child. I always thought it ironic that Hitler's empire, the place of history's greatest perpetrators was the place where I conceived again. When I mentioned it to Reverend Norpucker one Sunday after church, he replied, "God works in mysterious ways, my dear. After all, it is the country of *your* ancestors."

Soon our lives began to return to normal. In late August Papa offered to pay for Georgina's tuition at Holy Names Academy. Thankfully her health had improved and she appeared to be adapting to life in America very well. She had become part of our extended family and we all loved her tremendously.

Lizzie and Ernest were married on the second Saturday in October at Weyer's lodge in Friday Harbor. Cloudless and crisp with the advent of autumn, it was an auspicious day for a wedding. A small crowd gathered that festive afternoon, arriving by sailboat, ferry and airplane. The ambiance was casual and the guests sipped champagne in the lodge's backyard garden before the ceremony commenced. In the sky above, a canopy of oaks, suitably donned in cardinal, rust and amber leaves provided an exquisite outdoor sanctuary. The altar's backdrop was a nature arbor of wild grapes set against an ancient stone wall which Little Bull explained had been built by the Indians to mark a grave site. Bouquets of orange dahlias, yellow chrysanthemums and golden sunflowers surrounded a satin-covered platform upon which sat a rustic table. A six-foot high cross of birch branches stood alongside the altar and Little Bull's dream catcher hung from a tree branch nearby.

At the sound of the wedding march played by Little Bull on his flute, Tobi walked Lizzie down the cobblestone path to the altar as I, her matron of honor, stood proudly by. Our stunning bride donned her mother's bridal gown, which had been altered to fit her smaller figure. Crowned by her own wreath of flowers, her gleaming black hair hung loose and her bouquet continued the autumn theme.

Little Bull assisted Reverend Norpucker during the ceremony. Their acknowledgments were an interesting combination of Indian parable and traditional Christian prose. After the vows were said and the rings were exchanged, Jonathan sang Stephen Foster ballads, his sweet soprano voice ringing out like tinkling wind chimes. At the end of the ceremony, Lizzie turned to the smiling crowd and raised her hand.

"I have something I want to share with you. Over there, to the left of the altar, you will see a flower arrangement, which isn't like the rest. That bouquet is an exact replica of my mother's bridal bouquet. Shortly after my mother's death, I was going through her things when I came upon a letter that she'd written me. I'd like to read that to you now."

I watched with curiosity as the beaming bride and groom walked hand-in-hand to a large bouquet of yellow rose buds and white gardenias. Ernest held the arrangement while Lizzie pulled a slip of paper from her sleeve and began to read.

July 4, 1937

My beloved Lizzie,

Happy birthday, my darling daughter. Isn't life amazing? We come to this world to learn and to gain wisdom through our perceptions and deeds. Then we cross to the other side, as though this journey called life is only a stepping stone over a meandering stream to spiritual freedom. My time here will be over when you find this. I sense my death from within, from a place of internal knowing. So I leave you with eternal love and helpful advice: Find your father and learn from him. He taught me the joyful path of giving. A young girl will come into your life, a girl who has lived and died many times. Nurture and care for her. Never forget your friends for they are the cornerstone of your world, the foundations who will keep you from crumbling. Last but not least, please know I am always with you.

Love always, Moma

The guests were mystified. My mother wept as Father comforted her. Tobi sat next to Father, his dark, stoic face touched by raw emotion. Next to Tobi, the Gersteins appeared stunned. Jonathan just gave me a wink, as if to say, "This is no surprise."

An unsuspected wind whipped up a dust devil of dried leaves, which whirled and spun from one end of the garden to the other. Then an eerie whistle came from around the corner of the stone wall, long and low with a rhythm of its own. Lizzie shuddered and lifted her chin to the sky, issuing a loud cry. There was a stir and the pitter-patter of rain filled our ears, but we were not touched by water. Instead, the enormous oak to my left was dropping its leaves in droves. A carpet of living color fell over the wedding guests, crowning our heads with crimson and gold. The circle of neighboring oaks followed suit, littering the wedding party as nature's music rose into a rustling storm. People around me began to sigh, smile, and sing while holding their hands up to catch the bounty with rejoicing enthusiasm. When the trees had completed their symphony, there was not one leaf left on their limbs, nor was there a placid face in the crowd. Our joyous laughter rose as a final measure to Claudia's song.

Without thinking, I whispered her name, "Claudia." Georgina

looked at me, searchingly with those vivid blue eyes of hers, reaching for my hand.

"*Und ich*, Emily, ***I am the young girl***," she murmured.

"I know, Georgina. I know."

Ernest and Lizzie's wedding was only the first of many salubrious celebrations at the lodge. As Mr. Weyer had no heirs, the lodge had been bequeathed to Elizabeth Tobi Coomes in the event of her marriage. The deceased tycoon's two airplanes were left to Father with his remaining stocks, bonds and other monetary assets placed in a trust fund designed to preserve Indian burial grounds. It was Father's decision as to who would be the trust fund administrator. Tobi Irons, the only full-blooded Indian that Father knew, seemed the obvious choice. He had participated in the political arena for decades and was ripe for a new challenge.

Lizzie and Ernest were overjoyed by their good fortune and immediately began to make plans for their future. In the weeks following the wedding, Lizzie, Mother and I set to work organizing and sorting the entire contents of Weyer's estate. An estate sale produced enough money to invest in new paint, furniture and drapes, in addition to the cost of placing a series of advertisements in America's more prominent travel magazines. By February, we'd successfully completed our task. On March 1st, an elegant resort called Little Bull Lodge opened on San Juan Island, run by a young couple by the name of Strong. Two weeks later, on March 14th, I entered Virginia Mason Hospital, six days past my due date. Jacqueline Elizabeth Miller was born eight hours later, healthy, hollering and happily welcomed. David was beaming with pride and I, well, I just wanted to take a long nap.

A year has passed since the end of the war. Ernest and Lizzie are doing a fine job of running their business. The resort draws clientele from all over the Northwest who come for retreats, symposiums and family reunions. Their guests often include movie stars, corporate CEOs and other wealthy patrons who are looking for a private get-away. With her usual knack for efficiency, Lizzie manages the reservations and household staff. Her first baby is due any day now. Pregnancy becomes Lizzie, but the busy schedule would have taken its toll had it not been for Georgina's help. She is the little sister we never had.

Ernest loves their life on the island. He has found his niche in nature by keeping the Japanese gardens and 20 acres of grounds in tip-top shape. He is in the process of putting in a trout pond and a Byzantine hedge maze. An English rose garden is due for planting in Spring. The gardens have become a tourist focal point of the islands. Mind you, it helps when your sister writes for *Sunset* Magazine. The lodge and its history were last month's feature article.

David is in charge of the lodge's restaurant, planning and supervising the menus. Breakfast is served in the atrium and the Great Hall dinners are always a five course affair. Little Bull is the resident mystic and storyteller. Every evening around the huge hearth in the Samish Room, he tells the fables of his people while the patrons play chess, listen to jazz or simply gaze into the fire and dream. Once again, Little Bull has found his calling by teaching the white man to respect his people.

With my darling baby Jacqueline on my hip, I walk along the beach, singing nursery rhymes and keeping a look-out for Orca. The deep blue waters of the Puget Sound are calm today, rolling toward the shore in a timeless primordial rhythm. The story of our existence is told in the rushing of the wave, its lap and lick upon the land, the hovering of the billowy clouds and bursting yellow beams of the afternoon sun. Sea gulls gather on the sand, bickering over a bit of dried salmon. Among them is a tiny meadow lark, outnumbered, but overcoming the odds while fighting for her morsel of sustenance. The creature's perseverance is truly remarkable to me.

As I look back on my life, I have no regrets, though had I been able, I would have altered some of my loved ones' destinies. Claudia would have been so proud of Lizzie and all that she has accomplished. It's a shame she won't be here when her grandchild is born. My friends who are no longer with us, particularly Tommy Mason, have left a sore spot on my heart. And of course, no one will ever replace my dear brother Jack, though in some ways, our little Jacqueline reminds me of him. She has his golden hair and stunning blue eyes.

Yet I am amazed by life's magic. Tomorrow a young Hawaiian woman will be arriving in Washington. She is planning to relocate to Seattle. Though our family learned of her plight less than two months ago, Mother and Father have promised to take her in. Just 20-years-old, she is penniless, orphaned and the mother of my daughter's cousins, twin baby boys, George and Jack Jr. Her name is Kanui and she was Jackie's lover during the war.

As our illustrious leader, President Roosevelt, once said: *This generation of Americans has a rendezvous with destiny.* I know this is true for me. Life's inevitable head winds constantly move me toward my destiny, inspiring a feisty endurance, which rises from within me as I push against my own howling resistance. I recall Amelia's words, *Courage is the price that life extracts for granting peace.* Courage is the essence of existence. We must take risks, raise our face to the mighty jowls of fear and swallow our bitter trepidation in order to gain our time of peace. With courage as the ultimate price, Ginny refused to be humbled, instead rising above her lowly station in life. Papa faced his arrogant demons of bigotry when he handed me the coins of his courage for Georgina. David evolved into his own man by daring to leave home. Mother rejected the virulent seeds of Papa's prejudice despite the cost of his scorn. Jackie paid for the path of self-respect, but was nabbed by death on the way. Claudia lived and loved with the knowledge of her own imminent demise while Lizzie sustained innumerable losses and came away richer than ever. And I, I lived through it all as a witness and participant, overwhelmed by those and many other incorruptible human spirits around me. The unpredictable maelstroms of fate have left me with invaluable lessons, poignant truths and wonderful people with whom I share my life. I am, perhaps, most grateful for my friend, Lizzie, for she taught me the meaning of faith, the value of courage and the mystery of being a woman.

1. *Always Another Dawn* reveals many social themes such as racism, chauvinism, nationalism and patriotism. Which theme do you believe is most significant for this story?

2. In the first paragraph of the book Emily describes Lizzie's eyes as showing a 'wistful yearning for something lost.' What do you believe she has lost?

3. After Lizzie moves into Emily's home, she and Grandmother Ginny quickly take a liking for to another. What thread binds these two women?

4. Emily complains her family is full of secrets. Give some examples of these secrets. What is your reaction to this family?

5. Lizzie and Emily are dual protagonists. Who of the two do you identify with most and why?

6. Papa Joseph appears to be losing touch with reality as the story progresses. How do his family myths contribute to Papa's outrageous behavior?

7. How are our youth today like the Nazi sympathizers (Gerry Gordon and Dick Potter) in this story? Why do you think this is a trend in America?

8. Emily's response to her miscarriage was numbness. Is this a family pattern or does she lack compassion for herself?

9. Later in the story, the Strong family invites the Gersteins over for Christmas. Do you think this is an act of charity or a result of true friendship?

10. The writer has tried to epitomize the enduring results of trauma on a family. How does Melanie in particular react as a result of her only brother's death?

11. How do you feel when Emily attacks the German in the Edelweiss restaurant?

12. Claudia apparently knew of her premature death. Do you believe it is possible for people to anticipate such things?

13. Did you know women were used in the war for live target-towing? Now knowing this, how do you feel about the way women have or have not been portrayed in our history of WWII?

14. How does Emily's retrieval of Georgina change her view of herself?

15. Did this story ever cause you to laugh or cry?